Praise for #1 *New York Times* Bestselling Author Sandra Brown

"[Brown] is a masterful storyteller, carefully crafting tales that keep readers on the edge of their seats."

—*USA Today*

"Brown deserves her own genre."   —*Dallas Morning News*

"Sandra Brown proves herself top-notch."

—Associated Press

"Suspense that has teeth."   —Stephen King

"Sandra Brown just might have penned her best and most ambitious book ever... *Seeing Red* is an exceptional thriller in every sense of the word, a classic treatment of the costs of heroism and the nature of truth itself. Not to be missed."

—*Providence Journal*

"Sandra Brown is a publishing icon."

—*New York Journal of Books*

"[Brown] remains at the top of the suspense field."

—*Publishers Weekly*

"Brown's storytelling gift is surprisingly rare."

—*Toronto Sun*

BEST
KEPT
SECRETS

SANDRA BROWN

BEST KEPT SECRETS

GRAND CENTRAL
PUBLISHING

NEW YORK   BOSTON

Copyright © 1989 by Sandra Brown
Excerpt from *Thick as Thieves* copyright © 2020 by Sandra Brown Management, Ltd.

Grand Central Publishing
Hachette Book Group
1290 Avenue of the Americas, New York, NY 10104
grandcentralpublishing.com
twitter.com/grandcentralpub

First trade paperback edition: March 2014
Reissued: October 2020

Grand Central Publishing is a division of Hachette Book Group, Inc. The Grand Central Publishing name and logo is a trademark of Hachette Book Group, Inc.

The publisher is not responsible for websites (or their content) that are not owned by the publisher.

The Hachette Speakers Bureau provides a wide range of authors for speaking events. To find out more, go to www.hachettespeakersbureau.com or call (866) 376-6591.

ISBNs: 978-1-5387-5190-9 (trade paperback reissue), 978-1-4555-4625-1 (ebook)

Printed in the United States of America

LSC-C

10 9 8 7 6 5 4 3 2 1

BEST
KEPT
SECRETS

Chapter 1

It wasn't so much the cockroach that made her scream as the chipped fingernail. The cockroach was small. The chip was a dilly. On her manicured nail it looked as deep and jagged as the Grand Canyon.

Alex swatted at the cockroach with the laminated card that displayed the motel's limited room service menu. The reverse side advertised the Friday night Mexican buffet and The Four Riders, a country and western band currently performing in the Silver Spur Lounge nightly from seven till midnight.

Her swipe at the cockroach missed by a mile and it scuttled for cover behind the wood veneer dresser. "I'll get you later."

She found a nail file in the bottom of the cosmetic case she had been about to unpack when the metal clasp had wrecked her fingernail and the cockroach had come out to inspect the new tenant of room 125. The room was located on the ground floor of the Westerner Motel, three doors down from the ice and vending machines.

Once the nail had been repaired, Alex gave herself one last, critical look in the dresser mirror. It was important that she make a stunning first impression. They would be astonished when she told them who she was, but she wanted to create an even stronger impact.

She wanted to leave them stupefied, speechless, and defenseless.

They would undoubtedly make comparisons. She couldn't prevent that; she just didn't want to come out on the short end of their mental measuring sticks. If she could help it, they would find no flaws in Celina Gaither's daughter.

She had carefully chosen what to wear. Everything— clothes, jewelry, accessories—was in excellent taste. The overall effect was tailored but not severe, smart but not trendy; she exuded an aura of professionalism that didn't compromise her femininity.

Her goal was to impress them first, then surprise them with what had brought her to Purcell.

Until a few weeks ago, the town of thirty thousand had been a lonely dot on the Texas map. As many jackrabbits and horned toads lived there as people. Recently, town business interests had generated news, but on a comparatively small scale. By the time Alex's job was done, she was certain Purcell would capture newspaper headlines from El Paso to Texarkana.

Concluding that nothing about her appearance could be improved upon short of an act of God or very expensive plastic surgery, she shouldered her handbag, picked up her eel attaché case, and, making certain she had her room key, closed the door to room 125 behind her.

During the drive downtown, Alex had to creep through two school zones. Rush hour in Purcell began when school dismissed. Parents transported their children from school to dentists' offices, piano lessons, and shopping centers. Some might even have been going home, but the sluggish traffic and clogged intersections indicated that no one was staying indoors that day. She didn't actually mind the stop-and-go traffic. The delays gave her an opportunity to gauge the personality of the town.

Black and gold streamers fluttered from the marquee outside Purcell High School. The caricature of a black panther snarled at the passing cars on the highway and temporary letters spelled out POUNCE PERMIAN. On the field inside the stadium, the football team was working out and running plays. The marching band, its instruments flashing in the sun, was rehearsing Friday night's halftime show on a practice field.

The activity looked so innocent. For a moment, Alex regretted her mission and what its outcome would most likely mean for the community. She dismissed her guilty feelings quickly, however, when she reminded herself why she was here. A harvest of rejection, as well as her grandmother's harsh accusations, were stored in her mind if she ever, even for a second, forgot what had brought her to this point in her life. She could ill afford the slightest sentimental regrets.

Downtown Purcell was almost deserted. Many of the commercial buildings and offices facing the square were closed and barred. Foreclosure signs were too plentiful to count. Graffiti was scrawled across plate-glass windows that had once been filled with enticing merchandise. There was still a hand-lettered sign on the door of a deserted laundry. Someone had scratched out the *r*, so that the sign now read, 3 shi ts/$1.00. It crudely summed up the economic climate in Purcell County.

She parked in front of the county courthouse and fed coins into the meter at the curb. The courthouse had been built of red granite quarried in the hill country and hauled by rail to Purcell ninety years earlier. Italian stonecutters had carved pretentious gargoyles and griffins in every available spot as if the amount of decoration justified the expense of their commission. The results were ostentatious, but gaudiness was one of the edifice's attractions. Atop its dome the national and Texas state flags flapped in the brisk north wind.

Having worked in and about the state capitol of Austin for the last year, Alex wasn't intimidated by official buildings. She took the courthouse steps with a determined stride and pulled open the heavy doors. Inside, the plaster walls showed peeling paint and signs of general disrepair. The aggregate tile floor had faint cracks in it that crisscrossed like the lines in the palm of an ancient hand.

The ceiling was high. The drafty corridors smelled of musty record books, industrial-strength cleaning solution, and an overdose of perfume that emanated from the district attorney's secretary. She looked up expectantly as Alex entered the outer office.

"Hi, there. You lost, honey? I love your hair. Wish I could wear mine pulled back in a bun like that. You have to have real tiny ears. Wouldn't you know it, I've got jug handles sticking out from the sides of my head. Do you put henna on it to give it those reddish highlights?"

"Is this District Attorney Chastain's office?"

"Sure is, honey. Whatcha need him for? He's kinda busy today."

"I'm from the Travis County D.A.'s office. Mr. Harper called on my behalf, I believe."

The wad of chewing gum inside the secretary's cheek got a rest from the pounding it had been taking. "You? We were expecting a man."

"As you can see..." Alex held her arms out at her sides.

The secretary looked vexed. "You'd think Mr. Harper would have mentioned that his assistant was a lady, not a man, but shoot," she said, flipping her hand down from a limp wrist, "you know how men are. Well, honey, you're right on time for your appointment. My name's Imogene. Want some coffee? That's a gorgeous outfit, so high-fashion. They're wearing skirts shorter these days, aren't they?"

At the risk of sounding rude, Alex asked, "Are the parties here yet?"

Just then, masculine laughter erupted from the other side of the closed door. "That answer your question, honey?" Imogene asked Alex. "Somebody prob'ly just told a dirty joke to let off steam. They're just bustin' a gut to know what this hush-hush meeting is all about. What's the big secret? Mr. Harper didn't tell Pat why you were coming to Purcell, even though they were friends in law school. Is it something to do with ME getting that gambling license?"

"ME?"

"Minton Enterprises." She said it as though she was surprised Alex was not familiar with the name.

"Perhaps I shouldn't keep them waiting any longer," Alex suggested tactfully, sidestepping Imogene's question.

"Shoot, just listen to me running off at the mouth. Did you say you wanted some coffee, honey?"

"No, thank you." Alex followed Imogene toward the door. Her heart started beating double-time.

"Excuse me." Imogene interrupted the conversation by poking her head into the room. "District Attorney Harper's assistant is here. Y'all sure are in for a treat." She turned back toward Alex. One set of eyelashes, gummy with navy blue mascara, dropped over her eye in a broad, just-between-us-girls wink. "Go on in, honey."

Alex, bracing herself for the most crucial meeting in her life, entered the office.

It was obvious from the relaxed atmosphere that the men in the room had been expecting another man. The moment she crossed the threshold and Imogene pulled the transomed door closed, the man seated behind the desk sprang to his feet. He ground out a burning cigar in the thick, glass ashtray and reached for his suit coat, which had been draped over the back of his chair.

"Pat Chastain," he said, extending his hand. " 'Treat' is an understatement. But then, my good buddy Greg Harper always did have an eye for the ladies. Doesn't surprise me a bit that he's got a good-lookin' woman on his staff."

His sexist remark set her teeth on edge, but she let it slide. She inclined her head in acknowledgment of Chastain's compliment. The hand she clasped in a firm handshake was so loaded down with gold-nugget jewelry it could have anchored a fair-sized yacht. "Thank you for arranging this meeting, Mr. Chastain."

"No problem, no problem. Glad to be of service to both you and Greg. And call me Pat." Taking her elbow, he turned her toward the other two men, who had come to their feet out of deference to her. "This here is Mr. Angus Minton and his son, Junior."

"Gentlemen." Confronting them, meeting them eye to eye for the first time, had a strange and powerful impact on her. Curiosity and antipathy warred inside her. She wanted to analyze them, denounce them. Instead, she behaved in the expected civilized manner and extended her hand.

It was clasped by one studded with calluses. The handshake bordered on being too hard, but it was as open and friendly as the face smiling at her.

"A pleasure, ma'am. Welcome to Purcell County."

Angus Minton's face was tanned and weathered, ravaged by blistering summer sun, frigid blue northers, and years of outdoor work. Intelligent blue eyes twinkled at her from sockets radiating lines of friendliness. He had a boisterous voice. Alex guessed that his laugh would be as expansive as his broad chest and the beer belly that was his only sign of indulgence. Otherwise, he seemed physically fit and strong. Even a younger, larger man would be loath to pick a fight with him because of his commanding presence. For all his strength, he looked as guileless as an altar boy.

His son's handshake was softer, but no less hearty or friendly. He enfolded Alex's hand warmly, and in a confidence-inspiring voice, said, "I'm Junior Minton. How do you do?"

"How do you do?"

He didn't look his forty-three years, especially when he smiled. His straight white teeth flashed and a devilish dimple cratered one cheek, suggesting that he behaved no better than any given occasion called for him to. His blue eyes, a shade deeper than his father's but just as mischievous, held hers long enough to intimate that they were the only two in the room who mattered. She withdrew her hand before Junior Minton seemed ready to relinquish it.

"And over yonder is Reede, Reede Lambert."

Alex turned in the direction Pat Chastain had indicated and located the fourth man, whom she hadn't noticed until now. Flouting etiquette, he was still slouched in a chair in the corner of the room. Scuffed cowboy boots were crossed at the ankles, their toes pointing ceilingward and insolently wagging back and forth. His hands were loosely folded over a western belt buckle. He unlinked them long enough to raise two fingers to the brim of a cowboy hat. "Ma'am."

"Mr. Lambert," she said coolly.

"Here, sit yourself down," Chastain offered, pointing her toward a chair. "Did Imogene offer you some coffee?"

"Yes, but I told her I didn't care for any. I'd like to get to the purpose of the meeting, if we could."

"Sure enough. Junior, pull that other chair over here. Angus." Chastain nodded for the older man to sit back down. When everyone was reseated, the district attorney returned to his chair behind the desk. "Now, Miss—Well, I'll be damned. During all the introductions, we failed to get your name."

Alex held center stage. Four pairs of eyes were trained on her, curiously waiting to hear her name. She paused for dramatic effect, knowing that divulging it would cause a profound reaction. She wanted to witness and catalog their individual reactions. She wished she could see Reede Lambert better. He was sitting partially behind her, and the cowboy hat hid all but the lowest portion of his face.

She took a breath. "I'm Alexandra Gaither, Celina's daughter."

A stunned silence followed the announcement.

Pat Chastain, befuddled, finally asked, "Who's Celina Gaither?"

"Well, I'll be a sonofabitch." Angus flopped backward in his chair like a collapsing inflatable toy.

"Celina's daughter. My God, I can't believe it," Junior whispered. "I can't believe it."

"Somebody want to fill me in, please?" Pat said, still confused. Nobody paid him any attention.

The Mintons openly stared at Alex, searching her face for resemblances to her mother, whom they had known so well. From the corner of her eye, she noticed that the toes of Lambert's boots were no longer wagging. He drew his knees in and sat up straight.

"What on earth have you been doing with yourself all these years?" Angus asked.

"How many years has it been?" Junior wanted to know.

"Twenty-five," Alex answered precisely. "I was only two months old when Grandma Graham moved away from here."

"How is your grandma?"

"She's currently in a Waco nursing home, dying of cancer, Mr. Minton." Alex saw no merit in sparing their sensibilities. "She's in a coma."

"I'm sorry to hear that."

"Thank you."

"Where have y'all been living all this time?"

Alex named a town in central Texas. "We lived there all my life—at least, as far back as I can remember. I graduated high school there, went to the University of Texas, and then, straight into law school. I passed the bar a year ago."

"Law school. Imagine that. Well, you turned out fine, Alexandra, just fine. Didn't she, Junior?"

Junior Minton turned on his charming smile full blast. "I'd say so. You don't look a thing like you did last time I saw you," he told her teasingly. "Best as I recall, your diaper was wet and you didn't have a single hair on your head."

Considering the reason for this prearranged meeting, his flirting made Alex uneasy. She was glad when Pat Chastain intervened again. "I hate to butt into such a touching reunion, but I'm still in the dark."

Angus enlightened him. "Celina was a classmate of Junior's and Reede's. They were best friends, actually. Rarely did you see one of them without the other two when they were in high school. Crazy kids."

Then, his blue eyes turned cloudy and he shook his head sorrowfully. "Celina died. Tragic thing." He took a quiet moment to collect himself. "Anyway, this is the first time we've heard a word about Alexandra since her grandma, Celina's mother, moved away with her." Smiling, he slapped his thighs. "Damned if it's not great to have you back in Purcell."

"Thank you, but—" Alex opened her briefcase and took out a manila envelope. "I'm not back to stay, Mr. Minton. Actually, I'm acting in an official capacity." She passed the envelope across the desk to the district attorney, who looked at it with puzzlement.

"Official capacity? When Greg called me and asked if I'd help out his top prosecutor, he said something about reopening a case."

"It's all in there," Alex said, nodding down at the envelope. "I suggest that you peruse the contents and thoroughly acquaint yourself with the details. Greg Harper requests the full cooperation and assistance of your office and local law enforcement agencies, Mr. Chastain. He assured me that you would comply with this request for the duration of my investigation." She closed her attaché with a decisive snap, stood, and headed for the door.

"Investigation?" District Attorney Chastain came to his feet. The Mintons did likewise.

"Are you working with the racing commission?" Angus asked. "We were told we'd be carefully scrutinized before they granted us a gambling license, but I thought we had already passed muster."

"I thought it was all over except for the formalities," Junior said.

"As far as I know, it is," Alex told them. "My investigation has nothing to do with the racing commission, or the granting of your horse-racing license."

After a moment, when she didn't elaborate, Chastain asked, "Well, then, what *does* it have to do with, Miss Gaither?"

Drawing herself up to her full height, she said, "I am reopening a twenty-five-year-old murder case. Greg Harper asked for your help, Mr. Chastain, since the crime was committed in Purcell County."

She looked into Angus's eyes, then into Junior's. Finally, she stared down hard at the crown of Reede Lambert's hat. "Before I'm finished, I'm going to know which one of you killed my mother."

Chapter 2

Alex peeled off her suit jacket and tossed it onto the motel bed. Her underarms were damp and her knees were ready to buckle. She was nauseated. The scene in the D.A.'s office had shaken her more than she wanted to admit.

She had left Pat Chastain's office with her head held high and her shoulders back. She hadn't walked too fast, but she hadn't dawdled. She had smiled good-bye to Imogene, who had obviously been eavesdropping through the door because she stared at Alex bug-eyed, her mouth agape.

Alex's exit line had been well rehearsed, well timed, and perfectly executed. The meeting had gone just as she had planned it, but she was vastly relieved that it was over.

Now, she peeled off one cloying piece of clothing after another. She would love to think that the worst was behind her, but she feared it was yet to come. The three men she had met today wouldn't roll over and play dead. She would have to confront them again, and when she did, they wouldn't be so overjoyed to see her.

Angus Minton seemed as full of goodwill as Santa Claus,

but Alex knew that nobody in Angus's position could be as harmless as he tried to pretend. He was the richest, most powerful man in the county. One didn't achieve that status solely through benign leadership. He would fight to keep what he'd spent a lifetime cultivating.

Junior was a charmer who knew his way around women. The years had been kind to him. He'd changed little from the photographs Alex had seen of him as an adolescent. She also knew that he used his good looks to his advantage. It would be easy for her to like him. It would also be easy to suspect him of murder.

Reede Lambert was the toughest for her to pigeonhole because her impressions of him were the least specific. Unlike the others, she hadn't been able to look him in the eye. Reede the man looked much harder and stronger than Reede the boy from her grandma's picture box. Her first impression was that he was sullen, unfriendly, and dangerous.

She was certain that one of these men had killed her mother.

Celina Gaither had not been murdered by the accused, Buddy Hicks. Her grandmother, Merle Graham, had drummed that into little Alex's head like a catechism all her life.

"It'll be up to you, Alexandra, to set the record right," Merle had told her almost daily. "That's the least you can do for your mother." At that point she usually glanced wistfully at one of the many framed photographs of her late daughter scattered throughout the house. Looking at the photographs would invariably make her cry, and nothing her grand-daughter did could cheer her.

Until a few weeks ago, however, Alex hadn't known who

Merle suspected of killing Celina. Finding out had been the darkest hour of Alex's life.

Responding to an urgent call from the nursing home doctor, she had sped up the interstate to Waco. The facility was quiet, immaculate, and staffed by caring professionals. Merle's lifetime pension from the telephone company made it affordable. For all its amenities, it still had the gray smell of old age; despair and decay permeated its corridors.

When she had arrived that cold, dismal, rainy afternoon, Alex had been told that her grandmother was in critical condition. She entered the hushed private room and moved toward the hospital bed. Merle's body had visibly deteriorated since Alex had visited only the week before. But her eyes were as alive as Fourth of July sparklers. Their glitter, however, was hostile.

"Don't come in here," Merle rasped on a shallow breath. "I don't want to see you. It's because of you!"

"What, Grandma?" Alex asked in dismay. "What are you talking about?"

"I don't want you here."

Embarrassed by the blatant rejection, Alex had glanced around at the attending physician and nurses. They shrugged their incomprehension. "Why don't you want to see me? I've come all the way from Austin."

"It's your fault she died, you know. If it hadn't been for you…" Merle moaned with pain and clutched her sheet with sticklike, bloodless fingers.

"Mother? You're saying I'm responsible for Mother's death?"

Merle's eyes popped open. "Yes," she hissed viciously.

"But I was just a baby, an infant," Alex argued, desperately wetting her lips. "How could I—"

"Ask them."

"Who, Grandma? Ask who?"

"The one who murdered her. Angus, Junior, Reede. But it was you...you...you..."

Alex had to be led from the room by the doctor several minutes after Merle lapsed into a deep coma. The ugly accusation had petrified her; it reverberated in her brain and assaulted her soul.

If Merle held Alex responsible for Celina's death, so much of Alex's upbringing could be explained. She had always wondered why Grandma Graham was never very affectionate with her. No matter how remarkable Alex's achievements, they were never quite good enough to win her grandmother's praise. She knew she was never considered as gifted, or clever, or charismatic as the smiling girl in the photographs that Merle looked at with such sad longing.

Alex didn't resent her mother. Indeed, she idolized and adored her with the blind passion of a child who had grown up without her parents. She constantly worked toward being as good at everything as Celina had been, not only so she would be a worthy daughter, but in the desperate hope of earning her grandmother's love and approval. So it came as a stunning blow to hear from her dying grandmother's lips that she was responsible for Celina's murder.

The doctor had tentatively suggested that she might want to have Mrs. Graham taken off the life support systems. "There's nothing we can do for her now, Ms. Gaither."

"Oh, yes, there is," Alex had said with a ferocity that

shocked him. "You can keep her alive. I'll be in constant touch."

Immediately upon her return to Austin, she began to research the murder case of Celina Graham Gaither. She spent many sleepless nights studying transcripts and court documents before approaching her boss, the district attorney of Travis County.

Greg Harper had shifted the smoking cigarette from one corner of his lips to the other. In the courtroom, Greg was the bane of guilty defendants, lying witnesses, and orderly judges. He talked too loud, smoked too much, drank in abundance, and wore five-hundred-dollar pinstriped suits with lizard boots that cost twice that much.

To say that he was flashy and egomaniacal would be gross understatements. He was shrewd, ambitious, ruthless, relentless, and profane, and would therefore probably carve out quite a niche for himself in state politics, which was his driving ambition. He believed in the reward system and appreciated raw talent. That's why Alex was on his staff.

"You want to reopen a twenty-five-year-old murder case?" he asked her when she stated the purpose of the conference she'd requested. "Got a reason?"

"Because the victim was my mother."

For the first time since she'd known him, Greg had asked a question he didn't already know the answer to—or at least have a fairly good guess. "Jesus, Alex, I'm sorry. I didn't know that."

She gave a slight, dismissive shrug. "Well, it's not something one advertises, is it?"

"When was this? How old were you?"

"An infant. I don't remember her. She was only eighteen when she was killed."

He ran his long, bony hand down his even longer, bonier face. "The case remains on the books as officially unsolved?"

"Not exactly. There was a suspect arrested and charged, but the case was dismissed without ever going to trial."

"Fill me in, and make it short. I'm having lunch with the state attorney general today," he said. "You've got ten minutes. Shoot."

When she finished, Greg frowned and lit a cigarette from the smoldering tip of one he'd smoked down to the filter. "Goddamn, Alex, you didn't say that the Mintons were involved. Your granny really believes that one of them iced your mother?"

"Or their friend, Reede Lambert."

"By any chance, did she provide them with a motive?"

"Not specifically," Alex said evasively, loath to tell him that Merle had cited her, Alex, as the motive. "Apparently, Celina was close friends with them."

"Then why would one of them kill her?"

"That's what I want to find out."

"On the state's time?"

"It's a viable case, Greg," she said tightly.

"All you've got is a hunch."

"It's stronger than a hunch."

He gave a noncommittal grunt. "Are you sure this isn't just a personal grudge?"

"Of course not." Alex took umbrage. "I'm pursuing this from a strictly legal viewpoint. If Buddy Hicks had gone on trial and been convicted by a jury, I wouldn't put so much stock in what Grandma told me. But it's there in the public records."

"How come she didn't raise hell about the murder when it happened?"

"I asked her that myself. She didn't have much money and she felt intimidated by the legal machinations. Besides, the murder had left her drained of energy. What little she had went into rearing me."

It was now clear to Alex why, since her earliest recollections, her grandmother had pushed her toward the legal profession. Because it was expected of her, Alex had excelled in school and had ultimately graduated from the University of Texas Law School in the top ten percent of her class. The law was the profession Merle had chosen for her, but thankfully it was a field that intrigued and delighted Alex. Her curious mind enjoyed delving into its intricacies. She was well prepared to do what she must.

"Grandmother was just a widow lady, left with a baby to raise," she said, building her case. "There was precious little she could do about the judge's ruling at Hicks's competency hearing. With what money she had, she packed up, left town, and never went back."

Greg consulted his wristwatch. Then, anchoring his cigarette between his lips, he stood up and pulled on his suit jacket. "I can't reopen a murder case without a shred of evidence or probable cause. You know that. I didn't snatch you out of law school 'cause you were stupid. Gotta confess, though, that your shapely ass had something to do with it."

"Thanks."

Her disgust was obvious and it wasn't because of his sexism, which was so brassy she knew it was insincere. "Look,

Alex, this isn't a teensy-weensy favor you're asking of me," he said. "Because of who these guys are, we're talking earth-shattering shit here. Before I stick my neck out, I've got to have more to go on than your hunch and Granny's ramblings."

She followed him to the door of his office. "Come on, Greg, spare me the legal lingo. You're only thinking of yourself."

"You're goddamn right I am. Constantly."

His admission left her no room to maneuver. "At least grant me permission to investigate this murder when I'm not actively involved in other cases."

"You know what a backlog we've got. We can't get all the cases to court as it is now."

"I'll work overtime. I won't shirk my other responsibilities. You know I won't."

"Alex—"

"Please, Greg." She could see that he wanted her to withdraw the request, but she wouldn't capitulate to anything less than a definite no. Her preliminary research had piqued her interest as a prosecutor and litigator, and her desperate desire to prove her grandmother wrong and absolve herself of any guilt further motivated her undertakings. "If I don't produce something soon, I'll drop it and you'll never hear of it again."

He studied her intent face. "Why don't you just work out your frustrations with hot, illicit screwing like everybody else? At least half the guys in town would accommodate you, married or single." She gave him a withering look. "Okay, okay. You can do some digging, but only in your spare time. Come up with something concrete. If I'm going to win votes, I can't look or act like a goddamn fool, and neither can anybody else in this office. Now I'm late for lunch. 'Bye."

Her caseload was heavy, and the time she had had to

spend on her mother's murder had been limited. She read everything she could get her hands on—newspaper accounts, transcripts of Buddy Hicks's hearing—until she had the facts memorized.

They were basic and simple. Mr. Bud Hicks, who was mentally retarded, had been arrested near the murder scene with the victim's blood on his clothing. At the time of his arrest, he had had in his possession the surgical instrument with which he had allegedly killed the victim. He was jailed, questioned, and charged. Within days there was a hearing. Judge Joseph Wallace had declared Hicks incompetent to stand trial and had confined him to a state mental hospital.

It seemed like an open-and-shut case. Just when she had begun to believe that Greg was right, that she was on a wild-goose chase, she had discovered a curious glitch in the transcript of Hicks's hearing. After following up on it, she had approached Greg again, armed with a signed affidavit.

"Well, I've got it." Triumphantly, she slapped the folder on top of the others cluttering his desk.

Greg scowled darkly. "Don't be so friggin' cheerful, and for crissake, stop slamming things around. I've got a bitchin' hangover." He mumbled his words through a dense screen of smoke. He stopped puffing on the cigarette only long enough to sip at a steaming cup of black coffee. "How was your weekend?"

"Wonderful. Far more productive than yours. Read that."

Tentatively, he opened the file and scanned the contents with bleary eyes. "Hmm." His initial reading was enough to grab his attention. Leaning back in his chair and propping his feet on the corner of his desk, he reread it more carefully. "This is from the doctor at the mental hospital where this Hicks fellow is incarcerated?"

"Was. He died a few months ago."

"Interesting."

"Interesting?" Alex cried, disappointed with the bland assessment. She left her chair, circled it, and stood behind it, gripping the upholstered back in agitation. "Greg, Buddy Hicks spent twenty-five years in that hospital for nothing."

"You don't know that yet. Don't jump to conclusions."

"His last attending psychiatrist said that Buddy Hicks was a model patient. He never demonstrated any violent tendencies. He had no apparent scx drive, and in the doctor's expert opinion, he was incapable of committing a crime like the one that cost my mother her life. Admit that it looks fishy."

He read several other briefs, then muttered, "It looks fishy, but it's sure as hell not a smoking gun."

"Short of a miracle, I won't be able to produce any concrete evidence. The case is twenty-five years old. All I can hope for is enough probable cause to bring it before a grand jury. A confession from the real killer—because I'm convinced, beyond a shadow of a doubt, that Bud Hicks did not murder my mother—is a pipe dream. There's also the slim possibility of smoking out an eyewitness."

"Slim to none, Alex."

"Why?"

"You've done enough homework, so you should know. The murder took place in a barn on Angus Minton's ranch. Say his name anywhere in that county and the ground trembles. He's a big enchilada. If there was an eyewitness, he wouldn't testify against Minton because he'd be biting the hand that feeds him. Minton runs about a dozen enterprises in an area of the state where they're gasping their last breath, economically speaking.

"Which brings us to another delicate area, in a case rid-dled with delicate areas." Greg slurped his coffee and lit another cigarette. "The governor's racing commission just gave Minton Enterprises the green light on building that horse-racing track in Purcell County."

"I'm well aware of that. What bearing does it have?"

"You tell me."

"None!" she shouted.

"Okay, I believe you. But if you start slinging accusations and casting aspersions on one of Texas's favorite sons, how do you think that's going to sit with the governor? He's damn proud of his racing commission. He wants this pari-mutuel thing to get off the ground without a hitch. No controversy. No bad press. No shady deals. He wants everything above reproach and squeaky clean.

"So, if some smart-ass prosecutor starts shooting off her mouth, trying to connect somebody his hand-picked com-mission has given their coveted blessing to with a murder, the governor is going to be royally pissed off. And if said prose-cutor works in this office, who do you think he's going to be the most pissed off at? *Moi.*"

Alex didn't argue with him. Instead, she calmly said, "All right. I'll resign from this office and do it on my own."

"Jesus, you're theatrical. You didn't let me finish." He pressed his intercom button and bellowed to his secretary to bring him more coffee. While she was carrying it in, he lit another cigarette.

"On the other hand," he said around a gust of smoke, "I can't stand that bastard who's living in the governor's man-sion. I've made no secret of it, and it works both ways, though the sanctimonious sonofabitch won't admit it. It would tickle me pissless to watch him squirm. Can you imagine him justifying why his commission picked, from the hordes of applicants, somebody associated with a murder?" He chuckled. "I get a hard-on just thinking about it."

Alex found Greg's motivation distasteful, but she was ecstatic that he was granting her permission. "So, I can reopen the case?"

"The case remains unsolved because Hicks was never brought to trial." He lowered his feet, and his chair rocked forward jarringly. "I have to tell you, though—I'm doing this against my better judgment, and only because I trust your gut instincts. I like you, Alex. You proved yourself when you were interning here as a law student. Great ass aside, you're good to have in our corner."

He looked down at the material she'd compiled and fiddled with a corner of one folder. "I still think you've got a personal grudge against these guys, the town, whatever. I'm not saying it's unjustified. It's just not something you can build a case around. Without this shrink's affidavit, I would have turned down your request. So, while you're out there where the buffalo roam and the deer and antelope play, remember that my ass is in a sling, too." He raised his eyes and stared at her balefully. "Don't fuck up."

"You mean, I can go to West Texas?"

"That's where it happened, isn't it?"

"Yes, but what about my caseload?"

"I'll put interns on the preparations and ask for postponements. Meanwhile, I'll talk to the D.A. in Purcell. We were in law school together. He's perfect for what you're trying to do. He's not too bright, and he married above himself, so he's always striving to please. I'll ask him to give you whatever assistance you need."

"Don't be too specific. I don't want them forewarned."

"Okay."

"Thank you, Greg," she said earnestly.

"Not so fast," he said, snuffing her enthusiasm. "If you trap yourself out there, I'll disclaim you. The attorney general has made no secret that I'm his heir apparent. I want the job, and I'd like nothing better than to have a good-looking, smart broad as chief of one of my departments. That goes down good with the voters." He pointed a nicotine-stained finger at her. "But if you fall on your ass now, I never knew you, kiddo. Got that?"

"You're an unscrupulous son of a bitch."

He grinned like a crocodile. "Even my mama didn't like me much."

"I'll send you a postcard." She turned to leave.

"Wait a minute. There's something else. You've got thirty days."

"What?"

"Thirty days to come up with something."

"But—"

"That's as long as I can spare you without the rest of the natives around here getting restless. That's longer than your hunch and flimsy leads warrant. Take it or leave it."

"I'll take it."

He didn't know that she had a much more pressing deadline, a personal one. Alex wanted to present her grandmother with the name of Celina's killer before she died. She wasn't even concerned that her grandmother was in a coma.

Somehow, she would penetrate her consciousness. Her last breath would be peaceful, and Alex was certain she would at last praise her granddaughter.

Alex leaned across Greg's desk. "I know I'm right. I'll bring the real killer to trial, and when I do, I'll get a conviction. See if I don't."

"Yeah, yeah. In the meantime, find out what sex with a real cowboy is like. And take notes. I want details about spurs and guns and stuff."

"Pervert."

"Bitch. And don't slam—ah, *shit*!"

Alex smiled now, recalling that meeting. She didn't take his insulting sexism seriously because she knew she had his professional respect. Wild man that he was, Greg Harper had been her mentor and friend since the summer before her first semester of law school, when she had worked in the prosecutor's office. He was going out on a limb for her now, and she appreciated his vote of confidence.

Once she had gotten Greg's go-ahead, she hadn't wasted time. It had taken her only one day to catch up on paperwork, clear her desk, and lock up her condo. She had left Austin early, and made a brief stop in Waco at the nursing home. Merle's condition was unchanged. Alex had left the number of the Westerner where she could be reached in case of an emergency.

She dialed the D.A.'s home number from her motel room.

"Mr. Chastain, please," she said in response to the woman's voice who answered.

"He's not at home."

"Mrs. Chastain? It's rather important that I speak with your husband."

"Who is this?"

"Alex Gaither."

She heard a soft laugh. "You're the one, huh?"

"'The one'?"

"The one who accused the Mintons and Sheriff Lambert of murder. Pat was in a tailspin when he got home. I've never seen him so—"

"Excuse me?" Alex interrupted breathlessly. "Did you say *Sheriff* Lambert?"

Chapter 3

The sheriff's department was located in the basement of the Purcell County Courthouse. For the second time in as many days, Alex parked her car in a metered slot on the square and entered the building.

It was early. There wasn't much activity in the row of offices on the lower level. In the center of this warren of cubicles was a large squad room, no different from any other in the nation. A pall of cigarette smoke hovered over it like a perpetual cloud. Several uniformed officers were gathered around a hot plate where coffee was simmering. One was talking, but when he saw Alex, he stopped in midsentence. One by one, heads turned, until all were staring at her. She felt glaringly out of place in what was obviously a male domain. Equal employment hadn't penetrated the ranks of the Purcell County Sheriff's Department.

She held her ground and said pleasantly, "Good morning."

"Mornin'," they chorused.

"My name is Alex Gaither. I need to see the sheriff, please." The statement was superfluous. They already knew who she was and why she was there. Word traveled fast in a town the size of Purcell.

"He expectin' you?" one of the deputies asked belligerently, after spitting tobacco juice into an empty Del Monte green bean can.

"I believe he'll see me," she said confidently.

"Did Pat Chastain send you over?"

Alex had tried to reach him again that morning, but Mrs. Chastain had told her that he'd already left for his office. She tried telephoning him there and got no answer. Either she had missed him while he was in transit, or he was avoiding her. "He's aware of why I'm here. Is the sheriff in?" she repeated with some asperity.

"I don't think so."

"I haven't seen him."

"Yeah, he's here," one officer said grudgingly. "He came in a few minutes ago." He nodded his head toward a hallway. "Last door on your left, ma'am."

"Thank you."

Alex gave them a gracious smile she didn't feel in her heart and walked toward the hallway. She was conscious of the eyes focused on her back. She knocked on the indicated door.

"Yeah?"

Reede Lambert sat behind a scarred wooden desk that was probably as old as the cornerstone of the building. His booted feet were crossed and resting on one corner of it. Like yesterday, he was slouching, this time in a swivel chair.

His cowboy hat and a leather, fur-lined jacket were hanging on a coat tree in the corner between a ground-level window and a wall papered with wanted posters held up by yellowing, curling strips of Scotch tape. He cradled a chipped, stained porcelain coffee mug in his hands.

"Well, g'morning, Miss Gaither."

She closed the door with such emphasis that the frosted-glass panel rattled. "Why wasn't I told yesterday?"

"And spoil the surprise?" he said with a sly grin. "How'd you find out?"

"By accident."

"I knew you'd show up sooner or later." He eased himself upright. "But I didn't figure on it being this early in the morning." He came to his feet and indicated the only other available chair in the room. He moved toward a table that contained a coffee maker. "You want some?"

"Mr. Chastain should have told me."

"Pat? No way. When things get touchy, our D.A.'s a real chickenshit."

Alex caught her forehead in her hand. "This is a nightmare."

He hadn't waited for her to decline or accept his offer of coffee. He was filling up a cup similar to his. "Cream, sugar?"

"This isn't a social call, Mr. Lambert."

He set the cup of black coffee on the edge of the desk in front of her and returned to his chair. Wood and ancient springs creaked in protest as he sat down. "You're getting us off to a bad start."

"Have you forgotten why I'm here?"

"Not for a minute, but do your duties prohibit you from drinking coffee, or is it a religious abstinence?"

Exasperated, Alex set her purse on the desk, went to the table, and spooned powdered cream into her mug.

The coffee was strong and hot—much like the stare the sheriff was giving her—and far better than the tepid brew she'd drunk in the coffee shop of the Westerner Motel earlier. If he had brewed it, he knew how to do it right. But then, he looked like a very capable man. Reared back in his chair, he did not look at all concerned that he'd been implicated in a murder case.

"How do you like Purcell, Miss Gaither?"

"I haven't been here long enough to form an opinion."

"Aw, come on. I'll bet your mind was made up not to like it before you ever got here."

"Why do you say that?"

"It would stand to reason, wouldn't it? Your mother died here."

His casual reference to her mother's death rankled. "She didn't just die. She was murdered. Brutally."

"I remember," he said grimly.

"That's right. You discovered her body, didn't you?"

He lowered his eyes to the contents of his coffee mug and stared into it for a long time before taking a drink. He tossed it back, draining the mug as though it were a shot of whiskey.

"Did you kill my mother, Mr. Lambert?"

Since she hadn't been able to accurately gauge his reaction the day before, she wanted to see it now.

His head snapped up. "No." Leaning forward, he braced his elbows on the desk and gave her a level stare. "Let's cut through the bullshit, okay? Understand this right now, and it'll save us both a lot of time. If you want to interrogate me, Counselor, you'll have to subpoena me to appear before the grand jury."

"You're refusing to cooperate with my investigation?"

"I didn't say that. This office will be at your disposal per Pat's instructions. I'll personally help you any way I can."

"Out of the goodness of your heart?" she asked sweetly.

"No, because I want it over and done with, finished. You understand? So you can go back to Austin where *you* belong, and leave the past in the past where *it* belongs." He got up to refill his coffee mug. Over his shoulder he asked, "Why'd you come here?"

"Because Bud Hicks did not murder my mother."

"How the hell do you know? Or did you just ask him?"

"I couldn't. He's dead."

She could tell by his reaction that he hadn't known. He moved to the window and stared out, sipping his coffee reflectively. "Well, I'll be damned. Gooney Bud is dead."

"Gooney Bud?"

"That's what everybody called him. I don't think anybody knew his last name until after Celina died and the newspapers printed the story."

"He was retarded, I'm told."

The man at the window nodded. "Yeah, and he had a speech impediment. You could barely understand him."

"Did he live with his parents?"

"His mother. She was half batty herself. She died years ago, not too long after he was sent away."

He continued to stare through the open slats of the blinds with his back to her. His silhouette was trim, broad-shouldered, narrow-hipped. His jeans fit a little too well. Alex berated herself for noticing.

"Gooney Bud pedaled all over town on one of those large tricycles," he was saying. "You could hear him coming blocks away. That thing clattered and clanged like a peddler's wagon. It was covered with junk. He was a scavenger. Little girls were warned to stay away from him. We boys made fun of him, played pranks, things like that." He shook his head sadly. "Shame."

"He died in a state mental institution, incarcerated for a crime he didn't commit."

Her comment brought him around. "You've got nothing to prove that he didn't."

"I'll find the proof."

"None exists."

"Are you so sure? Did you destroy the incriminating evidence the morning you ostensibly found Celina's body?"

A deep crease formed between his heavy eyebrows. "Haven't you got anything better to do? Don't you already have a heavy enough caseload? Why did you start investigating this in the first place?"

She gave him the same catchall reason she had given Greg Harper. "Justice was not served. Buddy Hicks was innocent. He took the blame for somebody else's crime."

"Me, Junior, or Angus?"

"Yes, one of the three of you."

"Who told you that?"

"Grandma Graham."

"Ah, now we're getting somewhere." He hooked one thumb into a belt loop, his tanned fingers curling negligently over his fly. "While she was telling you all this, did she mention how jealous she was?"

"Grandma? Of whom?"

"Of us. Junior and me."

"She told me the two of you and Celina were like the three musketeers."

"And she resented it. Did she tell you how she doted on Celina?"

She hadn't had to. The modest house Alex had grown up in had been a veritable shrine to her late mother. Noting her frown, the sheriff answered his own question. "No, I can see that Mrs. Graham failed to mention all that."

"You think I'm here on a personal vendetta."

"Yeah, I do."

"Well, I'm not," Alex said defensively. "I believe there are enough holes in this case to warrant reinvestigation. So does District Attorney Harper."

"That egomaniac?" he snorted contemptuously. "He'd indict his own mother for selling it on street corners if it would move him any closer to the attorney general's office."

Alex knew his comment was partially true. She tried another tack. "When Mr. Chastain is better acquainted with the facts, he'll agree that there's been a gross miscarriage of justice."

"Pat had never even heard of Celina until yesterday. He's got his hands full chasing down wetbacks and drug dealers."

"Do you blame me for wanting justice? If your mother had been stabbed to death in a horse barn, wouldn't you do everything possible to see that her killer was punished?"

"I don't know. My old lady split before I was old enough to remember her."

Alex felt a pang of empathy for him that she knew she couldn't afford. No wonder the pictures she'd seen of Reede had been of a very intense lad with eyes much older than his years. She'd never thought to ask her grandmother why he looked so serious.

"This is an untenable situation, Mr. Lambert. You are a

suspect." She stood up and retrieved her purse. "Thank you for the coffee. I'm sorry to have bothered you so early in the morning. From now on, I'll have to rely on the local police department for assistance."

"Wait a minute."

Alex, already making her way toward the door, stopped and turned. "What?"

"There is no police department."

Dismayed by that piece of information, she watched as he reached for his hat and coat. He stepped around her, pulled open the door for her, then followed her out.

"Hey, Sam, I'm leaving. I'll be across the street." The deputy nodded. "This way," Reede said, taking Alex's elbow and guiding her toward a small, square elevator at the end of the hall.

They got into it together. The door creaked when he pulled it closed. The sound of grinding gears wasn't very reassuring. Alex hoped it would make the trip.

She tried to help it along by concentrating hard on their ascent. All the same, she was fully aware of Reede Lambert standing so close to her that their clothing touched. He was studying her.

He said, "You resemble Celina."

"Yes, I know."

"Your size, your mannerisms. Your hair's darker, though, and it has more red in it. Her eyes were brown, not blue like yours." His gaze moved over her face. "But there's a striking resemblance."

"Thank you. I think my mother was beautiful."

"Everybody thought so."

"Including you?"

"Especially me."

The elevator jerked to an abrupt stop. Alex lost her balance and fell against him. Reede caught her arm and supported her long enough for her to regain her balance, which might have taken a little too long, because when they separated, Alex felt light-headed and breathless.

They were on the first floor. He shrugged into his jacket as he guided her toward a rear exit. "My car's parked out front," she told him as they left the building. "Should I put more money in the meter?"

"Forget it. If you get a ticket, you've got friends in high places."

His smile wasn't as orthodontist perfect as Junior Minton's, but it was just as effective. It elicited a tickle in the pit of her stomach that was strange and wonderful and scary.

His quick grin emphasized the lines on his face. He looked every day of his forty-three years, but the weathered markings fit well on his strong, masculine bone structure. He had dark blond hair that had never known a stylist's touch. He pulled on his black felt cowboy hat and situated the brim close to his eyebrows, which were a shade or two darker than his hair.

His eyes were green. Alex had noticed that the moment she had walked into his office. She had reacted as any woman would to so attractive a man. He had no paunch, no middle-aged softness. Physically, he looked two decades younger than he actually was.

Alex had to keep reminding herself that she was a prosecutor for the sovereign state of Texas, and that she should be looking at Reede Lambert through the eyes of a litigator, not a woman. Besides, he was a generation older than she.

"Were you out of clean uniforms this morning?" she asked as they crossed the street.

He wore plain denim Levi's—old, faded, and tight—like the jeans rodeo cowboys wore. His jacket was brown leather, and fitted at the waist like a bomber jacket. The fur lining, which folded out to form a wide collar, was probably coyote. As soon as they'd stepped into the sunlight, he'd slid on aviator glasses. The lenses were so dark that she could no longer see his eyes.

"I used to dread the sight of a uniform, so when I became sheriff, I made it clear that they'd never get me in one of those things."

"Why did you always dread the sight of one?"

He smiled wryly. "I was usually trying to outrun it, or at least avoid it."

"You were a crook?"

"Hell-raiser."

"You had run-ins with the law?"

"Brushes."

"So what turned you around, a religious experience? A scare? A night or two in jail? Reform school?"

"Nope. I just figured that if I could outchase the law, I could outchase the lawbreakers." He shrugged. "It seemed a natural career choice. Hungry?"

Before she had a chance to answer, he pushed open the door of the B & B Café. A cowbell mounted above it announced their entrance. It was the place where things were happening, it seemed. Every table—red Formica with rusted chrome legs—was full. Reede led her to a vacant booth along the wall.

Greetings were called out to him by executives, farmers,

roughnecks, cowboys, and secretaries, each distinguished by his attire. Everyone except the secretaries wore boots. Alex recognized Imogene, Pat Chastain's secretary. As soon as they passed her table, she launched into an animated, whispered explanation of who Alex was to the women seated with her. A hush fell over the room as word traveled from one table to the next.

No doubt this microcosm of Purcell gathered every morning at the B & B Café during coffee-break time. A stranger in their midst was news, but the return of Celina Gaither's daughter was a news bulletin. Alex felt like a lightning rod, because she certainly attracted electric currents. Some, she sensed, were unfriendly.

A Crystal Gayle ballad about love lost was wafting from the jukebox. It competed with "Hour Magazine" on the fuzzy black-and-white TV mounted in one corner. Male impotence was being discussed to the raucous amusement of a trio of roughnecks. The nonsmoking movement hadn't reached Purcell, and the air was dense enough to cut. The smell of frying bacon was prevalent.

A waitress in purple polyester pants and a bright gold satin blouse approached them with two cups of coffee and a plate of fresh, yeasty doughnuts. She winked and said, "Mornin', Reede," before ambling off toward the kitchen, where the cook was deftly flipping eggs while a cigarette dangled between his lips.

"Help yourself."

Alex took the sheriff up on his offer. The doughnuts were still warm, and the sugary glaze melted against her tongue. "They had this waiting for you. Is this *your* table? Do you have a standing order?"

"The owner's name is Pete," he told her, indicating the cook. "He used to feed me breakfast every morning on my way to school."

"How generous."

"It wasn't charity," he said curtly. "I swept up for him in the afternoons after school."

She had unwittingly struck a sore spot. Reede Lambert was defensive about his motherless childhood. Now, however, wasn't the time to probe for more information. Not with nearly every eye in the place watching them.

He devoured two doughnuts and washed them down with black coffee, wasting neither food, nor time, nor motion. He ate like he thought it might be a long time before his next meal.

"Busy place," she commented, unself-consciously licking glaze off her fingers.

"Yeah. The old-timers like me leave the new shopping mall and fast food places out by the interstate to the newcomers and teenagers. If you can't find who you're looking for anyplace else, he's usually at the B & B. Angus'll probably be along directly. ME's corporate headquarters is just one block off the square, but he conducts a lot of business right here in this room."

"Tell me about the Mintons."

He reached for the last doughnut, since it was obvious that Alex wasn't going to eat it. "They're rich, but not showy. Well liked around town."

"Or feared."

"By some, maybe," he conceded with a shrug.

"The ranch is only one of their businesses?"

"Yeah, but it's the granddaddy. Angus built it out of nothing but acres of dust and sheer determination."

"What exactly do they do out there?"

"Basically, they're a racehorse training outfit. Thoroughbreds mostly. Some Quarter Horses. They board up to a hundred and fifty horses at a time, and get them ready for the track trainers."

"You seem to know a lot about it."

"I own a couple of racehorses myself. I board them out there permanently." He pointed down to her half-empty coffee cup. "If you're finished, I'd like to show you something."

"What?" she asked, surprised by the sudden shift in topic.

"It's not far."

They left the B & B, but not before Reede said good-bye to everyone he'd said hello to when they came in. He didn't pay for the breakfast, but was saluted by Pete the cook and given an affectionate pat by the waitress.

Reede's official car, a Blazer truck, was parked at the curb in front of the courthouse. The space was reserved for him, marked with a small sign. He unlocked the door, helped Alex up into the cab of the four-wheel-drive vehicle, then joined her. He drove only a few blocks before pulling up in front of a small house. "That's it," he said.

"What?"

"Where your mother lived." Alex whipped her head around to stare at the frame dwelling. "The neighborhood isn't what it was when she lived here. It's gone to pot. There used to be a tree there, where the sidewalk dips slightly."

"Yes. I've seen pictures."

"It died a few years ago and had to be cut down. Anyway,"

he said, slipping the truck back into gear, "I thought you'd want to see it."

"Thank you." As he pulled the Blazer away from the curb, Alex kept her eyes on the house. The white paint had grayed. Hot summer suns had faded the maroon awnings over the front windows. It wasn't attractive, but she swiveled her head and kept it in sight as long as she could.

That's where she had lived with her mother for two short months. In those rooms, Celina had fed her, bathed her, rocked her, and sang her lullabies. There, she had listened for Alex's crying in the night. Those walls had heard her mother's whispered vows of love to her baby girl.

Alex didn't remember, of course. But she knew that's how it had been.

Tamping down the stirring emotions, she picked up the conversation they had been having when they had left the B & B. "Why is this proposed racetrack so important to the Mintons?"

He glanced at her as though she'd lost her senses. "Money. Why else?"

"It sounds like they've got plenty."

"Nobody ever has enough money," he remarked with a grim smile. "And only somebody who's been as poor as me can say that. Look around." He gestured at the empty stores along the main thoroughfare they were now traveling. "See all the empty businesses and foreclosure notices? When the oil market went bust, so did the economy of this town. Just about everybody worked in an oil-related occupation."

"I understand all that."

"Do you? I doubt it," he said scornfully. "This town needs that racetrack to survive. What we don't need is a wet-behind-the-ears, blue-eyed, redheaded female lawyer in a fur coat to come along and screw things up."

"I came here to investigate a murder," she lashed out, stung by his unexpected insult. "The racetrack, the gambling license, and the local economy have no relevance to it."

"Like hell they don't. If you ruin the Mintons, you ruin Purcell County."

"If the Mintons are proven guilty, they've ruined themselves."

"Look, lady, you're not going to uncover any new clues about your mother's murder. All you're going to do is stir up trouble. You won't get any help from locals. Nobody's gonna speak out against the Mintons, because the future of this county is riding on them building that racetrack."

"And you top the list of the loyal and close-mouthed."

"Damn right!"

"Why?" she pressed. "Do the Mintons have something on you? Could one of them place you in that horse barn well before you 'discovered' my mother's body? What were you doing there at that time of day, anyway?"

"What I did every day. I was shoveling shit out of the stables. I worked for Angus then."

She was taken aback. "Oh, I didn't know that."

"There's a lot you don't know. And you're far better off that way."

He whipped the Blazer into his parking slot at the courthouse and braked, pitching her forward against her seat belt. "You'd do well to leave the past alone, Miss Gaither."

"Thank you, Sheriff. I'll take that under advisement."

She got out of the truck and slammed the door behind her. Cursing beneath his breath, Reede watched her walk up the sidewalk. He wished he could relax and just enjoy the shape of her calves, the enticing sway of her hips, and all else that had immediately captured his notice when she had entered Pat Chastain's office yesterday afternoon. Her name, however, had robbed him of the luxury of indulging in pure, masculine appreciation.

Celina's daughter, he thought now, shaking his head in consternation. It was little wonder that he found Alex so damned attractive. Her mother had been his soul mate from the day in grade school when some snotty kid had hurtfully taunted her because she no longer had a daddy after her father's sudden death of a heart attack.

Knowing how ridicule about one's parents could hurt, Reede had rushed to Celina's defense. He had fought that battle and many others for her in the ensuing years. With Reede as the bearer of her colors, no one dared speak a cross word to her. A bond had been forged. Their friendship had been extraordinary and exclusive, until Junior had come along and been included.

So he knew he shouldn't be surprised that the assistant D.A. from Austin had churned up such emotions inside him. Perhaps his only cause for alarm should be their intensity. Even though Celina had borne a child, she had died a girl. Alexandra was the embodiment of the woman she might have become.

He'd like to pass off his interest as purely nostalgic, a tender reminder of his childhood sweetheart. But he'd be lying to himself. If he needed any help defining the nature of his interest, all he had to do was acknowledge the warm pressure that had developed inside his jeans as he had watched her lick sugar off her fingertips.

"Christ," he swore. He felt as ambiguous toward this woman as he'd felt toward her mother, just before she had been found dead in that stable.

How could two women, twenty-five years apart, have such a pivotal impact on his life? Loving Celina had almost ruined him. Her daughter posed just as real a threat. If she started digging into the past, God only knew what kind of trouble would be stirred up.

He intended to trade his sheriff's job for one that would generate wealth and status. He sure as hell didn't want his future shadowed by a criminal investigation.

Reede hadn't worked his butt off all these years to let the payoff slip through his fingers. He'd spent his adult life over-compensating for his childhood. Now, when the respect he'd always wanted was within his grasp, he wasn't about to stand by and let Alex's investigation remind folks of his origins. The sassy lady lawyer could wreck him if she wasn't stopped.

The people who said material possessions weren't important already had plenty of everything. He'd never had anything. Until now. He was prepared to go to any length to protect it.

As he left his truck and reentered the courthouse, he cursed the day Alexandra Gaither had been born, just as he had on that day itself. At the same time, he couldn't help but wonder if her smart mouth wouldn't be good for something besides spouting accusations and legal jargon.

He'd bet his next win at the track that it would.

Chapter 4

Judge Joseph Wallace was the Prairie Drugstore's best customer for Mylanta. He knew as he pushed away from the lunch table that he'd have to take a swig or two of the stuff before the afternoon was over. His daughter Stacey had prepared the meal for him—as she did every day of the week except Sunday when they went to the country club buffet. Stacey's dumplings, light and puffy as always, had landed like golf balls in his stomach.

"Something wrong?" She noticed that her father was absently rubbing his stomach.

"No, it's nothing."

"Chicken and dumplings is usually one of your favorites."

"Lunch was delicious. I've just got a nervous stomach today."

"Have a peppermint." Stacey passed him a cut-glass candy dish, conveniently kept on a dust-free cherrywood coffee table. He took out a wrapped piece of red-and-white-striped candy and put it in his mouth. "Any particular reason why your stomach is nervous?"

Stacey had become her father's caretaker when her

mother had died several years earlier. She was single and rapidly approaching middle age, but she had never exhibited any ambition beyond being a homemaker. Because she had no husband or children of her own, she fussed over the judge.

She had never been a raving beauty, and age hadn't ameliorated that unfortunate fact. Describing her physical attributes with tactful euphemisms was pointless. She was and always had been plain. Even so, her position in Purcell was well established.

Every important ladies' league in town had her name on its roster. She taught a girls' Sunday school class at the First Methodist Church, faithfully visited residents of the Golden Age Home each Saturday morning, and played bridge on Tuesdays and Thursdays. Her activities calendar was always full. She dressed expensively and well, though far too dowdily for her age.

Her etiquette was above reproach, her decorum refined, her temperament serene. She had weathered disappointments in a style that was noble and worthy of admiration. Everybody assumed that she was happy and content.

They were wrong.

Judge Wallace, a sparrow of a man, pulled on his heavy overcoat as he made his way toward the front door. "Angus called me last night."

"Oh? What did he want?" Stacey asked as she pulled the collar of her father's coat up around his ears to guard against the wind.

"Celina Gaither's daughter turned up yesterday."

Stacey's busy hands fell still, and she took a step away from her father. Their eyes met. "Celina Gaither's daughter?" The voice coming from her chalky lips was high and thin.

"Remember the baby? Alexandra, I believe."

"Yes, I remember, Alexandra," Stacey repeated vaguely. "She's here in Purcell?"

"As of yesterday. All grown up now."

"Why didn't you tell me this last night when I came in?"

"You were late coming home from the chili supper. I was already in bed. I knew you'd be tired, too, and there was no need to bother you with it then."

Stacey turned away and busied herself picking the empty cellophane wrappers out of the candy dish. Her father had an annoying habit of leaving the empties. "Why should the sudden appearance of Celina's daughter bother me?"

"No reason in particular," the judge said, glad he didn't have to meet his daughter's eyes. "On the other hand, it'll probably upset the whole damn town."

Stacey came back around. Her fingers were mutilating a piece of clear cellophane. "Why should it?"

The judge covered a sour belch with his fist. "She's a prosecutor in the D.A.'s office in Austin."

"Celina's daughter?" Stacey exclaimed.

"Helluva thing, isn't it? Who would have guessed that she would turn out that well, growing up with only Merle Graham for a parent."

"You still haven't said why she's come back to Purcell. A visit?"

The judge shook his head. "Business, I'm afraid."

"Does it have any bearing on the Mintons' gambling license?"

He looked away, and nervously fidgeted with a button on his coat. "No, she's, uh, she's gotten the D.A.'s okay to reopen her mother's murder case."

Stacey's bony chest seemed to cave in another inch. She groped behind her, searching for a place to land when she collapsed.

The judge, pretending not to notice his daughter's distress, said, "She had Pat Chastain arrange a meeting with the Mintons and Reede Lambert. According to Angus, she made this grandstand announcement that before she was finished, she would determine which one of them had killed her mother."

"*What?* Is she mad?"

"Not according to Angus. He said she appears to be razor sharp, in complete control of her faculties, and dead serious."

Stacey gratefully lowered herself to the arm of the sofa and laid a narrow hand against the base of her neck. "How did Angus react?"

"You know Angus. Nothing gets him down. He seemed amused by the whole thing. Said there was nothing to worry about—that she couldn't present any evidence to a grand jury because there isn't any. Gooney Bud was the culprit." The judge drew himself up. "And no one can question my ruling that the man was incompetent to stand trial."

"I should say not," Stacey said, rising to his defense. "You had no choice but to commit Gooney Bud to that hospital."

"I reviewed his medical records every year, took depositions from the doctors who treated him. That facility isn't a snake pit, you know. It's one of the finest hospitals in the state."

"Daddy, nobody is pointing a finger at you. Good Lord, all anybody has to do is review your record as judge. For more than thirty years, your reputation has remained unblemished."

He ran his hand over his thinning hair. "I just hate for this to come up right now. Maybe I should retire early, not wait till my birthday next summer to step down."

"You'll do no such thing, Your Honor. You'll stay on that bench until you're ready to retire, and not a day before. No little upstart fresh out of law school is going to run you off."

For all her starchy show of support, Stacey's eyes revealed her anxiety. "Did Angus say how the girl...what she looks like? Does she resemble Celina?"

"Some." The judge went to the front door and pulled it open. On his way out he regrettably mumbled over his shoulder, "Angus said she was prettier."

Stacey sat woodenly on the arm of the sofa for a long time after the judge left, staring into space. She completely forgot about cleaning the noon meal dishes.

"Hello, Judge Wallace. My name is Alex Gaither. How do you do?"

Introductions were unnecessary. He had known who she was the minute he had stepped into the office outside his chambers. Mrs. Lipscomb, his secretary, had nodded toward a chair against the opposite wall. Turning, he saw a young woman—twenty-five, if his calculations were correct—sitting in the straight chair with all the poise and self-confidence of royalty. It was an air she had inherited from her mother.

He hadn't had much personal interaction with Celina Gaither, but he knew all about her through Stacey. The girls had been classmates through eleven years of public schooling. Even whittling away Stacey's typical adolescent jealousy, he'd still painted an unflattering picture of a girl who knew she was beautiful, well liked, and who held all the boys in the class in the palm of her hand, including the only two who really mattered, Junior Minton and Reede Lambert.

Too many times to count, Stacey's heart had been broken because of Celina. For that reason alone the judge had despised her. And because this young woman was her daughter, he disliked her on sight.

"How do you do, Miss Gaither."

Judge Wallace shook her proffered hand, but no longer than was necessary to serve propriety. He found it difficult to consider this fashionable woman his colleague. He preferred lawyers who wore white shirts and worsted wool, not chic, short-skirted suits and fur. Viable members of the bar should emanate the faint smell of cigar smoke and leather-bound tomes, not a delicate perfume.

"Has District Attorney Chastain briefed you on why I'm here?"

"Yes. This morning. But I heard from Angus last night."

She tilted her head, as though to say that that information was interesting and worth storing away for future consideration. He could have kicked himself for volunteering it.

The truth was, he was rather dazzled. Angus Minton had been right. Alexandra Gaither was better looking than her mother.

When she moved her head, a shaft of sunlight coming through the window blinds set her dark hair afire. The collar of her fur coat brushed her cheek, giving her complexion a glow as fresh and delectable as ripe apricots. Stacey had a similar coat, but it turned her complexion the color of cold ashes.

"Could I have a moment with you in your chambers, Judge Wallace?" she asked politely.

Needlessly, he consulted his wristwatch. "I'm afraid that's out of the question. Actually, I just stopped by to pick up my messages. I've got an appointment out of the office for the rest of the afternoon." Mrs. Lipscomb started with surprise, a dead giveaway that he was lying.

Alex pondered the toes of her shoes for a moment. "I hate to insist, but I must. This is very important, and I'm anxious to get the investigation underway as soon as possible. Before I can move forward, I need to verify some facts with you. It won't take very long." The corners of her mouth turned up into a smile. "I'm certain your cooperation will be appreciated by my office in Austin."

Judge Wallace wasn't stupid; neither was Alex. She couldn't very well pull rank on him, but she could make him look bad with the Travis County D.A., who hobnobbed with the powers that be in the capitol.

"Very well, please come in." He shrugged off his overcoat, asked Mrs. Lipscomb to hold his calls, then followed Alex into his chambers. "Have a seat."

"Thank you."

His stomach was burning in the center of his gut like a crashed meteor. He'd drunk two swallows of antacid on his way back to the courthouse, but he could stand another kick. Alex didn't appear the least bit rattled. She sat down across the desk from him and gracefully shrugged out of her coat.

"Let's get to it, Miss Gaither," he said imperiously. "What do you want to know?"

Alex opened her briefcase and withdrew a sheaf of papers.

Inwardly, the judge groaned. "I've read the transcript of Bud Hicks's hearing, and I have some questions about it."

"Such as?"

"What was your rush?"

"I beg your pardon?"

"Bud Hicks was arraigned on a charge of first-degree murder and held without bail in the Purcell County jail. His competency hearing was held three days later."

"So?"

"Isn't that a rather brief period of time in which to weigh a man's future?"

The judge leaned back in his cordovan leather chair, which had been a gift from his daughter, hoping to impress the young attorney with his composure. "Maybe the docket was loaded and I was trying to clear it out. Or maybe it was a slack time and I was able to act quickly. I don't remember. It was twenty-five years ago."

She lowered her eyes to the notepad resting on her lap. "You had only two psychiatrists examine Mr. Hicks."

"His retardation was obvious, Miss Gaither."

"I'm not questioning that."

"He was, to put it unkindly, the town idiot. I don't mean to sound cruel, but that's what he was. He was tolerated. People saw him, but looked through him, if you know what I mean. He was a harmless fixture—"

"*Harmless?*"

Again the judge could have bitten his tongue. "Until the night he killed your mother."

"No jury convicted him of that, Judge."

Judge Wallace wet his lips, chagrined. "Of course." He

tried to avoid her level gaze so he could collect his thoughts. "I felt that two psychiatric analyses would be adequate, in this particular case."

"No doubt I would agree with you, *if* the analyses hadn't been so divergent."

"Or, if your mother hadn't been the victim of the crime," the judge said, getting in a shot.

She bristled. "I'm going to disregard that, Judge Wallace."

"Well, isn't that what this is all about? Or do you, for some reason unknown to me, want to question my integrity and undermine a judgment I made twenty-five years ago?"

"If you've got nothing to hide, then you've got no reason to believe that your excellent record will be marred by my asking a few questions, do you?"

"Proceed," he said stiffly.

"The two court-appointed psychiatrists disagreed on Mr. Hicks's mental condition the night of my mother's murder. This was the glitch that first intrigued me. After calling District Attorney Harper's attention to it, he agreed that the case should be reinvestigated.

"One psychiatrist clearly believed that Hicks was incapable of committing such an act of violence. The other said he was. Why didn't you seek a third, tie-breaking opinion?"

"It wasn't necessary."

"I disagree, Judge." She paused a moment, then looked up at him without lifting her head. "You were golf partners with the doctor who ruled in favor of. The other psychiatrist was from out of town. That was the first and only time he ever appeared in your court as an expert witness."

Judge Wallace's face became red with indignation. "If

you doubt my honesty, I suggest you consult with the doctors themselves, Miss Gaither."

"I've tried. Unfortunately, both are deceased." She met his hostile gaze coolly. "I did, however, consult with the last doctor to treat Mr. Hicks. He says you punished the wrong man, and has given me an affidavit to that effect."

"Miss Gaither." He rose partially from his chair and slapped the top of his desk. He was angry, but he also felt naked and vulnerable. The soft knock on his door was a godsend. "Yes?"

Sheriff Lambert strolled in.

"Reede!" Alex wouldn't have been surprised if the judge had rushed across the room and embraced him. He seemed that glad to see him. "Come in."

"Mrs. Lipscomb said you weren't to be disturbed, but when she told me who was with you, I convinced her that I might be of service."

"To whom?" Alex asked tartly.

Reede sauntered to the chair next to hers and dropped into it. Insolent green eyes moved over her. "To anybody who needs servicing."

Alex chose to ignore the double entendre and hoped he would ignore the mounting color in her face. She directed her attention to the judge.

"Miss Gaither was curious to know why I ruled Mr. Hicks incompetent to stand trial. Since she didn't know him, she can't appreciate how easily he fit the criteria of being unable to understand the charges against him and assist in his own defense."

"Thank you, Judge Wallace," she said, seething, "but I

know the criteria. What I don't know is why you made the ruling so hastily."

"I saw no need for a postponement," the judge replied, obviously more at ease now that Reede was there. "I told you earlier that most people in town merely tolerated Hicks. Your mother, to her credit, was kind to him. Gooney Bud latched on to her, in a pathetic way. I'm sure he was often a nuisance, the way he followed her around like a devoted little puppy. Right, Reede?"

The sheriff nodded. "Celina wouldn't let anybody pick on him when she was around. He used to give her presents, you know, mesquite beans, rocks, stuff like that. She always thanked him like he'd given her the crown jewels."

"I figure that Gooney Bud mistook her kindness for a deeper emotion," Judge Wallace said. "He followed her into the Mintons' stables that night and, uh, tried to force his attentions on her."

"Rape her?" Alex asked bluntly.

"Well, yes," the judge said, flustered. "And when she rebuffed him, he couldn't handle the rejection, and..."

"Stabbed her thirty times," Alex supplied.

"You force me to be insensitive, Miss Gaither." Joe Wallace looked at her reproachfully.

Alex crossed her legs. Her stockings made a slippery, silky sound that drew the sheriff's attention to them. She caught him staring at her hemline, but tried not to let it bother her as she continued to question the jittery judge.

"Let me make sure I understand. It's your contention that the murder wasn't premeditated, but a crime of passion?"

"As you said, it's conjecture."

"Okay, but for the sake of argument, let's say that's the

way it was. If Bud Hicks was acting out of extreme provocation, outrage, uncontrollable lust, wouldn't he have utilized a
pitchfork, or a rake, or something else that was handy? What
was he doing with a scalpel if he didn't enter that stable with
the intention of killing her?"

"That's easy," Reede said. Alex looked at him sharply. "A
mare had foaled that day. It was a difficult birth. We called
the vet in to assist."

"How? Did he have to do an episiotomy?" she asked.

"In the long run, no. We were finally able to pull the foal.
But Doc Collins's bag was right there. The scalpel could have
fallen out. I'm guessing, of course, but it's logical to assume
that Gooney Bud saw it and picked it up."

"That's a very broad assumption, Sheriff Lambert."

"Not so broad. As I've told you, Gooney Bud collected all
kinds of stuff like that."

"He's right, Miss Gaither," Judge Wallace hastened to say.
"Ask anybody. Something as shiny as a surgical instrument
would have attracted his attention the moment he went into
the stable."

"Was he in the stable that day?" she asked Reede.

"Yes. There were people coming and going all day, Gooney Bud among them."

Alex wisely decided that it was time to retreat and
regroup. She gave the judge a peremptory thank-you and left
the chambers. The sheriff followed her out. As soon as they'd
cleared the anteroom, she turned to confront him.

"From now on, I'll thank you not to coach whoever I'm
questioning."

He assumed an innocent look. "Is that what I was doing?"

"You know damn well it was. I've never heard such a

flimsy, farfetched explanation of a murder in my life. And I would eat alive any attorney who attempted to defend a client with it."

"Hmm, that's funny."

"Funny?"

"Yeah." She was subjected to another sly, arrogant once-over. "I was thinking you were the one who looked good enough to eat."

Blood rushed to her head. She attributed it to outrage. "Don't you take me seriously, Mr. Lambert?"

His insolence dissolved along with his insinuating smile. "You're damn right I do, Counselor," he whispered fiercely. "Damn right I do."

Chapter 5

———◦◉◦———

"Calm down, Joe." Angus Minton was angled back in his red leather recliner. He loved this chair. His wife, Sarah Jo, loathed it.

When he spotted Junior standing in the doorway of his den, he waved him inside. Covering the mouthpiece of the cordless phone, he whispered to his son, "Joe Wallace is in a tizzy."

"Now, Joe, you're jumping to conclusions and getting upset over nothing," he said into the mouthpiece. "She's just doing what she thinks is her job. After all, her mama was murdered. Now that she's got a law degree and a high-falutin' job as a prosecutor, she's on a crusade. You know how these young career women are."

He listened for a moment. No longer cajoling, he repeated, "Goddammit, Joe, calm down, you hear? Just keep your mouth shut, and all this will blow over. Leave Celina's daughter to me, to *us*," he said, winking at Junior.

"In a few weeks she'll go back to Austin with her tail tucked between her pretty, long legs and tell her boss she struck out. We'll get our racing license, the track will be built on schedule, you'll retire with a perfect record, and this time next year we'll be sitting over drinks, laughing about this."

After saying good-bye, he tossed the portable phone onto the end table. "Jesus, he's a pessimist. To hear him tell it, Celina's daughter put his scrawny neck through a noose and pulled it tight. Fetch me a beer, will ya?"

"Pasty's in the hall waiting to see you."

That piece of news did nothing to improve Angus's sour mood. "Shit. I guess now's as good a time as any. Go get him."

"Don't be too hard on him. He's shivering in his boots."

"For what he did, he ought to be," Angus grumbled.

Junior returned a few seconds later. Pasty Hickam shuffled along behind him, head bowed in contrition, battered cowboy hat in hand. He had come by his nickname by imbibing a whole bottle of Elmer's glue on a dare. His real name had been long forgotten. The deed must have occurred at some point in elementary school, because Pasty had forsaken education before reaching the ninth grade.

He'd ridden the rodeo circuit for several years, but never successfully. What purses he won were small, and quickly expended on drink, gambling, and women. His job at the Minton ranch had been his first venture into gainful employment, and it had endured for almost thirty years, a surprise to everybody. Angus tolerated Pasty's occasional binges. This time, however, he'd gone too far.

Angus let him stand and sweat for several interminable moments before he barked, "Well?"

"Ang...Angus," the old ranch hand stuttered, "I know what you're gonna say. I...fucked up sumthin' royal, but I swear to God I didn't mean to. You know how it's said that all cats look gray in the dark? Well, damned if it ain't true of horses, too. 'Specially if you've got a pint of Four Roses sloshing around in yore gut." He smiled, revealing that what few teeth he had remaining were black with decay.

Angus wasn't amused. "You're wrong, Pasty. That isn't what I was going to say. What I was going to say is that you're fired."

Junior shot up out of the leather love seat. "Dad!" Angus shot him a hard look that quelled any further interference.

Pasty's face turned pale. "You cain't mean that, Angus. I've been here nigh on thirty years."

"You'll get fair severance pay—a damned sight more than you deserve."

"But... but—"

"You put a colt into a paddock with ten high-strung fillies. What if he'd mounted one of them? That one from Argentina was in there. Any idea what that horse is worth, Pasty—over half a million. If she'd been injured or come in foal by that randy colt..." Angus blew out a gust of air. "Jesus, I can't even bear to think about the mess that would've put us in. If one of the other hands hadn't caught your mistake, I could have been out millions, and the reputation of this ranch would have been shot to hell."

Pasty swallowed with difficulty. "Give me one more chance, Angus. I swear—"

"I've heard this speech before. Clear your stuff out of the bunkhouse and drop by the office at the end of the week. I'll have the bookkeeper draft you a check."

"Angus—"

"Good-bye and good luck, Pasty."

The old cowboy glanced plaintively at Junior, but knew before looking that there would be no help coming from that quarter. Junior kept his eyes lowered. Eventually Pasty left the room, tracking mud with each step.

When they heard the front door close, Junior got up and headed for the refrigerator built into the paneling. "I didn't know you were going to fire him," he said resentfully.

"No reason you should."

He carried a beer to his father and twisted off the cap of another for himself. "Was it necessary? Couldn't you have yelled at him some, taken away some of his responsibilities, docked his pay? For crissake, Dad, what's an old guy like that gonna do?"

"He should have thought of that before he put the colt in that pasture. Now, let's drop it. I didn't enjoy doing it. He's been around here a long time."

"He made a mistake."

"Worse, he got caught!" Angus shouted. "If you're gonna run this business, boy, you gotta grow steel balls. The job isn't always fun, you know. There's more to it than taking clients out to fancy dinners and flirting with their wives and daughters." Angus took a swig of beer. "Now, let's talk about Celina's girl."

Junior, resigned to accepting Pasty's harsh punishment, even if he didn't agree with it, dropped into an easy chair and sipped at his bottle of beer. "She went to see Joe, huh?"

"Yeah, and notice that she didn't waste any time doing it, either. Joe's jittery as hell. He's afraid his spotless tenure as judge is about to be flushed down the toilet."

"What did Alexandra want with him?"

"She asked some questions about why he rushed up

Gooney Bud's incompetency hearing. Reede came to Joe's rescue, which was a smart move on his part."

"Reede?"

"Never asleep at the switch, is he?" Angus removed his boots and dropped them over the padded arm of his chair. They hit the floor with a heavy thud. He had gout, and his big toe was giving him trouble. He massaged it thoughtfully while looking at his son. "What did you think of the girl?"

"I tend to agree with Joe. She's a threat. She thinks one of us killed Celina, and she's bound and determined to find out who."

"She struck me that way, too."

"Of course, she's got nothing on any of us."

"Of course."

Junior looked at his father warily. "She's sharp."

"As a tack."

"And no slouch in the looks department."

Father and son shared a bawdy laugh. "Yeah, she is good-lookin'," Angus said. "But then, so was her mama."

Junior's smile faded. "Yes, she was."

"Still miss her, don't you?" Angus shrewdly studied his son.

"Sometimes."

Angus sighed. "I don't suppose you can lose a close friend like that without it having a lasting effect on you. You wouldn't be human, otherwise. But it's foolish of you to pine for a woman who's been dead all these years."

"I've hardly pined," Junior countered. "Since the day I figured out how this operates," he said, touching the fly of his pants, "it hasn't gone inactive for long."

"That's not what I'm talking about," Angus said, frowning. "Anybody can get laid on a regular basis. I'm talking about your life. Commitment to something. You were upset for a long time after Celina died. It took you a while to pull your shit together. Okay, that was understandable."

He pushed the footstool of his chair and sat up straight, pointing a blunt finger at Junior. "But you stalled, boy, and you haven't worked up a full head of steam since. Look at Reede. He took Celina's death hard, too, but he got over her."

"How do you know he got over her?"

"Do you see him moping around?"

"I'm the one who's had three wives, not Reede."

"And that's something to be proud of?" Angus shouted, his temper snapping. "Reede's made his life count for something. He's got a career—"

"Career?" Junior interrupted with a contemptuous snort. "I'd hardly call being sheriff of this pissant county a career. Big fuckin' deal."

"What would you call a career? Screwing the entire female membership of the country club before you die?"

"I do my fair share of work around here," Junior argued. "I spent all morning on the phone with that breeder in Kentucky. He's this close to buying that colt by Artful Dodger out of Little Bit More."

"Yeah, what did he say?"

"That he's seriously thinking about it."

Angus came out of his chair, booming his approval. "That's great news, son. That old man's a tough son of a bitch, I've heard tell. He's a crony of Bunky Hunt's. Feeds his horses caviar and shit like that after they win." Angus slapped Junior on the back and ruffled his hair as though he were three, instead of forty-three.

"However," Angus said, his frown returning, "that just

emphasizes how much we stand to lose if the racing commission rescinds that license before the ink on it is even dry. One breath of scandal and we're history. So, how are we gonna handle Alexandra?"

"Handle her?"

Favoring his ailing toe, Angus hobbled toward the refrigerator to get another beer. "We can't wish her away. The way I see it," he said, twisting off the bottle cap, "we'll just have to convince her that we're innocent. Upstanding citizens." He gave an elaborate shrug. "Since that's exactly what we are, it shouldn't be that hard to do."

Junior could tell when the wheels of his father's brain were turning. "How will we go about that?"

"Not we—you. By doing what you do best."

"You mean—?"

"Seduce her."

"Seduce her!" Junior exclaimed. "She didn't strike me as being a prime candidate for seduction. I'm sure she can't stand our guts."

"Then, that's the first thing we gotta change...*you* gotta change. Just seduce her into liking you...at first. I'd do it myself if I still had the proper equipment." He gave his son a wicked smile. "Think you can handle such an *unpleasant* chore?"

Junior grinned back. "I'd damn sure welcome the opportunity to try."

Chapter 6

The cemetery gates were open. Alex drove through them. She had never been to her mother's grave, but she knew the plot number. It had been jotted down and filed among some official papers that she'd found when she had moved her grandmother into the nursing home.

The sky looked cold and unfriendly. The sun was suspended just above the western horizon like a giant orange disk, brilliant but brassy. Tombstones cast long shadows across the dead grass.

Using discreet signposts for reference, Alex located the correct row, parked the car, and got out. As far as she could tell, she was the only person there. Here on the outskirts of town, the north wind seemed stronger, its howl more ominous. She flipped up the collar of her coat as she made her way toward the plot.

Even though she was searching for it, she wasn't prepared to see the grave. It rushed up on her unexpectedly. Her impulse was to turn away, as though she'd happened upon an atrocity, something horrible and offensive.

The rectangular marker was no more than two feet high.

She wouldn't have ever noticed it if it weren't for the name. It gave only her mother's date of birth, and date of death—nothing else. Not an epitaph. Not an obligatory "In loving memory of." Nothing but the barest statistical facts.

The scarcity of information broke Alex's heart. Celina had been so young and pretty and full of promise, yet she'd been diminished to anonymity.

She knelt beside the grave. It was set apart from the others, alone at the crest of a gradual incline. Her father's body had been shipped from Vietnam to his native West Virginia, courtesy of the United States Army. Grandfather Graham, who had died when Celina was just a girl, was buried in his hometown. Celina's grave was starkly solitary.

The headstone was cold to the touch. She traced the carved letters of her mother's first name with her fingertip, then pressed her hand on the brittle grass in front of it, as though feeling for a heartbeat.

She had foolishly imagined that she might be able to communicate with her supernaturally, but the only sensation she felt was that of the stubbly grass pricking her palm.

"Mother," she whispered, testing the word. "Mama. Mommy." The names felt foreign to her tongue and lips. She'd never spoken them to anyone before.

"She swore you recognized her just by the sound of her voice."

Startled, Alex spun around. Pressing a hand to her pounding heart, she gasped in fright. "You scared me. What are you doing here?"

Junior Minton knelt beside her and laid a bouquet of fresh flowers against the headstone. He studied it for a moment, then turned his head and smiled wistfully at Alex.

"Instinct. I called the motel, but you didn't answer when they rang your room."

"How did you know where I was staying?"

"Everybody knows everything about everybody in this town."

"No one knew I was coming to the cemetery."

"Deductive reasoning. I tried to imagine where I might be if I were in your shoes. If you don't want company, I'll leave."

"No. It's all right." Alex looked back at the name carved into the cold, impersonal gray stone. "I've never been here. Grandma Graham refused to bring me."

"Your grandmother isn't a very warm, giving person."

"No, she isn't, is she?"

"Did you miss having a mother when you were little?"

"Very much. Particularly when I started school and realized that I was the only kid in my grade who didn't have one."

"Lots of kids don't live with their mothers."

"But they know they've got one." This was a subject she found difficult to discuss with even her closest friends and associates. She didn't feel inclined to discuss it with Junior Minton at all, no matter how sympathetic his smile.

She touched the bouquet he'd brought and rubbed the petal of a red rose between her cold fingertips. In comparison, the flower felt like warm velvet, but it was the color of blood. "Do you bring flowers to my mother's grave often, Mr. Minton?"

He didn't answer until she was looking at him again. "I was at the hospital the day you were born. I saw you before they had washed you up." His grin was open, warm, disarming. "Don't you think that should put us on a first-name basis?"

It was impossible to erect barriers against his smile. It would have melted iron. "Then, call me Alex," she said, smiling back.

His eyes moved from the crown of her head to the toes of her shoes. "Alex. I like that."

"Do you?"

"What, like your name?"

"No, bring flowers here often."

"Oh, that. Only on holidays. Angus and I usually bring something out on her birthday, Christmas, Easter. Reede, too. We split the cost of having the grave tended."

"Any particular reason why?"

He gave her an odd look, then answered simply, "We all loved Celina."

"I believe one of you killed her," she said softly.

"You believe wrong, Alex. I didn't kill her."

"What about your father? Do you think he did?"

He shook his head. "He treated Celina like a daughter. Thought of her that way, too."

"And Reede Lambert?"

He shrugged as though no elaboration was necessary. "Reede, well..."

"What?"

"Reede could never have killed her."

Alex settled deeper into her fur coat. The sun had set, and it was getting colder by the moment. When she spoke, her breath fogged the air in front of her face. "I spent some time in the public library this afternoon, reading back issues of the local newspaper."

"Anything about me?"

"Oh, yes, all about your Purcell Panther football days."

As he laughed, the wind lifted his fair hair. His was a much lighter blond than Reede's, and it was finer, better controlled. "That must have made for some fascinating reading."

"It did. You and Reede were cocaptains of the team."

"Hell, yeah." He crooked his arm as though showing off muscled biceps. "We thought we were invincible, real hot snot."

"Her junior year, my mother was the homecoming queen. There was a picture of Reede kissing her during halftime."

Studying that photograph had made Alex feel very strange. She'd never seen it before. For some reason her grandmother had chosen not to keep it among her many others, perhaps because Reede Lambert's kiss had been audacious, full-fledged, and proprietary.

Undaunted by the cheering crowd in the stadium, his arm had been curved possessively around Celina's waist. The pressure of the kiss had angled her head back. He looked like a conqueror, especially in the muddy football uniform, holding his battle-scarred helmet in his other hand.

After staring at the photograph for several minutes, she began to feel that kiss herself.

Coming back to the present, she said, "You didn't become friends with my mother and Reede until later on, isn't that right?"

Junior pulled up a blade of grass and began to shred it between his fingers. "Ninth grade. Until then, I attended a boarding school in Dallas."

"By choice?"

"By my mother's choice. She didn't want me picking up what she considered to be undesirable habits from the kids of oil-field workers and cowhands, so I was packed off to Dallas every fall.

"My schooling was a bone of contention between Mother and Dad for years. Finally, when I was about to go into high school, he put his foot down and said it was time I learned there were other kinds of people besides the 'pale little bastards'—and that's a quote—at prep school. He enrolled me in Purcell High School that fall."

"How did your mother take it?"

"Not too well. She was definitely against it, but there wasn't much she could do about it. Where she came from—"

"Which is?"

"Kentucky. In his prime, her old man was one of the most successful breeders in the country. He'd bred a Triple Crown winner."

"How did she meet your father?"

"Angus went to Kentucky to buy a mare. He brought it and my mother back with him. She's lived here for over forty years, but she still clings to Presley family traditions, one of which was to send all the offspring to private school.

"Not only did Dad enroll me at Purcell, he also insisted that I go out for the football team. The coach wasn't too keen on the idea, but Dad bribed him by promising to buy new uniforms for the team if he'd take me on, so..."

"Angus Minton makes things happen."

"You can bank on that," Junior said with a laugh. "He never takes no for an answer, so I went out for football. I'd never even touched one, and I nearly got the crap kicked out of me that first day of practice. The other boys naturally resented me."

"For being the richest kid in town?"

"It's a tough job, but somebody's got to do it," he said with an engaging grin. "Anyway, when I got home that night,

I told Dad that I hated Purcell High School and football with equal amounts of passion. I told him I preferred pale little bastards any day of the week over bullies like Reede Lambert."

"What happened?"

"Mother cried herself sick. Dad cussed himself into a frenzy. Then he marched me outside and threw footballs at me till my hands bled from catching them."

"That's terrible!"

"Not really. He had my interests at heart. He knew, even if I didn't, that out here, you've got to play, eat, drink, and sleep football. Say," he interjected, "I'm rambling on. Aren't you cold?"

"No."

"Sure?"

"Yes."

"Want to go?"

"No, I want you to keep rambling."

"Is this a formal interrogation?"

"Conversation," she replied, tartly enough to make him grin.

"At least put your hands in your pockets." Taking one of her hands in each of his, he guided them to the deep pockets of her coat, tucked them inside, and patted them into place. Alex resented the intimate gesture. It was presumptuous of him and, considering the circumstances, highly inappropriate.

"I gather you made the football team," she said, deciding to ignore his touch.

"Junior varsity, yes, but I didn't play, not a single game, until the very last one. It was for the district championship."

He lowered his head and smiled reflectively. "We were

down by four points. A field goal wouldn't have done us any good. There were only a few seconds left on the clock. We had the ball, but it was fourth down and miles to go because of penalties. Both the A- and B-string wide receivers had been injured in the previous quarters."

"My God."

"I told you, football's a blood-drawing sport out here. Anyway, they were carting the star running back off the field on a stretcher when the coach looked toward the bench and barked my name. I nearly wet my pants."

"What happened?"

"I shrugged off my poncho and ran out to join the team in a time-out huddle. Mine was the only clean jersey on the field. The quarterback—"

"Reede Lambert." Alex knew that from the newspaper accounts.

"Yeah, my nemesis. He groaned audibly when he saw me coming, and even louder when I told him the play the coach had sent in with me. He looked me right between the eyes and said, 'If I throw you the goddamn football, preppie, you fuckin' well better catch it.'"

For a moment Junior was silent, steeped in the memory. "I'll never forget that as long as I live. Reede was laying down the terms."

"The terms?"

"Of our becoming friends. It was then or never that I had to prove myself worthy of his friendship."

"Was that so important?"

"You bet your ass. I'd been in school here long enough to know that if I didn't hack it with Reede, I'd never be worth shit."

"You caught the pass, didn't you?"

"No, I didn't. In all fairness, I can't say that I did. Reede threw it right here," he said, pointing at his chest, "right between the numbers on my jersey. Thirty-five yards. All I had to do was fold my arms over the football and carry it across the goal line."

"But that was enough, wasn't it?"

His smile widened until it germinated into a laugh. "Yep. That marked the beginning of it."

"Your father must have been ecstatic."

Junior threw back his head and howled with laughter. "He jumped the fence, hurdled the bench, and came charging out onto the field. He swooped me up and carried me around for several minutes."

"What about your mother?"

"My mother! She wouldn't be caught dead at a football game. She thinks it's barbaric." He chuckled, tugging on his earlobe. "She's damned near right. But I didn't care what anybody thought about me, except Dad. He was so proud of me that night." His blue eyes shone with the memory.

"He'd never even met Reede, but he hugged him, too, football pads and all. That night was the beginning of their friendship, too. It wasn't too long after that that Reede's daddy died, and he moved out to the ranch to live with us."

For several moments, his recollections were private. Alex allowed him the introspective time without interruption. Eventually he glanced up at her and did a double take.

"Jesus, you looked like Celina just then," he said softly. "Not so much your features, but your expression. You have that same quality of listening." He reached out and touched her hair. "She loved to listen. At least she made the person talking think she did. She could sit so still and just *listen* for hours." He withdrew his hand, but he didn't seem happy about it.

"Is that what first attracted you to her?"

"Hell, no," he said with a leering smile. "The first thing that attracted me to her was a ninth-grade boy's adolescent lust. The first time I saw Celina in the hall at school, she took my breath, she was so pretty."

"Did you chase after her?"

"Hey, I was dumbstruck, not crazy."

"What about this mad crush you had on her?"

"She belonged to Reede then," he said unequivocally. "There was never any question about that." He stood up. "We'd better go. Regardless of what you say, you're freezing. Besides, it's getting spooky out here in the dark."

Alex, still befuddled by his last statement, let him assist her up. She turned to brush the dry grass off the back of her skirt and noticed the bouquet again. The green waxed paper wrapped around the vivid petals fluttered in the brisk wind. It made a dry, rattling sound. "Thank you for bringing the flowers, Junior."

"You're welcome."

"I appreciate your thoughtfulness to her over the years."

"In all honesty, I had an ulterior motive for coming here today."

"Oh?"

"Uh-huh," he said, taking both her hands. "To invite you out to the house for drinks."

Chapter 7

She had been expected. That much was evident from the moment Junior escorted her across the threshold of the sprawling two-story house on the Minton ranch. Eager to study her suspects in their own environment, she had agreed to follow Junior home from the cemetery.

As she entered the living room, however, she couldn't help wondering if perhaps she was being manipulated, rather than the other way around.

Her determination to proceed with caution was immediately put to the test when Angus strode across the spacious room and shook her hand.

"I'm glad Junior found you and convinced you to come," he told her as he helped her out of her coat. He tossed the fur jacket at Junior. "Hang that up, will ya?" Looking at Alex with approval, he said, "I didn't know how you'd take our invitation. We're pleased to have you."

"I'm pleased to be here."

"Good," he said, rubbing his hands together. "What'll you have to drink?"

"White wine, please," she said. His blue eyes were friendly, but she found them disquieting. He seemed to see beyond the surface and lay bare the emotional insecurities she kept heavily camouflaged with competency.

"White wine, huh? Can't stand the stuff myself. Just as well be drinking soda pop. But that's what my wife drinks. She'll be down directly. You sit there, Alexandra."

"She likes to be called Alex, Dad," Junior said as he joined Angus at the built-in wet bar to mix himself a scotch and water.

"Alex, huh?" Angus carried a glass of wine to her. "Well, I guess that name suits a lady lawyer."

It was a backhanded compliment, at best. She let her thank-you suffice for both the remark and the wine. "Why did you invite me here?"

He seemed momentarily nonplussed by her directness, but answered in kind. "There's too much water under the bridge for us to be enemies. I want to get to know you better."

"That's the reason I came, Mr. Minton."

"Angus. Call me Angus." He took a moment to study her. "How come you wanted to be a lawyer?"

"So I could investigate my mother's murder."

The answer came to her lips spontaneously, which astonished not only the Mintons, but Alex herself. She had never verbalized that as being her goal before. Merle Graham must have spoon-fed her doses of determination, along with her vegetables.

With that public admission also came the private realization that she was her own chief suspect. Grandmother Graham had said she was ultimately responsible for her mother's death. Unless she could prove otherwise, she would carry that guilt with her for the rest of her life. She was in Purcell County to exonerate herself.

"You certainly don't mince words, young lady," Angus said. "I like that. Pussyfooting is a waste of my time."

"Of mine, too," Alex said, remembering her concurrent deadlines.

Angus harrumphed. "No husband? No kids?"

"No."

"Why not?"

"Dad," Junior said, rolling his eyes, embarrassed by his father's lack of tact.

Alex was amused, not offended. "I don't mind, Junior, really. It's a common question."

"Got an answer to it?" Angus took a swig from his long-neck.

"No time or inclination."

Angus grunted noncommittally. "Around here, we've got too much time and not enough inclination." He shot Junior a withering glance.

"Dad's referring to my failed marriages," Junior told their guest.

"Marriages? How many have there been?"

"Three," he confessed with a wince.

"And no grandbabies to show for any of them," Angus grumbled like a foul-natured bear. He aimed a chastising index finger at his son. "And it's not like you don't know how to breed."

"As usual, Angus, your manners in front of company are deplorable."

Simultaneously, the three of them turned. A woman was standing in the open doorway. Alex had painted a mental picture of what Angus's wife would be like—strong, assertive, feisty enough to meet him toe to toe. She would typify the coarse, horsy type who rode to hounds and spent more time wielding a quirt than a hairbrush.

Mrs. Minton was the antithesis of Alex's mental picture. Her figure was willowy, her features as dainty as those on a Dresden figurine. Graying blond hair curled softly about a face as pale as the double strand of pearls she was wearing around her neck. Dressed in a full-skirted mauve wool jersey dress that floated around her slender body as she walked, she came into the room and sat down in a chair near Alex's.

"Honey, this is Alex Gaither," Angus said. If he was put off by his wife's reprimand, he didn't show it. "Alex, my wife, Sarah Jo."

Sarah Jo Minton nodded and, in a voice as formal and cool as her acknowledgment of the introduction, said, "Miss Gaither, a pleasure, I'm sure."

"Thank you."

Her pallid face lit up and her straight, thin lips curved into a radiant smile when she accepted a glass of white wine from Junior, who had poured it without being asked. "Thank you, sweetheart."

He bent down and kissed his mother's smooth, proffered cheek. "Did your headache go away?"

"Not entirely, but my nap helped it. Thank you for inquiring." She reached up to stroke his cheek. Her hand, Alex noted, was milky white and looked as fragile as a flower ravaged by a storm. Addressing her husband, she said, "Must you bring talk of breeding into the living room, instead of keeping it in the stable, where it belongs?"

"In my own house, I'll talk about anything I goddamn

well please," Angus answered, though he didn't seem angry at her.

Junior, apparently accustomed to their bantering, laughed and circled Sarah Jo's chair to sit on the arm of Alex's. "We weren't talking about breeding, per se, Mother. Dad was just lamenting my inability to keep a wife long enough to produce an heir."

"You'll have children with the right woman when the time comes." She spoke to Angus as much as to Junior. Then, turning to Alex, she asked, "Did I overhear you say you'd never been married, Miss Gaither?"

"That's right."

"Strange." Sarah Jo sipped her wine. "Your mother certainly never lacked for male companionship."

"Alex didn't say she lacked for male companionship," Junior corrected. "She's just choosy."

"Yes, I chose a career over marriage and having a family. For the time being, anyway." Her brow beetled as an original idea occurred to her. "Did my mother ever express any interest in having a career?"

"Not that I ever heard her mention," Junior said, "though I guess all the girls in our class went through that stage of wanting to be Warren Beatty's leading lady."

"She had me so early," Alex said with a trace of regret. "Maybe an early marriage and a baby prevented her from pursuing a career."

Junior placed his finger beneath her chin and raised it, until she was looking at him. "Celina made her own choices."

"Thank you for saying that."

He dropped his hand. "I never heard her say she wanted to be anything other than a wife and mother. I remember the day we talked about it specifically. You should, too, Dad. It was summertime, and so hot you told Reede to take the day off after he'd mucked out the stables. The three of us decided to take a picnic out to that old stock pond, remember?"

"No." Angus left his chair in pursuit of another beer.

"I do," Junior said dreamily, "like it was yesterday. We spread a quilt under the mesquite trees. Lupe had packed us some homemade tamales to take with us. After we'd eaten them we stretched out on our backs, Celina between Reede and me, and stared up at the sky through the branches of those mesquites. They hardly cast a shade. The sun and our full bellies made us drowsy.

"We watched buzzards circling something and talked about chasing them down to find out what had died, but we were too lazy. We just lay there, talking, you know, about what we were going to be once we grew up. I said I wanted to be an international playboy. Reede said that if I did, he was gonna buy stock in a company that made condoms and get rich. He didn't care what he turned out to be, so long as he was rich. All Celina wanted to be was a wife." He paused a moment and looked down at his hands. "Reede's wife."

Alex started.

"Speaking of Reede," Angus said, "I think I hear his voice."

Chapter 8

Lupe, the Mintons' housekeeper, showed Reede in. Alex turned in time to see him come through the doorway. Junior's startling revelation had left her dazed.

From Grandma Graham, she'd heard that Reede and Celina had been high school sweethearts. The photograph of him crowning her homecoming queen bore that out. But Alex hadn't known that her mother had wanted to marry him. She knew her expression must reflect her shock.

He took in the room at a glance. "Well, isn't this a cozy little scene."

"Hey, Reede," Junior said from his position near Alex, which suddenly seemed all too close and familiar, for a reason she couldn't explain. "What brings you out? Drink?"

"Come on in." Angus signaled him into the room. Sarah Jo ignored him as though he was invisible. That mystified Alex, since he had once lived with them like a member of the family.

He laid his coat and hat in a chair and moved toward the

bar to accept the drink that Angus had poured for him. "I came to check on my mare. How is she?"

"Fine," Angus told him.

"Good."

There followed a strained silence while everyone seemed to contemplate the contents of their glasses. Finally, Angus said, "Something else on your mind, Reede?"

"He came out here to warn you about what you say to me," Alex said. "The same way he did Judge Wallace earlier this afternoon."

"When somebody asks me a direct question, I'll do my own answering, Counselor," he said testily. He threw back his drink and set down the glass. "See y'all later. Thanks for the drink." He stamped from the room, pausing only long enough to pick up his hat and coat.

Surprisingly, it was Sarah Jo who filled the silence once Reede had slammed out the front door. "I see his manners haven't improved any."

"You know Reede, Mother," Junior said with a casual shrug. "Another glass of wine?"

"Please."

"Have another drink together," Angus said. "I want to speak to Alex in private. Bring your wine if you want," he told her.

She had been helped out of her chair and escorted into the hallway before she quite knew how it had come about. As they moved down the hall, she looked around.

The walls were covered with red flocked wallpaper and held framed photographs of racehorses. A massive Spanish chandelier loomed threateningly overhead. The furniture was dark and bulky.

"Like my house?" Angus asked, noticing that she was dawdling to take in her surroundings.

"Very much," she lied.

"Designed and built it myself when Junior was still in diapers."

Without being told, Alex knew that Angus had not only built but decorated the house. Nothing in it reflected Sarah Jo's personality. Doubtless she countenanced it because she'd been given no choice.

The house was atrociously ugly, but it was in such appalling and unapologetic bad taste that it had a crude charm all its own, much like Angus.

"Before this house was here, Sarah Jo and I lived in a lineman's shack. You could see daylight through the walls of that damn thing. Nearly froze us out in the winter, and in the summer, we'd wake up with an inch of dust covering our bed."

Alex's initial reaction to Mrs. Minton had been dislike. She seemed distracted and self-absorbed. Alex could, however, sympathize with a younger Sarah Jo who had been plucked like an exotic flower out of a gracious, refined culture and replanted into one so harsh and radically different that she had withered. She could never adapt here, and it was a mystery to Alex why either Angus or Sarah Jo thought she could.

He preceded her into a paneled den that was even more masculine than the rest of the house. From their mountings on the walls, elk and deer gazed into space with resigned brown eyes. What space they didn't take up was filled with photographs of racehorses wearing the Minton colors standing in the winners' circles of racetracks all over the country. Some were fairly current; others appeared to be decades old.

There were several gun racks with a firearm in each slot. A flagpole with the state flag had been propped in one corner. A framed cartoon read: "Tho I walk through the valley of the Shadow of Death, I will fear no evil...'cause I'm the meanest son of a bitch in the valley."

The moment they entered the room, he pointed her toward a corner. "Come over here. I want to show you something."

She followed him to a table that was draped with what looked like an ordinary white bed sheet. Angus unfurled it.

"My goodness!"

It was an architectural model of a racetrack. Not a single detail had been overlooked, from the color-coded seating in the stands, to the movable starting gate, to the diagonal stripes painted in the parking lot.

"Purcell Downs," Angus boasted with the chest-expanding pride of a new father. "I realize you're only doing what you feel like you've got to do, Alex. I can respect that." His expression was belligerent. "But you don't realize how much is at stake here."

Alex defensively folded her arms across her midriff. "Why don't you tell me?"

Needing no more encouragement, Angus launched into a full explanation of how he wanted the track to be built, enumerating its various features. There would be no corners cut, no scrimping. The entire complex was to be a first-class facility from the stables to the ladies' restrooms.

"We'll be the only full-scale track between Dallas/Fort Worth and El Paso, and three hundred or so miles from each. It will be a good stopover for travelers. I can envision Purcell becoming another Las Vegas in twenty years, springing up out of the desert like a gusher."

"Isn't that being a little optimistic?" Alex asked skeptically.

"Well, maybe a bit. But that's what folks said when I started this place. That's what they said when I built my practice track and drew up plans for an indoor swimming pool for the horses. I don't let skepticism bother me. You gotta dream big if you want big things to happen. Mark my words," he said, jabbing the air between them for emphasis. "If we get that license to build this track, the town of Purcell will explode."

"Not everybody would like that, would they? Some might want to keep the community small."

Stubbornly, Angus shook his head. "Several years ago, this town was booming."

"Oil?"

"Yessiree. There were ten banks. *Ten.* More than in any other town this size. Per capita, we were the richest city in the country. Merchants had more business than they could handle. The real estate market was hot. Everybody prospered." He paused to take a breath. "You want something to drink? A beer? A Coke?"

"Nothing, thank you."

Angus took a beer from the refrigerator, twisted off the cap, and took a long drink. "Then, the bottom fell out of the oil market," he resumed. "We told ourselves that it was temporary."

"To what extent did the oil market affect you?"

"I hold a hefty percentage in several wells and one natural gas company. But thank God, I'd never invested more than I could afford to lose. I'd never liquidated my other businesses to support an oil well."

"Still, that drop in the price of oil must have caused you a substantial financial setback. Weren't you upset?"

He shook his head. "I've won and lost more fortunes than you are years old, young lady. Hell, I really don't mind being broke. Being rich is more fun, but being broke is more exciting. It's got built-in challenges.

"Sarah Jo," he said, sighing thoughtfully, "doesn't agree with me, of course. She likes the security of having money collecting dust in a vault. I've never touched her money or Junior's inheritance. I promised her I never would."

Talking about inheritances was foreign to Alex. She couldn't even conceive of it. Merle Graham had supported them on her salary from the telephone company, and then on her pension after her retirement. Alex's grades had been high enough to earn her a scholarship at the University of Texas, but she'd worked after classes to keep herself dressed and fed so her grandmother wouldn't have those expenses to complain about.

She had received financial assistance for law school, too, because her grades were so impressive. Working in public service didn't provide her with luxuries. She'd struggled with her conscience for weeks before rewarding herself with the fur coat for passing the bar. It was one of the few extravagances she had ever allowed herself.

"Do you have enough capital to finance the racetrack?" she asked, bringing her mind back around.

"Not personally."

"Minton Enterprises?"

"Not by itself. We've formed a group of investors, individuals, and businesses that would profit from having the track built here."

He sat down in his red leather recliner and pointed her into a chair. "During the oil boom, everybody got a taste of wealth. They're greedy for it again."

"That's hardly a flattering assessment of the population of Purcell—a group of avaricious carnivores waiting to gobble up horse-racing money."

"Not avaricious," he said. "Everybody would get his fair share, starting with the major investors, and working down to the guy who owns the self-serve filling station on the nearest corner. It wouldn't mean just individual gain, either. Think of the schools and hospitals and public facilities the town could build with that increased revenue."

He leaned forward and curled his hand into a fist, as though grasping at something. "That's why this racetrack is so damned important. It would set Purcell back on its feet and then some." His blue eyes sparkled with enthusiasm for his argument. "Well, what do you think?"

"I'm not a moron, Mr. Minton, uh, Angus," she corrected. "I realize what the track could mean to the county's economy."

"Then, why don't you drop this ridiculous investigation?"

"I don't think it's ridiculous," she retaliated sharply.

Studying her, he absently scratched his cheek. "How could you think that I killed your mama? She was one of Junior's best friends. She was in and out of this house on a daily basis. Not so much after she got married, but certainly before then. I couldn't have lifted a finger to hurt that girl."

Alex wanted to believe him. Despite the fact that he was a suspect in a criminal case, she admired him very much. From what she had read and gathered through conversation, he had started with nothing and built an empire.

His brusqueness was almost endearing. He had a persuasive personality. But she couldn't let his colorful persona influence her. Her admiration for Angus wasn't as strong as her need to know how she, an innocent baby, had prompted someone to murder her mother.

"I can't drop the investigation," she said. "Even if I wanted to, Pat Chastain—"

"Listen," he said, scooting forward. "You bat those big baby blues of yours at him, tell him you made a mistake, and by this time tomorrow, I guarantee that he won't even remember what you came here for."

"I wouldn't do—"

"Okay, then leave Pat to me."

"Angus," she said loudly, "you're missing my point." When she was assured she had his attention, she said, "As strongly as you believe in your racetrack, I believe that my mother's murder case was mishandled. I intend to see that rectified."

"Even though the future of a whole town is at stake?"

"Come on," she cried in protest. "You make it sound like I'm taking bread from starving children."

"Not as bad as that, but still—"

"*My* future is at stake, too. I can't go on with the rest of it until the case is resolved to my satisfaction."

"Yes, but—"

"Hey, time out." Junior opened the door suddenly and poked his head inside. "I've had a great idea, Alex. Why don't you stay for supper?"

"Damn you, Junior," Angus thundered, pounding the arm of his chair with his fist. "You wouldn't recognize a business discussion if it bit you in the ass. We're talking seriously here. Don't ever interrupt me when I'm in a private conference again. You know better than that."

Junior swallowed visibly. "I didn't know your conversation was so private or so serious."

"Well, you damned well should have, shouldn't you? For crissake, we were—"

"Angus, please, it's all right," Alex said quickly. "Actually, I'm glad Junior interrupted. I just now noticed how late it is. I need to be going."

She couldn't stand to watch a grown man get a dressing down from his father, especially in front of a female guest. She was embarrassed for both of them.

Most of the time, Angus was a good ol' boy. But not always. He had an explosive temper when crossed. Alex had just witnessed how short his fuse was and just how slight a transgression it took to ignite it.

"I'll see you out," Junior offered woodenly.

She shook hands with Angus. "Thank you for showing me the model. Nothing you've said has diverted me, but you've clarified some things. I'll keep them in mind as I pursue the case."

"You can trust us, you know. We're not killers."

Junior walked her to the front door. After he had held her coat for her, she turned to face him. "I'll be in touch, Junior."

"I certainly hope so." He bent over her hand and kissed it, then turned her palm up and kissed it, too.

She took it back quickly. "Do you flirt like this with every woman you meet?"

"Just about." He flashed her an unrepentant grin. "Are you susceptible?"

"Not in the least."

His grin widened, indicating to her that he wasn't convinced and knew that she wasn't either. After saying another quick good night, she left.

Her car was cold. She shivered inside her coat. As she

drove down the private road toward the highway, she noticed the outbuildings on either side of it. Most were stables. There was a faint light burning inside one of them. Reede's Blazer was parked at the door. On impulse, Alex pulled up beside it and got out.

Sarah Jo's bedroom in Kentucky had been duplicated at her Texas home, down to the silk cord tiebacks on the drapes. When the house had been built, she had agreed to let Angus have his heavy, dark furniture, his red leather upholstery, and his hunting trophies in other rooms, but she had flatly refused to let his revolting frontier motif defile their bedroom.

Cheerfully, he had agreed. He liked her fussy, feminine, frilly things around him at night. He'd often told her that if he'd wanted to marry a cowgirl, he wouldn't have had to go all the way to Kentucky to find one.

"Mother, may I come in?" Junior opened the bedroom door after a tentative knock.

"Darling, please do." Sarah Jo smiled, evidently quite pleased over her son's visit.

Junior found her propped up on a mountain of satin pillows, wearing a lace night jacket, smelling of expensive face cream, and reading the biography of some foreign statesman of whom he'd never heard. He'd never even heard of the country from which the man hailed. Probably no one except his mother had.

She took off her reading glasses, laid the book aside, and patted the quilted satin comforter. With a brisk shake of his head, Junior declined to sit down. Instead he remained standing at the foot of the bed, hands in pockets, jingling change, resenting this nightly ritual that was a carryover from his childhood.

Long ago, he'd outgrown the need or desire to kiss his mother good night, but Sarah Jo continued to expect it. Her feelings would be hurt if he didn't. He and Angus went out of their way to spare Sarah Jo's feelings, which were always tenuous.

"It always smells good in here," he commented for lack of anything else to say. The dressing down he'd received in front of Alex still smarted. He was impatient to leave the house and go to one of the local nightspots where he wouldn't have to concentrate on his problems.

"Sachets. I keep them in all my drawers and closets. When I was a girl, we had a maid who made them from crushed dried flowers and herbs. They smelled wonderful," she said reminiscently. "Now I have to order them. They use artificial scents in them these days, but I still think they're pretty."

"How's the book?" Junior was already bored with the subject of sachets.

"Quite interesting."

He seriously doubted it, but he smiled down at her. "Good. I'm glad you're enjoying it."

Sarah Jo sensed his melancholy mood. "What's wrong?"

"Nothing."

"I can tell when something's wrong."

"Nothing out of the ordinary. I got on Dad's bad side by interrupting his discussion with Alex."

Sarah Jo made a moue of displeasure. "Your father still hasn't learned how to conduct himself when there's company in the house. If he can be rude enough to cart a guest out of the living room during the cocktail hour, you can be rude enough to interrupt a discussion."

She bobbed her head as though she had said her piece and that settled the matter. "What were they discussing so privately, anyway?"

"Something about her mother's death," he said nonchalantly. "Nothing to worry about."

"Are you sure? Everybody seemed so tense tonight."

"If there's any cause for alarm, Dad'll take care of it, the way he always does. It's certainly nothing for you to worry about."

He had no intention of telling his mother about Alex's investigation. The men in Sarah Jo's life knew she hated being exposed to anything upsetting or unpleasant, and protected her from it.

Angus never discussed business with her, especially when it was bad. She was disappointed when their horses didn't perform well at the track and celebrated when they did, but beyond that, neither the ranch, nor any of the subsidiary companies comprising Minton Enterprises, held much interest for her.

Indeed, nothing held much interest for Sarah Jo, with the possible exception of Junior. She was like a beautiful doll, sealed inside a sterile room, never exposed to light or any other corrupting element—especially life itself.

Junior loved his mother, but recognized that she wasn't well liked. By contrast, everybody liked Angus. A few of his friends' wives, out of loyalty and obligation, were friendly to Sarah Jo. If not for them, she wouldn't have any acquaintances in Purcell at all.

She'd certainly never gone out of her way to cultivate a

friendship. She thought most of the locals were vulgar and coarse, and she made no attempt to conceal her low opinion of them. She seemed perfectly content to reside in this room, surrounded by the soft, pretty, uncomplicated things she liked and understood best.

Junior knew she was the object of derision and gossip. It was said that she drank. She didn't, except for two glasses of wine before dinner. Some, who didn't understand her delicate sensibilities, thought she was odd. Others thought she was just plain "off."

Admittedly, she was distracted a good deal of the time, as though mentally reliving the privileged childhood she treasured. She had never quite recovered from the premature death of a beloved brother, and had still been mourning it when she had met Angus.

Junior wondered if she had married his father to escape unpleasant memories. He could find no other grounds for two such mismatched people to base a marriage on.

Junior was eager to get on his way to having a good time, but he lengthened tonight's visit, curious to know his mother's opinion of their guest that evening. "What did you think of her?"

"Who, Celina's daughter?" Sarah Jo asked absently. Her brows drew together into a slight frown. "She's very attractive physically, though I don't find such flamboyant coloring flattering to a woman."

Thoughtfully, she fingered the fine lace on the bodice of her bed jacket. "She's certainly intense, isn't she? Much more serious-minded than her mother. Celina was a silly little thing, God knows. As I recall, she was always laughing." She paused and cocked her head to one side, as though listening to distant laughter. "I don't remember ever seeing that girl when she wasn't laughing."

"There were plenty of times. You just didn't know her that well."

"Poor darling. I know you were crushed when she died. I know what it's like to lose someone you love. It's sheer misery."

Her voice, so soft, changed suddenly, as did her expression. No longer a shrinking violet, her features hardened with resolve. "Junior, you must stop letting Angus embarrass you, especially in front of other people."

He gave a careless shrug. This was familiar territory. "He doesn't mean anything by it. It's just a habit of his."

"Then, it's up to you to break him of it. Darling, don't you see," she said, "that's what he wants you to do. He wants you to stand up to him. Angus only understands one tone of voice—harsh.

"He doesn't know how to be soft-spoken and genteel, like us. You have to talk to him in a way he understands, like Reede does. Angus wouldn't dare speak to Reede in the condescending way he does to you because he respects Reede. And he respects him because Reede doesn't kowtow to him."

"Dad thinks Reede can do no wrong. To this day, it sticks in his craw that Reede left ME. He'd much rather have Reede than me around to manage things. I never do anything to his liking."

"That's simply not true!" Sarah Jo objected, showing more spirit than she had in weeks. "Angus is very proud of you. He just doesn't know how to show it. He's such a hard man. He's had to be tough to accomplish everything he's done. He wants you to be tough, too."

Junior grinned, doubling up his fists. "Okay, Mother, tomorrow morning I'll come out slugging."

She giggled. His resilience and sense of humor had always delighted her. "Not literally, I hope, but that's the spirit Angus wants to see in you."

Laughter was a good note to leave on. Junior seized the opportunity, said his good night, gave her his promise to drive safely, and left. On the stairs, he met Angus, who was carrying his boots and limping. "When are you going to see a doctor about that toe?"

"What good's a goddamn doctor, except to take your money? I ought to shoot off the sonofabitch and be done with it."

Junior smiled. "Okay, but don't get blood on the carpet. Mother would have a fit."

Angus laughed, all traces of anger gone. It was as if the episode in his den had never happened. He placed his arm across Junior's shoulders and gave them a quick squeeze. "I knew I could depend on you to get that girl out here. It worked out just like I hoped it would. We've put her on the defensive and planted seeds of doubt. If she's smart, and I believe she is, she'll call this thing off before too much damage has been done."

"What if she doesn't?"

"If she doesn't, we'll cross that bridge, too," Angus said darkly. Then he smiled and affectionately slapped Junior on the cheek. "Good night, boy."

Junior watched his father hobble across the landing. Feeling much better, he whistled softly beneath his breath on his way downstairs. Angus wouldn't be disappointed in him this time. The job he had been assigned suited him to a tee.

His experience in handling women was legendary. The challenges that Alex presented would just make the chase that much more exciting and fun. She was a damned attractive woman. Even if Angus hadn't told him, he would have wooed her anyway.

Doing it just right, however, would take some time and thought. He would give himself a few days to come up with a sure-fire strategy. In the meantime, there were lesser worlds to conquer. He saluted his handsome image in the hallway mirror on his way out the front door.

Chapter 9

Like the house, the stable was built of stone. The interior was like any other that Alex had seen, except that it was spotlessly clean. Two rows of stalls were divided by a wide center aisle. It smelled, not unpleasantly, of hay and leather and horseflesh.

Low wattage night-lights placed between the stalls made it easy for her to see where she was going—toward a brighter light that was burning in a stall about midway down. Quietly she made her way toward it, passing an open tack room and a door that was labeled PHYSICAL THERAPY. Through a wide opening she also saw a round pen with a walker that would exercise several horses at one time.

Before she saw him, she heard Reede, speaking in a low murmur to the occupant of the stall. Drawing even with it, she looked inside. He was hunkered down, sitting on the heels of his boots, rubbing his large hands up and down the animal's back leg.

His head was bent to one side as he concentrated on his

task. His fingers pressed a spot which was obviously sensitive. The horse sniffed and tried to withdraw.

"Easy, easy."

"What's the matter with him?"

He didn't turn around or show the slightest surprise at the sound of her voice. Apparently, he had known all along that she was standing there and was just being obtuse. He gently lowered the injured leg and, standing, patted the animal's rump. "It's a her." He shot her a suggestive smile. "Or aren't you old enough to tell the difference?"

"Not from this angle."

"Her name is Fancy Pants."

"Cute."

"It fits her. She thinks she's smarter than me, smarter than anybody. Fact is, she's too smart for her own good. She goes too far, too fast, and as a result, she ends up getting hurt." He scooped up a handful of grain and let the horse eat it from his hand.

"Oh, I get it. That's a veiled reference to me." He admitted it with a shrug. "Should I take it as a threat?"

"You can take it any way you want it."

Again, he was playing word games, implying double meanings. Alex didn't rise to the bait this time. "What kind of horse is she?"

"A pregnant one. This is the mares' barn."

"They're all kept here?"

"Away from the others, yeah." The mare nuzzled his chest and he smiled as he scratched behind her ears. "Mamas and babies cause a ruckus in a stable."

"Why?"

He shrugged his shoulders, indicating there was no clear-cut explanation. "I guess it's like the nursery floor at the hospital. Everybody goes a little nuts over a newborn."

He ran his hand over the mare's smooth belly. "This is her first time, and she's nervous about being a mother. She got a little skittish the other day when they were walking her and injured her metatarsal."

"When will she foal?"

"In the spring. She's got a while yet. Give me your hand."

"What?"

"Your hand." Sensing her reservation, he impatiently drew her into the stall with him until she was standing as close to the mare as he. "Feel."

He covered her hand with his and flattened it against the mare's sleek coat. The hair was coarse and short, and the vitality and strength of muscle beneath it was evident to the touch.

The animal snuffled and took a hesitant step forward, but Reede shushed her. The stall seemed close and over-heated. The fecund smell of new life in the making perme-ated the square enclosure. "She's warm," Alex commented breathlessly.

"She sure is."

Reede moved closer to Alex and maneuvered her hand, together with his, down the contours of the mare's body to her swollen underbelly. Alex gave a soft exclamation of sur-prise when she felt movement.

"The foal." Reede was so close his breath disturbed strands of her hair and she smelled the scent of his cologne, mingled with that of the stable.

A swift kick against her palm made Alex laugh with

spontaneous delight. She also gave a start of surprise and bumped against Reede. "So active."

"She's breeding me a winner."

"She belongs to you?"

"Yes."

"What about the sire?"

"I paid dearly for his services, but he was worth it. Good-looking stallion from Florida. Fancy Pants took to him right away. I think she was sorry when it was over. Maybe if he was around all the time, I wouldn't have to worry about her getting out of line."

The pressure in Alex's chest was such that she could barely breathe. Her inclination was to rest her cheek against the mare's side and continue to listen to Reede's lulling voice. Thankfully, her reason reasserted itself before she did anything so foolish.

She pulled her hand from beneath his and turned. He was standing so close to her that her clothes brushed against his, and she had to tilt her head back until it was resting against the horse in order to look into his face.

"Do all owners have access to the stables?"

Reede stepped back and allowed her to move toward the opening.

"Since I used to work for the Mintons, I guess they feel they can trust me."

"What kind of horse is she?" Alex said, reverting to her original question.

"A Quarter Horse."

"A quarter of what?"

"'A quarter of what?'" He tossed back his head and laughed. Fancy Pants danced aside. "Jesus, that's good. A quarter of what?" He unfastened the chain that had secured the mare to a metal ring in the wall, and then joined Alex outside the stall, carefully closing the gate behind him. "You don't know much about horses, do you?"

"Obviously not," she replied tightly.

Her embarrassment seemed to amuse him for only a moment. Then, frowning, he asked, "Was coming out here your idea?"

"Junior invited me."

"Ah, that figures."

"Why should it figure?"

"He's always hot on the trail of the newest available broad."

Blood surged through Alex's veins. "I am not available to Junior, or to anybody else. Neither am I a broad."

He subjected her to a slow and ridiculing once-over. "No, I guess you're not. Too much lawyer and not enough woman. Don't you ever relax?"

"Not when I'm working on a case."

"And that's what you were doing over drinks?" he asked scornfully. "Working on your case?"

"That's right."

"They've sure got funny methods of investigation in the Travis County D.A.'s office." He turned his back on her and swaggered toward the opposite end of the building.

"Wait! I'd like to ask you a few questions."

"Subpoena me," he tossed over his shoulder.

"Reede!" Impulsively, she struck out after him and grabbed the sleeve of his leather jacket. He stopped, glanced down where her fingers were curled into the age-softened leather, then came around slowly and stared at her with eyes as green and sharp as jungle spears.

She let go of his sleeve and fell back a step. She wasn't frightened; rather, she was shocked at herself. She hadn't intended to call his name like that, and she certainly hadn't intended to touch him, especially after what had happened in the stall.

Wetting her lips nervously, she said, "I want to talk to you. Please. Off the record. To satisfy my own curiosity."

"I know the technique, Counselor. I've used it myself. You play chummy with the suspect, hoping that he'll drop his guard and tell you something he's trying to hide."

"It's not like that. I just want to talk."

"About what?"

"About the Mintons."

"What about them?"

Standing with his feet widespread, pelvis tipped slightly forward, he slid his hands into the back pockets of his jeans, which pulled his jacket open across his chest. The stance was intimidatingly manly. It aroused her as much as it annoyed her. Alex tried to suppress both responses. "Would you say that Angus and Sarah Jo have a happy marriage?"

He blinked and coughed. "What?"

"Don't look at me like that. I'm asking for your opinion, not an analysis."

"What the hell difference does it make?"

"Sarah Jo's not the kind of woman I would have expected Angus to marry."

"Opposites attract."

"That's too pat. Are they . . . close?"

"Close?"

"Close, as in intimate."

"I've never thought about it."

"Of course you have. You lived here."

"Apparently, my mind doesn't operate on the same prurient track as yours." He took a step closer and lowered his voice. "But, we could change that."

Alex refused to let him provoke her, which she knew came closer to his intention than seduction. "Do they sleep together?"

"I guess so. It's none of my business what they do or don't do in bed. Furthermore, I don't care. I only care about what goes on in my bed. Why don't you ask me about that?"

"Because I don't care."

Again, he gave her a slow, knowing grin. "I think you do."

"I hate being patronized, Mr. Lambert, just because I'm a woman prosecutor."

"Then stop being one."

"A woman?"

"A prosecutor."

Mentally, she counted to ten. "Does Angus see other women?"

She could see annoyance building up behind his green eyes. His patience with her was wearing thin. "Do you take Sarah Jo for a passionate woman?"

"No," Alex replied.

"Do you figure that Angus has a healthy sexual appetite?"

"If it matches his other appetites, I'd say yes."

"Then, I guess you've got your answer."

"Has their relationship affected Junior?"

"How the hell should I know? Ask him."

"He'd only make some glib, dismissive comment."

"Which would be a nice way of telling you that you're interfering with business that doesn't concern you. I'm not as nice as he is. Butt out, lady."

"This does concern me."

He withdrew his hands from his hip pockets and folded his arms across his chest. "I can hardly wait to hear this rationalization."

She didn't let his sarcasm daunt her. "His parents' relationship might explain why Junior has had three failed marriages."

"That's something else that's none of your business."

"It is my business."

"How so?"

"Because Junior loved my mother."

The words reverberated down the corridor of the quiet stable. Reede's head went back with a snap, as if he'd sustained a quick, unexpected uppercut on the chin. "Who told you that?"

"He did." She watched him closely, adding softly, "He said you both loved her."

He stared at her for a considerable time, then shrugged. "In one way or another. So?"

"Is that why Junior's marriages didn't work? Because he was still carrying a torch for my mother?"

"I have no idea."

"Take a wild guess."

"Okay." Arrogantly, he angled his head to one side. "I don't think Celina had shit to do with Junior's marriages. It's just that he can't fuck for recreation without feeling guilty about it later, so to ease his conscience, he takes a wife every few years."

His statement was intended to offend her, and it did. She tried not to show how much. "Why do you think he feels guilty about it?"

"Genetics. He's got generations of southern chivalry flowing through his veins. That makes for a guilty conscience where the ladies are concerned."

"What about you?"

A Cheshire-cat grin lifted one corner of his mouth. "I never feel guilty for anything I do."

"Even murder?"

His grin collapsed and his eyes turned dark. "Get the hell out of here."

"Have you ever been married?"

"No."

"Why not?"

"None of your goddamn business. Anything else, Counselor?"

"Yes. Tell me about your father."

Gradually, Reede lowered his arms to his sides. He gave her a hard, cold stare. Alex said, "I know your father died while you were still in high school. Junior mentioned it today. When he died, you came to live here."

"You have a morbid curiosity, Miss Gaither."

"I'm not curious. I'm looking for facts pertinent to my investigation."

"Oh, sure. Pertinent stuff like Angus's sex life."

She gave him a reproving look. "Motives are what I'm after, Sheriff Lambert. As a law officer, you can identify with that, can't you? Ever hear of motive and opportunity?" His eyes turned even colder. "I need to establish your frame of mind the night of my mother's death."

"That's bullshit. What has that got to do with my old man?"

"Maybe nothing, but you tell me. If it's irrelevant, why are you so touchy about it?"

"Did Junior tell you how my old man died?" She shook her head. Reede snorted a bitter laugh. "I can't imagine why not. The nasty details made big news around here. People talked about it for years."

He bent at the waist so they were standing eye to eye. "He choked to death on his own vomit, too drunk to save himself. That's right, look shocked. It was pretty goddamned horrifying, especially when the principal of the high school called me out of class to tell me."

"Reede." In an attempt to stop the flow of sarcastic words, Alex raised her hand. He swatted it aside.

"No, if you're so anxious to open all the closet doors and expose the skeletons, here it is. But brace yourself, baby, this one's a dilly.

"My daddy was the town drunk, a laughingstock, a worthless, pathetic, sorry excuse for a human being. I didn't even cry when I heard he'd died. I was glad. He was a miserable, scummy son of a bitch who never did a single goddamn thing for me except make me ashamed that he was my father. And he wasn't any happier about that than I was. Dickweed— that's what he called me, usually right before he clouted me alongside the head. I was a liability to him.

"But, like a fool, I kept pretending, wishing, that we were a family. I was always after him to come watch me play ball. One night he showed up at a game. He created such a scene stumbling up the bleachers, tearing down one of the banners when he fell, that I wanted to die of embarrassment. I told him never to come again. I hated him. *Hated*," he repeated, rasping the word.

"I couldn't invite friends to my house because it was such a pigsty. We ate out of tin cans. I didn't know there were things like dishes on the table and clean towels in the bathroom until I was invited to other kids' houses. I made myself as presentable as possible when I went to school."

Alex regretted having lanced this festering wound, but she was glad he was talking freely. His childhood explained a lot about the man. But he was describing an outcast, and that didn't mesh with what she knew about him.

"I've been told that you were a ringleader, that the other kids gravitated to you. You made the rules and set the mood."

"I bullied myself into that position," he told her. "In grade school, the other kids made fun of me, everybody except Celina. Then I got taller and stronger and learned to fight. I fought dirty. They stopped laughing. It became much safer for a kid to be my friend than my enemy."

His lip curled with scorn. "This'll knock your socks off, Miss Prosecutor. I was a thief. I stole anything that we could eat or that might come in useful. You see, my old man couldn't keep a job for more than a few days without going on a binge. He'd take what he'd earned, buy himself a bottle or two, and drink himself unconscious. Eventually, he gave up trying to work. I supported us on what I could earn after school doing odd jobs, and on what I could get away with stealing."

There was nothing she could say. He had known there wouldn't be. That's why he'd told her. He wanted her to feel rotten and small-minded. Little did he know that their childhoods hadn't been that dissimilar, although she'd never gone without food. Merle Graham had provided for her physical needs, but she'd neglected her emotional ones. Alex had grown up feeling inferior and unloved. Empathetically she said, "I'm sorry, Reede."

"I don't want your goddamn pity," he sneered. "I don't want anybody's. That life made me hard and mean, and I like it that way. I learned early on to stand up for myself because it was for damn sure nobody else was going to go to bat for me. I don't depend on anybody but myself. I don't take anything for granted, especially people. And I'm damned and determined never to sink to the level of my old man."

"You're making too much out of this, Reede. You're too sensitive."

"Uh-huh. I want people to forget that Everett Lambert ever lived. I don't want people to associate me with him. Ever."

He clenched his teeth and hauled her up to just beneath his angry face by the lapels of her coat. "I've lived down the unfortunate fact that I was his son for forty-three years. Now, just when folks are about to forget it, you come along and start asking nosy questions, raising dead issues, reminding everybody that I crawled up out of the gutter to get where I am."

He sent her backward with a hard push. She caught herself against the gate of a stall. "I'm sure that no one holds your father's failures against you."

"You don't think so? That's the nature of a small town, baby. You'll find out how it is soon enough, because they'll start comparing you to Celina."

"That won't bother me. I'll welcome the comparisons."

"Are you so sure?"

"Yes."

"Careful. When you round a blind corner, you'd better know what's waiting for you."

"Care to be less oblique?"

"It could go one of two ways. Either you won't measure up to her, or you'll find out that being like her isn't all that terrific."

"Well, which is it?"

His eyes swept over her. "Like her, looking at you reminds a man that he is one. And like her, you use that to your advantage."

"Meaning?"

"She was no saint."

"I didn't expect her to be."

"Didn't you?" he asked silkily. "I believe you did. I think you've created this fantasy mother in your head and you expect Celina to fulfill it for you."

"That's ridiculous." Her strenuous denial sounded juvenile and obstinate. More calmly, she said, "It's true that Grandma Graham thought the sun rose and set on Celina. I was brought up to believe she was everything a young woman should be. But I'm a woman myself now, and mature enough to realize that my mother was made of flesh and blood, with flaws, just like everybody else."

He studied her face for a moment. "Just remember that I warned you," he said softly. "You should go back to the Westerner, pack up your designer clothes and your legal briefs, and head for Austin. Leave the past alone. Nobody around here wants to remember that blight on Purcell's history—particularly with that license hanging in the balance. They'd much rather leave Celina lying dead in this stable than—"

"*This* stable?" Alex gasped. "My mother was killed here?"

It was clear to her that he hadn't intended to let that slip. He cursed beneath his breath before answering curtly, "That's right."

"Where? Which stall?"

"It doesn't mat—"

"Show me, damn you! I'm sick to death of your half answers and evasions. Show me where you found her body that morning, Sheriff." She enunciated the last word carefully, reminding him that it was his sworn duty to protect and serve.

Without another word, he turned and strode toward the door through which she had entered the barn. At the second stall in the row, he halted. "Here."

Alex came to a full stop, then moved forward slowly until she was even with Reede. She turned to face the stall. There was no hay in it, just the rubber-covered floor. The gate had been removed because no horse was occupying the stall. It looked innocent, almost sterile.

"There hasn't been a horse boarded in this stall since it happened." Scornfully, he added, "Angus has a sentimental streak."

Alex tried to envision a bloody corpse lying in the stall, but couldn't. She raised inquiring eyes to Reede.

The skin seemed more tautly stretched across his cheekbones, and the vertical lines that framed his mouth appeared more pronounced than they had a few moments ago, when he had been angry. A visit to the scene of the crime wasn't as easy for him as he wanted to pretend.

"Tell me about it. Please."

He hesitated, then said, "She was lying diagonally, her

head in that corner, her feet about here." He touched a spot with the toe of his boot. "She was covered with blood. It was in her hair, on her clothes, everywhere." Alex had heard jaded homicide detectives discussing gory murder sites with more emotion. Reede's voice was hollow and monotonal, but his features were stark with pain. "Her eyes were still open."

"What time was that?" she asked huskily.

"When I found her?" She nodded, finding it difficult to speak. "Dawn. Around six-thirty."

"What were you doing here at that time of day?"

"I usually started mucking the stables around seven. That particular morning I was worried about the mare."

"Oh, yes, the one that had foaled the day before. So, you had come to check on her and the foal?"

"That's right."

Tears were shimmering in her eyes as she raised them to his. "Where were you the night before?"

"Out."

"All night?"

"Since supper time, yes."

"Alone?"

His lips narrowed with irritation. "If you want more answers, Counselor, bring the case to trial."

"I plan to."

As she brushed past him on her way to the door, he caught her arm and drew her up against him. He felt hard and powerfully male. "Miss Gaither," he growled in irritation and impatience, "you're smart. Drop this. If you don't, somebody's likely to get hurt."

"Namely?"

"You."

"How?"

He didn't actually move; he just inclined his body closer to hers. "There are any number of ways."

It was a threat, only subtly veiled. He was physically capable of killing a woman, but what about emotionally?

He seemed to have a low opinion of women in general, but according to Junior, he had loved Celina Graham. At one time, she had wanted to marry Reede. Maybe everyone, including Reede, had taken for granted that they would marry until Celina had married Al Gaither and gotten pregnant with Alex.

Alex didn't want to believe that Reede could have killed Celina under any circumstances, but she certainly didn't want to believe he had killed Celina because of her.

He was chauvinistic, arrogant, and as testy as a rattler. But a killer? He didn't look like one. Or was it just that she'd always had a weakness for dark blond hair and green eyes; for tight, faded jeans and worn leather coats with fur collars; for men who could wear cowboy boots without looking silly; for men who walked and talked and smelled and sounded and felt consummately male?

Reede Lambert was all of that.

Disturbed more by his effect on her senses than by his cautionary words, she pulled her arm free and backed toward the door.

"I have no intention of dropping this investigation until I know who killed my mother and why. I've waited all my life to find out. I won't be dissuaded now."

Chapter 10

Reede let loose a string of curses the minute Alex left the stable. Pasty Hickam had overheard them from his hiding place in a nearby stall.

He hadn't planned to eavesdrop on their conversation. When he had come into the barn earlier, he'd only been looking for a place where it was dark and warm and solitary, where he'd have some privacy to nurse his damaged pride, cultivate his resentment of his former employer, and suck on his bottle of cheap rye as if it was mother's milk.

Now, however, his ennui had vanished and his mind was concocting a nefarious plan. Sober, Pasty was merely crotchety. Drunk, he was mean.

He'd barely been able to contain himself as he listened to what that gal from Austin had to say to the sheriff, and vice versa. Lordy be, she was Celina Gaither's daughter, here to investigate her mama's killing.

Thanks to her, and a benevolent God he didn't even believe in, he had been given a golden opportunity to get revenge on Angus and that useless son of his.

He'd busted his ass on this place, worked for miserly wages, and gone without completely when Angus was so broke he couldn't pay him, but he'd stuck it out. He had gone through thick and thin with the bastard, and what thanks did he get? Fired and booted out of the bunkhouse that had been home for almost thirty years.

Well, fortune had finally smiled on Pasty Hickam. If he played his cards right, he could finally have some money for his "retirement fund." Ruby Faye, his current lover, was always after him about never having any money to spend on her. "What's the fun of having an affair if I don't get something out of it besides the thrill of cheating on my husband?" she was fond of saying.

Monetary compensation, however, would be icing on the cake. Revenge would be sweet enough. It was past time that somebody kicked Angus where it hurt.

His impatience was at a near-frantic pitch by the time Reede finished examining his mare and left the stable. Pasty waited several moments to make sure he was alone before leaving the empty stall where he'd been curled up in the fresh hay. He moved down the shadowed corridor toward the wall telephone. He cursed a horse that nickered, spooking him. For all his meanness, courage had never been his strong suit.

He called Information first, then quickly punched out the digits of the number before he could forget them. Maybe she hadn't had time to get there, he thought anxiously after he'd asked the clerk to ring her room. But she answered on the fifth ring, a trifle breathlessly, like she might have come in while the phone was ringing.

"Miz Gaither?"

"Yes, who's this?"

"You don't need to know. I know you, and that's enough."

"Who is this?" she demanded, with what Pasty thought was false bravado.

"I know all about your mama's murder."

Pasty cackled to himself, enjoying the sudden silence. He couldn't have gotten her attention any sooner or any better if he'd walked up and bit her on her tittie.

"I'm listening."

"I cain't talk now."

"Why not?"

"Cause I cain't, that's why."

It was risky to go into it with her now over the telephone. Somebody might pick up another extension somewhere on the ranch and overhear him. That could prove to be unhealthy.

"I'll call you back."

"But—"

"I'll call you back."

He hung up, enjoying her anxiety. He remembered the way her mama used to sashay around, like she owned the world. Many a summer day, he'd ogled her lustfully while she frolicked in the swimming pool with Junior and Reede. They'd put their hands all over her and call it roughhousing. But she was too good to even cast an eye in Pasty's direction. He hadn't minded that she got herself killed. He sure as hell hadn't interfered and stopped it when he could have.

He remembered that night and everything that had happened like it was yesterday. It was a secret that he'd kept all this time. Now it would be divulged. And it was gonna tickle him to death to tell that prosecutor all about it.

Chapter 11

—◦◦◦—

Are you waiting to give me a parking ticket?" Alex asked as she got out of her car and locked it. She was feeling chipper this morning, due to the unexpected telephone call she had received the night before. Maybe the caller was the eyewitness she'd been praying for. But it could have been a crank call, too, she realistically reminded herself.

If he was genuine, it would be a tragedy if he named Reede Lambert as Celina's murderer. He looked extremely attractive leaning against the parking meter. Actually, since the meter was listing to the right, it might have been leaning on Reede.

"I should change my mind since you're being a smart-ass, but I'm such a nice guy..." He slipped a canvas hood over the meter. In blue letters it was labeled, CITY OF PURCELL—OFFICIAL CAR. "Take this with you when you leave and use it from now on. It'll save you some change."

He turned and started up the sidewalk toward the courthouse. Alex fell into step beside him. "Thanks."

"You're welcome." They climbed the stairs and went

inside. "Come down to my office," he said. "I've got something to show you."

Curious, she followed his lead. They hadn't parted on the best of terms the night before. Yet this morning, he was going out of his way to be hospitable. Deciding that was out of character, Alex couldn't help but be suspicious of his motives.

When they reached the lower level, everyone in the squad room stopped what he was doing to stare. The scene became as still as a photograph.

Reede gave the room one slow, meaningful sweep of his eyes. Activity was immediately resumed. He hadn't spoken a single word, but it was apparent that he wielded tremendous authority over his staff. They either feared or respected him. Alex suspected the former.

Reede stepped around her, swung open a door to the left of the staircase, and moved aside so she could go in. She stepped into a small, square, windowless, cheerless office. It was as cold as a meat locker. There was a desk so dented and scarred it looked like it had been made from scrap metal. The particleboard top was ink-stained, and holes had been chipped out of it. Sitting on it were an overflowing ashtray and a black, no-frills telephone. Behind it was a swivel chair she had little confidence in.

"It's yours to use if you want it," Reede told her. "I'm sure you're accustomed to fancier office space."

"No. Actually, my cubicle in Austin is not much larger than this. Whom should I thank?"

"The city of Purcell."

"But it was somebody's idea. Yours, Reede?"

"So what if it was?"

"So," she said, drawing out the word in an effort to ignore the chip he carried on his shoulder, "thank you."

"You're welcome."

Trying to temper the animosity between them, she smiled and said teasingly, "Now that we're in the same building, I can keep a closer eye on you."

He pulled the door shut as he backed out. "You've got it backwards, Counselor. I can keep a closer eye on *you*."

Alex tossed down her ballpoint pen and vigorously rubbed her chilled arms. The electric space heater she had bought at the hardware store was on full blast, but it wasn't helping much. The square little office was frigid and seemed to be the only dank, damp spot in this otherwise arid climate.

Earlier she had bought office supplies: paper, pencils, pens, paper clips. The office was hardly comfortable, but at least it was functional. It was also much more centrally located than her room at the Westerner Motel.

After checking to see that the heater was indeed working at its maximum, she bent over her notes again. It had taken all afternoon to compile and arrange them according to the individuals involved.

Beginning with her profile on Angus, she reread the briefs. Unfortunately, they were no more concrete or factually based than they had been the first dozen times she'd read them.

What she had was conjecture and hearsay. What few facts she had, she had known when she left Austin. So far, this trip had been a waste of taxpayers' money, and almost a week of Greg's deadline had elapsed.

For the time being, she decided to let the question of opportunity wait. She had to establish motives. All she had learned so far was that the three men had adored Celina. Adoration was hardly motivation for murder.

She had nothing—no evidence, not even a viable suspect. She was certain that Buddy Hicks hadn't killed her mother, yet she was no closer to discovering who had.

After spending time alone with Angus, Junior, and Reede, Alex was convinced that getting a confession would be tantamount to a miracle. Contrition and repentance didn't fit their personality profiles. Nor would one testify against the other. The loyalties were solidly forged, though it was obvious their friendship wasn't what it had once been, which in itself was a clue. Had Celina's death splintered their clique, yet kept them bound to one another?

She still hoped that the person who had called a few nights before was an actual eyewitness. She had waited for days for another call, one that hadn't come, which was a strong indication that it had been a prank.

Apparently, the only people near the stable that night had been Gooney Bud, the killer, and Celina. Gooney Bud was dead. The killer wasn't talking. And Celina—

Alex was suddenly inspired. Her mother couldn't talk—at least, not in the literal sense—but she *might* have something valuable to tell.

The idea made Alex sick to her stomach. She propped her forehead on the palms of her hands and closed her eyes. Did she have the fortitude to do it?

She groped for alternatives, but came up empty-handed. She needed evidence, and she could think of only one place to look for it.

Before she could change her mind, she switched off the heater and left the office. Avoiding the unreliable elevator, she jogged up the stairs, hoping that she would catch Judge Joe Wallace before he left for the day.

She anxiously checked her wristwatch. It was almost five o'clock. She didn't want to put this off until tomorrow. Now that her mind was made up, she wanted to act on her decision before she had the time and opportunity to back out.

The corridors on the second floor were deserted. Jurors had been dismissed for the day. Trials were in recess until tomorrow. Her footsteps echoed loudly as she made her way toward the judge's chambers adjacent to the empty courtroom. His secretary was still in the anteroom, and none too pleased to see her.

"I need to speak with the judge immediately." Alex was out of breath after quickly climbing two flights of stairs, and her voice was tinged with desperation.

"He's fixin' to leave for the day," she was told with a lack of apology. "I can make an appoint—"

"This is vitally important, or I wouldn't bother him at this time of day."

Alex wasn't intimidated by Mrs. Lipscomb's censorious stare or the retiring sigh she emitted as she left her desk and moved to the connecting door. She knocked discreetly, then went inside, closing the door behind her. Alex paced impatiently until she returned.

"He's agreed to see you. Briefly."

"Thank you." Alex rushed past her and into the chambers.

"Well, what is it this time, Miss Gaither?" Judge Wallace barked at her the instant she crossed the threshold. He was pulling on his overcoat. "You seem to have a nasty habit of showing up without an appointment. As you can see, I'm leaving. My daughter Stacey doesn't like to hold dinner, and it would be rude of me to expect her to."

"I apologize to both of you, Judge. As I told your secretary, it's urgent that I talk to you this afternoon."

"Well?" he demanded cantankerously.

"Could we sit down?"

"I can talk standing up. What do you want?"

"I want you to issue a court order to have my mother's body exhumed."

The judge sat down then. Or rather, he dropped down into the chair in front of which he was standing. He stared up at Alex with undisguised dismay.

"I beg your pardon?" he wheezed.

"I believe you heard me, Judge Wallace, although if it's necessary to repeat my request, I will."

He waved his hand. "No. Good Lord, no. Hearing it once was bad enough." He cupped each knee with a hand and continued to stare up at her, apparently thinking she was certifiable. "Why would you want to do such a ghastly thing as that?"

"I don't *want* to. I wouldn't ask for a court order if I didn't think exhumation was absolutely necessary."

Having recovered some of his aplomb, he ungraciously indicated a chair. "You might as well sit. Explain your reasons."

"A crime was committed, but I can find no incriminating evidence."

"I told you you wouldn't," he exclaimed. "You didn't listen. You came charging in here, slinging unfounded accusations, bent on getting vengeance."

"That's not true," she denied evenly.

"That's how I read it. What does Pat Chastain have to say about this?"

"The D.A. is unavailable. It seems he's spontaneously taken a few days' vacation and gone hunting."

The judge harrumphed. "Sounds like a damn good idea to me."

It sounded cowardly to Alex, and she'd been ready to chew nails when the aloof Mrs. Chastain had informed her of it. "Will you permit me to look for evidence, Judge?"

"There is no evidence," he stressed.

"My mother's remains might provide some."

"She was autopsied when she was killed. That was twenty-five years ago, for crissake."

"With all due respect to the coroner at that time, he might not have been looking for clues when the cause of death was so readily apparent. I know an excellent forensic specialist in Dallas. We use him frequently. If there is anything to be found, he'll find it."

"I can guarantee you that he won't."

"It's worth a try, isn't it?"

He gnawed at the corner of his lip. "I'll take your request under advisement."

Alex recognized a brush-off when she saw one. "I'd appreciate an answer tonight."

"Sorry, Miss Gaither. The best I can do is think about it overnight and give you an answer in the morning. Between now and then, I hope you'll change your mind and withdraw the request."

"I won't."

He stood up. "I'm tired, hungry, and damned perturbed

that you've put me in this awkward position." He aimed an accusatory index finger at her. "I don't like messes."

"Neither do I. I wish this weren't necessary."

"It isn't."

"I believe it is," she countered stubbornly.

"In the long run, you'll be sorry you ever asked me for this. Now, you've taken up enough of my time. Stacey will be worried. Good night."

He marched from the room. A few seconds later, Mrs. Lipscomb appeared in the doorway. Her eyelids were fluttering with indignation. "Imogene told me you'd mean trouble around here."

Alex swept past her and returned to her temporary office, only long enough to retrieve her belongings. The drive out to the Westerner took longer than usual because she got caught up in Purcell's rush hour. To further complicate the snarled traffic, it began to sleet.

Knowing she wouldn't want to go out again, she picked up a box of carryout fried chicken. By the time she spread the meal on the round table near the windows of her room, the food was cold and tasted like cardboard. She promised herself that she would buy some fruit and healthy snack food to supplement her unbalanced diet, and maybe a bouquet of fresh flowers to brighten the dismal room. She debated taking down the lurid painting of the bullfighter that dominated one wall. The swirling red cape and slavering bull were real eyesores.

Loath to review her notes again, she decided to switch on the TV. The HBO movie she watched was a comedy she didn't have to think about. She was feeling better by the time it was over, and decided to take a shower.

She had just dried off and wrapped her wet hair in a towel when someone knocked on her door. Pulling on her long, white terry-cloth robe and knotting the tie at her waist, she peered through the peephole.

She opened the door as far as the chain lock would allow. "What are you, the Welcome Wagon?"

"Open the door," Sheriff Lambert said.

"What for?"

"I need to talk to you."

"About what?"

"I'll tell you when I get inside." Alex didn't move. "Are you going to open the door, or what?"

"I can talk to you from here."

"Open the friggin' door," he shouted. "I'm freezing my balls off."

Alex slid the chain out of its mooring, then pulled the door open and stood aside. Reede stamped his feet and brushed off the ice pellets that were clinging to the fur collar of his coat.

He looked her up and down. "Expecting someone?"

Alex crossed her arms over her middle, a gesture meant to convey her annoyance. "If this is a social call—"

"It isn't." He caught his finger between his teeth and pulled off one leather glove, then the other. He slapped the felt cowboy hat against his thigh to shake off the sleet, then ran a hand through his hair.

He tossed the gloves into the crown of his hat, set the hat down on the table, and lowered himself into a chair. He eyed the remains of her supper, then took a bite out of an untouched drumstick. Munching, he asked, "You don't like our fried chicken?"

He was slouched in the chair, looking like he had settled in for the night. Alex remained standing. She felt absurdly exposed in the robe, even though it covered her from jaw to ankles. Having a motel towel wrapped around her head didn't help boost her self-confidence.

She tried to appear indifferent to him and her own disha-bille. "No, I didn't like the fried chicken, but it was conve-nient. I didn't want to go out to eat."

"Smart decision on a night like this. The roads are getting treacherous."

"You could have told me that over the phone."

Ignoring that, he leaned far to one side and looked past her at the television screen, where an unclothed couple were carnally involved. The camera moved in for a close-up of the man's lips against the woman's breast.

"No wonder you're mad that I interrupted."

She smacked the power button with her palm. The screen went blank. "I wasn't watching."

When she turned around, he was looking up at her, smiling. "Do you always open your door to any man who knocks on it?"

"I didn't open my door until you swore at me."

"Is that all a man has to do, talk dirty?"

"You're the highest-ranking law enforcement officer in this county. If I can't trust you, who can I trust?" She was thinking she would trust a used car salesman in a green poly-ester suit before she would trust Reede Lambert. "And was it really necessary to strap that on when you came calling?"

He followed the direction of her gaze down to the holster riding just below his belt. He stretched his booted feet far out in front of him and crossed them at the ankles. Templing his fingers, he peered at her over their tips. "I never know when I might have to use it."

"Is it always loaded?"

He hesitated, his eyes lowering to the vicinity of her breasts. "Always."

They were no longer talking about the pistol in his holster. But more than what was actually being said, the tone of the conversation made her distinctly uncomfortable. She shifted her weight from one bare foot to the other and dampened her lips, only then realizing that she had already removed her makeup. Somehow, that made her feel even more vulnerable. That, and his motionless, broody stare.

"Why did you come here tonight? What couldn't wait until morning?"

"An urge."

"An urge?" she repeated huskily.

He languidly got up out of the chair and moved forward until he stood only inches in front of her. He slipped his rough hand into the parting of her robe and encircled her neck with it. "Yeah, an urge," he whispered. "An urge to throttle you."

Uttering a frustrated grunt, Alex removed his hand and stepped aside. By choice, he let her go. "Judge Wallace called me tonight and told me about the court order you asked him for."

Her heart, which had been beating furiously, slowed down, but she muttered a curse of aggravation. "Isn't anything private in this town?"

"Not much, no."

"I don't think I could sneeze without everybody within the city limits offering me a Kleenex."

"You're in the spotlight, all right. What do you expect, going around asking to dig up a body?"

"You make it sound so whimsical."

"Well, isn't it?"

"Do you think I'd disturb my mother's grave if I didn't think it was a vital step toward solving her murder?" she asked heatedly. "My God, do you think it was easy for me to even voice the request? And why did the judge feel it necessary to consult you, *you*, of all people?"

"Why not me? Because I'm a suspect?"

"Yes!" she cried. "Discussing this case with you is highly unethical."

"I'm the sheriff, remember?"

"I never forget it. That's still no excuse for Judge Wallace to go behind my back. Why is he so nervous about having the body exhumed? Is he afraid a forensic investigation will reveal something he helped to cover up?"

"Your request presented him with a problem."

"I'll just bet it did! Who is he trying to protect by keeping that coffin sealed?"

"You."

"Me?"

"Celina's body can't be exhumed. She was cremated."

Chapter 12

Reede couldn't figure out why he had elected to go to the seediest tavern along the highway for a drink when he had a perfectly good bottle of whiskey at home. Maybe it was because his frame of mind matched the dark, murky atmosphere of the honky-tonk.

He felt like shit.

He signaled for the bartender to pour him another drink. The Last Chance Bar was the kind of place that refilled glasses; customers didn't get a clean one with each round.

"Thanks," Reede said, watching the whiskey splash into his glass.

"You staking us out undercover, or what?" the bartender quipped.

Without moving anything but his eyes, Reede looked up at him. "I'm having a drink. Is that all right with you?"

The silly grin collapsed. "Sure, Sheriff, sure." The bartender backed away to the opposite end of the bar, where he'd been carrying on a conversation with two friendlier patrons.

Reede noticed that one booth across the room was

occupied by women. Surrounding the pool table was a trio of guys whom he recognized as wild well controllers. They were usually a rowdy bunch who partied hard between each dangerous gig. For the time being, they were peaceable enough.

Pasty Hickam and Ruby Faye Turner were cuddled in another booth. Reede had heard in the B & B that morning that Angus had canned the old ranch hand. Pasty had made a damn stupid mistake, but Reede thought the punishment was severe. Apparently, Pasty was being consoled by his latest flame. Reede had doffed his hat in their general direction when he had come in. They gave every appearance of wanting to be ignored as much as he wanted to ignore them.

It was a slow night at the Last Chance, which suited the sheriff just fine for professional as well as personal reasons.

He had gulped his first drink, barely tasting it. This one he sipped because he needed it to last longer. Nursing it delayed going home. Being alone didn't hold much appeal for Reede. Neither did passing time in the Last Chance, but it was better than the first option. At least, tonight it was.

The whiskey had started a slow fire in his belly. It had made the twinkling Christmas lights, strung year-round over the bar, seem brighter and prettier. The dinginess of the place wasn't so obvious when viewed through whiskey fumes.

Since he was beginning to mellow, he decided this would be his last drink of the night, another reason to savor it. Reede never drank to the point of intoxication. Never. He'd had to clean up after his old man had puked up everything but his toenails too many times for him to think that getting shit-faced was fun.

When he was just a kid, he remembered thinking that he might grow up to be a jailbird or a monk, an astronaut or a post-hole digger, a zookeeper or a big game hunter, but one thing he was *not* going to be was a drunk. They already had one of those in the family, and that was one too many.

"Hiya, Reede."

The sound of the breathy, feminine voice interrupted his contemplation of the amber contents of his glass. He raised his head and immediately saw a plump set of tits.

She was wearing a skin-tight black T-shirt with BORN BAD spelled out in glittering red letters. Her jeans were so tight she had difficulty climbing onto the bar stool. She managed, but not without jiggling her breasts and pressing Reede's thigh in the process. Her smile was as brilliant as a zirconium ring, and not nearly as genuine. Her name was Gloria, Reede remembered, just in time to be courteous.

"Hi, Gloria."

"Buy me a beer?"

"Sure." He called out the order to the bartender. Glancing pointedly over his shoulder, Reede called her attention to the group of friends she'd left sitting in the booth across the dim tavern.

"Don't mind them," she said, flirtatiously tapping his arm where it rested on the bar. "It's every girl for herself after ten o'clock."

"Ladies' night out?"

"Hmm." She tipped the long-neck to her glossy lips and drank. "We were headed for Abilene to see the new Richard Gere movie, but the weather turned so bad, we said what the hell, and decided to stay in town. Wha'chu been up to tonight? You on duty?"

"For a while. I'm off now." Reluctant to be drawn into conversation, he returned to his drink.

Gloria wasn't going to be dismissed that easily. She scooted as close to him as the bar stool would allow and threw her arm across his shoulders. "Poor Reede. It must get awful lonesome riding around by yourself all the time."

"I'm working when I'm riding around."

"I know, but still..." Her breath fanned his ear. It smelled like beer. "It's no wonder you frown so much." A sharp fingernail plowed the deep furrow between his eyebrows. He jerked his head back, away from her touch. She snatched her hand back and uttered a soft, wounded sound.

"Look, I'm sorry," he muttered. "My mood's as bad as the weather. It's been a long day. Guess I'm just tired."

Rather than putting her off, that encouraged her. "Maybe I could cheer you up, Reede," she said with a timorous smile. "Anyway, I'd sure like to try." Again she moved close, sandwiching his upper arm between her cushiony breasts. "I've had the wildest crush on you since I was in seventh grade. Don't make out like you didn't know," she said with a scolding pout.

"No, I didn't know that."

"Well, I did. But you were taken then. What was that girl's name? The one that loony killed in the stable?"

"Celina."

"Yeah. You were real gone on her, weren't you? By the time I got to high school, you were at Texas Tech. Then I got married and started having kids." She didn't notice that he wasn't interested in her chatter. " 'Course, the husband's long gone, and the kids are old enough now to take care of themselves. I guess there never was much chance for you to know I had a crush on you, was there?"

"I guess not."

She leaned so far forward, her perch on the stool became precarious. "Maybe it's time you did, Reede."

He glanced down at her breasts, which were making teasing, brushing contact with his arm. As a result, her nipples made hard, distinct impressions against her T-shirt. Somehow, the blatancy wasn't as enticing as Alex's innocent, bare toes peeking out from beneath her terry-cloth bathrobe. Knowing that there was nothing but Gloria under the black T-shirt didn't excite him as much as wondering what, if anything, was under Alex's white robe.

He wasn't aroused, not even a little. He wondered why.

Gloria was pretty enough. Black hair curled around her face and emphasized dark eyes that were now lambent with invitation and promise. Her lips were parted and wet, but he wasn't sure he could kiss them without sliding off. They were coated with cherry-red lipstick. Involuntarily, he compared them to lips free of makeup, but still pink and moist, kissable and sexy, without making any attempt to be.

"I gotta be going," he said suddenly. He unhooked his boot heels from the rungs of the stool and came to his feet, fishing in the pocket of his jeans for enough bills to cover the price of his drinks and her beer.

"But, I thought—"

"Better get back to your group, or you're liable to miss the party."

The wild well control boys had ventured toward the women, who were making no secret of being on the prowl and out for a good time. The merging of the two groups had been as inevitable as a hard freeze by morning. The delay had been calculated to build the anticipation. Now, however, sexual innuendos were being swapped at a rate to match the stock exchange on a busy day.

"Nice seeing you, Gloria."

Reede pulled his hat down low over his brows and left, but not before catching her wounded expression. Alex's face had held that same devastated, disbelieving expression when he had told her that her mother's body had been cremated.

Seconds after he had uttered the words, she recoiled against the wall, clutching the lapels of her robe to her throat as if she was warding off something evil. "Cremated?"

"That's right." He watched her face turn pale, and her eyes turn glassy.

"I didn't know. Grandma never said. I never thought…"

Her voice dwindled into nothingness. He remained silent and unmoving, figuring that she needed time to digest that sobering piece of information.

He had mentally cursed Joe Wallace for dumping such a rotten task on him. The goddamn coward had called him, fit to be tied, whining and carrying on, asking what he should tell her. When Reede suggested that Alex be told the truth, the judge had interpreted it as volunteering and had been all too willing to abdicate the responsibility.

Alex's numbness hadn't lasted long. Her senses returned abruptly, as though she'd been jarred into consciousness by a thought. "Did Judge Wallace know?"

Reede remembered shrugging with feigned indifference. "Look, all I know is that he called me and said that what you wanted to do was impossible, even if he had handed down a court order, which he would have been reluctant to do."

"If he knew my mother's body had been cremated, why didn't he tell me himself this afternoon?"

"My guess would be that he didn't want a scene on his hands."

"Yes," she murmured distractedly, "he doesn't like messes. He told me so." She looked at him without expression. "He sent you to do his dirty work. Messes don't bother you."

Reede, declining to comment, pulled on his gloves and replaced his hat. "You've had a jolt. Are you going to be okay?"

"I'm fine."

"You don't look fine."

Her blue eyes were filled with tears and her mouth trembled slightly. She clasped her hands at her waist, as though forcibly holding herself together. That's when he had wanted to put his arms around her and hold her close, wet hair, damp towel, bathrobe, bare toes, and all.

That's when he had moved forward and, before he even realized what he was doing, forcibly pulled her arms out to her sides. She had resisted, as though wanting to cover a bleeding wound.

Before she reconstructed that barrier, he slid his arms around her and pulled her against him. She was dewy and warm and fragrant, fragile in her grief. She seemed to wilt against him. Her arms dangled listlessly at her sides.

"Oh, God, please don't make me go through this," she had whispered, and he had felt her breasts tremble. She rolled her head toward him, until her face was making an impression on his chest and he could feel her tears through his clothes.

He had angled his head to secure hers against him. The towel wrapping her hair unwound and fell to the floor. Her hair was damp and fragrant against his face.

He told himself now that he hadn't kissed it, but he knew

his lips had brushed her hair and then her temple, and rested there.

At that point, a severe case of lust had seized him, and it had been so powerful it was a wonder to him now that he hadn't acted on it.

Instead he had left, feeling like crap for having to tell her something like that and then slinking out like a snake. Staying with her had been out of the question. His desire to hold her hadn't been nobly inspired, and he didn't try to kid himself into believing it was. He'd wanted gratification. He had wanted to cover that hurting, courageous smile with hot, hard kisses.

He swore to his dashboard now as he drove the Blazer down the highway, heading in the opposite direction from home. Sleet froze on the windshield before the wipers could whisk it off. He was driving too fast for the weather conditions—the pavement was like an ice rink—but he kept going.

He was too old for this. What the hell was he doing entertaining sexual fantasies? He hadn't consciously done that since he and Junior had jerked off while drooling over centerfolds. Yet, at no time in recent memory had his fantasies been so vivid.

Completely forgetting who Alex was, he had envisioned his hands parting that white bathrobe and finding underneath it smooth, ivory flesh; hard, pink nipples; soft, auburn hair. Her thighs would be soft, and between them she would be creamy.

Cursing, he squeezed his eyes shut for a moment. She wasn't just *any* woman who happened to be eighteen years younger than himself. She was Celina's daughter, and he was old enough to be her daddy, for crissake. He wasn't, but he could have been. He very well could have been. Knowing that made his stomach feel a little queasy, but it did nothing to decrease the thick hard-on now testing the durability of his fly.

He wheeled the truck into the deserted parking lot, cut the engine, and bounded up the steps to the door. He tried it, and when he discovered it was locked, pounded on it with his gloved fists.

Eventually, the door was opened by a woman as broad-breasted as a pigeon. She was wearing a long, white satin peignoir that might have looked bridal had there not been a black cigarette anchored in the corner of her lips. In her arms she was holding an apricot-colored cat. She was stroking his luxurious fur with an idle hand. Woman and cat glared at Reede.

"What the hell are you doing here?" she demanded.

"Why do most men come here, Nora Gail?" Rudely, he brushed past her and went inside. If he'd been anybody else, he would have been shot right between the eyes with the pistol she kept hidden in the garter belt she always wore.

"Obviously, you haven't noticed. Business was so slow tonight, we closed early."

"Since when has that mattered to you and me?"

"Since you started taking advantage. Like now."

"Don't give me any lip tonight." He was already at the top of the stairs, heading toward her private room. "I don't want conversation. I don't want to be entertained. I just want to be screwed, okay?"

Propping her fist on a generous and shapely hip, the madam's voice dripped sarcasm as she called up to him, "Do I have time to put the cat out first?"

———⊙———

Alex was unable to sleep, so she was awake when the telephone rang. It still alarmed her because of the hour. Instead of turning on the nightstand lamp, she groped in the darkness for the receiver and brought it to her ear. "Hello," she croaked, her voice hoarse from crying earlier. "Hello," she repeated.

"Hidy, Miz Gaither."

Her heart raced with excitement, but she said crossly, "You again? I hope you're ready to talk, since you woke me from a sound sleep." She'd learned from Greg that reluctant witnesses were often more prone to talk when you diminished the importance of what they might have to say.

"Don't go gettin' hoity-toity with me, little lady. I know sumthin' you want to know. Bad."

"Such as?"

"Such as who did in yore mama."

Alex concentrated on regulating her breathing. "I think you're bluffing."

"I ain't."

"Then, tell me. Who was it?"

"You think I'm stupid, lady? You think Lambert ain't bugged yore telephone?"

"You've seen too many movies." All the same, she looked suspiciously at the receiver she held in her hand.

"You know where the Last Chance is?"

"I'll find it."

"Tomorrow evenin'." He specified a time.

"How'll I know you?"

"I'll know you."

Before she could say anything else, he hung up. Alex sat on the edge of the bed for a moment, staring into the darkness. She recalled Reede's warning about getting hurt. Her imaginative mind conjured up all the horrible things that could happen to a woman alone. By the time she lay back down, her palms were sweating and sleep was even more elusive.

Chapter 13

——◦◉◦——

"You'll never guess what she's up to now."

Purcell County's sheriff lifted the steaming coffee mug to his lips, blew into it, and sipped. It scorched his tongue. He didn't care. He needed a fix of caffeine in the worst way.

"Who are we talking about?" he asked the deputy who was standing in the doorway of his private office, wearing a goofy grin that annoyed the hell out of him. He didn't like guessing games, and he was especially in no mood for one this morning.

The deputy jerked his head in the direction of the other side of the building. "Our resident prosecutor with the baby blues, perky tits, and the legs that go on forever." He kissed the air with a noisy, juicy smack of his lips.

Reede slowly lowered his feet from the corner of his desk. His eyes glittered with a frigid light. "Are you referring to Miss Gaither?"

The deputy didn't have an overabundance of gray matter, but he knew when he'd gone too far. "Uh, yeah. I mean, yes, sir."

"Well?" Reede demanded darkly.

"That funeral parlor man, Mr. Davis, well, sir, he just called, raisin' Cain on account of her. She's over there now going through his files and all."

"*What?*"

"Yes, sir, that's what he said, Sheriff Lambert. He's good and pissed off because—"

"Call him back and tell him I'm on my way." Reede was already reaching for his coat. If the deputy hadn't side-stepped quickly, he'd have been run down as Reede rushed through the door.

He was impervious to the inclement weather that had kept schools and most businesses closed. They could handle snow, but an inch-thick sheet of ice covering everything was another matter. Unfortunately, the sheriff's office never closed.

Mr. Davis met him at the door, anxiously wringing his hands. "I've been in business for over thirty years and nothing like this—*nothing,* Sheriff Lambert—has ever happened to me before. I've had caskets disappear. I've been robbed. I even had—"

"Where is she?" Reede barked, cutting short the funeral director's litany.

The man pointed. Reede stamped toward the closed door and wrenched it open. Alex, seated behind a desk, looked up expectantly. "Just what the hell do you think you're doing?"

"Good morning, Sheriff."

"Answer my question." Reede slammed the door and strode into the room. "I've got a hysterical undertaker on my hands because of you, lady. How'd you get here, anyway?"

"I drove."

"You can't drive in this."

"I did."

"What is all this?" With an angry swipe of his hand, he indicated the files strewn across the desk.

"Mr. Davis's records for the year my mother was killed. He gave me permission to sort through them."

"You coerced him."

"I did no such thing."

"Intimidated him, then. Did he ask to see your search warrant?"

"No."

"Do you have one?"

"No. But I can get one."

"Not without probable cause."

"I want proof positive that Celina Gaither's body is not interred in that grave at the cemetery."

"Why didn't you do something sensible, like get a shovel and start digging?"

That silenced her. It took her a moment to recover. At last she said, "You're in a surly mood this morning. Rough night?"

"Yeah. I got laid, but it wasn't very good."

Her eyes dropped to the littered table. "Oh. I'm sorry to hear that."

"What, that I got laid?"

She gazed back up at him. "No, that it wasn't very good."

They shared a lengthy stare. His face looked as rugged and craggy as a mountain range, but it was one of the most appealing she'd ever encountered.

Whenever they were together, she was involuntarily aware of him, of his body, of the way she was drawn to him. She knew her attraction was unethical and reckless, from a professional standpoint, and compromising, from a personal one. He'd belonged to her mother first.

Yet, too often she wanted to touch him or to be touched by him. Last night she'd wanted him to hold her longer while she cried. Thankfully, he'd had better sense and had left.

Who had he gone to? Alex wondered. Where and when had the unsatisfactory lovemaking taken place? Had it been before or after he'd come to her motel room? Why hadn't it been any good?

Several moments elapsed before she lowered her head and resumed sorting through the files.

Not one to be ignored, he reached across the table and placed his hand beneath her chin, jerking it toward him. "I told you that Celina was cremated."

She jumped to her feet. "*After* you and Judge Wallace put your heads together and discussed it. That seems a little convenient to me."

"You enjoy imagining things."

"Why didn't Junior mention that Celina had been cremated when he saw me in the cemetery? I'm thinking that maybe she *is* buried there. That's why I'm going through all these files."

"Why would I lie about it?"

"To keep me from having the body exhumed."

"Again, why? What difference would that make to me?"

"Life imprisonment," she said tightly, "if the forensic report implicated you as her murderer."

"Ah…" At a loss for a word foul enough, he slammed his fist into his opposite palm and ground it against the tough flesh. "Is this what they teach you in law school—to start grasping at straws when all else fails?"

"Exactly."

He planted his hands firmly on the desk and leaned far across it. "You're not a lawyer, you're a witch hunter."

That stung because Alex did feel like one. This search had a vigilante desperation to it that left a bad taste in her mouth. She sat back down and laid her hands on top of the open files.

Turning her head away, she stared out at the winter landscape. The naked branches of the sycamore trees on the lawn were encased in tubes of ice. Sleet pellets made tiny pinging sounds against the windowpanes. The sky and everything below it were a dead, dismal gray. Lines of distinction were imprecise. The world was monochromatic—without light and shadows.

Some things, however, were black and white. Chief among them was the law.

"That might be true if there hadn't been a crime, Reede," she said, bringing her head back around. "But there was. Somebody went into that stable and stabbed my mother."

"With a scalpel. Right," he said scoffingly. "Can you envision Angus, Junior, or me wielding a surgical instrument? Why not kill her with our bare hands? Strangle her?"

"Because you're all too clever. One of you made it to look like a mentally unbalanced man had done it." She splayed her hand upon her chest and asked earnestly, "In my place, wouldn't you want to know who that someone was and why he did it? You loved Celina. If you didn't kill her—"

"I didn't."

"Then, don't you want to know who did? Or are you afraid that her killer will turn out to be somebody else you love?"

"No, I don't want to know," he said emphatically. "And until you obtain a search warrant—"

"Miss Gaither?" Mr. Davis interrupted, entering the room. "Is this what you're looking for? I found it in a file cabinet in my storeroom." He handed her a folder, then scuttled out under Reede's baleful stare.

Alex read the name typed across the top of the file. She glanced at Reede, then eagerly opened the cover. After scanning the first of several forms, she sank into her chair and reported huskily, "It says here that her body was cremated." Her heart feeling like lead, she closed the folder and rhetorically asked, "Why didn't my grandmother ever mention that?"

"She probably didn't think it was significant."

"She saved everything, Celina's clothes, her things. Why wouldn't she have taken the ashes?"

Suddenly, she leaned forward, rested her elbows on the table, and supported her head with both hands. Her stomach churned mutinously. Fresh tears were building behind her lids, making them sting. "God, this is morbid, but I've got to know. I've *got* to."

After taking a few deep breaths, she reopened the file and began to flip through the various forms. Reading one, she sucked in her breath sharply.

"What is it?"

She lifted the sheet out of the folder and handed it to Reede. "This is a receipt for all of mother's funeral expenses, including the cremation."

"So?"

"Look at the signature."

"Angus Minton," he read softly, thoughtfully.

"You didn't know?" He shook his head. "It appears that Angus paid for everything, and wanted to keep it a secret from everybody." Alex drew a shuddering breath and gazed at Reede inquisitively. "I wonder why."

———————

Across town, Stacey Wallace entered the room that served as her father's office away from the courthouse. He was bent over the desk, poring through a legal tome. "Judge," she chided him affectionately, "as long as you're taking the day off, you should really take it off."

"It's not an official day off," he grumbled, giving the wintry view through the window a disgusted glance. "I've needed to catch up on some reading. Today's the perfect day for it, since I can't get to the courthouse."

"You've been working too hard and worrying too much."

"You're not telling me anything that my ulcer hasn't already."

Stacey sensed that he was extremely upset. "What's wrong?"

"It's that Gaither girl."

"Celina's daughter? She's still pestering you?"

"She came to my office yesterday wanting a court order to have the body exhumed."

"My God!" Stacey exclaimed in a disbelieving whisper. She raised a pale hand to the base of her throat. "The woman sounds like a fiend."

"Fiendish or not, I had to deny the request."

"Good for you."

He shook his head. "I had no choice. The body had been cremated."

Stacey pondered that. "Seems like I remember that now. How'd she take that news?"

"I don't know. Reede delivered it."

"Reede?"

"I called him last night. He volunteered. I would guess she didn't take it well."

"Do Angus and Junior know about this?"

"I'm sure they do by now. Reede would have told them."

"Probably," Stacey murmured. For a moment she was quiet. Then she roused herself and asked, "Can I bring you anything?"

"Not so soon after breakfast, thanks."

"Some hot tea?"

"Not now."

"Cocoa? Why don't you let me—"

"Stacey, I said, no thanks." He spoke with more impatience than he intended.

"I'm sorry I bothered you," she said dejectedly. "If you need me, I'll be upstairs."

The judge gave her an absentminded nod and dipped back into the leather-bound legal volume. Stacey quietly closed the study door. Her hand listlessly trailed the banister rail as she went upstairs to her bedroom. She didn't feel well. Her abdomen was swollen and achy. She'd started her period that morning.

The mid-forties seemed a ludicrous time to be suffering cramps like a teenager, although Stacey supposed she should welcome these monthly fluxes. They were her only reminders that she was a woman. No children came to her asking for lunch money or help with homework. No husband demanded to know what she had cooked for dinner, or if she'd picked up his cleaning, or if he could expect sex that night.

Daily she lamented not having all that glorious chaos in her life. As regularly as some people said prayers, Stacey enumerated to God the amenities of life that he had denied her. She longed for the racket of children running through the house. She yearned to have a husband reach for her in the night, to nuzzle her breasts and satisfy her hungering, restless body.

Like a priest who takes up self-flagellation, she went to her bureau, opened the third drawer, and took out the photograph album with the embossed white leather cover.

She opened it with reverence. One by one, she fondled the precious mementos—a yellowed newspaper clipping with her picture, a small square paper napkin with silver letters spelling out two names in one corner, a crumbling rose.

She leafed through the plastic binders, gazing at the photographs pressed between them. The people posing for the pictures in front of the altar had changed very little over the years.

After nearly an hour of masochistic reverie, Stacey closed the album and replaced it in its sacred drawer. Stepping out of her shoes so as not to spoil the comforter on her bed, she lay down and drew her pillow against her chest, snuggling it against her curved body like a lover.

Hot, salty tears leaked from her eyes. She whispered a name, urgently and repeatedly. She ground the heel of her hand over her lower body to relieve the pain of emptiness inside her womb, which had been a receptacle for his body, but never his love.

Chapter 14

Hey, what the hell, you two?" Junior exclaimed, dividing his puzzled glance between Alex and Reede. Then, buffeted by a gust of wind, he moved out of the doorway and urged them inside. "Come in. I couldn't imagine who'd come calling on a day like this. Reede, you ought to have your head examined for dragging Alex all the way out here."

He was wearing an ancient pair of jeans with the knees worn through, a cotton sweater, and thick white socks. It looked like he hadn't been up very long. In one hand he was holding a steaming mug of coffee; in the other, a trashy paperback novel. His hair was appealingly mussed. Stubble shadowed the lower half of his face.

Having recovered from the surprise of finding them on his doorstep, he smiled down at Alex. She thought he looked terrific and figured that most of the women in the world would agree with her. He looked lazy and rich, sexy and rumpled, comfortable and cushy. He invited snuggling, and his slow smile suggested that's what he'd been doing when they had interrupted.

"I didn't drag her out here," Reede said touchily. "It was the other way around."

"I was willing to come alone," Alex snapped.

"Well, I wasn't willing to let you become a highway statistic in my county," he shouted. Turning to Junior, who was bemusedly taking in their heated exchange, Reede said, "To make a long story short, I drove her out here because she was determined to come and I was afraid she'd kill herself—or worse, somebody else—on these roads. So, here we are."

"Well, I'm damned glad you're here," Junior said. "I had resigned myself to spending a boring day here alone. I've got a great fire going in the living room, and all the makings for hot toddies. Follow me." He set off, but turned and added, "Oops, Reede, you know how Mother is about having the floors tracked up. Better take your boots off."

"Fuck that. Is Lupe in the kitchen? I'm gonna try and sweet-talk her out of some breakfast." Giving no regard to Sarah Jo's floors, he tramped toward the back of the house as though he still lived there.

Alex watched him disappear through a doorway. "Did he say *sweet talk*?" she asked caustically.

"Oh, he's in a sunny mood today," Junior remarked negligently. "You ought to see him when he's really pissed. Leave Reede to Lupe. She knows how he likes his eggs. He'll feel better once he eats."

Alex let him help her off with her coat. "I hope this isn't too much of an intrusion."

"Hell, no. I wasn't kidding when I said I'm glad you're here." He threw his arm across her shoulders. "Let's—"

"Actually," Alex said, shrugging off his arm, "this isn't a social call."

"Business, huh?"

"Yes, and extremely important. Is Angus here?"

"He's in his den." His smile was still in place, but it had stiffened.

"Is he busy?"

"I don't think so. Come on, I'll take you back."

"I hate to tear you away from your novel."

He glanced dubiously at the torrid cover. "Doesn't matter. It was getting monotonous."

"What's it about?"

"A legendary cock's sojourn through most of the bedrooms in Hollywood, both male and female."

"Oh, really?" Alex inquired, feigning interest. "Can I borrow it when you're finished?"

"Shame on you," he exclaimed. "I'd be corrupting the morals of a minor, wouldn't I?"

"You're not that much older than I am."

"Compared to Reede and me, you're a baby," he told her as he opened the door to the den. "Dad, we've got company."

Angus glanced up from his newspaper. In the span of several seconds his face registered surprise, irritation, then a smile.

"Hello, Angus. I hate to disturb you on a sleep-in morning like today."

"No problem. There's not much going on. We can't exercise racehorses outdoors when the ground's frozen." He left his red leather recliner and crossed the room to welcome her. "You're a bright spot on a gloomy day, that's for damn sure, hey, Junior?"

"I've already told her as much."

"But as I've told Junior," she hastened to say, "this isn't a social visit."

"Oh? Sit down, sit down." Angus waved her toward a tufted leather love seat.

"I'll just—"

"No, Junior, I'd like for you to stay," Alex said before he could withdraw. "This concerns all of us."

"Okay, shoot." Junior straddled the overstuffed arm of the love seat as though it were a saddle.

"I spoke to Judge Wallace again yesterday." Alex thought she saw both men tense, but it was so fleeting, she could have imagined it.

"Any particular reason why?" Angus asked.

"I wanted to have my mother's body exhumed."

There was no mistaking their reaction this time. "Jesus, girl, why in hell would you want to do something like that?" Angus shuddered.

"Alex." Junior reached for her hand, laid it on his thigh, and massaged the back of it. "Isn't this getting a little out of hand? That's . . . that's gruesome."

"The case is gruesome," she reminded him as she eased her hand off his thigh. "Anyway, as I'm sure you know, what I asked for is impossible. My mother's body was cremated."

"That's right," Angus said.

"Why?" Her eyes were bright and intensely blue in the dim room. They reflected the fire burning in the fireplace, making them appear accusatory.

Angus resettled in his chair and hunched his shoulders defensively. "It seemed the best way to handle things."

"I fail to see how."

"Your grandmother planned to leave town with you as soon as everything was tidied up. She made no secret of it.

So I decided to have Celina's body cremated, thinking that Merle might want to take the, uh, remains with her."

"*You* decided? By what right, Angus? Under whose authority? Why was it left to you to decide what would happen to Celina's body?"

His brows beetled with displeasure. "You think I had her body cremated to destroy evidence, is that it?"

"I don't know!" she exclaimed, rising from the love seat.

She moved to the window and stared out at the empty paddocks. Lights shone through the doors of various stables, where horses were being groomed, fed, and exercised. She had thoroughly researched Minton Enterprises. Angus had millions invested in this facility. Was he reticent because he had so much to lose if she won an indictment, or because he was guilty, or both?

Eventually, she turned to face the men. "You've got to admit, in retrospect, that it seems an odd thing for you to have done."

"I only wanted to relieve Merle Graham of that responsibility. I felt I should because her daughter had been killed on my property. Merle was out of her mind with grief and had you to take care of. If what I did seems suspicious now, that's just too damn bad, young lady. I'd make the same decision if I had to do it again today."

"I'm sure Grandma Graham appreciated what you did. It was an unselfish thing to do."

Shrewdly, Angus looked at her and said, "But you wish you could believe it was entirely unselfish."

She looked him straight in the eye. "Yes, I do."

"I respect your honesty."

For a moment there was no sound in the room other than the friendly, crackling noise of burning firewood. Alex broke the awkward silence. "I wonder why Grandma didn't take the remains."

"I wondered about that myself when I offered them to her. I think it was because she couldn't face the fact that Celina was dead. An urn of ashes was tangible proof of something she couldn't accept."

Knowing how obsessed her grandmother had been with Celina's life, his explanation was feasible. Besides, unless Merle came out of her coma and Alex posed the question to her, she had no alternative but to accept as truth what Angus told her.

He was absently massaging his big toe through his sock. "I couldn't see storing her ashes in a mausoleum. I never could stand vaults and tombs. Goddamn spooky things. The very thought of them gives me the creeps. Went to New Orleans once. All those cement graves sitting on top of the ground...ugh."

He shook his head in repugnance. "I'm not afraid of dying, but when I go, I want to become part of the living again. Dust to dust. That's the natural cycle.

"So it seemed fitting to buy a cemetery plot and have Celina's ashes buried in the soil she grew up on. Guess you figure I'm a crazy old man, Alex, but that's how I felt about it then, and that's how I feel about it now. I didn't tell anybody because I was embarrassed. It was so sentimental, you see."

"Why not just scatter the ashes somewhere?"

He pulled on his earlobe as he pondered the question. "I thought about it, but I reckoned you might turn up one day and want to see where your mama was laid."

Alex felt her spirit slump, along with her posture. Lowering her head, she studied the toes of her suede boots, which were still damp from walking through the sleet. "I guess you think I'm a ghoul for wanting to open her grave. Reede did."

Angus made a dismissive gesture. "Reede's trigger-happy when it comes to forming opinions. Sometimes he's wrong."

She drew a shaky breath. "This time he is. Believe me, it wasn't an easy thing to even consider, much less ask for. I just thought that an extensive forensic investigation might shed some light..."

Her voice trailed off. She lacked the will and conviction to continue. Yesterday she had thought that an exhumation might provide the physical evidence she needed. As it had turned out, she was no closer to learning the truth, and all she had to show for her efforts was the traumatic upheaval she'd put herself and everyone else through.

Angus's explanation sounded so damned plausible and guileless. Paying all the funeral expenses, making all the arrangements, had been an act of charity to alleviate her grandmother's grim responsibility and financial burden.

Alex earnestly wanted to believe that. As Celina's daughter, it made her feel good inside. As a prosecutor, however, it left her empty-handed and frustrated and more suspicious than ever that something had been swept under the rug.

"You ready to go back to town, or what?"

Reede was standing in the doorway with his shoulder propped against the frame, insolently maneuvering a toothpick from one side of his mouth to the other. He might have eaten breakfast, but his tone of voice let her know that his foul disposition remained intact.

"Yes, I'm ready, if you'd be so kind as to drive me."

"Good. The sooner I get back to work the better. Somebody's got to ride herd on the crazy sons of bitches out driving in this."

"As long as you're out here, why don't you spend the day by the fireplace?" Junior suggested to Alex. "We could pop popcorn. Celina used to love that. Maybe we could talk Lupe out of a batch of pralines. I could drive you back later when the roads have cleared."

"It sounds wonderful, Junior, thank you, but I've got work to do."

He wheedled charmingly, but she remained adamant. The Mintons walked her and Reede to the door. She didn't see Sarah Jo. If she were even aware that she had guests in the house, she made no effort to present herself.

Angus looped Alex's arm through his as they made their way down the hall. He spoke softly. "I know this is difficult for you, girl."

"Yes, it is."

"Heard anything about your grandma?"

"I phone the nursing home every day, but there's been no change."

"Well, holler if you need anything, you hear?"

Alex gazed at him with genuine puzzlement. "Angus, why are you being so nice to me?"

"Because of your mama, because I like you, and mainly, because we've got nothing to hide."

When he smiled at her, Alex realized that it was easy to see where Junior had come by his charm. He and Reede were engaged in their own conversation. Alex overheard Reede say, "Ran into one of your old girlfriends last night at the Last Chance."

Her ears picked up at the mention of the tavern where she had an appointment later that day.

"Oh, yeah?" Junior was saying. "Who was that?"

"Gloria something. Forgot her married name. Curly black hair, dark eyes, bit tits."

"Gloria Tolbert. How'd she look?"

"Horny."

Junior gave a dirty and masculine laugh. "That's Gloria. Takes a strong man to keep her satisfied."

"You ought to know," Reede said drolly.

"Well, what happened last night, you lucky bastard? Did you leave a contented smile on Gloria's pretty face?"

"You know I never discuss my love life."

"That's just one of your traits that irritates the hell out of me."

Alex turned around in time to see Junior playfully sock Reede in the gut. His fist bounced back like he'd struck a drum.

"Is that the best you can do, ol' man?" Reede taunted. "Admit it, Minton, you're losing it."

"Like hell I am." Junior took a swipe at Reede's head. The blow was dodged just in time. Reede tried to catch Junior behind the knee with his boot. They fell against the hall table, almost toppling a ceramic vase.

"Okay, boys, cut it out before you break something," Angus said indulgently, speaking to them as though they were still in grade school.

Alex and Reede pulled on their coats and he opened the door. The frigid wind swirled inside. Junior said, "Sure you can't stay here where it's cozy?"

"I'm afraid not," Alex replied.

"Shoot. Well, good-bye then." He pressed her hand between his and kissed her cheek.

Father and son watched as Reede assisted Alex over the icy stone walkway to where his Blazer was parked. He helped her up into the truck, then went around to the driver's side and vaulted in.

"Brrr," Junior said, shutting the door. "Ready for a hot toddy, Dad?"

"Not yet," Angus answered with a scowl. "It's too early in the day to be drinking hard liquor."

"Since when have you taken into consideration the time of day when you wanted a drink?"

"Get in here. I want to talk to you." Limping to favor his toe, he led his son back into his den. "Stoke up that fire, will ya?"

When the flames were licking fresh logs, Junior faced his father. "What is it? Not business, I hope. I'm taking an official day off," he said around a yawn, stretching like a sleek cat.

"Alex Gaither."

Junior pulled down his arms and frowned. "She was all fired up about that burial business when she came in, wasn't she? But you brought her around."

"I only told her the truth."

"You made it sound as convincing as a good lie."

"Will you be serious for once?" Angus barked.

Junior looked baffled. "I thought I was."

"You listen to me," Angus said sternly, aiming a finger at his son. "Only a damn fool would laugh off her determination to get to the bottom of this thing. Even if she is a good-looking woman, she means business. She looks soft, but she isn't. She's tough as boot leather when it comes to this murder case."

"I'm aware of that," Junior said sulkily.

"Ask Joe Wallace if you don't believe it."

"I do. I just find it hard to take her seriously when she looks as good as she does."

"You do, huh? Well, I don't see you doing anything about that, either."

"I asked her out here for drinks, and she came."

"What have you done since then?"

"What do you want me to do? Court her like some snot-nosed kid? Go the flowers and chocolates route?"

"Yes, goddammit!"

"She'd never fall for that," Junior snorted, "even if I could do it with a straight face."

"You listen to me, boy. You've got life good. You drive a new Jag every year, wear a big, diamond-studded Rolex, go skiing, deep-sea fishing, and to the horse races whenever you feel like it, and you gamble big.

"But if this little lady has her way, she'll bust us. Yeah," he said, reading his son's frown correctly, "you might have to go out and get a job for once in your life."

Angus reined in his temper and continued in a more conciliatory tone. "She hasn't got a prayer of turning up any evidence. I think she knows that. She's throwing darts into the dark and hoping to hit one of us in the ass. Sooner or later, hopefully, her arm'll get tired."

Junior chewed on his lip and said glumly, "She probably wants a court trial as much as we want a racetrack. That'd be a real coup for her. It'd launch her career."

"Damn," Angus grumbled. "You know how I feel about that. I don't like all this career bullshit. Women don't belong in courtrooms."

"Where would you keep them? In bedrooms?"

"Nothing wrong with that."

Junior laughed shortly. You won't get an argument from me, but I imagine you would from millions of working women."

"Alex might not be working for long. It wouldn't surprise me if her career was riding on the outcome of this investigation."

"How do you mean?"

"I know all about Greg Harper. He's ambitious, sees himself in the attorney general's seat. He likes his people to win convictions. Now, if I've got him figured right, he's letting Alex do this because he smells blood, our blood. If we got our tails in a crack over this murder business, he'd get his name in the headlines and gloat every step of the way because there's no love lost between him and the governor. The governor's nose would be rubbed in shit and so would the racing commission's.

"On the other hand, if Alex fails to smoke out any skeletons in our closet, Harper'll have to eat crow. Rather than do that, he'll boot Alex out. And we'll be there with open arms to catch her when she falls," he said, jabbing the air for emphasis.

"I see you've got it all worked out," Junior remarked dryly.

Angus made a grunting sound. "Damn right I do. One of us better be concentrating on more than the fine way she fills out a sweater."

"I thought that's what you wanted me to do."

"You gotta do more than gawk and lust from afar. A love affair would be the best thing that could happen to Alex."

"How do you know she's not involved in one?"

"Because unlike you, I don't leave things to chance. I made it my business to find out. I've had her checked out."

"You cagey old bastard," Junior whispered with grudging admiration.

"Humph. You gotta know what cards the other guy's holding, son, or it does you no good to have a winning hand."

While the fire in the grate popped cheerfully, Junior contemplated all that Angus had said. Then, focusing a narrow gaze on his father, he asked, "Where would you have this love affair lead? To marriage?"

Angus slapped Junior's knee and chortled. "Would that be so bad?"

"Would you approve?"

"Why not?"

Junior wasn't sharing the laugh. He moved to the fire, away from his father's touch and conniving smile. Absently, he poked at the burning logs.

"I'm surprised," he said softly. "You didn't think Celina would make a suitable wife for me. I remember the ruckus you raised when I told you I wanted to marry her."

"You were eighteen then, boy!" Angus shouted. "Celina was a widow with a baby."

"Yes. Alex. And look how fine she turned out. She could have been my stepdaughter."

Angus's brows drew together over the bridge of his nose. They were a dependable gauge of his temper. The steeper the vee, the angrier he was. "There were other considerations."

Junior spun around. "Like what?"

"That was twenty-five years ago, another time, another person. Alex isn't her mother. She's got more beauty, and a hell of a lot more brains. If you were half the man you're supposed to be—if, for once, you'd think with your head instead of your pecker—you'd see how valuable it'd be to have her standing by your side."

Junior blushed with anger. "I *can* see all that. I just wanted to make damn certain before I started a courtship that you would approve of it this time. Whether you want to believe it or not, I loved Celina. And if I start romancing Alex, I might just fall in love with her, too. For real. Not for you, not for the corporation, but for myself."

He stamped toward the door. Angus called his name sharply. Out of habit, Junior stopped and turned around. "You resent this lecture, don't you, boy?"

"Yes," he stormed. "I'm a grown man, not a boy. I don't need your coaching. I know how to handle Alex, or any other woman you can name."

"Oh, you do?" Angus asked silkily.

"Yeah, I do."

"Then why did Alex leave you today and go off with Reede?"

Upstairs, Sarah Joe eavesdropped on the raging conversation. When Junior slunk into the living room and she heard the clatter of glassware, she silently closed the door to her sanctum and leaned back against it. Her chest rose and fell with a heavy, despairing sigh.

It was happening again.

There seemed to be no escaping this nightmare. Junior was going to have his heart broken again, this time by Celina's daughter because she would come between Junior and his father and his best friend. History was repeating itself. The house was in an uproar, and all because of that girl.

Sarah Jo knew she wouldn't be able to stand it. No, she was quite sure she wouldn't. The first time, she had failed to protect Junior from heartache. She wouldn't be able to protect him this time, either.

And that broke her heart.

Chapter 15

She'd had every opportunity to be mugged, raped, or murdered, or any combination thereof, in the Last Chance. Not to mention the chances she'd taken on the roads there and back. Luckily, she had left unscathed, except for her riled temper.

Entering her motel room, Alex slung her handbag and coat in the chair, furious with herself for chasing after what was obviously a red herring. Greg Harper would have a field day if he ever found out she'd been so gullible.

That afternoon, she had called him. He wasn't impressed with her findings so far, and made another pitch for her to return to Austin and reconcile herself to the past. She had held him to the time he'd allotted her.

His disfavor with her lack of results was one reason she had put so much stock in her clandestine meeting tonight. Greg would feel different if she could produce an eyewitness to the murder.

She should have known the instant she pulled into the parking lot of the bar that it didn't hold much promise. Three bulbs were missing from the Texas lone star that blinked off and on above the door. She had hesitated to even go inside the place.

Every head in the room had turned. The men were a rough bunch. They were drawn to her like coyotes to fresh meat. The women looked even rougher, and glowered at her with the blatant unfriendliness of potential rivals. She was tempted to turn and run, but remembering what had taken her there, she walked boldly to the bar.

"White wine, please."

That generated a snicker from everybody within hearing distance. Taking her glass with her, she moved to a booth and slid into the bench that would afford her the best view of the room. Sipping self-consciously, she let her gaze move from one face to another, trying to ascertain which belonged to the voice on the telephone.

Then, to her horror, she realized that some of the men took her close scrutiny of them as encouragement. From then on, she confined her stares to the bottom of her wine glass, wishing that her informant would hurry up and join her and end the suspense. On the other hand, she dreaded meeting him. If he were among this crowd, she didn't think he'd be someone she would enjoy getting to know.

Billiard balls clacked and clattered. She got an overdose of George Strait and Waylon Jennings. She inhaled clouds of smoke, even though she wasn't smoking. And still she sat alone.

Finally, a man who had been seated at the bar when she had come in slid off his stool and moved in the general direction of her booth. He took his own sweet time, stopping at the jukebox to make his selections and pausing beside the pool table to heckle one of the players about a bad shot.

His wandering seemed aimless and casual, but his gaze kept drifting toward her. Her midsection tightened. Instinctively, she knew that his final destination would be her booth.

It was. He propped his hip against the back of the padded bench across the table from her and smiled down as he tilted a long-neck beer bottle to his lips. "You waitin' for somebody?"

His voice sounded different, but then, both times he'd called her, he'd been whispering. "You know I am," she replied in a cold undertone. "Why'd you take so long to come over?"

"I was building up my courage," he said, slurping another draft of beer. "Now that I'm here, wanna dance?"

"Dance?"

"Yeah, dance. You know, a one an' a two." He used the spout of his beer bottle to push up the brim of his cowboy hat. His eyes slithered over her.

Her reaction was negative and chilling. "I thought you wanted to talk."

He seemed momentarily nonplussed, then gave her a slow, sly grin. "We can talk all you want to, honey." He set his bottle of beer on the table and extended his hand down to her. "My truck's right outside."

He was just a cowboy on the make! Alex didn't know whether to laugh or scream. Hastily gathering up her things, she headed for the door. "Hey, wait a minute. Where're you goin'?"

She left him and everybody else at the Last Chance wondering. Now, pacing the worn carpet of her motel room, she berated herself for being such a fool. She wouldn't put it past Reede or one of the Mintons to pay an out-of-work cowboy a few bucks to call her and deliberately throw her off track.

She was still stewing several minutes later when her telephone rang. She yanked it up. "Hello."

"Do you think I'm crazy?" the familiar voice wheezed.

"Where were you?" she shouted. "I waited in that sleazy joint for almost an hour."

"Was the sheriff there the whole time?"

"What are you talking about? Reede wasn't there."

"Look, lady, I know what I seen. I got there just as you was goin' inside. Reede Lambert was tailin' you. Oh, he cruised on past, but made a U-turn down the road a piece. I didn't even stop. It wouldn't do at all for Lambert to see us talkin' together."

"Reede was following me?"

"Damn right. I didn't count on no law, especially Lambert, breathin' down my neck when I called you. He's thicker'n thieves with the Mintons. I've got a good mind to call off this whole goddamn thing."

"No, no," Alex said quickly. "I didn't know Reede was anywhere around. We'll meet someplace else. Next time, I'll be certain he's not trailing me."

"Well…"

"On the other hand, if what you've got to tell me isn't all that important…"

"I seen who done it, lady."

"Then where can we meet? And when?"

He named another bar, which sounded even more disreputable than the Last Chance. "Don't go inside this time. There'll be a red pickup parked on the north side of the building. I'll be in it."

"I'll be there, Mr.—Uh, can't you at least tell me your name?"

"Nope."

He hung up. Alex cursed. She bounced off the bed and went to the window, throwing open the drapes with the flourish of the bullfighter in the terrible artwork.

Feeling foolish, she saw that the only car near her room was her own. The familiar black-and-white Blazer was nowhere to be seen. She closed the drapes, went back to the phone, and angrily punched out another number. She was so furious at Reede for scaring off an eyewitness, she was shaking.

"Sheriff's office."

"I want to speak to Sheriff Lambert."

"He's already left for the day," she was informed. "Is it an emergency?"

"Do you know where he is?"

"At home, I reckon."

"What's that number, please?"

"We aren't s'posed to give it out."

"This is Ms. Gaither. I must speak with Sheriff Lambert tonight. It's very important. If necessary, I could track him through the Mintons, but I hate to disturb them."

Dropping important names worked miracles. She was given the telephone number without further delay. She intended to put an immediate halt to the sheriff's sneaky surveillance.

Her resolve vanished when a feminine contralto voice answered his telephone.

"It's a woman, asking for you." Nora Gail extended the telephone receiver to Reede. Her pencil-perfect eyebrows formed an inquisitive arch. He had been adding logs to the fireplace across the room. He brushed his hands on the seat of his jeans and pretended not to see the inquiry in her expression as he took the receiver from her.

"Yeah? This is Lambert."

"This is Alex."

He turned his back on his guest. "What do you want?"

"I want to know why you were following me tonight."

"How do you know I was?"

"I...I saw you."

"No, you didn't. What the hell were you doing in that honky-tonk?"

"Having a drink."

"And you picked the Last Chance?" he asked scoffingly. "Baby, you hardly look like its typical barfly. That place is reserved for shit kickers and roughnecks looking for fun with dissatisfied housewives. So either you went there to get laid, or to keep a secret appointment. Which was it?"

"I was there on official business."

"So, it was to meet somebody. Who? You'd be wise to tell me, Alex, because whoever it was got scared off when he saw me."

"You admit that you were trailing me?" Reede remained stubbornly silent. "That's just one of many topics we'll address first thing in the morning."

"Sorry. Tomorrow's my day off."

"It's important."

"That's your opinion."

"Where will you be?"

"I said no, Counselor."

"You don't have a choice."

"The hell I don't. I'm off duty tomorrow."

"Well, I'm not."

He cursed and blew out an exasperated breath, making certain she heard both. "If the ground's thawed out, I'll be at the Mintons' practice track."

"I'll find you."

Without another word, he dropped the receiver back into the cradle. He'd trapped her and he knew it. He'd heard her breathing falter when he'd asked how she'd known he had followed her. Whoever she had planned on meeting had chickened out. Who? Junior? It was disturbing how much he disliked that idea.

"Who was that?" Nora Gail asked, adjusting the lush white mink coat around her shoulders. Her beaded sweater had a low neckline. She amply filled it...and then some. In the cleft of her breasts nestled an opal as big around as a silver dollar. The gold chain suspending it in that magnificent setting was half an inch wide and studded with small, brilliant diamonds.

She took a black cigarette out of an eighteen-carat gold box. Reede picked up her matching lighter and held it to the tip of the cigarette. She curved her hand around his. The rings on her plump, pampered hand glittered. "Thank you, sugar."

"Don't mention it." He tossed the lighter back onto the kitchen table and returned to his chair across from her.

"That was Celina's girl, wasn't it?"

"What if it was?"

"Ah." She pulled her lips into a ruby pucker and blew a stream of smoke toward his ceiling. "Her ears must have been burning." Tilting her hand downward, she pointed with her cigarette at the letter lying on the table. "What do you think about it?"

Reede picked up the letter and reread it, though its message had been crystal clear the first time. It urged Alexandra Gaither to cease and desist in her investigation. The letter strongly suggested that she suspend all efforts to prosecute Angus Minton, Junior Minton, and Reede Lambert on any criminal charges.

The character of each man mentioned was given a glowing review by the undersigned, who were a group of concerned citizens—among them, his guest. They were concerned not only for their esteemed colleagues who found themselves in this unfortunate circumstance, but also for themselves and their business interests, should the racetrack license be revoked in light of Ms. Gaither's unfounded investigation.

In summation, the letter admonished her to retreat immediately and let them get down to the business of profiting well off the increased revenue a racetrack would mean to their community.

After reading the letter a second time, Reede refolded it and stuffed it into the unsealed envelope. It had been addressed to Alex in care of the Westerner Motel.

He didn't comment on the contents. Instead, he asked, "Did you instigate it?"

"I bounced the idea off a few of the others."

"It sounds like one of your brainstorms."

"I'm a careful businesswoman. You know that. The others thought it was a good idea and took it from there. We all approved the final draft. I suggested that we get your input before we mail it to her."

"Why's that?"

"You've spent more time with her than anybody else in town. We thought you might guess what her reaction will be."

He studied her impassive features for a long moment. She was as sly as a fox. She hadn't gotten as rich as she was by being dumb or careless. Reede liked her, always had. He slept with her on a regular basis to their mutual satisfaction. But he didn't trust her.

Feeding someone like her too much information would not only be unethical, it would be just plain stupid. He had enough street smarts to know better, and it would take more than an extended viewing of her spectacular cleavage to loosen his tongue.

"Your guess is as good as mine how she'll react," he said noncommittally. "She probably won't react at all."

"Meaning?"

"Meaning, I doubt she'll pack her bags and head for Austin the minute she reads this."

"Courageous, is she?"

Reede shrugged.

"Stubborn?"

He gave a sardonic smile. "You could say that, yeah. She's damned stubborn."

"I'm curious about this girl."

"Why?"

"Because you frown every time her name comes up." She sent another stream of acrid smoke ceilingward as she regarded him closely. "You're frowning now, sugar."

"Habit."

"Does she look like her mother?"

"Not much," he said shortly. "There's a resemblance, that's all."

Her smile was slow, feline, crafty. "She bothers you, doesn't she?"

"Hell, yes, she bothers me," he shouted. "She's trying to send me to prison. Wouldn't that bother you?"

"Only if I was guilty."

Reede clenched his teeth. "All right, I've read your letter and given you my opinion. Why don't you haul your ass out of my house?"

Unperturbed by his anger, she leisurely ground out her cigarette in his tin ashtray and pulled her fur coat around her as she stood up. She gathered up her cigarettes, lighter, and the envelope addressed to Alex, and replaced them in her handbag. "I know from experience, Mr. Reede Lambert, that you think my ass is quite something."

Reede's temper abated. Laughing with chagrin, he squeezed a handful of fanny through her clothing and snarled, "You're right. It is."

"Friends?"

"Friends."

As they stood facing each other, she smoothed her hand down his belly and cupped his sex. It was full and firm, but unaroused. "It's a cold night, Reede," she said in a sultry voice. "Want me to stay?"

He shook his head. "We agreed a long time ago that in order to remain friends, I'd come to you to get laid."

She drew a pretty frown. "Why'd we agree to that?"

"Because I'm the sheriff and you run a whorehouse."

Her laugh was guttural and sexy. "Goddamn right, I do. The best and most profitable one in the state. Anyway, I see I took good care of you the other night." She'd been massaging him through his jeans, with no results.

"Yeah, thanks."

Smiling, the madam dropped her hand and moved toward

the door. She addressed him over her shoulder. "What was the urgency? I don't recall seeing you in such a dither since you heard about a certain soldier boy in El Paso, name of Gaither."

Reede's eyes turned a darker, more menacing green. "No urgency. Just horny."

She smiled her knowing smile and patted his stubbled cheek. "You'll have to lie better than that, Reede, honey, to put one over on me. I've known you too long and too well." Her voice drifted back to him as she stepped into the darkness beyond his door. "Don't be a stranger, sugar, you hear?"

Chapter 16

It was no longer sleeting, but it was still very cold. Patches of thin ice crunched beneath Alex's boots as she carefully made her way from her parked car toward the practice track. The brilliant sunshine, which had not deigned to appear for the last several days, now blinded her. The sky was a vivid blue. Jets, looking no larger than pinpoints, trailed puffy lines that sometimes crisscrossed, matching the miles of white fencing on the Minton ranch that divided the compound into separate pens and paddocks.

The ground between the gravel road and the practice track was uneven. Tire tracks had worn permanent ruts in it over the years. It was muddy in spots where ice had already surrendered to the sun's rays.

Alex had dressed appropriately in old boots and jeans. Even though her hands were gloved in kid leather, she raised her fists to her mouth and blew on them for additional warmth. She took a pair of sunglasses out of her coat pocket and slid them on to combat the sunlight. From behind their tinted lenses, she watched Reede. He was standing at the rail clocking the horses between the timing poles placed every sixteenth of a mile.

She held back a moment to study him unobserved. Instead of the leather bomber jacket, he had on a long, light-colored duster. One boot was propped on the lowest rail of the fence, a stance that drew attention to his narrow buttocks and long thighs.

The boot she could see was scuffed and well worn. His jeans were clean, but the hems were frayed, their denim threads bleached white. It occurred to her that the flies of all his jeans were similarly worn, and she was shocked to realize that she knew that.

His wrists were propped on the top fence rail, his hands dangling over the other side. He was wearing leather gloves, the same ones he'd had on when he'd pulled her against him the other night and held her while she cried. It was odd, and deliciously disturbing, to reflect on how his hands had moved over her back with nothing except a terry-cloth robe separating them from her nakedness. A stopwatch lay in the palm of the hand that had cupped her head and pressed it against his chest.

He had on the cowboy hat she'd first seen him in, pulled down low over his brows. Dark blond hair brushed the collar of his coat. When he turned his head, she noticed that the angles of his profile were sharp and clear. There were no indecisive shapes, no subtle contours. When he breathed, a vapor formed around the lips that had kissed her damp hair after he'd told her about Celina's body.

"Let 'em go," he shouted to the practice riders. His voice was as masculine as all his features. Whether he was shouting orders or making innuendos, it never failed to elicit a response low in her body.

As the horses came around—four, in all—their hooves pounded and raised clumps of turf that a track conditioner had loosened earlier that morning. Flaring nostrils sent up billows of steam.

When the riders slowed them to a walk, they were directed back toward the stables. Reede called out to one. "Ginger, how's he doing?"

"I've been holding him back. He's bouncy."

"Give him his head. He wants to run. Walk him around once, then let him go again."

"Okay."

The diminutive rider, who Alex hadn't initially realized was a young woman, tipped the bill of her cap with her quirt and nudged her splendid mount back onto the track.

"What's his name?"

Reede's head came around. He speared Alex with eyes shaded against the sun only by the brim of his hat and a natural squint that had left him with appealing crow's-feet at the outer corners of his eyes. "She's a girl."

"The horse?"

"Oh. The horse's name is Double Time."

Alex moved up beside him at the rail and rested her forearms on it. "Is he yours?"

"Yes."

"A winner?"

"He keeps me in pocket change."

Alex watched the rider crouched over the saddle. "She seems to know just what to do," she remarked. "That's a lot of horse for such a tiny person to handle."

"Ginger's one of the Mintons' best gallop boys—that's what they're called." He returned his attention to the horse and rider as they came around the track at a full-out gallop. "Atta boy, atta boy," he whispered. "Comin' through like a pro." He whooped when Double Time streaked past them, a blur of well-coordinated muscle, agility, and immense strength.

"Good work," Reede told the rider when she brought the horse around.

"Better?"

"Several seconds better."

Reede had more encouraging words for the horse. He patted him affectionately and spoke in a language the animal seemed to understand. The stallion pranced off friskily, tail fanning, knowing that a rewarding breakfast was awaiting him in the stable for having performed so well for his owner.

"You seem to have a real rapport with him," Alex observed.

"I was there the day his sire covered the mare. I was there when he was foaled. They thought he was a dummy, and wanted to put him down."

"A what?"

"A dummy's a foal that was deprived of oxygen during the birthing." He shook his head as he watched the horse enter the stable. "I didn't think so. I was right. His lineage indicated he had every chance to be good, and he has been. Never a disappointment. Always runs his heart out, even when he's outclassed."

"You've got good reason to be proud of him."

"I guess."

Alex wasn't fooled by his pretended indifference. "Do they always run the horses full out like that?"

"No, they're breezing them today, seeing how they run

against each other. Four days a week, they're galloped once or twice around the track. Comparable to a jog. Two days after breezing them, they're just walked."

He turned and headed toward a saddled horse that was tied to a fence post. "Where are you going?"

"Home." He mounted with the loose-limbed grace of a range cowboy.

"I need to talk to you," Alex cried in consternation.

He bent down and extended his hand. "Get on." From beneath the brim of his hat, green eyes challenged her.

She pushed her sunglasses higher on the bridge of her nose and approached the horse with an outward show of confidence she didn't actually feel.

Clasping Reede's hand was the tough part. He hauled her up with very little effort, though it was left to her to get situated between his buttocks and the sloping back of the saddle.

That was disconcerting enough, but when he kneed the horse forward, Alex threw herself against his broad back. Out of necessity, her arms encircled his waist. She was careful to keep her hands well above his belt. Her mind wasn't as easy to control. It kept straying to his damned, well-worn fly.

"Warm enough?" he asked her over his shoulder.

"Yes," she lied.

She had thought his long white duster with the steep pleat in the back was all for show. She'd never seen one outside a Clint Eastwood western. Now, however, she realized the coat was designed to keep a rider's thighs warm.

"Who were you meeting in the bar last night?"

"That's my business, Reede. Why did you follow me?"

"That's my business."

Impasse. For the time being, she let it go. She had a file

of questions she wanted to ask him, but it was difficult to keep her mind on her task when her open cleft kept bumping into his hips with each rocking motion of the horse. She blurted out the first question that came to mind. "How did you and my mother get to be such close friends?"

"We grew up together," he said dismissively. "It started out on the jungle gym on the school playground and evolved as we got older."

"It never became awkward?"

"Nope. We had no secrets from each other. We'd even played doctor a few times."

"'I'll show you mine if you'll show me yours'?"

He grinned. "You must've played doctor, too."

Alex didn't rise to the bait, knowing that he was trying to sidetrack her. "I guess the two of you eventually grew out of that stage."

"We didn't play doctor anymore, no, but we talked about everything. No subject was taboo between Celina and me."

"Isn't that the kind of relationship a girl usually has with another girl?"

"Usually, but Celina didn't have many girlfriends. Most of the girls were jealous of her."

"Why?" Alex already knew the answer. She knew even before he shrugged, a move that rubbed his shoulder blade against her breast. Alex was hardly able to speak. She had to force herself to ask. "It was because of you, wasn't it? Her friendship with you?"

"Maybe. That, and the fact that she was by far the prettiest girl around. Most of the girls considered her a rival, not a friend. Hold on," he warned her before guiding the horse into a dry gully.

Inertia pushed her forward, closer to him. Instinctively, she hugged his torso tighter. He made a grunting sound. She asked, "What's the matter?"

"Nothing."

"You sounded...uncomfortable."

"If you were a guy sitting astride a horse taking a steep incline and were being crammed against the pommel of the saddle so that your manhood pushed into your lap, you'd be uncomfortable, too."

"Oh."

"Jesus," he swore beneath his breath.

Until the ground leveled out, there was an awkward silence between them, broken only by the horse's clumping tread as he carefully picked his way over the rocky ground. To hide her embarrassment and keep the cold wind off her, Alex buried her face in the flannel-lined collar of his coat. Eventually, she said, "So, Mother came to you with all her problems."

"Yes. When she didn't, and I knew something was wrong, I went to her. One day she was absent from school. I got worried and went to her house during lunch break. Your grandmother was at work, so Celina was there alone. She'd been crying. I got scared and refused to leave until she told me what was wrong."

"What was the matter?"

"She got her period for the first time."

"Oh."

"From what I gathered, Mrs. Graham had made her feel ashamed of it. She'd told her all kinds of horror stories about Eve's curse—crap like that." There was disapproval in his voice. "Was she that way with you?"

Alex shook her head no, but didn't remove it from the

protection of his collar. His neck was warm, and smelled like him. "Not that severe. Maybe Grandma had become more enlightened by the time I reached puberty." Until Reede reined in the horse and dismounted, Alex hadn't realized that they'd reached a small frame house. "What about Mother?"

"I consoled her and told her that it was normal, nothing to be ashamed of, that she had officially become a woman." He looped the reins around a hitching post.

"Did it work?"

"I guess so. She stopped crying and—"

"And...?" Alex prodded him to continue, knowing that he had omitted the most important part of the story.

"Nothing. Swing your leg over." He reached up to help her down, taking her around the waist with sure, strong hands and lifting her to the ground.

"Something, Reede."

She clutched the sleeves of his coat. His lips were drawn into a thin, stubborn line. They looked chapped and consummately masculine. She remembered looking at the newspaper picture of him kissing Celina when he crowned her homecoming queen. As before, Alex's stomach swelled and receded like a wave far out in the gulf.

"You kissed her, didn't you?"

He made an uneasy movement with his shoulder. "I'd kissed her before."

"But that was the first real kiss, wasn't it?"

He released her and, crossing the shallow front porch, thrust open the door. "You can come in or not," he said over his shoulder, "it's up to you."

He disappeared through the door, leaving it open.

Despondent but curious, Alex followed. The front door opened directly into the living room. Through an arched opening on her left, she could see a dining area and kitchen. A hallway on the opposite side presumably led into a bedroom, where she could hear him rummaging about. Absently, she closed the front door, removed her glasses and gloves, and looked around.

The house had the stamp of a bachelor. Furniture had been arranged for comfort and convenience, not with any decorative flair. He'd set his hat on a table and tossed his coat and gloves onto a chair. Other surfaces were clear, but the bookshelves were cluttered, as though straightening up amounted to cramming anything lying around onto a shelf. There were cobwebs in the corners of the ceiling that caught the sunlight as it poured in through the dusty venetian blinds.

He caught her looking up at one of the cobwebs as he reappeared, carrying a pair of aviator sunglasses. "Lupe sends one of her nieces out here every few weeks. It's about that time." It was an explanation, but hardly an excuse or apology. "Want some coffee?"

"Please."

He went into the kitchen. Alex continued to walk around the room as she stamped circulation back into her frozen feet. Her attention was drawn to a tall trophy in one of the built-in bookshelves. "Most Valuable Player" was engraved on it in block letters, along with Reede's name and the date.

"Is this the right color?" He had moved up behind her. When she turned he was holding a mug of coffee out to her. He had remembered to add milk.

"Fine, thanks." Inclining her head toward the trophy, she asked, "Your senior year, right?"

"Hmmm."

"That's quite an honor."

"I guess so."

Alex noticed that he resorted to that catchall phrase when he wanted the conversation to end. He remained an enigma in all other respects. "You're not sure it was an honor?"

He dropped into an easy chair and thrust his feet out in front of him. "I felt then, and still feel, that I had a good team backing me up. The other nominated players were just as valuable as me."

"Junior?"

"He was one of them, yeah," he replied, instantly defensive.

"But you won the award and Junior didn't."

His eyes glared at hers. "Is that supposed to be significant?"

"I don't know. Is it?"

He gave a scoffing laugh. "Stop playing lawyer games with me and say what's on your mind."

"Okay." She leaned against the padded arm of the sofa and considered him carefully as she asked, "Did Junior resent your getting named most valuable player?"

"Ask him."

"Maybe I will. I'll also ask Angus if he minded."

"Angus couldn't have been prouder the night of the awards banquet."

"Except if his son had been named most valuable player instead of you."

Reede's expression turned stony. "You're full of shit, you know that?"

"I'm sure Angus was proud of you, glad for you, but you can't expect me to believe that he wouldn't have rather seen Junior get the trophy."

"Believe whatever you goddamn want to. It makes no difference to me." He emptied his coffee mug in three swallows, set it on the low coffee table in front of him, then stood up. "Ready?"

She set her coffee down, too, but she made no move to leave. "Why are you so touchy about this?"

"Not touchy, bored." He leaned down to put his face close to hers. "That trophy is a twenty-five-year-old, tarnished piece of junk that's good for nothing except to collect dust."

"Then, why have you kept it all these years?"

He plowed his fingers through his hair. "Look, it doesn't mean anything now."

"But it did then."

"Precious little. Not enough to get me an athletic scholarship, which I was counting on to go to college."

"What did you do?"

"I went anyway."

"How?"

"A loan."

"A government loan?"

"No, a private one," he answered evasively.

"Who lent you the money—Angus?"

"So? I paid back every friggin' cent of it."

"By working for him?"

"Until I left ME."

"Why'd you leave?"

"Because I'd paid him back and wanted to do something else."

"That was as soon as you got out of college?"

He shook his head. "The air force."

"You were in the air force?"

"Four years of officers' training during college, then active duty after graduation. For six years my ass belonged to Uncle Sam. Two of those years were spent bombing gooks in Vietnam."

Alex hadn't known he'd been involved in the war, but she should have guessed. He'd been at draftable age during the height of it. "Did Junior serve, too?"

"Junior at war? Can you picture that?" he asked with a rough laugh. "No, he didn't go. Angus pulled some strings and got him into the reserves."

"Why not you, too?"

"I didn't want him to. I wanted to go into the air force."

"To learn to fly?"

"I already knew how to fly. I had my pilot's license before I had my driver's license."

She contemplated him for a moment. The information was coming too fast and furious to absorb. "You're just full of surprises this morning, aren't you? I didn't know you could fly."

"No reason you should, Counselor."

"Why aren't there any pictures of you in uniform?" she asked, indicating the bookcase.

"I hated what I was doing over there. No mementos of wartime, thanks." He backed away from her, picked up his hat, gloves, and coat, then went to the front door and ungraciously pulled it open.

Alex remained where she was. "You and Junior must have missed each other while you were serving your six years in the air force."

"What's that supposed to mean? Do you think we're queer for each other?"

"No," she said with diminishing patience. "I just meant

that you're good friends who, up till that point, had spent a lot of time together."

He slammed the door closed and slung down his outer-wear. "By then we were used to being apart."

"You spent four years of college together," she pointed out.

"No, we didn't. We were attending Texas Tech at the same time, but since he was married—"

"Married?"

"Another surprise?" he asked tauntingly. "Didn't you know? Junior got married just a few weeks after we gradu-ated from high school."

No, Alex hadn't known that. She hadn't realized that Junior's first marriage had come on the heels of high school graduation, and consequently, so soon after Celina's murder. The timing seemed strange.

"For a long while, then, you and Junior didn't see much of each other."

"That's right," was Reede's clipped response.

"Did my mother's death have anything to do with that?"

"Maybe. We didn't—couldn't talk about it."

"Why?"

"It was too damned hard. Why the hell do you think?"

"Why was it hard to be around Junior and talk about Celi-na's death?"

"Because we'd always been a trio. One of us was suddenly missing. It didn't feel right to be together."

Alex weighed the advisability of pressing him on this, but decided to take the plunge. "You were a trio, yes, but if it was ever odd man out, the odd man was Junior, not Celina. Right? You and she were an inseparable duo before you became an inseparable trio."

"You keep the hell out of my life," he ground out. "You don't know a damn thing about it, about me."

"There's no need for you to get mad, Reede."

"Oh, no? Why shouldn't I get mad? You want to resurrect the past, everything from my first real kiss to some fucking football trophy that has about as much value as a pile of horse shit, but I'm not supposed to get mad."

"Most people enjoy reminiscing."

"I don't. I want to leave my past in the past."

"Because it's hurtful?"

"Some of it."

"Is it hurtful to remember the first time you kissed my mother for real?"

He strode toward the sofa and bridged her hips with his hands, keeping his arms stiff. His voice changed from a ranting pitch to pure silk. "That kiss sure as hell intrigues you, doesn't it, Counselor?"

He overwhelmed her. She could say nothing.

"Well, if you're so interested in how I kiss, maybe you should experience it firsthand."

He pushed his hands inside her coat and linked them together at the small of her back. Giving a swift yank, he pulled her to her feet. She caught herself against his chest, gasping soundlessly before he bent his head down low and covered her lips with his.

At first she was so stunned she didn't move. When she realized what was happening, she placed both her fists firmly against his chest. She tried to turn her head aside, but he trapped her jaw in one hand and held it still. His lips expertly rubbed hers apart, then he thrust his tongue between them. He kissed her thoroughly, sweeping her mouth with his tongue and making stabbing motions toward the back of her throat. His lips were chapped. She felt their roughness against hers as well as the thrilling contrast of their sleek lining.

She might have uttered a small whimper of surprise and need. Her body might have become pliant enough to conform to his. He might have made a low, hungry, growling sound deep in his throat. Then again, she might have imagined it all.

But she didn't imagine the feathering sensation between her thighs, or the tingling in her breasts, or the heat spreading through her middle like melting butter. She didn't mistake the rare and wonderful taste of his mouth, or the scent of wind and sunlight that clung to his hair and clothing.

He raised his head and looked into her dazed eyes. His own mirrored her bewilderment. But the smile that lifted one corner of his mouth was sardonic. "Just so you don't feel cheated," he murmured.

He pecked a series of soft, quick kisses across her damp lips, then ran his tongue over them lightly and teasingly. He probed the corner of her lips with the tip of his tongue, and the suggestive caress caused a ribbon of sensation in her belly to slowly uncurl.

Then he sealed his open mouth upon hers again. His tongue sank into it, as invasive as her response was involuntary. He stroked her mouth with deeply satisfying leisure while his hands moved over her back, then up her sides to her breasts. He rubbed them softly with the heels of his hands, creating a hunger inside her for him to touch their crests.

Instead, he slid his hands down to her bottom, cupped it, and tilted her hips forward against his. He matched the motions of his tongue with his hips, an ebb and flow that whetted her appetite for fulfillment and eroded her resistance.

Before she could submit to the delicious weakness stealing through her, he abruptly released her. His face still close, he whispered, "Curious to know what I usually do next?"

Alex stepped back, mortified over how close she had come to total capitulation. She wiped his kiss off her lips with the back of her hand. He merely smirked. "No, I didn't think so."

He put on his sunglasses and hat, giving the brim a tug that pulled it low over his eyes. "From now on, Counselor, I suggest you save your cross-examination for the courtroom. It's much safer."

The Derrick Lounge was far worse than the Last Chance. Alex approached it from the south, so when she rounded the corner of the building and saw a battered, rusty, red pickup parked there, she breathed a sigh of relief. She'd already made up her mind that if the eyewitness wasn't there, she wasn't going to hang around waiting on him.

When she had left the Westerner Motel, she'd made certain she wasn't followed. She felt ridiculous playing such cat-and-mouse games, but she was willing to go to any lengths to speak to this man who claimed to be an eyewitness to her mother's murder. If this meeting produced nothing but a telephone prankster looking for new thrills, it would be the crowning touch to a perfectly horrible day.

The longest horseback ride in history had been the one she'd made with Reede back to the practice track where she'd left her car. "Have a nice day," he had called mockingly after she slid from the saddle.

"Go to hell," had been her angry response. As he wheeled his horse around, she could hear him chuckling.

"Arrogant bastard," she whispered to herself now as she got out of her car and moved toward the pickup. She could see the driver sitting behind the steering wheel, and although she was glad he had shown up, she wondered how she would feel if he cited Reede as the man who had killed her mother. It was a disquieting possibility.

She went around the hood of the truck, her shoes crunching noisily in the loose gravel. The Derrick Lounge hadn't spent any money on outdoor lighting, so it was dark at the side of the building. No other vehicles were parked nearby.

Alex entertained a moment's trepidation as she reached for the door handle. Forcibly quelling her uneasiness, she slid inside and pulled the door closed behind her.

Her eyewitness was an ugly little man. He had stark, Indianlike cheekbones with pockmarked craters scooped out beneath them. He was unkempt, and smelled like he didn't shower frequently. He was scrawny and wrinkled and grizzled.

He was also dead.

Chapter 17

When it registered why he just sat there staring at her with a vacuous, unfocused, and somewhat surprised expression, Alex tried to scream, but nothing came out. Her mouth had turned to cotton. Reaching behind her, she tried to open the pickup door. It stubbornly resisted.

After frantically tugging on the handle, she gave it her shoulder. It swung open so suddenly that she almost fell out. In her scrambling haste to put distance between her and the bloody corpse, the toe of her shoe got caught in the gravel. She stumbled and fell, landing hard on the heels of her hands and scraping her knees.

She cried out in pain and fear and tried to stand. Plunging headlong into the darkness, she was suddenly blinded by a pair of headlights and petrified by the blasting of a horn.

Reflexively, she raised her hand to shield her eyes. Against the backdrop of brilliant light, she made out the outline of a man approaching her. Before she could run or utter a peep, he said, "You get around, don't you?"

"Reede!" she cried in a mix of relief and terror.

"What the hell are you doing here?"

He didn't sound at all sympathetic. That enraged her. "I could ask you the same question. That man," she said, pointing a shaky finger toward the pickup, "is dead."

"Yeah, I know."

"You know?"

"His name is, uh, *was* Pasty Hickam. He's a ranch hand who used to work for Angus." He peered through the bug-splattered windshield and shook his head. "Jesus, what a mess."

"Is that all you can say?"

He turned on her. "No, I could say that the only reason I'm not taking you in on suspicion of murder is because whoever phoned in the tip that Pasty was sitting in his pickup with his throat cut didn't mention that there was a broad with him."

"Somebody tipped you?"

"That's right. Any idea who?"

"I guess whoever knew I was coming here to meet him," she shouted. Then, when another thought struck her, she became still and quiet. "How'd you get here so fast, Reede?"

"You think I headed him off and put a knife to his throat?" he asked with an incredulous laugh.

"It's possible."

Holding her stare, he called for one of his deputies. Alex hadn't realized until then that there was someone with him. She became aware of a couple of things at once—the wail of an approaching siren, the appearance of curious customers, who were rushing out the door of the bar to see what the commotion was about.

"Escort her back to her motel," Reede curtly instructed the deputy. "See that she gets inside her room."

"Yes, sir."

"Keep an eye on her till daylight. Make sure she doesn't go anywhere."

Alex and the sheriff exchanged a hostile stare before she allowed the deputy to lead her back to her car.

"Sheriff?" The deputy tapped hesitantly on the door before daring to open it. The word around the office that morning was that Reede was in a bitch of a mood, and only partially because of Pasty Hickam's death the night before. Everybody was walking on eggshells.

"What is it?"

"I've got some papers for you to sign."

"Give them here." Reede eased up from his half-reclining position in the swivel chair and reached for the stack of official documents and letters. He scrawled his signature where it was called for.

"How's Ruby Faye this morning?"

Pasty's lover had been found in her mobile home when the sheriff arrived there to question her, beaten to a pulp. Before passing out, she named her cuckolded husband as the culprit.

"Lyle did almost as good a number on her as he did on Pasty. She's gonna have to stay in the hospital a week or so. The kids have been packed off to her mama's house."

Reede's expression turned even surlier. He had no tolerance for men who physically abused women, no matter what the provocation. He had been on the receiving end of too many beatings from his old man to stomach domestic violence.

He passed the paperwork back to the clerk. "Any feedback on that APB?"

"No, sir. I'll let you know. And you told me to remind you that you're scheduled to testify in Judge Wallace's court this afternoon."

"Shit, I would've forgotten. Okay, thanks." The deputy gratefully withdrew, but Reede had mentally dismissed him from his mind even before the door clicked shut.

He couldn't hold a thought for longer than a few seconds this morning. The image of Alex left little room for any others.

Swearing liberally, he left his chair and moved to the window. Outside, it was another sunny day. He was reminded of yesterday, when he'd pulled her up on that horse with him and the sunlight had turned her hair a deep, mahogany red. That's what he must have been thinking about when he'd started shooting off his mouth about that stupid football trophy.

Why, for crissake, had he kept it all this time? Every time he looked at it his emotions were split right down the middle, the way they'd been the night he had received it. His elation had been dampened because Junior hadn't been named most valuable player. Crazy as the notion was, he had wanted to apologize to Angus and Junior for winning the award. He'd deserved it because he was the better athlete, but winning over Junior had tainted the prize.

Alex had figured all that out by herself. She was smart, all right. But she wasn't as tough as she pretended to be. She'd had the daylights scared out of her last night, and justifiably so. Pasty had never been a pretty sight, but dead, with blood congealing on his down jacket, he was even uglier.

Maybe it had been good for her to see that. Maybe she wouldn't be so eager to uncover secrets that were none of her concern. Maybe Pasty's grisly murder would scare her out of investigating Celina's. Maybe she'd leave Purcell and never come back.

That possibility should have cheered him. It didn't. It made him angrier with her and with himself.

Kissing her yesterday had been a dumb move. He had let her provoke him. He'd lost his temper. He hadn't been in control of himself. The excuse relieved his conscience, just enough for him to live with what had happened. At the same time, however, it scared the hell out of him. Alex had pushed him over the edge of sound reason. Only one other person had ever been able to do that—Celina.

How had the clever little witch tricked him into mentioning that kiss, he wondered. He hadn't thought about it in years, but all of a sudden, it had been vivid in his mind.

It had been a hot September day, he remembered, when he had gone to check on Celina after she had failed to report to school. The old window air-conditioning unit had labored to cool the stifling little house without much success. The air was hot and humid, instead of hot and dry.

Celina wasn't acting like herself. She had let him in, but had acted subdued, as though this first rite of passage into womanhood had robbed her of girlish animation. Her eyes had been puffy from crying. He had been scared that something was terribly wrong.

When she had told him about her period, he'd been so relieved he had wanted to laugh. He hadn't, though. Her bleak expression had quashed any levity. He had put his arms around her, held her tenderly, stroked her hair, and reassured her that it was something wonderful, not shameful. Seeking comfort, she had wrapped her arms around his waist and nuzzled her face against his collarbone.

For a long time, they had just clung to each other, as they had so many times in the past when it seemed that the two of them were at odds with the rest of the world. But he felt a need to solemnize this occasion, to officially mark her departure from childhood.

He had kissed her cheek first. Tears had left it damp and salty. He kissed his way down. She caught her breath suddenly, and held it, until he pressed his lips firmly upon hers. It was a fervent but chaste kiss.

He had kissed other girls using his tongue. The Gail sisters were already adept at French kissing, and had been eager to share their expertise with him. At least once a week he met the three of them in the abandoned VFW hall and took turns kissing them, feeling their breasts, and slipping his hand into the elastic legs of their cotton panties to touch the hair between their thighs. They quarreled over which one got to undo his pants and fondle him first.

Those sweaty, sordid interludes made life with his father bearable. They were also the only secret he kept from Celina. What he did with the Gail sisters would probably embarrass her if she knew. It might also make her mad. Either way, it was better that she didn't know about the condemned VFW hall and what he did there.

But when he felt Celina's mouth beneath his, and heard that little catch in her throat, he had wanted to kiss her the correct way—the good and exciting and forbidden way. Unable to resist the temptation, his body had overruled his mind.

He'd barely touched the seam of her lips with the tip of

his tongue before he felt them separate. Heart pounding, blood boiling, he drew her closer and pushed his tongue into her mouth. When she didn't recoil, he moved it around. She clutched his waist. Her small, pointed breasts burned like brands against his chest.

God, he had thought he was going to die of pleasure. It was immense. The experience rocked the foundations of his adolescent soul. His body had vibrated with volcanic energy. He had wanted to go on kissing Celina Graham forever. But when his penis became so engorged it pressed against her middle, he pushed her away and began babbling apologies.

Celina had stared at him for several seconds, wide-eyed and breathless, then threw herself against him, wrapped her arms around his neck, and told him that she was glad he had kissed her like that. She loved him. He loved her. They were going to get married someday, and nothing was going to come between them, ever.

Now Reede, rubbing his eyes tiredly, returned to his desk and flopped down into the creaky chair. He had been furious with Alex for calling forth memories he had strived for years to keep at bay. It had been his intention to punish and insult her with that kiss.

But, dammit, he hadn't counted on her feeling so good against him—all fur coat and soft wool and warm skin. He hadn't expected her mouth to taste so goddamn sweet. That sweetness still lingered on his tongue. How could he have guessed that her breasts would be that full and soft?

He sure as hell hadn't bargained on his body becoming embarrassingly, instantly aroused for Celina's daughter. It was harder than he'd ever gotten for the Gail sisters—harder than he'd ever gotten period. Hell, he was still hard.

That was just one reason why the impetuous embrace had left him feeling mad as hell at her and not much kinder toward himself. Alex Gaither, the woman he had kissed like crazy yesterday, had all but accused him of two murders, first Celina's, then Pasty's. Even if she couldn't make those allegations stick, she could still spoil all his plans for the future.

He was so close to realizing his dreams. He was about to be where he'd worked hard all his life to get. She could mess it up royally. She didn't even have to finger him. If she indicted any one of them, she would snatch his future away from him before he had fully grasped it. For that, he could easily choke her.

But when he thought about putting his hands on her again, it wasn't to choke her.

"They told me you were in."

"Did they also tell you that I'm due in court in a few minutes, and that between now and then I'm too busy to see anyone?"

Alex stepped into Reede's office and closed the door behind her. "They mentioned it."

"Where'd you get the idea that you're exempt?"

"I thought you'd want to question me about the man who got killed."

"You aren't really a suspect. You were just at the wrong place at the wrong time, something you have a bad habit of doing."

"You don't think there's a connection between me and his murder?"

"No, but obviously you do." Propping his feet on the

corner of his desk and stacking his hands behind his head, he said, "Let's hear it."

"I think you already know it. Pasty Hickam witnessed Celina's murder."

"How do you know?"

"He told me over the telephone."

"He was a legendary liar. Ask anybody."

"I believed him. He sounded nervous and terribly afraid. We made an appointment to meet at the Last Chance, but when he saw you following me, he got frightened off."

"So, that makes me Celina's killer?"

"Or someone who's covering up for the killer."

"Let me tell you what's wrong with your theory." He lowered his feet to the floor. "Angus fired Pasty the other day. He was on a revenge trip, something you should be able to relate to, Counselor. He made up some cock-and-bull story that you wanted to believe because so far, your investigation hasn't turned up one goddamn scrap of concrete evidence.

"You think the two murders are connected, right? Wrong," he said. "Think about it. Last night's killing doesn't match Celina's murder. The M.O.'s wrong. The guy who cut Pasty a new smile found out Pasty was humping his wife while he was working over at the potash plant near Carlsbad. We've got an APB out on him."

It sounded so plausible that Alex squirmed under his direct gaze. "Isn't it possible that this ranch hand witnessed my mother's murder? He kept quiet until now out of fear of retribution, or simply because no one ever conducted a thorough investigation. Knowing what he did got him killed before he could identify the killer. That's what I choose to believe."

"Suit yourself. But waste your time on it, not mine." Reede

made to stand up, but she said, "That's not all." Resigned, he sat back down.

Alex took an envelope out of her purse and handed it to him. "This came in the mail this morning. It was addressed to me at the motel."

Reede scanned the letter quickly and handed it back to her. She stared at him in amazement. "You don't seem very disturbed by it, Sheriff Lambert."

"I've already read it."

"*What?* When?"

"Day before yesterday, if I'm remembering right."

"And you let them send it?"

"Why not? It's not obscene. I figure even the postmaster general would agree that it meets postal regulations. It's got the correct amount of postage on it. As far as I can tell, that letter isn't illegal, Counselor."

Alex wanted to reach across his desk and slap the gloating smile off his face. The impulse was so strong she had to curl her hand into a fist to keep from doing so.

"Did you read between the lines? The people who signed this, all"—she paused to count the signatures—"all fourteen of them, have threatened to run me out of town."

"Surely not, Miss Gaither," he said, feigning shock. "You're just being paranoid because you found Pasty. That letter simply underlines what I've been telling you all along. Angus and Junior Minton mean a lot to this town. So does that racetrack.

"You get somebody's attention quicker by kicking him in the bank account than you do by kicking him in the nuts. You've put some sizable investments in jeopardy. Did you expect folks to stand by and watch all their dreams go down the tubes because of your vindictiveness?"

"I'm not being vindictive. I'm conducting a valid and long-overdue investigation into a severe miscarriage of justice."

"Spare me."

"The district attorney of Travis County sanctioned my investigation."

His eyes drifted over her insultingly as he drawled, "In exchange for what?"

"Oh, that's good. Very professional, Sheriff. When you run out of viable ammunition, you resort to throwing sexist rocks at my character."

With angry, jerky motions, she stuffed the letter back into the envelope and replaced it in her purse, snapping the catch firmly.

"I don't have to explain my reasons to you. Just understand this," she enunciated. "I won't quit until I can draw some satisfactory conclusions about my mother's murder."

"Well, I wouldn't worry about being mugged, if I were you," Reede told her with an air of boredom. "As I've explained, Pasty's killing had absolutely nothing to do with you. The people who signed that letter are pillars of the community—bankers, businessmen, professionals. They're hardly types who would accost you in a dark alley.

"Although," he went on, "I'd recommend that you stop cruising in hotbeds of trouble like you have the last two evenings. If you've just got to have it, there are a couple of fellas I could recommend."

She released a slow, contemptuous breath. "Do you dislike all professional women, or is it me in particular?"

"It's you in particular."

His bluntness was an affront. She was tempted to remind him that his kiss yesterday hadn't conveyed dislike, but she didn't. She didn't want to remind him of it. She hoped to forget it herself, pretend that it had never happened, but she couldn't. It had left her feeling drastically and irrevocably altered.

No, she couldn't forget it. The best she could hope for was to learn to cope with the memory of it, and the addictive craving it had instigated.

His statement hurt her deeply. She heard herself asking, "Why don't you like me?"

"Because you're a meddler. I don't like people who meddle in other people's business."

"This *is* my business."

"How could it be? You were peeing in your diapers when Celina was killed," he shouted.

"I'm glad you brought that up. Since I was only two months old at the time, what was she doing out at the ranch that night?"

His stunned reaction to the question was swiftly covered. "I forget. Look, I'm due—"

"I doubt you ever forget anything, Reede Lambert, much as you pretend that you do. What was she doing there? Please tell me."

He stood up. So did Alex. "Junior had invited her for supper, that's all."

"Was it a special occasion?"

"Ask him."

"I'm asking you. What was the occasion? And don't tell me you don't remember."

"Maybe he felt sorry for her."

"Sorry? Why?"

"For being cooped up with a kid, not getting out. Her

social life had gone to zilch. She was only eighteen, for cris-sake." He stepped around her and headed for the door.

Alex wasn't ready to let it go at that. His answer was too pat. She caught his arm and forced him to face her. "Were you there at dinner that night?"

"Yeah, I was there." He jerked his arm free.

"The entire evening?"

"I left before dessert."

"Why?"

"I don't like cherry pie."

She groaned with frustration. "Answer me, Reede. Why did you leave?"

"I had a date."

"With whom? Does she still live here in town?"

"What the hell difference does it make?"

"She's your alibi. I'd like to talk to her."

"Forget it. I'll never drag her into this."

"You might have to, or plead the Fifth."

"Don't you ever give up?" he asked through bared teeth.

"Never. Did you return to the ranch that night?"

"No."

"Not at all?"

"No."

"Not even to sleep?"

"I told you, I had a date." He put his face close enough to hers that she could feel his breath against her lips. "And she was hot."

He gave a terse bob of his head to emphasize his point, then turned to leave. "I'm due in court. Close the door on your way out, will ya?"

Chapter 18

———◈———

"Miss Gaither?"

"Yes?"

Alex didn't feel like having company. Her latest altercation with Reede had left her drained. After last night, her nerves were shot. Neither Reede's glib explanation of the Hickam man's murder or any amount of her own sound reasoning had convinced her that she wasn't in danger.

So, when someone knocked on her motel room door, she had approached it cautiously and looked through the peephole. A strange, but evidently harmless, couple were on her threshold. She opened the door and looked at them expectantly.

Suddenly, the man stuck out his hand. Startled, Alex jumped back. "Reverend Fergus Plummet." Feeling foolish, Alex shook hands with him. "Did I frighten you? I'm dreadfully sorry. I didn't mean to."

The reverend's mannerisms were so deferential, his tone of voice so sympathetic, he hardly posed a threat. He had a slight build and was shorter than average, but held himself erect with almost military posture. His black suit was shiny in spots and inadequate for the season. He wore no overcoat and nothing to cover his wavy dark hair, which was fuller than current fashion dictated. In a community where almost every male from the age of twelve wore either a cowboy hat or bill cap, it looked odd to see a man without one.

"This is my wife, Wanda."

"Hello, Mrs. Plummet, Reverend."

Mrs. Plummet was a large woman, with a notable bosom that she'd tried to minimize by covering it with a drab olive cardigan sweater. Her hair was pulled back into a knot on the back of her head, which she kept meekly lowered. Her husband had referred to her with no more personal regard than he might give a lamppost.

"How'd you know my name?" Alex asked, curious about the couple.

"Everybody does," he replied with a brief smile. "There's talk going around town about you."

The minister had a Bible tucked under one arm. Alex couldn't imagine what a minister was doing at her door— recruiting new members?

"I guess you're wondering why I'm here," he said, correctly reading her puzzled expression.

"Frankly, yes. Would you like to come in?"

They stepped into the room. Mrs. Plummet seemed ill at ease and unsure where to sit until her husband pointed her to a corner of the bed. He took the only chair. Alex sat down on the edge of the bed, but far enough away from Mrs. Plummet for both of them to be comfortable.

The preacher gazed about him. He seemed to be in no hurry to disclose the reason he was there. Finally, and with a trace of impatience, Alex asked, "Is there something I can do for you, Reverend Plummet?"

Closing his eyes, he raised his hand heavenward and evoked a blessing. "May heaven's rich blessings pour down on this beloved daughter of God," he intoned in a deep, vibrating voice.

He began to pray with loud earnestness. Alex had the wildest impulse to giggle. Merle Graham had seen to it that she was raised with traditional Protestant beliefs. They had attended church regularly. Though she had never embraced the fundamentalist dogma her grandmother adhered to, Alex's Christian faith was well cemented.

"Please, Reverend Plummet," she interrupted when his prayer extended into overtime, "I've had a very long day. Could we get to the point of your visit, please?"

He looked rather piqued over her interruption, but said with a mysterious air, "I can assist you with your investigation of Minton Enterprises."

She was stunned. She had never expected him to be connected in any way to her investigation. She reminded herself, however, to proceed with caution. She was, after all, extremely skeptical. What deep, dark secrets could this weird little man know about Celina, Reede Lambert, or the Mintons? Ministers were privy to confidences, but experience had taught her that professional ethics usually prevented them from revealing any confessions. They strictly abided by the rules of privileged information, and only imparted it in life-threatening situations.

It didn't seem likely that either Angus or Junior would bare his soul to a mousy little man like Plummet. Based wholly on outward appearance, he would have a minimal amount of influence with the Almighty. The thought of Reede Lambert confessing a sin was preposterous.

She responded with a professional detachment that Greg Harper would have been proud of: "Oh, really? How can you do that? Did you know my mother?"

"Unfortunately, no. But I can speed along your investigation just the same. We—my congregation of saints and I—believe that you're on our side. And our side is God's side."

"Th-thank you," she stammered, hoping that was the correct response.

Obviously, it was. It earned a soft amen from Mrs. Plummet, who had been silently praying all this time.

"Reverend Plummet," Alex said uncertainly, "I'm not sure you understand. I'm here at the behest of the district attorney's office to—"

"The Lord uses people as his holy instruments."

"—to investigate the murder of my mother, which occurred here in Purcell twenty-five years ago."

"God be *praised*...that this *wrong*...will soon be set *right*!" He shook his fists heavenward.

Alex was flabbergasted. She gave a nervous laugh. "Yes, well, I hope so, too. But I fail to see how my investigation concerns you and your ministry. Do you have inside knowledge of the crime?"

"Oh, that I did, Miss Gaither," Plummet wailed. "Oh, that I did, so that we could speed along God's work and punish the iniquitous."

"The iniquitous?"

"Sinners!" he shouted fervently. "Those who would corrupt this town and all the innocent children of God living here. They want to build Satan's playground, fill the precious veins of our children with narcotics, their sweet mouths with foul liquor, their fertile little minds with carnality."

From the corner of her eye, Alex glanced at Mrs. Plummet, who sat with her head bowed, her hands folded in her lap, her knees and ankles decorously pressed together, as though they had been glued that way.

"Are you referring to Purcell Downs?" Alex asked tentatively.

Just as she had feared, the very words opened up a wellspring of evangelical fervor. Prophecies came spewing out of the preacher's mouth like a fountain run amok. Alex endured a sermon on the evils of horse-race gambling and all the ungodly elements that accompanied it. But when Plummet began to tout her as a missionary sent to Purcell to vanquish the sons of Satan, she felt compelled to bring the fiery sermon to a halt.

"Reverend Plummet, please." After several attempted interruptions he stopped speaking and looked at her blankly. She licked her lips anxiously, not wanting to offend him, but wanting to make herself explicitly clear.

"I have absolutely nothing to do with whether or not Minton Enterprises is granted a gambling license. The fact is that they've already been approved by the racing commission. All that remains are the formalities."

"But the Mintons are under investigation for murder."

Choosing her words carefully, and omitting any direct reference to the Mintons, she said, "If enough evidence or probable cause is found as a result of my investigation, the case could be brought before the grand jury. It would be up to it to bring forth an indictment. In any instance, the parties involved are to be presumed innocent until proven guilty, in accordance with our Constitution."

She held up a hand to stave off his interruption. "Please, let me finish. Whatever happens regarding the proposed race-track after I conclude my investigation will be the responsibility of the racing commission. I will have nothing to do with its final decision on this or any other application for a gambling license.

"Actually, it's coincidental that the Mintons are personally involved with both issues simultaneously. I reopened my mother's murder case because, as a public prosecutor, I was dissatisfied with its resolution, and thought that it warranted further investigation. I do not hold a personal grudge against this town, or anyone in it."

Plummet was squirming with the need to speak, so she let him. "You don't want to see gambling come to Purcell, do you? Aren't you against this device of the devil that snatches food from children's mouths, destroys marriages, and plunges the weak onto paths bound for hell and damnation?"

"My views on pari-mutuel betting—or anything else, for that matter—are none of your business, Reverend Plummet." Alex came to her feet. She was tired, and he was a wacko. She'd given him more time than he deserved. "I must ask you and Mrs. Plummet to leave now."

He wasn't an educated and eloquent churchman, who had researched the issue and drawn enlightened conclusions. There were well-founded arguments for both sides. But whether pari-mutuel gambling came to Purcell County or not, Alex had nothing to do with it.

"We're not giving up," Plummet said, following her to the door. "We're willing to make any sacrifice to see that God's will is carried out."

"God's will? If it's God's will that the Mintons be denied

that gambling license, then nothing you do will help or hin-
der, right?"

He couldn't be trapped with logic. "God uses us to do his
work. He's using you, though you might not know it yet." His
eyes smoldered with fanatical fire. It gave Alex goose bumps.
"You are the answer to our prayers. Oh, yes, Miss Gaither,
the answer to our prayers. Call on us. You've been anointed
by God, and we're your humble and willing servants."

"I, uh, I'll keep that in mind. Good-bye."

Reverend Plummet's theology was warped. He gave her
the creeps. She couldn't get her door closed behind him fast
enough. As soon as she did, her telephone rang.

Chapter 19

"How does dinner and dancing sound?" Junior Minton asked without preamble.

"Like a fairy tale."

"It's not. Just say yes."

"You're inviting me out for dinner and dancing?"

"It's the monthly fete at the Purcell Horse and Gun Club. Please say you'll go with me. Otherwise, it'll be boring as hell."

Alex laughed. "Junior, I doubt you're ever bored. Especially when there are women around. Do most of them fall for your b.s.?"

"Almost without exception. If you go with me tonight, it'll be unanimous."

"Tonight?"

"Sure, tonight. Did I fail to mention that? Sorry I couldn't give you more notice."

"You're actually serious?"

"Would I joke about something as important as the monthly get-together at the Horse and Gun Club?"

"Of course you wouldn't. Forgive my flippancy."

"All's forgiven if you'll go."

"I really can't. I'm exhausted. Last night—"

"Yeah, I heard about that. Jeez, that must've been awful, you finding Pasty Hickam that way. I want to help take your mind off it."

"I appreciate your consideration, but I can't go."

"I refuse to take no for an answer."

While talking, she had struggled out of her dress and was now standing in her slip and stockings, cradling the telephone receiver between her shoulder and her ear while trying to pull on her robe. The housekeeper always turned off the heat after she cleaned the room. Every evening Alex had a frigid homecoming to dread.

She glanced toward the alcove where her clothes were hanging. "I really can't go, Junior."

"How come?"

"All my dressy clothes are in Austin. I don't have anything to wear."

"Surely a lady as articulate as you isn't resorting to that cliché."

"It happens to be the truth."

"And the occasion calls for casual. Wear that leather skirt you had on the other day. It's a knockout."

Alex had finally managed to wriggle herself into the robe without dropping the phone. She sat down on the edge of the bed and snuggled deeper into the terry cloth. "I still have to say no."

"Why? I know it's rude to put you on the spot like this, but I'm not going to be gracious and let you bow out without giving me a valid reason."

"I just don't think it would be a good idea for us to socialize."

"Because you're hoping I'll soon be a resident of the Huntsville State Prison?"

"No!"

"Then, what?"

"I don't *want* to send you to prison, but you *are* a key suspect in a murder case."

"Alex, you've had time to form an opinion of me. Do you honestly believe that I could commit such a violent crime?"

She remembered how Reede had laughed at the notion of Junior going to war. He was lazy, unambitious, a philanderer. Violent outbursts didn't fit into his image. "No, I don't," she replied softly. "But you're still a suspect. It wouldn't do for us to be seen fraternizing."

"I like that word," he snarled. "It sounds dirty, incestuous. And for your peace of mind, I do all my fraternizing privately. That is, except for a few times, when I was younger. Reede and I used to—"

"Please," she groaned, "I don't want to know."

"Okay, I'll spare you the lurid details, on one condition."

"What?"

"Say you'll go tonight. I'll pick you up at seven."

"I can't."

"Alex, Alex," he moaned dramatically, "look at it this way. During the course of the evening I'll have a drink or two, possibly more. I might start reminiscing, get maudlin, say something indiscreet. When I do, you'll be there to hear it. No telling what stunning confessions I might blurt out in my inebriation. Consider this evening one long interrogation. It's part of your job to wear down the defenses of your suspects, isn't it?

"You'd be shirking your duty if you didn't take advantage of every opportunity to rout out the truth. How can you self-ishly languish in the luxury of the Westerner Motel while a suspect is shooting off his mouth over drinks at the Horse and Gun Club? Shame on you. You owe this to the taxpay-ing public who're footing the bill for this investigation. Do it for your country, Alex."

Again, she groaned dramatically. "If I consent to go, will you promise not to make any more speeches?"

"Seven o'clock."

She could hear the triumph in his voice.

The moment she entered the clubhouse, she was glad she had come. There was music and laughter. She caught snatches of several conversations, none of which were centered around Celina Gaither's murder. That in itself was a refreshing change. She looked forward to several hours of relaxation, and felt that the break had been earned.

Nevertheless, she rationalized being there. Not for a min-ute did she believe that Junior would make a public spectacle of himself while under the influence. She wasn't likely to hear any startling confessions.

All the same, something beneficial might come out of the evening. The exclusivity of the Horse and Gun Club sug-gested that only Purcell's upper crust were members. Reede had told her that the people who had signed the letter she had received were local businessmen and professionals. It was conceivable that she would meet some of them tonight, and get a feel for the extent of their animosity.

More important, she would have an opportunity to mingle with locals, people who knew the Mintons and Reede well and might shed light on their characters.

Junior had picked her up in his red Jaguar. He'd driven it with a lack of regard for the speed limit. His festive mood had been contagious. Whether she was acting in a professional capacity or not, it felt good to be standing beside the handsomest man in the room, with his hand riding lightly, but proprietorially, on the small of her back.

"The bar's this way," he said close to her ear, making himself heard over the music. They wended their way through the crowd.

The club wasn't glitzy. It didn't resemble the slick, neon nightclubs that were bursting out like new stars in the cities, catering to yuppies who flocked to them in BMWs and designer couture.

The Purcell Horse and Gun Club was quintessentially Texan. The bartender could have been sent over by Central Casting. He had a handlebar mustache, black bow tie and vest, and red satin garters on his sleeves. A pair of longhorns, which spanned six feet from polished tip to polished tip, were mounted above the ornately carved nineteenth-century bar.

The walls were adorned with pictures of racehorses, prizewinning bulls with testicles as large as punching bags, and landscapes where either yucca or bluebonnets abounded. In almost every instance the paintings featured an obligatory windmill, looking lonesome and stark against the sunstreaked horizon. Alex was Texan enough to find it comfortable and endearing. She was sophisticated enough to recognize its gaucheness.

"White wine," she told the bartender, who was unabashedly giving her a once-over.

"Lucky son of a bitch," he muttered to Junior as he served them their drinks. The grin beneath the lavish mustache was lecherous.

Junior saluted him with his scotch and water. "Ain't I just?" He propped his elbow on the bar and turned to face Alex, who was seated on the stool. "The music's a little too country and western for my taste, but if you want to dance, I'm game."

She shook her head. "Thanks, but no. I'd rather watch."

A few songs later, Junior leaned close and whispered, "Most of them learned to dance in a pasture. They still look like they're trying to avoid stepping in a pile of cow shit."

The wine had taken effect. Her eyes were bright, her cheeks flushed. Feeling a pleasant buzz, she tossed her hair over her shoulder and laughed.

"Come on," he said, placing his hand beneath her elbow and helping her off the stool. "Mother and Dad are at their table."

Alex moved with him along the perimeter of the dance floor to the cluster of tables set up for dining. Sarah Jo and Angus were seated at one. He was puffing on a cigar. Sarah Jo was idly waving the offensive smoke away from her face.

Alex had been apprehensive about wearing the russet leather skirt and matching, leather-trimmed sweater, but she felt more comfortable in them than she would have wearing Sarah Jo's burgundy satin dress and looking out of place in a room where people were stamping out "Cotton-Eyed Joe," yelling "bullshit" in the appropriate places, and drinking beer straight from opaque amber bottles.

"Hello, Alex," Angus said around his cigar.

"Hello. Junior was hospitable enough to invite me," she said as she sat down in the chair Junior was holding out for her.

"I had to do some arm-twisting," he told his parents, taking the chair next to her. "She plays hard to get."

"Her mother certainly didn't."

Sarah Jo's cool, catty remark momentarily stifled the conversation. It served to counteract the potency of Alex's glass of wine. Her giddiness fizzled and went flat as day-old soda. She nodded toward Sarah Jo and said, "Hello, Mrs. Minton. You look lovely tonight."

Even though her dress was inappropriate, she did look lovely in it. *Not vibrant*, Alex thought. Sarah Jo could never look vivacious and animated. Her beauty had an ethereal quality, as though her visitation on earth was temporary and tenuous. She gave Alex one of her vague, secretive smiles and murmured a thank-you as she took a sip of wine.

"Heard you were the one who discovered Pasty's body."

"Dad, this is a party," Junior said. "Alex won't want to talk about something nasty like that."

"No, it's all right, Junior. I would have brought it up myself, sooner or later."

"I don't reckon it was coincidence that you met him at that honky-tonk and climbed into his pickup with him," Angus said, rolling the cigar from one corner of his lips to the other.

"No." She paraphrased for them her telephone conversations with Pasty.

"That cowboy was a liar, a fornicator, and, worse than all his other vices put together, he cheated at poker," Angus said with some vehemence. "In the last few years he'd gone plumb goofy and irresponsible. That's why I had to let him go. I figure you've got better sense than to put any stock in what he told you."

In the middle of his monologue, Angus signaled the waiter to bring another round of drinks. "Oh, sure, Pasty might've seen who went into that stable with Celina, but the one he saw was Gooney Bud."

Having said his piece, and giving Alex no opportunity to dispute it, he launched into a glowing review of a jockey from Ruidoso that he wanted to ride for them. Since the Mintons were her hosts, Alex graciously let the topic of Pasty Hickam die for the moment.

When they'd finished their drinks, Angus and Junior offered to go through the barbecue buffet for the ladies. Alex would just as soon have gone through the line herself. She found it difficult to make small talk with Sarah Jo, but after the men withdrew, she valiantly made an attempt.

"Have you been members of the club for a long time?"

"Angus was one of the charter members," Sarah Jo supplied distractedly. She kept her eyes on the couples doing the two-step in an eternal circle around the dance floor.

"He seems to have a finger in just about every pie in town," Alex remarked.

"Hmm, he likes to know everything that's going on."

"And be a part of it."

"Yes. He makes things happen and spreads himself thin." She gave a delicate sigh. "Angus has this need to be well liked, you see. He's always politicking, as though it matters what other people think."

Alex folded her hands beneath her chin and propped her elbows on the table. "You don't believe it matters?"

"No." Her entrancement with the dancers ended. For the first time that evening, she looked directly at Alex. "Don't you read too much into the way Junior treats you."

"Oh?"

"He flirts with every woman he meets."

Alex slowly lowered her hands to her lap. Anger roiled inside, but she managed to keep her voice low and level. "I resent your implication, Mrs. Minton."

Sarah Jo lifted one shoulder indifferently. "Both of my men are charming and they know it. Most women don't realize that their flirting is meaningless."

"I'm sure that's true of Angus, but I don't know about Junior. Three ex-wives might disagree with you about his flirting."

"They were all wrong for him."

"What about my mother? Would she have been wrong for him?"

Sarah Jo fixed her empty stare on Alex again. "Absolutely wrong. You're a lot like her, you know."

"Am I?"

"You enjoy causing dissonance. Your mother was never content to leave bothersome things alone. The only difference is that you're even better at making trouble and creating ill will than she was. You're direct to the point of being tactless, a trait I've always attributed to bad breeding." She lifted her eyes to someone who had moved up behind Alex.

"Good evening, Sarah Jo."

"Judge Wallace." A sweet smile broke across Sarah Jo's face. One would never guess she had had her stinger out seconds earlier. "Hello, Stacey."

Alex, her face hot with indignation over Sarah Jo's

unwarranted criticism, turned around. Judge Joe Wallace was staring down at her with disapproval, as though her being there was a breach of the club's standards.

"Miss Gaither."

"Hello, Judge Wallace." The woman standing beside him looked at Alex with a censure that matched his, though for what reason, Alex couldn't guess. Obviously, Junior was the only friendly face she was going to find in this crowd.

The judge gave the woman's arm a nudge and they moved toward another table. "Is that his wife?" Alex asked, following their progress.

"Good heavens, no," Sarah Jo said. "His daughter. Poor Stacey. Eternally dowdy."

Stacey Wallace was still staring at Alex with such malice that she was captivated by it. She didn't break her stare until Junior's knee bumped hers when he resumed his seat and set two plates of food on the table.

"I hope you like ribs and beans." His gaze followed the direction of hers. "Hey, Stacey." He winked at her and raised his hand in a friendly wave.

The woman's puckered mouth relaxed into a faltering smile. Blushing, she raised her hand to her neckline like a flustered girl and called back shyly, "Hi, Junior."

"Well?"

Though she was still curious about the judge and his chameleon daughter, Junior's one-word inquiry brought Alex's head around. "Sorry?"

"Do you like ribs and beans?"

"Watch me," she laughed, spreading the napkin over her lap.

She did unladylike damage to her plate of food, but her

healthy appetite earned her a compliment from Angus. "Sarah Jo eats like a bird. Don't you like the ribs, honey?" he asked, looking into her plate, which had barely been disturbed.

"They're a little dry."

"Want me to order you something else?"

"No, thank you."

After they'd eaten, Angus took a fresh cigar from his pocket and lit it. Fanning out the match, he said, "Why don't you two dance?"

"Are you game?" Junior asked.

"Sure." Alex pushed back her chair and stood up. "But this kind of dancing isn't my forte, so nothing too fancy, please."

Junior drew her into his arms and, disobeying her request, executed a series of intricate turns and dips. "Very nice," he said, smiling down at her when they lapsed into a more sedate two-step. Using the arm he had placed around her waist, he pulled her tighter against him. "Very, *very* nice."

Alex let him hold her close because it felt good to have two strong arms around her. Her partner was handsome and charming and knew how to make a woman feel beautiful. She was a victim of his charm, but knowing it was her safety net.

She could never actually fall for a glib charmer like Junior, but small doses of attention from one was fun temporarily, especially since every time she was around Reede, her confidence and ego took a beating.

"Is Reede a club member?" she asked casually.

"Are you kiddin'?"

"He hasn't been invited to join?"

"Oh, sure, as soon as he won sheriff the first time. It's just that he feels more at home in another crowd. He doesn't give a fuck—excuse me—for society stuff." He stroked her back. "You seem more relaxed than when I picked you up. Having fun?"

"Yes, but you got me here under false pretenses," she accused. "You're a long way from becoming drunk and talkative."

His smile was unrepentant. "Ask me anything."

"Okay. Who's the man over there, the one with the white hair?" Junior identified him by name. Her instincts proved correct. His name had been among those at the bottom of her letter. "Introduce us when the band takes its next break."

"He's married."

She shot him a look. "My interest in him isn't romantic."

"Ah, good, good."

He did as she asked. The banker she had picked out of the crowd seemed disconcerted when Junior introduced her. As she shook hands with him, she said, "I received your letter, Mr. Longstreet."

Her straightforwardness surprised him, but he recovered admirably. "I see that you're taking it to heart." He slid a knowing glance toward Junior.

"Don't let my being here tonight with Junior fool you. I can appreciate what he, his father, and Mr. Lambert mean to Purcell and its economy, but that does not mean I'll suspend my investigation. It'll take more than a letter to scare me off."

Clearly irritated, Junior spoke to her out of the side of his mouth as he escorted her back onto the dance floor a few minutes later. "You could have warned me."

"About what?"

"That you are armed and dangerous. Longstreet's a big wheel who shouldn't be put on the defensive. What's all this about a letter, anyway?"

She explained, reciting as many of the names as she could recall. "I hoped to meet some of them here tonight."

He pulled a deep frown, regarding her with asperity. Eventually, however, he shrugged and fashioned a beguiling smile. "And here I thought I'd swept you off your feet." Sighing in resignation, he added, "Well, I'd just as well help you out. Want to meet the rest of your adversaries?"

Trying to make it appear as casual as possible, Junior moved her through the crowd, introducing her to those there who had signed their names to that subtly threatening letter.

A half hour later they moved away from a couple who owned a chain of convenience stores throughout West Texas. They had invested heavily in Purcell Downs and were the most demonstratively hostile. By that time, though, word had gotten around who Junior's date was, so they'd been laying for her.

"There, that's everybody," he told her.

"Thank God," Alex whispered. "Are the knives still sticking out of my back?"

"You're not going to let that old biddy's rapier tongue get to you, are you? Look, she's a dried-up old shrew who hates any woman who doesn't have a mustache as thick as hers."

Alex smiled in spite of herself. "She all but said, 'Be on the next stage leaving town . . . or else.'"

He squeezed her arm. "Come on, let's dance again. It will take your mind off your troubles."

"I need to repair the damages," she said, slipping out of his grasp. "Excuse me."

"Okay. The little girls' room is thataway." He pointed down a narrow hallway.

There was no one in the powder room when she went in, but when she came out of the cubicle, the judge's daughter was standing in front of the dressing table, staring at her reflection in the mirror. She turned and faced Alex.

Alex smiled. "Hi."

"Hello."

Alex moved to the sink and washed her hands. "We haven't been formally introduced. I'm Alex Gaither." She plucked two coarse paper towels from the dispenser.

"Yes, I know."

Alex dropped the used towels into the wastepaper basket. "You're Judge Wallace's daughter." She attempted to break the ice in an atmosphere that was glacial and getting colder by the second. The woman had dropped all vestiges of the shy, insecure maiden she had assumed when Junior had spoken to her. Her face was stony and uncompromisingly antagonistic. "Stacey, wasn't it?"

"Yes. Stacey. But the last name isn't Wallace. It's Minton."

"Minton?"

"That's right. I am Junior's wife. His *first* wife."

Chapter 20

I can see that's news to you," Stacey said, laughing humorlessly at Alex's dumbfounded expression.

"Yes," she replied in a hollow tone. "No one's mentioned that."

Stacey's composure, always intact, deserted her. Flattening a hand on her meager bosom, she cried out, "Do you have any idea the damage you're doing?"

"To whom?"

"To me," she shouted, pounding her chest. Immediately she dropped her hand and rolled her lips inward, as though mortified by her outburst. She closed her eyes momentarily. When she opened them, they were filled with animosity, but she appeared to have regained control of herself. "For twenty-five years I've had to live down the generally held belief that Junior Minton married me on the rebound from your mother."

Alex didn't state the obvious, but guiltily lowered her eyes.

"I see that you hold to that belief, too."

"I'm sorry, Miss . . . Stacey. May I call you Stacey?"

"Of course," she replied stiffly.

"I'm sorry that my investigation has distressed you."

"How could it not? You're dredging up the past. By doing so, you're airing my dirty linen for all the town to see. Again."

"I had no idea who Junior's first wife was, or that she even lived in Purcell."

"Would it have mattered?"

"Probably not," Alex answered with rueful honesty. "I can't see that your marriage to Junior has any bearing on the case. It's a peripheral association that I can't help."

"What about my father?" Stacey asked, switching subjects.

"What about him?"

"This petty investigation of yours is going to cause him embarrassment. It already has."

"How so?"

"The fact that you're questioning his original ruling."

"I'm sorry. I can't help that, either."

"Can't—or won't?" Stacey held her arms straight at her sides and shuddered with revulsion. "I abhor people who trample on the reputations of others for their own personal gain."

"Is that what you think I'm doing?" Alex asked, taking umbrage. "Do you think I devised this investigation to advance my career?"

"Didn't you?"

"No," she answered, firmly shaking her head. "My mother was murdered in that stable. I don't believe that the man accused of it was capable of committing that crime. I want to know what really happened. I *will* know what happened. And I'll make the one responsible pay for making me an orphan."

"I was prepared to give you the benefit of the doubt, but I see it's only revenge you want, after all."

"I want justice."

"No matter what it costs other people?"

"I've already apologized for any unhappiness it causes you."

Stacey made a scoffing sound. "You want to publicly crucify my father. Don't deny it," she snapped when Alex started to object. "No matter how much you deny it, you're leaving him open to ridicule. At the very least, you're accusing him of making a serious error in judgment."

To deny that would be a lie. "Yes, I believe he made a bad judgment in the case of Buddy Hicks."

"Daddy's got forty impeccable years on the bench that vouch for his wisdom and integrity."

"If my investigation is petty, as you call it, it won't affect his record, will it, Mrs. Minton? A lofty judge couldn't possibly be brought down by a lowly public prosecutor with nothing except spite and vengeance for ammunition. Evidence would be necessary to support my allegations."

"You don't have any."

"I believe I will before I'm finished. If your father's reputation suffers as a result..." She drew a deep breath and raised a weary hand to her forehead. Her expression was earnest, her words heartfelt. "Stacey, I don't want to ruin your father's career or besmirch his tenure on the bench. I don't want to hurt anybody's feelings or cause any innocent bystander grief or embarrassment. I only want to see justice done."

"Justice," Stacey sneered, her eyes narrowing with malice. "You've got no right to even speak the word. You're just like your mother—pretty, but shallow. Single-minded and selfish.

Uncaring of other people's feelings. Unable to see beyond your own superficial desires."

"I take it you didn't like my mother very much," Alex remarked, her voice laced with sarcasm.

Stacey took her seriously. "I hated her."

"Why? Because Junior was in love with her?"

Alex reasoned that if Stacey were going to hit below the belt, she might as well, too. It worked. Stacey fell back a step and groped for the dressing table to support herself. Reflexively, Alex extended a helping hand, but the judge's daughter recoiled from her touch.

"Stacey, I know that Junior married you only a few weeks after my mother was killed. You must realize how odd that strikes me."

"It might have seemed sudden, but we'd been dating for years."

That surprised Alex. "You had?"

"Yes. And for most of that time, we'd been lovers."

Stacey threw that piece of news at Alex like a dart, sharply and triumphantly. All it served, however, was to make Alex pity her more. She had the full picture now of a plain girl, hopelessly in love with the affable and handsome football hero, willing to sacrifice anything, including her pride, to have even scraps of his attention. She would do anything to keep him near her. "I see."

"I doubt it. Just like Junior, you're blind to the truth."

"What is the truth, Stacey?"

"That Celina was wrong for him. Like everybody else, she constantly compared him to Reede. Junior always came out in second place. I didn't care how he measured up to anybody. I loved him for what he was. Junior didn't want to believe it, but in spite of your father and you, Celina would have always loved Reede."

"If she loved him so much, why did she marry my father?" That question had been plaguing Alex for days.

"Celina and Reede had a falling out the spring of our junior year. As soon as school was out for the summer, she went to visit cousins in El Paso."

"That's where she met my father." Alex knew this much of the story from her grandmother. "He was going through boot camp at Fort Bliss. Soon after they were married, he got shipped to Vietnam."

Stacey sneered, "And after he died, she wanted to take back up with Reede, but he wouldn't have her. That's when she kindled Junior's hopes. She knew he'd always wanted her, but he never would have pursued it, on account of Reede. It was disgraceful how she played up to Junior, involving him with her pregnancy. She might have toyed with the idea of marrying him, but it never would have happened as long as Reede Lambert drew breath.

"Your mother kept Junior dangling by a thread of hope. She made his life miserable. She would have gone on making him miserable if she had lived." The former Mrs. Minton drew a choppy breath that caused her shapeless chest to stagger as it rose and fell. "I was glad when Celina died."

A spark of suspicion leaped into Alex's eyes. "Where were you that night?"

"At home unpacking. I'd just returned from a week's vacation in Galveston."

Would she lie over something so easily checked? "You married Junior right away."

"That's right. He needed me. I knew that I was only a

panacea for his grief, just like I'd always known when he made love to me that it was Celina he really wanted. But I didn't care if he used me. I wanted to be used. I cooked his meals, took care of his clothes, nurtured him in bed and out."

Her expression changed as she lapsed into a private reverie. "I overlooked the first time he was unfaithful to me. I was crushed, naturally, but I could understand how easily it had happened. Whenever we went out, women flocked to him. What man could resist such a strong temptation? The affair didn't last long before he lost interest." She clasped her hands and studied them as she spoke softly. "Then there was another. And another. I would have tolerated all his lovers if only he'd stayed married to me.

"But he asked me for a divorce. At first I refused. He kept on and on, telling me that he hated hurting me with his affairs. When I was left no option, I granted the divorce. It broke my heart, but I gave him what he wanted, knowing, *knowing,*" she repeated with emphasis, "that no other woman would ever be as right for him as I was. I thought I'd die with the pain of loving him too well."

She shook herself out of the reflective mood and beaded on Alex. "And I still have to stand by and watch him move from woman to woman, all the time searching for what I can and want to give him. I had to watch him dance and flirt with you tonight. You! My God," she sobbed, tilting her face toward the ceiling and pressing her fist to her forehead, eyes squeezed shut. "You want to ruin him, and he still can't see beyond your pretty face and body."

She lowered her hand and glared at Alex. "You are poison, Miss Gaither. I feel the same way about you tonight as I did twenty-five years ago." Closing the distance between them and putting her narrow, angular face close to Alex's, she hissed, "I wish you'd never been born."

Alex's attempts to compose herself after Stacey's departure had been in vain. Her face was pale and she was trembling as she walked out of the powder room.

"I was about to come in and get you." Junior was waiting for Alex in the hallway. At first he didn't notice her troubled expression. When he did, he was instantly concerned. "Alex? What's the matter?"

"I'd like to leave now."

"Are you sick? What's—"

"Please. We'll talk on the way."

Without further argument, Junior took her arm and steered her toward the cloakroom, where he asked the attendant for their coats. "Wait here." Alex watched him reenter the club, skirt the dance floor, and move to the table where they had eaten dinner. After a brief exchange with Angus and Sarah Jo, he returned in time to claim their coats.

He hustled her outside and into the red Jaguar. He waited until they were a good distance from the club and the car's heater was pumping warm air before he addressed her across the plush interior. "All right, what gives?"

"Why didn't you tell me that you were married to Stacey Wallace?"

He stared at her until it became a driving hazard, then turned his head and fixed his eyes on the road ahead. "You didn't ask."

"How glib."

She laid her head against the cold passenger window, feeling like she'd just sustained a beating with a chain and was due to enter the ring for round two. Just when she thought she had finished sorting through all the pieces of the various liaisons of Purcell, another intricate twist emerged.

"Is it important?" Junior asked.

"I don't know." She turned her shoulders toward him and rested the back of her head on the window. "You tell me. Is it?"

"No. The marriage lasted less than a year. We parted friends."

"*You* parted friends. She's still in love with you."

He winced. "That was one of our problems. Stacey's love is obsessive and possessive. She shackled me. I couldn't breathe. We—"

"Junior, you screwed around," she interrupted impatiently. "Spare me the banal explanations. I really don't care."

"Then why'd you bring it up?"

"Because she confronted me in the powder room and accused me of ruining her father's life with this investigation."

"For crissake, Alex, Joe Wallace is a big crybaby. Stacey mothers him. I don't doubt for a minute that he's whined and carried on about you something awful in front of her. It's a ploy to get her sympathy. They feed each other's neuroses. Don't worry about it."

Alex didn't like Junior Minton very much at that moment. His cavalier attitude toward a woman's—*any* woman's—love reduced him in Alex's eyes. She'd watched him tonight, doing just as Stacey had described, moving from woman to woman. The young and old, attractive and homely, married and unattached, all seemed to be fair game. He was charming with each, like a mall Easter bunny working the crowd, doling out treats to greedy children who didn't realize they'd be better off without them.

He seemed to take their fawning as his due. Alex had never found that kind of conceit commendable or appealing. Junior took for granted that he would elicit a response from every woman he spoke to. Flirting was an involuntary action to him, as natural as breathing. It would never occur to him that someone might misinterpret his intentions and suffer emotional pain.

Perhaps if she hadn't had the conversation with Stacey, Alex would have smiled indulgently, as all the other women had, and accepted his suaveness as part of his personality. But instead, she now felt irritable toward him and wanted him to know she couldn't be so blithely dismissed. "It wasn't just the judge Stacey took issue with. She said I was stirring up memories of her marriage to you, airing her dirty linen. I get the impression that being your ex has been a real trial for her."

"That's not really my problem, is it?"

"Maybe it should be."

Her harsh backlash surprised him. "You sound mad at me. Why?"

"I don't know." The flare of her temper had been short and sweet. Now, she felt drained. "I'm sorry. Maybe it's just that I always pull for the underdog."

He reached across the car and covered her knee with his hand. "An admirable quality that hasn't escaped my notice." Alex picked up his hand and dropped it back onto the leather seat between them. "Uh-oh, I'm not off the hook yet."

She resisted his smile. "Why did you marry Stacey?"

"Is this really what you want to talk about?" He wheeled the car up to the breezeway of the Westerner Motel and shifted the gear into Park.

"Yes."

Frowning, he cut the engine and laid his arm along the seat, turning toward her. "It seemed like the thing to do at the time."

"You didn't love her."

"No shit."

"But you made love to her." He raised an inquisitive eyebrow. "Stacey told me that you'd been lovers for a long time before you got married."

"Not lovers, Alex. I took her out every now and then."

"How often?"

"You want it plain?"

"Shoot."

"I called on Stacey whenever I got horny and the Gail sisters were busy, or had their periods, or—"

"The who?"

"The Gail sisters. Another story." He waved off the questions he could see rising in her mind.

"I've got all night." She settled more comfortably against her door.

"Doesn't anything escape you?"

"Very little. What about these sisters?"

"There were three of them—triplets, in fact. All named Gail."

"That stands to reason."

"No, it wasn't their last name. Their names were Wanda Gail, Nora Gail, and Peggy Gail."

"Is this a joke?"

He drew an *x* across his chest. "Cross my heart. Reede had already initiated them, so to speak, before I arrived on the scene. He introduced me to them." He snickered, as though recalling a particularly sordid incident of his youth. "In short, the Gail sisters put out. They liked putting out. Every guy in Purcell High School must have had them at least once."

"Okay, I get the picture. But when they were unavailable, you called on Stacey Wallace, because she put out, too."

He looked at her levelly. "I've never coerced a woman. She was willing, Alex."

"Only for you."

He shrugged an admission.

"And you took advantage of that."

"Name me one guy who wouldn't."

"You've got a point," she said dryly. "I would venture to say that you're the only man Stacey's ever been with."

He had the grace to look a little ashamed. "Yeah, I'd say so, too."

"I felt sorry for her tonight, Junior. She was hateful to me, but I couldn't help but feel sorry for her."

"I never understood why she latched onto me, but she shadowed me from the day I enrolled into Purcell High School. She was a brainy kid, you know. Always the teachers' favorite because she was so conscientious and never got into trouble." He chuckled. "They'd *never* believe what she was willing to do in the backseat of my Chevy."

Alex gazed distractedly into space, not really listening. "Stacey despised Celina."

"She was jealous of her."

"Mainly because when you made love to Stacey, she knew it was my mother you were wishing for."

"Jesus," he swore softly, his smile collapsing.

"That's what she said. Is that true?"

"Celina was always with Reede. That's just the way it was. It was a fact of life."

"But you did want her, even though she belonged to your best friend?"

After a lengthy pause, he admitted, "I'd be lying if I said otherwise."

Very softly, Alex said, "Stacey told me something else. It was an offhanded comment, not a revelation. She said it as though it was common knowledge—something I should already know."

"What?"

"That you wanted to marry my mother." She refocused on him and asked huskily, "Did you?"

He averted his head for a second, then said, "Yes."

"Before or after she got married and had me?"

"Both." When he saw her apparent confusion, he said, "I don't think a man could look at Celina and not want her for his own. She was beautiful and funny and had this way of making you think you were special to her. She had…" He groped for the adequate word. "Something," he said, closing his fist around the elusive noun, "something that made you want to possess her."

"Did you ever possess her?"

"Physically?"

"Did you ever sleep with my mother?"

His expression was baldly honest and terribly sad. "No, Alex. Never."

"Did you ever try? Would she have?"

"I don't think so. I never tried. At least, not very hard."

"Why not, if you wanted her so much?"

"Because Reede would have killed us."

Stunned, she gazed at him. "Do you really think so?"

He shrugged as his disarming smile moved into place. "Figure of speech."

Alex wasn't so sure. It had sounded literal when he said it.

He scooted along the seat of his Jaguar until they were sitting very close. He slid his fingers up through her hair, laid his thumb along her neck, and stroked it lightly.

"That's sure a dreary subject. Let's change it," he whispered, brushing an airy kiss across her mouth. "How about leaving the past for a while and thinking about the present?" His eyes wandered over her face while his fingertips touched each feature. "I want to sleep with you, Alex."

For a moment, she was too stunned to speak. "You're not serious?"

"Wanna bet?"

He kissed her in earnest then. At least, he tried to. Tilting his head, he rested his lips upon hers, pressed, tested, pressed harder. When she didn't respond, he pulled back and gave her a puzzled look.

"No?"

"No."

"Why not?"

"You know without my telling you. It would be crazy. Wrong."

"I've done crazier things." He lowered his hand to the front of her sweater and fingered a patch of soft suede. "Wronger things, too."

"Well, I haven't."

"We'd be good together, Alex."

"We'll never know."

He ran his thumb along her lower lip, tracking its slow progress with his eyes. "Never say never." He bent his head and kissed her again—affectionately, not passionately—then returned to the driver's side of the car and got out.

At the door, he gave her a chaste good-night kiss, but his expression was indulgent and amused. Alex knew he thought she was just being coy and that wearing her down was only a matter of time.

She was so befuddled by his come-on that it was several minutes before she noticed that the red message light on her telephone was blinking. She called the motel's front desk, retrieved her message, and called the specified number. Even before the doctor got on the line, she knew what he would say. Nevertheless, his words shocked her.

"Miss Gaither, I'm terribly sorry. Mrs. Graham passed away earlier this evening without ever regaining consciousness."

Chapter 21

Alex knocked and waited until Reede called out, "Come in," before entering his office. "Good morning. Thank you for seeing me on such short notice."

She sat down in the chair in front of his desk. Without asking, he poured her a cup of coffee to her liking and placed it in front of her. She thanked him with a nod.

"I'm sorry about your grandmother, Alex," he said as he resumed his seat in the creaky swivel chair.

"Thank you."

Alex had been away for a week, handling the details of her grandmother's funeral. Only Alex, a handful of former co-workers, and a few of the nursing home patients had attended the chapel service. After the burial, Alex had begun the unwelcome chore of clearing out her grandmother's room at the nursing home. The staff had been kind, but there was a waiting list, so they had needed the room emptied immediately.

It had been an emotionally stressful week. As she had sat staring at the modest casket, while organ music played softly in the background, she had felt an overwhelming sense of defeat. She had failed to fulfill the promise she had made to herself and to her grandmother: She hadn't produced Celina's murderer in time.

More defeating than that, she had failed to win her grandmother's absolution and love. That had been her last chance; she wouldn't have another.

She had given serious consideration to throwing in the towel, telling Greg that he'd been right, and that she should have taken his advice from the beginning. He would enjoy seeing her humility, and he would immediately assign her another case.

That would have been the easier course. She would never have to enter the city limits of Purcell again, or cope with the hostility that flew at her like missiles from everyone she met, or look into the face of this man, who generated myriad ambiguous feelings inside her.

From a legal viewpoint, she still had a case too weak to stand up in court. But from a personal perspective, she couldn't quit. She had become intrigued by the men who had loved her mother. She *had* to know which one of them had killed her, and whether or not she was responsible for her mother's murder. She would either have to deny her guilt, or learn to live with it, but she couldn't let it go forever unresolved.

So, she had returned to Purcell. She was staring into the pair of green eyes that had haunted her thoughts for a week, and they were as compelling and disturbing as she remembered.

"I wasn't sure you'd be back," he told her bluntly.

"You should have been. I told you I wouldn't give up."

"Yeah, I remember," he said grimly. "How was the dance the other night?"

His question came out of the blue and evoked a knee-jerk response. "How did you know I went?"

"Word gets around."

"Junior told you."

"No."

"I can hardly stand the suspense," Alex said. "How did you find out I went to the Horse and Gun Club?"

"One of my deputies clocked Junior doing eighty-one that night out on the highway. Around eleven o'clock, he said. He saw you in the car with him." He was no longer looking at her, but studying the toes of his boots. "You sure were in a hell of a hurry to get back to your motel."

"I was ready to leave the club, that's all. I wasn't feeling well."

"The barbecue didn't sit well with you? Or was it the people? Some of them make me sick to my stomach, too."

"It wasn't the food or the people. It was, well, one person: Stacey Wallace ... Minton." Alex closely watched for his reaction. His face remained impassive. "Why didn't anyone tell me that Stacey had been married to Junior?"

"You didn't ask."

Miraculously, she was able to hold her temper in check. "Didn't it occur to anybody that their hasty marriage might be significant?"

"It wasn't."

"I reserve the right to decide the significance of it myself."

"Be my guest. Do you think it's significant?"

"Yes, I do. The timing of Junior's first marriage always

struck me as strange. It's even stranger that the bride turned out to be the judge's daughter."

"That's not strange at all."

"Coincidental, certainly."

"Not even that. Stacey Wallace had been in love, or lust, with Junior since the day she first laid eyes on him. Everybody knew it, including Junior. She certainly made no secret of her devotion. When Celina died, Stacey saw her chance and seized it."

"Stacey didn't strike me as an opportunist."

"Grow up, Alex. We're all opportunists when we want something bad enough. She loved the guy," he pointed out impatiently. "He was sick over Celina's death. I guess Stacey figured her love could make his hurt go away, that it would be enough."

"It wasn't."

"Obviously. She couldn't make Junior love her back. She sure as hell couldn't weld his zippers shut." Vexed, he gnawed on the corner of his lip. "Who spilled the beans about this? Junior?"

"Stacey herself. She confronted me in the powder room and accused me of upsetting her life by reopening this case."

"Gutsy lady," he said, nodding approval. "I always liked her."

"Oh, really? Did you sleep with her, too? Or did the Gail sisters keep you satiated?"

"The Gail sisters, huh?" He barked a short laugh. "I know Stacey didn't talk to you about Purcell's notorious triplets."

"Junior filled in the gaps."

"Must have been quite an evening."

"Most revealing."

"Oh, yeah?" he drawled. "What'd you reveal?"

She ignored this well-placed insinuation. "Reede, what was the rush? Junior wasn't in love with Stacey. For the sake of argument, let's say he talked himself into marrying her. Why did they marry when they did?"

"Maybe she wanted to be a June bride."

"Don't make fun of me!" She shot out of her chair and moved to the window.

He whistled low and long. "Boy, are you ever in a rotten mood."

"I just buried my only living relative, remember?" she flared.

He cursed beneath his breath and raked his fingers through his hair. "For a minute there, I did forget. Look, Alex, I'm sorry. I remember how bad I felt when I buried my old man."

She turned to face him, but he was staring at nothing. "Angus and Junior were the only ones out of the whole god-damn town who came to my father's funeral. We didn't even hold it in a church or the funeral home, just at the grave site. Angus went back to work. Junior returned to school so he wouldn't miss a biology test. I went home.

"Not long after lunch, Celina came to my house. She had skipped school just to come and be with me. She knew I'd feel low, even though I hated the son of a bitch while he was alive. We lay down together on my bed and stayed there until it got dark. She knew if she didn't go home, her mother would get worried. She cried for me because I couldn't."

When he stopped speaking, there was a ponderous silence in the room. Alex was still standing by the window, motionless and transfixed by his story. Her chest hurt with heartache for the lonely young man he'd been.

"Was that the first time you made love to Celina?"

He looked straight at her, got out of his chair, and approached her. "Since you broached the subject of love lives, how's yours?"

The tension snapped, as did her temper. "Why don't you stop beating around the bush and come right out and ask?"

"Okay," he sneered. "Has Junior made it into your pants yet?"

"You bastard."

"Has he?"

"No!"

"I'll bet he's tried. He always tries." His laugh was deep and stirring. "Bingo." He raised his hand and stroked her cheek with the backs of his fingers. "You're blushing, Counselor."

She swatted his hand aside. "Go to hell."

She was furious with herself for blushing like a schoolgirl in front of him. It was none of his business who she slept with. What bothered her most, however, was that he didn't seem to care. If she had to describe that glint in his eyes she would call it amusement, possibly contempt, but certainly not jealousy.

To retaliate, she asked suddenly, "What did you and Celina quarrel about?"

"Celina and I? When?"

"The spring of your junior year. Why did she go to El Paso for the summer and start dating my father?"

"Maybe she needed a change of scenery," he said flippantly.

"Did you know how much your best friend loved her?"

His goading grin vanished. "Did Junior tell you that?"

"I knew before he told me. Did you know, at the time, that he loved her?"

He rolled his shoulders forward in a semblance of a shrug. "Nearly every guy in school—"

"I'm not talking about infatuation with a popular girl, Reede." She grabbed his shirtsleeve to show just how important this was to her. "Did you know how Junior felt about her?"

"What if I did?"

"He said you would have killed him if he'd tried anything with her. He said you would have killed them both if they had betrayed you."

"A figure of speech."

"That's what Junior said, too, but I don't think so," she said evenly. "There were a lot of passions stirring. Your relationships with each other were overlapping and complex."

"Whose relationships?"

"You and my mother loved each other, but you both loved Junior, too. Wasn't it a love triangle in the strictest sense of the word?"

"What the hell are you talking about? Do you think Junior and I are a couple of queers?"

Unexpectedly, he grabbed her hand and flattened it against his fly. "Feel that, baby? It's been hard more than it's been soft, but it's never been hard for a fag."

Stunned and shaken, she pried her hand away, subconsciously rubbing the palm of it against her thigh, as though it had been branded. "You have a redneck mentality, Sheriff Lambert," she said, supremely agitated. "I think you and Junior love each other the way Indian blood brothers do. But you're competitive, too."

"I don't compete with Junior."

"Maybe not consciously, but other people have pitted you against each other. And guess which one of you always came out on top? *You*. That bothered you. It still does."

"Is this more of your psychological bullshit?"

"It's not just my opinion. Stacey mentioned it the other night, and not at my prompting. She said people always compared the two of you, and that Junior always came in second."

"I can't help what people think."

"Your competitiveness came to a head over Celina, didn't it?"

"Why ask me? You've got all the answers."

"You had the edge there, too. Junior wanted to be Celina's lover, but you actually were."

A long silence followed. Reede regarded her with the concentration of a hunter who finally has his quarry in the cross hairs. The sunlight streaming through the blinds glinted in his eyes, on his hair, on his eyebrows, which were slanted dangerously.

Very quietly, he said, "Good try, Alex, but I'm not admitting anything."

He tried to move away then, but she caught his arms. "Well, weren't you her lover? What difference does it make if you say so now?"

"Because I never kiss and tell." His eyes slid down to her pulsing throat, then back up. "And you should be damned glad I don't."

Want surged through her, as warm and golden as the morning sunlight. She craved to feel his hard lips on hers again, the rough, powerful mastery of his tongue inside her mouth. She became dewy with desire and tearful with remorse for what she desperately wanted and couldn't have.

Eyes locked, neither realized that they were being observed from across the street. The sun was as good as a spotlight on them.

Willing herself out of the dubious present and into the disturbing past, she said, "Junior told me that you and Celina were more than just childhood sweethearts." It was a bluff, but she gambled on it working. "He told me everything about your relationship with her, so it really doesn't matter whether you admit it or not. When did you and she first... you know?"

"Fuck?"

The vulgarity, spoken in a low, thrumming rasp, sent shafts of heat through her. Never had that word sounded erotic to her before. She swallowed and made an almost imperceptible nod of acknowledgment.

Suddenly, he hooked his hand around the back of her neck and pulled her against him, placing her face directly beneath his. His eyes bore into hers.

"Junior didn't tell you shit, Counselor," he whispered. "Don't try your fancy, courtroom-lawyer bluffs on me. I've got eighteen years on you, and I was born smart. The tricks I've got up my sleeve, you've never even heard about. I'm damn sure not ignorant enough to fall for yours."

His fist clenched tighter around the handful of her hair he was holding. His breath felt hotter and came faster against her face. "Don't ever try to come between Junior and me again, you hear? Fight us both or fuck us both, but don't tamper with something outside your understanding."

His eyes narrowed with sinister intensity. "Your mama

had a bad habit of playing both ends against the middle, Alex. Somebody got a bellyful of it and killed her before she learned her lesson. You'd do well to learn it before something like that happens to you."

The morning was a washout in terms of discovering new clues. Nothing diverted her mind from the disturbing conversation she had had with Reede. If a deputy hadn't knocked on the office door and interrupted them, she didn't know whether she would have clawed at Reede's eyes or yielded to her stronger urge to press her body close to his and kiss him.

At noon she stopped trying to concentrate and crossed the street to have lunch at the B & B Café. Like most people who worked downtown, that had become her habit. No longer were conversations suspended when she went in. Every now and then she even merited a greeting from Pete if he wasn't too busy in the kitchen.

She dawdled over her meal as long as possible, scooting the yellow ceramic armadillo ashtray back and forth across her table and leafing through Pete's printed brochure on the proper way to prepare rattlesnake.

She was killing time, loath to return to the dingy little office in the basement of the courthouse and stare into space, recounting unsettling thoughts and reviewing hypotheses that seemed more farfetched by the hour. But one thought kept haunting her. Was there any connection between Celina's death and Junior's hasty marriage to Stacey Wallace?

Her mind was steeped in speculation when she left the café. Ducking her head against the cold wind, she walked toward the corner. The traffic light, one of the few down-town, changed just as she reached the corner. She was about to step off the cracked and buckled concrete curb when her arm was caught from behind.

"Reverend Plummet," she stated in surprise. Subsequent events had quickly dismissed him and his timid wife from her mind.

"Miss Gaither," he said in a censorious tone, "I saw you with the sheriff this morning." He could have tacked on any number of deadly sins to account for the accusation smolder-ing in his deep-set eyes. "You've disappointed me."

"I fail to see—"

"Furthermore," he interrupted with the rolling intonation of a sidewalk evangelist, "you've disappointed the Almighty." His eyes rounded largely, then closed to mere slits. "I warn you, the Lord will not tolerate being mocked."

She nervously moistened her lips and glanced around, hoping to see some avenue of escape, though she didn't know what form it might take. "I haven't meant to offend you or God," she said, feeling foolish for even making such a statement.

"You haven't locked the iniquitous behind bars yet."

"I haven't found any reason to. My investigation isn't com-plete. And just to set the record straight, Reverend Plummet, I didn't come here to lock anybody behind bars."

"You're being too soft on the ungodly."

"If by that you mean that I've approached this investiga-tion impartially, then yes, I have."

"I saw you this morning fraternizing with that son of the devil."

His maniacal eyes were arresting, if repellent. She caught herself staring into them. "You mean Reede?"

He made a hissing sound, as though the very name conjured up an evil spirit that must be warded off. "Don't be taken in by his wily devices."

"I assure you, I'm not."

He came a step closer. "The devil knows where women are weak. He uses their soft, vulnerable bodies as channels for his evil powers. They're tainted, and must be cleansed by a regular outpouring of blood."

He isn't only nutty, he's sick, Alex thought in horror.

He slapped his hand upon his Bible, causing Alex to jump. Raising his index finger into the air, he shouted, "Resist all temptation, daughter! I command every lascivious impulse to desert your head and mind and body. Now," he bellowed.

He slumped, as though the exorcism had totally drained him of energy. Alex stood transfixed by disbelief. Coming to her senses, she glanced around uneasily, hoping that no one had witnessed this madness and her unwitting involvement in it.

"As far as I know, I have no lascivious impulses. Now, I must go. I'm late." She stepped off the curb despite the fact that the traffic light was flashing instructions not to walk.

"God is counting on you. He's impatient. If you betray his trust—"

"Yes, well, I'll try harder. Good-bye."

He lunged off the curb and grabbed her by the shoulders. "God bless you, daughter. God bless you and your holy mission." Clasping her hand, he pressed a cheaply printed pamphlet into it.

"Thank you."

Alex worked her hand free and jogged across the street, quickly putting two lanes of traffic between her and the preacher. She trotted up the steps and barreled through the courthouse doors.

Glancing over her shoulder to see if Plummet had followed her, she ran right into Reede.

He caught her against his chest. "What the hell's the matter with you? Where have you been?"

She wanted to lean against him, feel his protective strength, until her heart stopped racing, but didn't allow herself the luxury. "Nowhere. I mean, I went out. To lunch. At the, uh, the B & B. I walked."

He studied her, taking in her windblown hair and ruddy cheeks. "What's that?" He nodded down at the pamphlet she was clutching in her white-knuckled hand.

"Nothing." She tried to stuff it into the pocket of her coat.

Reede snatched it out of her hand. He scanned the cover, flipped it open, and read the message heralding doomsday. "You into this?"

"Of course not. A sidewalk preacher handed it to me. You really should devote some attention to clearing the panhandlers off your city's streets, Sheriff," she said haughtily. "They're a nuisance."

She stepped around him and continued downstairs.

Chapter 22

————◦◉◦————

Nora Gail sat up and retrieved the filmy garment she'd worn into the room.

"Thanks," Reede said to her.

She gave him a reproving glance over her milky-white shoulder. Drolly she replied, "How romantic." After shoving her arms through the ruffled sleeves of the peignoir, she left the bed and moved toward the door. "I've got to go check on things, but I'll be back, and we can talk." Patting her beehive hairdo, she left the room.

Reede watched her go. Her body was compact now, but in a few years it would go to fat. The large breasts would sag. Her oversized nipples would look grotesque without any muscle tone supporting them. Her smooth, slightly convex belly would become spongy. Her thighs and ass would dimple.

Even though they were friends, he hated her at the moment. He hated himself more. He hated the physical necessity that propelled him through this travesty of intimacy with a woman.

They rutted, probably more mindlessly and heartlessly

than some species of animals. The release should have been cleansing and cathartic. It should have felt great. It didn't. It rarely did anymore, certainly not recently.

"Shit," he muttered. He would probably go on sleeping with her through their old age. It was convenient and uncomplicated. Each knew what the other was able to give and demanded nothing more. As far as Reede was concerned, passion was based on need, not desire, and sure as hell not on love.

He got off. So did she. She had often told him he was one of the few men who could make her come. He wasn't particularly flattered because that might be, and probably was, a lie.

Disgusted, he threw his legs over the side of the bed. There was a pack of cigarettes on the bedside table, courtesy of the house. The carefully rolled joints you had to pay for. He lit one of the cigarettes, something he rarely did anymore, and drew the tobacco deep into his lungs. He missed the post-coital cigarettes more than any others, maybe because the tobacco punished and polluted the body that continually betrayed him with a healthy sex drive.

He poured himself a drink from the bottle on the nightstand—that would be added to his bill, even if he did fuck the madam herself—and tossed it down in one swallow. Rebelling, his esophagus contracted. His eyes teared. The whiskey spread a slow, languid heat through his belly and groin. He began to feel marginally better.

He lay back down and stared at the ceiling, wishing he could sleep, but welcoming this coveted time of relaxation when he wasn't called on to speak, move, or think.

His eyes closed. An image of a face, bathed in sunlight and wreathed by loose, dark-auburn hair, was projected on the backs of his eyelids. His cock, which should have been limp with exhaustion, swelled and stretched with more pleasure than it had felt earlier tonight.

Reede didn't whisk the image away, as he usually did. This time he let it stay, evolve. The fantasy was welcomed and indulged. He watched her blue eyes blink with surprise at her own eroticism, watched her tongue nervously flick over her lower lip.

He felt her against him, her heart beating in time with his, her hair tangled in his fingers.

He tasted her mouth again, felt her tongue shyly flirting with his.

He didn't realize that he made a low moan or that his penis twitched reflexively. A drop of moisture pearled the tip. Yearning pressed down on him suffocatingly.

"Reede!"

The door to the room was flung open and the madam rushed back in, no longer looking cool and elegant.

"Reede," she repeated breathlessly.

"What the hell?" He swung his feet to the floor again and stood up in one economical motion. He didn't think to be embarrassed by his evident arousal. Something was desperately wrong.

As long as he'd known her, he'd never seen her rattled, but now, her eyes were wide with alarm. He was stepping into his briefs before she even started speaking.

"They just called."

"Who?"

"Your office. There's an emergency."

"Where?" Already standing in jeans and an unbuttoned shirt, he crammed his feet into his boots.

"The ranch."

He froze and swiveled his head toward her. "The *Minton* ranch?" She nodded. "What kind of emergency?"

"The deputy didn't say. Swear to God he didn't," she added hurriedly when she could see that Reede was about to question that.

"Personal or professional emergency?"

"I don't know, Reede. I got the impression that it's a combination of both. He just said you're wanted out there pronto. Is there anything I can do?"

"Call back and tell them I'm on my way." Grabbing his coat and hat, he pushed her aside and ran into the hallway. "Thanks."

"Let me know what happened," she called down to him, leaning over the banister, watching his hasty descent.

"When I can." Seconds later he slammed the door behind him, leaped over the porch rail, and hit the ground running.

———◆———

Alex was in a deep slumber, which was why she didn't associate the knocking on her door with reality. Subconsciously, she thought the racket was an extension of her dream. A voice finally roused her.

"Get up and open the door."

Groggily, she sat up and reached for the switch to the bedside lamp, which always seemed to elude her. When the lamp came on, she blinked against the sudden light.

"Alex, dammit! *Get up!*"

The door was vibrating with each fall of his fist. "Reede?" she croaked.

"If you're not up in ten seconds..."

She checked the digital clock on the nightstand. It was almost two in the morning. The sheriff was either drunk or crazy. Either way, she wasn't about to open her door to him in his present frame of mind. "What do you want?"

Alex couldn't account for the change in the sound of the thumping until the wood began to splinter, then shatter. Reede kicked the door open and let himself in.

"Just what the hell do you think you're doing?" she shouted, gathering the covers against her as she sat bolt upright.

"Coming to get you."

He grabbed her, covers and all, plucked her off the bed and stood her on her feet, then ripped the covers away from her grasping hands. She stood shivering in front of him, wearing only panties and a T-shirt, her usual sleeping ensemble. It would be difficult to say which of them was the more furious or riveted.

Alex recovered her voice first. "I hope you have a damn good reason for kicking in my door, Sheriff."

"I do." He crossed to the dresser, yanked open a drawer, and began riffling through articles of clothing.

"I'd like to hear it."

"You will." Another drawer fell victim to his searching hands. She moved beside him and pushed the drawer shut with her hip, almost slamming it on his fingers.

"What are you looking for?"

"Clothes. Unless you'd rather go out like that."

He gestured down toward the panties with their high, French-cut legs. The spot where the sheer lace panel tapered between her thighs seemed to capture his attention for several tense seconds before he dragged his eyes toward the alcove where her clothes were hanging. "Where are your jeans?" he asked, his voice thick.

"I'm not going anywhere. Do you know what time it is?"

He jerked the jeans off the hanger. It rocked on the rod, then fell unheeded to the floor. "Yes." None too gently, he tossed the jeans at her. "Put those on. These, too." He threw her casual boots at her feet, then faced her, hands on hips, looking mean. "Well? Want me to do it for you?"

She couldn't imagine what she had done to provoke him. It was obvious, however, that he was livid over something. If he wanted to play out this caveman game, let him. She would go along, but she wouldn't do it graciously.

Turning her back on him, she stepped into her jeans and wiggled them over her hips. She took a pair of socks from one of the ravaged bureau drawers, shook them out, then pulled them on. The boots came next. Finally, she turned and glared up at him.

"There, I'm dressed. Now, are you going to tell me what this is all about?"

"On the way."

He yanked a sweater from a hanger and moved toward her as he gathered the material up to the turtleneck. He pulled it over her head, then shoved her arms into the sleeves and tugged the hem to her hips. The narrow neck had trapped her hair. He lifted it out.

Instead of withdrawing his hands, he closed his fingers tightly around her scalp, then roughly tilted her head up and back. He was shaking with rage.

"I ought to break your neck."

He didn't. He kissed her—hard.

His lips crushed hers, bruised them against her teeth. He

thrust his tongue inside her mouth with no semblance of tenderness. It was an angry kiss, spawned by angry passion.

It ended abruptly. Her coat was lying across a chair. He tossed it at her. "Here."

Alex was too shaken to think of arguing. She put it on. He pushed her over the threshold. "What about the door?" she asked inanely.

"I'll send someone to fix it."

"At this time of night?"

"Forget the goddamn door," he roared. Cupping her bottom in his palm, he boosted her up into the cab of the Blazer, which he'd kept running. The light bar across the roof of it was flashing a tricolor code of emergency.

"How long before I get an explanation?" she asked as the Blazer careened onto the highway. Her seat belt did little good. She was thrown against him, and had to clutch his thigh to keep from being pitched onto the floorboard. "For heaven's sake, Reede, tell me what's happened."

"The Minton ranch has been set afire."

Chapter 23

S et afire?" she repeated in a thready voice.

"Drop the innocent act, will ya?"

"I don't know what you're talking about."

He banged his fist on the steering wheel. "How could you sleep through it?"

She stared at him, aghast. "Are you suggesting that I had something to do with it?"

Reede turned his attention back to the road. His face was taut and rigid in the greenish light emanating from the dashboard. The police radio discharged its scratchy static. The transmissions were loud and intrusive. There was no other traffic on the highway, so the siren wasn't necessary, but the lights overhead continued to whirl and flash, making Alex feel like she was caught in a weird kaleidoscope.

"I think you had a lot to do with it, you and your close friend and associate." Her bewilderment only seemed to infuriate him more. "Reverend Fergus Plummet," he shouted. "The preacher's a good friend of yours, isn't he?"

"Plummet?"

"'Plummet?'" he mimicked nastily. "When did the two of you cook up this idea, the evening he paid a visit to your motel room, or the other day, on the sidewalk in front of the B & B Café?"

She took a series of quick, shallow breaths. "How'd you know?"

"I know, okay? Who called who first?"

"He and his wife showed up at my room. I'd never heard of him before that. The man's a maniac."

"That didn't stop you from enlisting him to your cause."

"I did no such thing."

Swearing beneath his breath, he pulled the transmitter of his radio toward his mouth and notified one of his deputies at the scene that he was only minutes away.

"Ten-four, Reede. When you get here, go to barn number two."

"How come?"

"Don't know. Somebody said to tell you that."

"Ten-four. I'm at the gate now."

They turned off the highway and took the private road. Alex's stomach turned over when she saw a column of smoke rising from one of the horse barns. Flames were no longer visible, but the roof and those of the adjacent buildings were still being doused with fire hoses. Firemen, wearing slickers and rubber boots, were frantically trying to contain the fire.

"They got to it before it did too much damage," Reede informed her harshly.

Emergency vehicles were parked near the smoking stable and in front of the house. Nearly every downstairs window had been broken out. All exterior walls had dire warnings of Armageddon spray-painted on them.

"There were three carloads of them. Apparently they circled the premises several times, throwing rocks through the windows, but only after they'd done their real dirty work. You can see how well K-Mart did tonight in the spray-paint department." His lip curled snidely. "They dumped shit into the drinking troughs. Fine class of friends you've got there, Counselor."

"Was anybody hurt?" It was a horrendous scene. She was unable to draw sufficient air into her lungs.

"One of the gallop boys." Alex turned toward him for elaboration. "He heard the racket, rushed outside the bunkhouse, stumbled, fell, and broke his arm."

Barn number two was the one with the smoldering roof. Reede braked the Blazer in front and left her sitting in the truck when he went inside. Alex, feeling like each limb weighed a thousand pounds, shoved open the door and followed him through the wide doors, shouldering her way through the scurrying firemen.

"What's the matter?" she heard Reede demand as he jogged down the center aisle of the stable.

A horse was screaming, obviously in pain. It was the most hideous sound Alex had ever heard. Reede picked up speed.

The Mintons were gathered in a somber, pajama-clad huddle outside one of the stalls. Sarah Jo was weeping copiously. Angus was fervently, but ineffectually, patting her back. Junior was holding her hand and using his other to cover a yawn. Reede pushed them aside, but drew up short at the entrance to the stall.

"Jesus Christ." He cursed a stream of blue words, then let out a tortured roar that caused Alex to shrink back into the shadows.

A pot-bellied, bespectacled man stepped into Alex's line of vision. By all appearances, he'd come straight from his bed. His corduroy jacket had been pulled on over a pair of pajamas. Laying a hand on Reede's arm, he shook his balding head gravely. "There's nothing I can do for him, Reede. We'll have to put him down."

Reede stared at the man blankly, wordlessly. His chest rose and fell as though he were about to heave up his supper.

Sarah Jo's sobs increased. She covered her face with her hands. "Mother, please let me take you back to the house." Junior placed his arm around her waist and turned her away. Angus's arm dropped to his side. Mother and son moved slowly down the center aisle.

They were almost even with Alex before they noticed her. The instant Sarah Jo saw her, she released a high, keening sound and pointed an accusing finger. "*You*. You did this to us."

Alex recoiled. "I—"

"It's your fault, you meddlesome, spiteful little bitch!"

"Mother," Junior said, not in chastisement, but commiseration. Spent by her outburst, Sarah Jo collapsed against him. He gave Alex a penetrating look, but it seemed more puzzled than accusatory. Without speaking again, he moved on with Sarah Jo, whose head was now bent in misery against her son's chest.

"What happened, Ely?" Reede asked, seemingly unaware of the other drama.

"A falling beam must've landed square on him. He went down hard and broke his shoulder," the man called Ely said quietly. Apparently, he was a veterinarian.

"Give him some painkiller, for crissake."

"I already have. It's strong, but it can't anesthetize this." He gazed down at the suffering animal. "His femur's busted, too. I can only guess at his internal injuries. Even if I could patch him up, he'd likely be sickly from now on, and no use to you as a stud."

They stood silent a moment, listening to the pitiful sounds coming from the animal. At last Angus said, "Thank you, Ely. We know you've done all you could."

"I'm sorry, Angus, Reede," the vet said, meaning it. "Y'all go on outta here. I need to make a quick trip to the office and get the drug, then I'll come back and give him the injection."

"No." The word came hoarsely from Reede's lips. "I'll do it."

"You oughtn't to do that, Reede. The injection is—"

"I can't let him wait that long."

"It won't take me ten minutes."

"I said, I'll do it," Reede shouted impatiently.

Angus intervened, clapping the well-meaning vet hard on the shoulder to stem any further arguments. "Go on home, Ely. Sorry to have dragged you out for this."

"I'm damned sorry. I've been treating Double Time since he was foaled."

Alex's hand flew up to cover her mouth. Double Time was Reede's adored racehorse. The vet left by another door. He didn't see Alex.

Firemen shouted back and forth to each other outside. Other horses snorted fearfully, and restlessly tramped the floors of their stalls. Those sounds seemed distant and detached from the tense silence in that one single stall.

"Reede, you gonna be all right, boy?"

"Yes. Go see to Sarah Jo. I'll take care of this."

The older man looked ready to argue, but finally turned away. He gave Alex a hard, pointed look as he passed her, but said nothing before stamping out.

She wanted to cry as she watched Reede kneel in the hay. He rubbed the injured horse's muzzle. "You were good—the best," he whispered softly. "You gave it all you had, and then some." The animal nickered in what sounded like a plea.

Reede slowly came to his feet and reached for the pistol in his holster. He took it out, checked the chamber, and pointed it down at the racehorse.

"No!" Alex rushed out of the shadows and grabbed his arm. "Reede, no, don't. Let someone else."

She had seen hardened criminals, after being sentenced to death, turn on their prosecutors, the judge, the jury, and vituperatively swear vengeance, even if from beyond the grave.

But she had never seen such deadly intent on a face as when Reede looked down at her. His eyes were glazed with tears and hatred. With uncanny speed, he encircled her waist and drew her backward against his chest. She struggled. He cursed and increased the pressure of his arm across her midriff.

He took her right hand in his left and forcibly wrapped her reluctant fingers around the pistol, so that she was actually holding it when he aimed the barrel between the horse's eyes and pulled the trigger.

"*No!*"

She screamed the instant the pistol went off in her hand. The deadly sound seemed to ricochet off the stone walls of the stable and reverberate forever. Horses whinnied and tramped in fear. Someone outside shouted, and several of the firemen scrambled through the door to see what the shot meant.

Reede shoved Alex away from him. His voice crackling with rage, he said, "You should have done it clean like that in the first place, and spared him the agony."

"The fire's completely put out, Mr. Minton," the fire chief reported. "We checked all the wiring, insulation, everything in the roof. All the damage was superficial." He clicked his lips against his gums. "Damn shame about Reede Lambert's Thoroughbred, though."

"Thank you for all you've done. I've always said our fire department is the finest in West Texas."

Some of Angus's heartiness had been restored, though his features were heavy with fatigue. He was putting up a good front, as though he was determined not to let this be a setback. Alex could only admire his stamina and optimism.

He was sitting at the kitchen table with Junior, looking like he might have been wrapping up an all-night poker game instead of holding a wake for a destroyed racehorse and his vandalized property.

"Guess we'll be taking off, then." The fireman picked up his hard hat and moved toward the back door. "Someone will be out tomorrow to look for clues. It's a definite arson."

"We'll cooperate any way we can. I'm just glad you responded so quickly and kept the fire from spreading."

"So long." As the fireman went through the back door, he met Reede coming in. Reede ignored Alex, who was standing self-consciously against the wall, and poured himself a cup of coffee from the pot Lupe had brewed.

"The troughs are pure again. The horses won't be poisoned

by their own excrement," he said emotionlessly. "We got all the windows boarded up so you won't freeze tonight. There's still a lot of cleanup to do."

"Well," Angus sighed, coming to his feet, "we can't start on that till daylight, so I'm going up to bed. Thanks, Reede. You went above and beyond your duties as sheriff."

Reede bobbed his head in quick acknowledgment. "How's Sarah Jo?"

"Junior made her take a tranquilizer."

"She's sleeping now." Junior stood up also. "Would you like me to drive you back to town now, Alex? You've got no business being out here at this time of night."

"I wanted her to see her handiwork," Reede said.

"I had nothing to do with it!" she cried.

"Maybe not directly," Angus said sternly, "but this damn fool investigation of yours put things in motion. We've been fighting that loud-mouthed hellfire-and-damnation preacher for years. He was just looking for an excuse to pull a malicious stunt like this. You handed him a golden opportunity."

"I'm sorry if you see it that way, Angus."

The air was thick with tension. No one moved. Even the housekeeper stopped washing empty coffee cups. Finally, Junior stepped forward and took her arm. "Come on. It's getting late."

"I'll take her back," Reede said curtly.

"I don't mind."

"I'm going anyway."

"You'll just harp on what happened here."

"What the hell do you care what I say to her?"

"All right then, you take her home," Junior said testily. "You're the one who brought her, aren't you?" With that, he turned and left the room.

" 'Night, Reede, Alex." An unsmiling Angus followed his son out.

Reede tossed the dregs of his coffee into the sink. "Come on," her ordered her.

Retrieving her coat, she went outside with him and dejectedly climbed into his truck. She wanted to say something to break the dreadful silence, but couldn't bring herself to utter a single word. Reede seemed disinclined to converse. His eyes remained resolutely on the center stripe of the highway.

Finally, the growing knot of anxiety in her chest got to be too much and she blurted out, "I had nothing to do with what happened tonight."

He merely turned his head and looked at her, his expression one of patent disbelief.

"I think Junior believes me," she cried defensively.

"What the hell does he know? You've dazzled him. He took one look into those baby blues of yours and sank like a rock. He's up to his ass in sentimental bullshit about you being Celina's daughter. He remembers how he used to dote on you and wants to do it again—only in an entirely different way. The toy he wants to give you to play with now doesn't rattle."

"You're disgusting."

"It must have given you a thrill to see us coming close to blows over you."

She ground her teeth. "Think what you want to about my designs on Junior and his on me, but I won't have you thinking I was responsible for the damage done to his ranch tonight."

"You were responsible. You incited Plummet."

"Not intentionally. Plummet got it into his head that I was an answer to his prayers—that God sent me to purge Purcell of sinners, the Mintons, anyone connected to or a proponent of pari-mutuel gambling."

"He's crazier than I thought."

She rubbed her upper arms as though recollections of Plummet gave her chills. "You don't know the half of it. He says God is angry because I haven't locked all of you away. He accused me of fraternizing with the devil, meaning you." She refrained from telling him the sexual parallels Plummet had drawn.

Reede parked in front of her motel room. The door was still in shambles and standing ajar. "I thought you said you'd take care of that."

"Prop a chair under the doorknob till morning. You'll be all right."

He didn't turn off the Blazer's engine, but let it idle. The police radio crackled with its monotonous static, but there were no transmissions now. The noise was grating on her nerves.

"I'm sorry about Double Time, Reede. I know how attached to him you were."

His leather jacket made a squeaking sound against the upholstery when he shrugged indifferently. "He was insured."

Alex uttered a small cry of anguish and anger. He wouldn't let her apologize. He wouldn't let her feel sad or sorry because he wouldn't allow himself those emotions. She had witnessed the heartache he had suffered seconds before he put a bullet through the horse's brain. She had heard it when he talked about his father's pathetic funeral.

And that's what Reede couldn't forgive. More than once he had let down his guard and revealed to her that he was a feeling human being after all.

She balled her fists, pressed her wrists together, and thrust them across the console toward him. He looked at her with a dark, questioning frown. "What does that signify?"

"Handcuff me," she said. "Haul me in. Arrest me. Charge me with the crime. You said I was responsible."

"You are," he ground out, his previous rage returning. "Angus was right. If you hadn't come here and started snooping around, none of this would have happened."

"I refuse to take the blame for what happened tonight, Reede. It was the act of an unbalanced man and his misled followers. If my investigation hadn't been their catalyst, something else would have been. I've apologized for the horse. What more do you want from me?"

He gave her a sharp look. She withdrew her hands, snatching them back as though they'd been placed too close to the maws of some terrible beast, and she had realized it in the nick of time.

Inside her mouth was the taste of his kiss—whiskey- and tobacco-flavored. As though it were happening again, she felt the swirling search of his tongue, the possessive pressure of his fingers on her scalp, the solid presence of his thighs against hers.

"You'd better go inside, Counselor." His voice was quiet and husky.

He dropped the truck's transmission into reverse. Alex took his advice and got out.

Chapter 24

Alex groped for the ringing telephone. She answered it on the fifth ring and said groggily, "Hello?"

"Miss Gaither? I didn't wake you, did I? If so, I'm terribly sorry."

Alex shoved hair out of her eyes, licked her dry lips, blinked puffy eyes into focus, and struggled into a sitting position. "No, I was just, uh, doing some, uh, stuff." The nightstand clock said ten o'clock. She'd had no idea she was sleeping that late, but then, it had been almost dawn before she'd gone to bed. "I'm sorry, I'm not sure—"

"Sarah Jo Minton."

She couldn't hold back her exclamation of surprise. She could name at least a hundred people who might call her before Sarah Jo Minton would. "Are you...is everything all right?"

"I'm feeling well, but terribly ashamed for the horrible things I said to you last night."

The confession, spoken so contritely, shocked Alex. "You were understandably upset."

"Would you care to have tea with me this afternoon?"

Maybe she was still asleep, after all, and this was a dream. Nowadays, people said, "Let's do lunch," or "How 'bout a beer?" or "Let's get together for a drink." No one ever said, "Would you care to have tea?"

"That . . . that sounds nice."

"Good. Three o'clock."

"Where?"

"Why, here at the ranch, of course. I'll look forward to seeing you then, Miss Gaither. Good-bye."

Alex stared at the receiver for several seconds before slowly hanging it up. What in the world had prompted Sarah Jo Minton to invite her to tea?

———◆———

Dr. Ely Collins's office was probably the most cluttered room Alex had ever been in. It was clean but disorganized, and as unpretentious as the veterinarian.

"Thank you for agreeing to see me, Dr. Collins."

"No trouble. I was free this afternoon. Come on in. Sit down." He removed a stack of trade journals from the seat of the straight, wooden chair, making it available for Alex. He sat behind a desk cluttered with mountains of paperwork. "I wasn't all that surprised to hear from you," he remarked candidly.

"Why?"

"Pat Chastain called and said you'd probably get around to asking me some questions."

"I thought he was out of town."

"This was a couple of weeks ago, right after you got here."

"I see."

Alex had decided to utilize the hours before her appointment with Sarah Jo by questioning the veterinarian. When she'd phoned, he had readily agreed to see her.

"Are you familiar with the murder of Celina Gaither?" she began, intentionally playing down her personal involvement.

"Sure am. She was a sweet girl. Everybody was sick about it."

"Thank you. It was your father who attended the foaling at the Minton ranch earlier that day, wasn't it?"

"That's right. I took over his practice after he died."

"I'd like some background information. Do you work exclusively for the Mintons?"

"No, I'm not a resident vet. I have a practice. However, I must be honest and tell you that the Mintons give me so much business I could almost work for them exclusively. I'm out there nearly every day."

"It was the same with your father?"

"Yes, but if you're suggesting that I wouldn't rat on the Mintons at the risk of cutting off my meal ticket, you're wrong."

"I didn't mean to imply that."

"This is horse and cattle country. I have to turn down more business than I can accept. I'm an honest man. So was my daddy."

Alex apologized to him a second time, although it had crossed her mind that he might be reluctant to divulge information that would tend to incriminate his well-paying clients.

"Did your father talk to you about Celina's murder?"

"He cried like a baby when he heard that she'd been killed with one of his instruments."

"Dr. Collins positively identified the murder weapon as his scalpel?"

"There was never any question. Mama had given him that set of sterling-silver instruments for their twenty-fifth wedding anniversary. They had his initials engraved on the handles. That scalpel was his, all right. What he couldn't get over is that he'd been careless enough to lose it."

Alex scooted to the edge of her chair. "It would be unlike him to be careless with that scalpel if it was an engraved gift from his wife, wouldn't it?"

He scratched his cheek. "Daddy treasured those things—kept them in a velvet-lined box. I never could figure out how that scalpel fell out of his bag, except that the mare had everyone's attention that day. In all the commotion, I guess it just got jostled out."

"You were there?"

"I figured you already knew that. I'd gone along to observe and assist if Daddy needed me. 'Course, Reede was there, too. He had helped in other births."

"Reede was there?"

"All day."

"Did your father ever leave him alone with his black bag?"

Ely Collins gnawed the inside of his cheek. She could tell he didn't want to answer. "Daddy could have and wouldn't have given it a second thought," he said finally, "but don't get the notion I'm accusing Reede."

"No, of course not. Who else was in the stable that day?"

"Well, now, let's see." He tugged on his lower lip while he thought back. "Just about everybody, at one time or another—Angus, Junior, Reede, all the stable hands and gallop boys."

"Pasty Hickam."

"Sure. Everybody at the ranch was pulling for that mare. Even Stacey Wallace stopped by. As I recall, she'd just gotten back from a trip to the coast."

Everything inside Alex went still. She worked hard at keeping her expression impassive. "Did she stay long?"

"Who, Stacey? No. Said she had to go home and unpack."

"What about Gooney Bud? Was he around?"

"He meandered everywhere. I don't remember seeing him, but that doesn't mean he wasn't there."

"If you didn't see him, weren't you surprised when he turned up with the scalpel covered with Celina's blood?"

"Not really. Daddy hadn't noticed it was missing until they found it on Gooney Bud. We believed what they said—that it had fallen out of Daddy's bag, that Gooney Bud had seen it, picked it up, and killed your mother with it."

"But it's conceivable that someone, in the midst of all the confusion and concern for the mare and her foal, sneaked it out of your father's bag."

"Conceivable, sure."

He admitted it with reluctance because it implicated the men he worked for. Alex remembered how concerned he'd been the night before, over Reede's racehorse. Ely Collins was a friend to all three suspects. Alex had forced him to divide his loyalties between his own integrity and the men who made hand-tooled Lucchese boots affordable. The task was unpalatable, but necessary.

She stood up to leave and extended the doctor her hand. He shook it, and she said good-bye. "Oh, one more thing, Dr. Collins. Would you mind if I looked at the scalpel?"

He was taken aback. "I wouldn't mind at all, if I had it."

"You don't?"

"No."

"Your mother?"

"She never got it back."

"Even after Gooney Bud was incarcerated?"

"She and Daddy didn't press too hard to get it back because of what had happened with it."

"You mean, it's still floating around somewhere?"

"I don't know what happened to it."

The Minton ranch was a beehive of activity. Cleanup crews were sorting through debris and hauling it away. Fire inspectors were picking through the charred lumber and insulation, searching for clues into the origin of the fire.

Around the house, a sandblasting crew was erasing the apocalyptic messages spray-painted on the stone walls. The window openings were being measured for replacement glass.

Reede was in the thick of it, serving in several capacities at once. He was unshaven and unclean; he looked like he'd personally sifted through soot and ash searching for clues. His shirttail was out and unbuttoned; the sleeves had been rolled up. He was hatless, but was wearing leather work gloves.

He spotted Alex as she alighted from her car, but before he could speak, he was summoned by a fire inspector. "You might want to take a look at this, Sheriff."

Reede made an about-face and walked toward barn number two. Alex followed him. "A rock? What the hell does a rock have to do with the fire?" Reede was asking when she approached.

The fireman scratched his head through his Houston

Astros baseball cap. "Looks to me like the fire was an accident. What I mean is, whoever done all this was using something like a slingshot to knock out the windows and such."

"Like David going up against Goliath," Alex murmured. Reede's lips narrowed as he nodded in agreement.

The fireman said, "My guess is that this-here rock went flying, landed in one of the vents on the roof of the stable, and shorted out some of the wiring. That's what caused your fire."

"You don't think it was deliberately set?"

The investigator frowned. "Naw, I can't rightly say it looks that way. If I was gonna start a fire, I'd've pitched a Molotov cocktail or shot a flaming arrow." His frown reversed itself into a silly grin. "I wouldn't've thrown no rock."

Reede bounced the heavy rock in his palm. "Thanks." After the fireman ambled away, Reede said to Alex. "So much for holding Plummet on an arson charge."

Because the day was unseasonably warm, Reede smelled salty and sweaty, but it wasn't an offensive odor. In fact, she liked it. His dense chest hair fanned out over the upper part of his torso and funneled to a narrow line that disappeared into his belt. Up close she could see that perspiration had made it damp and curly. It whorled over the muscles and around his nipples, which the cooling breeze had drawn erect.

Noticing that made her warm inside. She raised her eyes to his face. A bead of sweat trickled from beneath his loose, windblown hair and ran into his eyebrow. She curbed the temptation to catch it on her fingertip. His day-old beard went well with the grime and sweat on his face.

It was an effort for her to keep her mind on business. "Have you arrested Plummet?"

"We tried," he said. "He's vanished."

"His family?"

"They're all at home, looking guilty as hell, but playing dumb about the preacher's whereabouts. I'm not worried about it. He won't go far. We'll run down the roster of his congregation. Somebody's hiding him. He'll surface sooner or later."

"When he does, I'd like to be there when you question him."

He tossed the rock to the ground. "What are you doing here?"

"I came to have tea with Sarah Jo." In response to his incredulous expression, she said, "Her idea, not mine."

"Well, have fun," he said sardonically. He turned his back on her and sauntered toward the barn.

Angus was standing on the porch of the house, feet widespread, overseeing the activity. As she approached, she tried not to let her apprehension show. She wasn't certain how she would be received.

"You're right on time," he said.

So, he knew she was expected. "Hello, Angus."

"Punctuality is a virtue. So's having guts. You've got 'em, little lady." He nodded his approval. "It took guts for you to show your face around here today." He appraised her through squinted eyes. "In that respect, you're a lot like your mama. She was no shrinking violet."

"No?"

He chuckled. "I saw her hold her own with those two hellions—Reede and Junior—many a time."

His chuckles faded into silent smiles of fond remembrance as he contemplated the horizon. "If she'd lived, she'd've become quite a woman." His eyes came back to Alex. "She'd've been like you, I guess. If I'd ever had a daughter, I'd have wanted her to be like you."

Discomfited by the unexpected statement, she said, "I apologize for being even remotely connected to this, Angus." She made a sweeping gesture that encompassed all the damage. "I hope Reede finds whoever did it. I hope they're prosecuted and convicted."

"Yeah, so do I. Most of it I can overlook." He glanced down at the broken window glass on the porch. "But that was a terrible waste of good horseflesh. I hate like hell that Reede lost him. He took pride in saving up enough to buy him."

"He seemed extremely upset," Alex said, turning to watch as Reede went to his truck and spoke into the radio transmitter.

"More like enraged. He's as jealous as a mama bear when it comes to anything that belongs to him. It's understandable, I guess, considering how he grew up. Didn't have a pot to piss in, not even anybody to look out for him. Lived on hand-me-downs and handouts. Once you've been a scavenger in order to survive, I reckon it's a tough habit to break. He's mean and testy 'cause at times his life depended on it."

Junior breezed through the front door then, beaming his famous smile. He was in an inappropriately jovial mood. Unlike Reede and Angus, his clothes were spotless. If he'd ever broken a sweat, one couldn't tell it by looking at him now.

After greeting Alex warmly, he said, "Y'all wouldn't believe the telephone conversation I just had. One of the owners called to check on her mare that's in foal. Bad news travels fast in racehorse circles," he informed Alex.

"Anyway, she had this high, falsetto voice and was saying,

'My poor baby must have been scared out of her wits.' I reassured her that the mare was in another barn, but she kept me on the phone for half an hour, making me swear that her baby and her baby's baby were okay."

He had imitated the woman's warbling, soprano voice. Angus and Alex were laughing. Suddenly, from the corner of her eye, Alex caught Reede watching them. He was standing perfectly still, and, though it was too far away to tell, she was certain he didn't like what he saw. His resentment seemed to ride the airwaves until they struck her with near-palpable force.

"I'd better go inside or I'll be late for tea," she told the men.

Junior laid a hand on her shoulder. "Mother wants to make amends for her outburst last night. She was tickled pink when you accepted her invitation. She's looking forward to seeing you."

Chapter 25

———◈———

Lupe took her coat and led her upstairs. The maid paused outside a door and gave it a soft tap.

"Come in."

Lupe swung the door open, but didn't go in. Taking that as her cue, Alex stepped across the threshold into a room that could have been a movie set. Her remark was spontaneous and genuine. "What a beautiful room!"

"Thank you. I like it." Sarah Jo looked beyond Alex's shoulder. "Close the door, please, Lupe. You know I can't stand that draft, and the racket those workers are making is deplorable. Bring up the tea tray right away."

"Yes, ma'am." The housekeeper withdrew, leaving them alone.

Alex stood near the door, feeling self-conscious in her low-heeled suede boots and long wool skirt. There was nothing wrong with her totally black ensemble, but it seemed glaringly modern and out of place in this ultrafeminine Victorian room, which smelled like a perfumery.

Her hostess looked as right in the setting as a whirling

ballerina in a musical jewelry box. The ruffles along the neckline of her white blouse were duplicated around her slender wrists. She was wearing a soft beige skirt that fanned out around her where she sat on a robin's-egg-blue damask divan near the window. The afternoon sunlight created a halo around her hair.

"Come in and sit down." She motioned toward a dainty chair near her.

Usually poised, Alex felt gauche as she crossed the carpeted floor. "Thank you for inviting me. This was a very good idea."

"It was mandatory that I apologize as soon as possible for what I said to you last night."

"Never mind. It's forgotten." Junior and Angus seemed to have forgiven her for the unwitting role she had played in the act of vandalism. In return, she could be forgiving toward Sarah Jo.

Curious, she took in her surroundings. "This truly is a lovely room. Did you decorate it yourself?"

Sarah Jo offered a laugh as frail as the hand she raised to her throat to fiddle with the ruffles. "My, yes. I wouldn't let one of those dreadful decorators inside my house. Actually, I copied my room back home item by item, as closely as I could. Angus says it's too fussy."

Alex searched discreetly for something masculine, a shred of evidence that a man had been inside the room. There was none. As though reading her mind, Sarah Jo said, "He keeps his things in another room, through there. Alex followed the direction of her gaze to a closed door.

"Come in, Lupe," Sarah Jo said at the housekeeper's soft knock. "Here's our tea."

While Lupe was arranging the silver service on the tea table, Alex asked conversationally, "You mentioned home, Mrs. Minton. Kentucky, right?"

"Yes, horse country. Hunt country. I loved it so."

Her wistful gaze drifted toward the window. The panorama didn't offer much to please the eyes, just miles of dun-colored earth, until it blurred into the horizon. They watched a tumbleweed roll across the stone patio and land in the swimming pool. The landscaping around it was as dead and brown as a cotton field after harvest.

"It's so barren here. I miss the green. Of course, we have acres of irrigated pasture for the horses, but somehow, it's not the same." Her head came back around slowly and she thanked the maid with a nod. Lupe withdrew. "How do you take your tea?"

"Lemon and sugar, please. One lump."

Sarah Jo practiced the ritual that Alex thought had died two generations ago. She did it meticulously. Her pale, translucent hands moved fluidly. Alex realized then why the custom had died in contemporary America. No one would have the time.

"Sandwich? Cucumber and cream cheese."

"Then, by all means," Alex replied with a smile.

Sarah Jo also added two tea cakes to the small plate before passing it to Alex, who had spread a lacy napkin over her lap. "Thank you."

She sipped her tea and pronounced it perfect. The sandwich was only a sliver of crust-trimmed bread, but the filling was cool and creamy. She hoped her stomach wouldn't make a rude noise when it greedily devoured the inadequate portion. She had slept through breakfast; it had seemed superfluous to eat lunch so soon before teatime.

Starting on one of the tea cakes, she asked, "Have you returned to Kentucky often for visits?"

Her hostess prepared her own tea and stirred it idly. "Only twice, for my parents' funerals."

"I didn't mean to bring up a sad topic."

"I have no family left, except for Angus and Junior. Anybody with character learns to live with losses." She replaced her cup and saucer on the table so carefully that the china didn't even clink. Keeping her head lowered, she looked up at Alex from beneath her brows. "Only you haven't, have you?"

Alex returned the uneaten half of the sugar cookie to her plate, knowing intuitively that they had reached the reason behind this invitation to tea. "Haven't what?"

"You haven't learned that it's best to let the dead remain dead."

The lines of battle had been drawn. Alex returned all the tea implements to the silver tray, even the spiderwebby napkin from her lap. "Are you referring to my mother?"

"Precisely. This investigation of yours has upset my entire household, Miss Gaither."

"I apologize for the inconvenience. The circumstances make it unavoidable."

"Thugs vandalized my property, threatening the health and life of every horse we own or board, thereby our livelihood."

"That was an unfortunate incident. I can't tell you how truly sorry I am for it," Alex said, appealing to the woman to understand. "*I* had nothing to do with it. You must believe that."

Sarah Jo drew a deep breath. The ruffles around her neck quivered with suppressed indignation and dislike. Her hostility was so palpable that Alex wondered again what possible reason she had had for inviting her here. The need to apologize had been a ruse. Apparently, Sarah Jo wanted to vent a long-harbored grudge.

"How much do you know about your mother and her relationships with Junior and Reede Lambert?"

"Only what my grandmother told me, coupled with what I've gathered since talking to people here in Purcell."

"They were like a unit," she said, lapsing into a faint, reflective voice, and Alex realized that she had slipped into her own private world. "A little club unto themselves. You rarely saw one without seeing the other two."

"I've noticed that in candid shots in their high school yearbooks. There are lots of pictures of the three of them." Alex had pored over the photographs on those glossy pages, looking for clues, anything, that might benefit her investigation.

"I didn't want Junior to get so deeply involved with them," Sarah Jo was saying. "Reede was a hoodlum, the son of the town drunk, of all things. And your mother...well, there were many reasons why I didn't want him to become attached to her."

"Name one."

"Mainly because of how it was between her and Reede. I knew Junior would always be her second choice. It galled me that she could even exercise a choice. She wasn't worthy of the right to choose," she said bitterly.

"But Junior adored her, no matter what I said. Just as I feared, he fell in love with her." Suddenly, her eyes focused sharply on her guest. "And I have a sick feeling that he'll fall in love with you, too."

"You're wrong."

"Oh, I'm sure you'll see to it that he does. Reede, too, probably. That would round out the triangle again, wouldn't it? Don't you want to pit them against each other, like she did?"

"No!"

Sarah Jo's eyes narrowed with malice. "Your mother was a tramp."

Up to this point, Alex had carefully controlled her tongue. But since her hostess was maligning her late mother, she dismissed her manners. "I take exception to that slanderous remark, Mrs. Minton."

Sarah Jo gave a negligent wave of her hand. "No matter. It's the truth. I knew she was common and coarse the first time I met her. Oh, she was pretty, in a lush, flamboyant way. Much like you."

Her eyes moved over Alex critically. Alex was tempted to get up and walk out. The only thing that kept her sitting in that spindly chair was the hope that Sarah Jo would inadvertently impart some scrap of valuable information.

"Your mother laughed too loud, played too hard, loved too well. Emotions were to her what a bottle of liquor is to a drunkard. She overindulged, and had no control over exhibiting her feelings."

"She sounds very honest," Alex said with pride. "The world might be better off if people openly expressed what they were feeling." Her words fell on deaf ears.

"Whatever a man needed or wanted her to be at the moment," Sarah Jo continued, "she was. Celina was an unconscionable flirt. Every man she met fell in love with her. She made certain of it. She would do anything to guarantee it."

Enough was enough. "I won't let you disparage a woman

who's not around to defend herself. It's ugly and cruel of you, Mrs. Minton." The room, which had been as fresh as a greenhouse when she had come in, now seemed suffocating. She had to get out. "I'm leaving."

"Not yet." Sarah Jo stood up when Alex did. "Celina loved Reede as much as she was capable of loving anyone except herself."

"What concern was that of yours?"

"Because she wanted Junior, too, and she let him know it. Your grandmother, that stupid woman, was giddy over the idea of a match between our children. As if I'd let Junior marry Celina," she sneered. "Merle Graham even called me once and suggested that we, as future in-laws, get together and become better acquainted. God, I would have sooner died! She was a telephone operator," she said, laughing scornfully.

"There was never any chance of Celina Graham becoming my daughter-in-law. I made that quite clear to your grandmother and to Junior. He moped and whined over that girl until I wanted to scream." She raised her small fists, as though she still might do so. "Why couldn't he see her for what she was—a selfish, manipulative little bitch? And now *you.*"

She stepped around the small tea table to confront Alex. Alex was taller, but Sarah Jo had years of cultivated anger to make her strong. Her delicate body was trembling with wrath.

"Lately, all he can talk about is you, just like it used to be with Celina."

"I have not led Junior on, Mrs. Minton. There could never be a romantic entanglement between us. We could be friends, maybe, once this investigation is resolved."

"Don't you see," Sarah Jo cried, "that's exactly how it was with her? She abused his friendship because he was clinging to the vain hope that it would develop into something deeper. All he is to you is a suspect in a murder case. You'll use him, just like your mother did."

"That simply isn't true."

Sarah Jo swayed, as though about to swoon. "Why did you have to come here?"

"I want to know why my mother was murdered."

"You're the reason!" she said, pointing a finger straight at Alex's heart. "Celina's illegitimate baby."

Alex fell back a step, sucking in a sharp, painful breath. "What did you say?" she gasped.

Sarah Jo composed herself. The suffusion of color in her face receded and it returned to its normal porcelain hue. "You were illegitimate."

"That's a lie," Alex denied breathlessly. "My mother was married to Al Gaither. I've seen the marriage license. Grandma Graham saved it."

"They were married, but not until after she came back from El Paso and discovered she was pregnant."

"You're a liar!" Alex gripped the back of the chair. "Why are you lying to me?"

"It's not a lie. The reason I'm telling you should be clear. I'm trying to protect my family from your vengeful destruction. Being the richest woman in this horrid, ugly little town is the only thing that makes it tolerable. I like being married to the most influential man in the county. I won't let you destroy everything Angus has created for me. I won't let you cause dissent in my family. Celina did. This time, I won't allow it."

"Ladies, ladies." Junior came into the room, laughing indulgently. "What is all the shouting about? See a spider?"

His manner changed drastically when he sensed the seething animosity between them. It was sulfuric, as real as the ozone in the air after lightning has struck nearby. "Mother? Alex? What's wrong?"

Alex stared at Sarah Jo, whose face was as serene and complacent as a cameo. Alex spun toward the door, sending the small chair toppling over. She rushed from the room and clambered down the stairs.

Junior gave his mother a searching look. She turned her back on him and returned to the divan, picked up her teacup, and took a sip.

Junior raced down the stairs after Alex and caught up with her at the front door, where she was unsuccessfully trying to work her arms into the sleeves of her coat.

He grabbed her upper arms. "What the hell is going on?"

Alex averted her head so he wouldn't see her tears. She tried to disengage his hands. "Nothing."

"You hardly look like you've been to a tea party."

"Tea, ha!" Alex said, tossing back her head. "She didn't invite me out here to drink tea." She sniffed and batted her eyes in an effort to keep the tears from falling. "I guess I should thank her for telling me."

"Telling you what?"

"That I was a biological accident." Junior's face went blank with shock. "It's true, then, isn't it?" Junior's hands fell away from her arms and he tried to turn away. Reversing their positions, Alex gripped his arm and forced him back around. "Isn't it?" Her tears finally overflowed her eyelids. "Say something, Junior!"

He looked uncomfortable with admitting the truth. It was Alex who verbally pieced together the scenario.

"Celina came back from El Paso. She'd had her fling with a soldier and was ready to reconcile with Reede. They probably would have, too, if it hadn't been for me, right?" She covered her face with her hands. "Oh, God, no wonder he hates me so much."

Junior pulled her hands away from her face and looked at her with sincere blue eyes. "Reede doesn't hate you, Alex. None of us did then, or do now."

She laughed shortly, bitterly. "I'll bet Albert Gaither hated the very thought of me. He was forced to get married." Her eyes went round, and she spoke in a rapid, short-winded, staccato voice. "This explains so much. So *much*. Why Grandma Graham was strict about my dating—who I went with, what time I got home, where I'd been.

"I resented her for being so inflexible because I'd never given her any reason to mistrust me. I guess her overprotectiveness was justified, wasn't it?" Her voice rose to a near-hysterical pitch. "Her daughter got knocked up, and twenty-five years ago, that was still a definite sin."

"Alex, stop this."

"That explains why Grandma never really loved me. I ruined Celina's life, and she never forgave me for it. Celina couldn't have Reede, couldn't have you, couldn't have a future. And all because of me. Oh, God!"

The curse, or prayer, was cried in a wailing voice. Alex turned away from him and yanked the door open. She ran across the porch and down the steps toward her car.

"Alex!" He started after her.

"What the hell's going on?" Angus demanded as Alex rushed past him toward her car.

"Leave her alone, you two." Sarah Jo was standing at the top of the stairs, where she had watched and overheard everything.

Junior spun around. "Mother, how could you? How could you hurt Alex that way?"

"I didn't tell her to hurt her."

"What'd you tell her?" Angus asked. He filled up the open doorway, baffled and impatient because no one was answering his questions.

"Of course it hurt her," Junior said. "You knew it would. Why tell her at all?"

"Because she needed to know. The only one who can hurt Alex is Alex herself. She's chasing an illusion. The mother she's looking for didn't exist in Celina Gaither. Merle filled her head with a lot of nonsense about how wonderful Celina was. She forgot to tell the girl how devious her mother was. It was time Alex found out."

"Shit!" Angus cursed. "Will somebody please tell me what the hell is going on?"

Chapter 26

Angus quietly closed the bedroom door behind him as he came in. Sarah Jo, propped against the pillows on their bed, laid her book aside and peered at him over the rims of the glasses that were perched on the tip of her nose. "Coming to bed so early?"

She looked about as harmful as a butterfly, but Angus knew that her frail appearance camouflaged an iron will. If she ever gave ground it was out of indifference, not defeat. "I want to talk to you."

"About what?"

"About what happened this afternoon."

She pressed her fingers to her temples. "It gave me quite a headache. That's why I didn't come down to dinner."

"Taken anything?"

"Yes. It's better now."

They had repeated this same exchange regarding her headaches nearly every day of their marriage.

"Don't sit on the bedspread," she scolded as he lowered himself to the edge of the bed. He waited until she had folded back the quilted satin spread, then sat down close to her hip. "My, you look so downcast tonight, Angus," she said with concern. "What's the matter? Not more maniacs on our property, I hope."

"No."

"Thank God the only horse that was injured belonged to Reede."

Angus let that pass without comment. Sarah Jo resented Reede, and Angus knew why. Her feelings toward him would never change, so berating her for the uncharitable remark would serve no purpose.

What he had come to discuss was a delicate subject. He took a moment to choose his words carefully. "Sarah Jo, about this afternoon—"

"I was quite upset by it," she said, drawing her lips into a pretty frown.

"*You* were upset?" Angus forcibly tamped down his impatience. He needed to hear her side of the story before jumping to conclusions. "What about Alex's feelings?"

"She was upset, too, naturally. Wouldn't you be if you'd found out you were a bastard?"

"No," he said with a gruff, humorless laugh. "Wouldn't surprise me if I was. I never checked to see if my parents had a marriage license, and it wouldn't have mattered to me if they didn't." His brows drew together. "But I'm an ornery old cuss, and Alex is a sensitive young woman."

"I felt that she was strong enough to take it."

"Obviously, she wasn't. She ran past me without even seeing me. She was practically in hysterics when she left."

Sarah Jo's smile crumpled. "Are you blaming me for telling her? Do you think it was wrong?"

When she looked up at him with that apprehensive, little-lost-girl look, his heart melted. It always had. Angus took her hand. He could have crushed it like a flower between his rough palms, but he had learned over the years not to exert too much pressure when he caressed her.

"I'm not blaming you for telling her, honey. I'm just questioning the wisdom of it. I wish you had discussed it with Junior and me before you did. It was something she could have gone throughout her life not knowing."

"I disagree," Sarah Jo argued petulantly.

"What difference does it make now if her mama and daddy weren't married until after she was in the oven? Hell, that's so commonplace now it's not even considered a sin anymore."

"It makes a difference in the way she views Celina. Up until now, she's had her on a pedestal."

"So what?"

"Celina hardly deserves a pedestal," Sarah Jo snapped. "I thought it was time everybody stopped pussyfooting around with Alex and set her straight about her mother."

"Why?"

"*Why?* Because she's trying to ruin us, that's why. I decided to stop catering to her and to fight back. I used the only ammunition I had." As usual, during scenes like this, Sarah Jo became overwrought. "I was only trying to protect you and Junior."

Actually, Angus thought, it had taken a tremendous amount of courage for Sarah Jo to confront a self-assured woman like Alex. He still thought Sarah Jo could have refrained from telling Alex about her folks, but her motive had been unselfish. She'd been protecting her family. Her valiant effort deserved better than his criticism. He leaned down and kissed her forehead.

"I appreciate your fighting spirit, but none of us needs your protection, honey." He laughed at the thought. "How could a little thing like you protect one of us big, strapping boys? I've got plenty of money and plenty of know-how to handle any little problem that crops up. A redhead that only stands five feet six inches tall is hardly worth a second's worry."

"If you could resurrect that odious Pasty Hickam, I'm sure he would disagree," she said. "Look what happened to him. Unlike you and Junior, and obviously, every other man, I'm immune to the girl's charms." Her voice developed an edge of desperation. "Angus, can't you see it? Junior is falling in love with her."

"I fail to see why that's so god-awful," he said with a beam-ing smile.

"It would be a disaster," Sarah Jo cried softly. "Her mother broke his heart. Don't you care about that?"

Frowning, Angus reminded her, "That was a long time ago. And Alex isn't like her mother."

"I'm not so sure." Sarah Jo stared into space.

"Alex isn't fickle and flighty like Celina was," he said. "She's a tad too bossy, but maybe Junior needs that. He walked all over his other wives, and they laid down and let him do it. Maybe he needs a wife who'll tell him what's what."

"Where is he, by the way? Is he still angry with me?" she asked anxiously.

"He was upset, but he'll get over it, like he always does. He said he was going out to get drunk."

They laughed together. Sarah Jo was the first to turn serious again. "I hope he'll drive safely."

"He, uh, will probably be spending the night out."

"Oh?"

"Wouldn't surprise me," Angus said. "Alex needs some time to sort herself out. Junior might be carrying a torch, but he's not dead from the waist down. He'll find a woman who'll give him the comfort he needs tonight."

His gaze lowered to his wife's décolletage, which was smooth and luminescent with the body powder she had used after her bath. "He's got a man's appetites, just like his daddy."

"Oh, Angus," she sighed wearily, as his hand waded through layers of lace in search of her breast.

"I could use some comforting myself."

"You men! Is that all you ever think about? You make me—"

"You make me horny."

"Don't use that kind of language. It's crude. And I don't want to do this tonight. My headache's coming back."

His kiss cut off any further objections. She submitted, as he knew she would. She always put up token resistance, but she never refused him. From the cradle, she had been coached to accept her marital duties, just as she had to properly serve tea.

That she responded to him out of a sense of obligation rather than passion didn't stop him from wanting her; it might even have enhanced his desire. Angus enjoyed a challenge.

He undressed quickly and lowered himself on top of her. He fumbled with the buttons on her gown and finally managed, with no assistance from her, to get it open. Her breasts were as pert and shapely as they had been on their wedding night, when he had first beheld and touched them.

He kissed them now with polite restraint. Her nipples were small. His stroking tongue was rarely successful in coaxing them erect. He doubted she knew they were supposed to get erect, unless some of those novels she read were more sexually explicit than he suspected.

She winced slightly when he entered her. He pretended not to see her grimace. He tried not to sweat or make a sound or do anything that she would consider nasty and unpleasant.

He saved all his raunchiness for the widow lady he supported in the neighboring county. She didn't mind his crude language. In fact, she hooted with laughter over some of his more colorful expressions.

She was as lusty a lover as he. She had large, dark, milky-tasting nipples that she would let him diddle with for hours if he wanted to. She even went down on him and let him go down on her. Each time he mounted her, her round thighs gripped his ass like a vise. She was a noisy comer, and the only woman he'd ever met who could laugh in downright joy while she was screwing.

They'd been together for over twenty years. She never asked for more of a commitment; she didn't expect one. They had a damn good time together, and he didn't know what he would do without her in his life, but he didn't love her.

He loved Sarah Jo. Or, at least, he loved what she was: dainty and pure and refined and beautiful. He loved her as an art collector would love a sculpture or priceless alabaster that was to be touched only on special occasions, and then with the utmost care.

Because she demanded it, he always wore a condom, and when he was done, he removed it carefully so her silk sheets wouldn't get soiled. While he was doing so tonight, he watched Sarah Jo fold down the hem of her nightgown, rebutton the buttons, and straighten the covers.

Angus got back in bed, kissed her cheek, and put his arms around her. He loved holding her tiny body against his, loved touching her smooth, fragrant skin. He wanted to cherish her. To his disappointment, she removed his arm and said, "Go on to sleep now, Angus. I want to finish this chapter."

She reopened her novel, which was no doubt as dry and lifeless as her lovemaking. Angus was ashamed of the disloyal thought as he rolled to his other side, away from the light of her reading lamp.

It never occurred to him to be ashamed of making the thirty-mile trip to his mistress's house, which he planned to do tomorrow night.

———◆———

Stacey dropped the ceramic mug. It crashed and broke on the tile kitchen floor. "Good Lord," she breathed, clutching together the lapels of her velour robe.

"Stacey, it's me."

The first knock on the back door had startled her so badly the mug had slipped from her hand. The voice speaking her name did nothing to restore her heart to its proper beat. For several moments she stood staring at the door, then rushed across the kitchen and pushed back the stiff, starched curtain.

"Junior?!"

She didn't have sufficient air to say his name aloud. Her

lips formed it soundlessly. Fumbling with the lock, she hastily unlatched the door and pulled it open, as though afraid he would vanish before she could do it.

"Hi." His smile was uncomplicated and open, as if he knocked on her back door every night about this time. "Did I hear something break?"

She reached up to touch his face and reassure herself he was really there, then shyly dropped her hand. "What are you doing here?"

"I came to see you."

She glanced past him, searching her backyard for a plausible reason for her ex-husband to be standing on the steps.

He laughed. "I've come alone. I just didn't want to ring the bell, in case the judge had already gone to bed."

"He has. He…uh, come in." Remembering her manners, she moved aside. Junior stepped in. They stood facing each other in the harsh kitchen light, which wasn't very flattering to Stacey, who had already cleaned her face and prepared for bed.

She had fantasized about him coming to her one night, but now that it had happened, she was immobilized and rendered mute by disbelief. Myriad professions of love and devotion rushed through her mind, but she knew he wouldn't welcome hearing them. She resorted to safe subjects.

"Dad went to bed early. His stomach was upset. I made him some warm milk. I decided to make cocoa out of what I had left over." Unable to take her eyes off him, she gestured nervously toward the stove, where the milk was about to scorch in the pan.

Junior went to the range and turned off the burner. "Cocoa, huh? Your cocoa? There's none better. Got enough for two cups?"

"Of... of course. You mean you're staying?"

"For a while. If you'll have me."

"Yes," she said with a rush of air. "Yes."

Usually adept in the kitchen, Stacey clumsily prepared two cups of cocoa. She couldn't imagine why he'd chosen tonight to come see her. She didn't care. It was enough that he was here.

When she handed him his cocoa, he smiled disarmingly and asked, "Do you have any spirits in the house?"

He followed her into the living room, where several bottles of liquor were stored in a cabinet, to be taken out only on the most special occasions.

"This isn't your first drink of the night, is it?" she asked as she tilted the spout of the brandy bottle against his mug of chocolate.

"No, it isn't." Lowering his voice, he whispered, "I smoked a joint, too."

Her lips pursed with stern disapproval. "You know how I feel about dope, Junior."

"Marijuana isn't *dope*."

"It is so."

"Ah, Stacey," he whined, bending down to kiss her ear. "An ex-wife has no right to scold."

The touch of his lips made her insides flutter. Her censure melted as quickly as ice cream in August. "I didn't mean to scold. I just wondered why, after all this time, you came to me tonight."

"I wanted to." She knew that to Junior's mind, that was reason enough. He sprawled on the sofa and pulled her down beside him. "No, leave the lamp off," he told her when she reached for the switch. "Let's just sit here and drink our cocoa together."

"I heard about the trouble out at the ranch," she said after a quiet moment.

"It's all cleaned up now. Can't tell it ever happened. It could have been a lot worse."

She touched him hesitantly. "You could have been hurt."

He set his empty cup on the coffee table and sighed. "You're still concerned for my safety?"

"Always."

"No one's ever been as sweet to me as you, Stacey. I've missed you." He reached for her hand and pressed it between his.

"You look worn out and troubled."

"I am."

"Over the vandalism?"

"No." He slumped deeper into the cushions of the couch and rested his head on the back of it. "This mess we're in about Celina's murder. It's depressing as hell." He tilted his head until it was lying on her shoulder. "Hmm, you smell good. It's a smell I've missed. So clean." He nuzzled her neck.

"What bothers you so much about this investigation?"

"Nothing specific. It's Alex. She and Mother had a row today. Mother let it slip that Celina got knocked up and had to get married to her soldier. It wasn't a pretty scene."

His arm slid around her waist. Automatically, Stacey lifted her hands to cradle his cheek and pressed his head against her breasts.

"I lied to her," she confessed in a small voice. "A lie of omission."

Junior mumbled with disinterest.

"I never told her I was in the barn the day Celina was killed."

"How come you did that?"

"I didn't want her hounding me with questions. I hate her for causing you trouble again, Junior."

"Alex can't help it. It's not her fault."

It was a familiar refrain, one that set Stacey's teeth on edge. Junior had often said the same thing about Celina. No matter how shabbily she treated him, he had never spoken a harsh, critical word against her.

"I hate this girl of Celina's as much as I did her," Stacey whispered.

The alcohol and strong Mexican grass had dulled Junior's thinking. "Never mind all that now. This feels good, doesn't it?" he murmured as his lips followed his hand inside her robe to her breast. His damp tongue glanced her nipple. "You always liked for me to do that."

"I still do."

"Really? And this? Do you still like this?" he asked, sucking her nipple into his mouth and pushing his hand into the furry, damp warmth between her thighs.

She groaned his name.

"I'll understand if you don't want me to." He pulled away slightly.

"No," she said quickly, guiding his head back down and clenching her thighs closed around his hand. "I do want you to. Please."

"Stacey, Stacey, your tender loving care is just what I need tonight. I could always count on you to make me feel better." He raised his head from her breast and gave her mouth a long, slow, thorough kiss. "Remember what always made me feel better than anything?" he asked, his lips resting on hers.

"Yes." She looked up at him solemnly. He smiled as beatifically as an angel. When he looked at her that way, she couldn't deny him anything—not when they were teenagers, not when they were married, not now, not ever.

Stacey Wallace Minton, the judge's proper, straitlaced daughter, immediately dropped to her knees in front of him, hastily opened his fly, and took him into her hungry mouth.

"Miz Gaither, ma'am? Miz Gaither? You in there?"

Alex had been dozing. Roused by the knocking on her door, which had been repaired, she woke up to find that she was sprawled on top of the bedspread, stiff and cold. Her eyes were swollen from crying.

"What do you want?" Her voice amounted to little more than a croak. "Go away."

"Is your phone off the hook, ma'am?"

"Damn." She swung her feet to the side of the bed. Her clothes were wrinkled and bunched around her. She shook them back into place as she walked to the window and pulled aside the drape. The motel's night clerk was standing at the door.

"I took the phone off the hook so I wouldn't be disturbed," she told him through the window.

He peered in at her, obviously glad to see that she was still alive. "Sorry to bother you then, ma'am, but there's this guy trying to get in touch with you. He's been arguin' with me, saying you couldn't be talking on your phone for this long."

"What guy?"

"Happer or Harris or something," he mumbled, consulting the slip of paper he'd brought with him. He held it closer to the light over her door. "Can't quite make out my writin' here…spellin' ain't so good."

"Harper? Greg Harper?"

"I reckon that's it, yes, ma'am."

Alex dropped the drape back into place, slid the chain lock free, and opened the door. "Did he say what he wanted?"

"Sure did. Said for me to tell you that you was to be in Austin tomorrow morning for a ten o'clock meeting."

Alex stared at the clerk, stupefied. "You must have gotten the message wrong. Ten o'clock tomorrow morning?"

"That's what he said, and I didn't git it wrong, 'cause I wrote it down right here." He showed her the slip of paper with the message scrawled in pencil. "The man's been callin' you all afternoon and was p.o.'d 'cause he couldn't git you. Finally, he said he was goin' out for the evenin' and for me to come to your room and hand-deliver the message, which I done. So, good night."

"Wait!"

"Look, I'm s'posed to be tending the switchboard."

"Did he say what kind of meeting this was, why it was so urgent?"

"Naw, only that you're s'posed to be there."

He stood there expectantly. With mumbled thanks, she pressed a dollar bill into his hand, and he loped off in the direction of the lobby.

Thoughtfully, Alex closed her door and reread the message. It made no sense. It wasn't like Greg to be so cryptic. It wasn't like him to call meetings that were virtually impossible to make, either.

When the bafflement began to wear off, the enormity of her dilemma set in. She had to be in Austin by ten o'clock in the morning. It was already dark. If she left now, she would have to drive most of the night, and would arrive in Austin in the wee hours.

If she waited until morning, she would have to leave dreadfully early and then be on a deadline to get there in time. Either choice was wretched, and she wasn't mentally or emotionally fit to make a decision.

Then, an idea occurred to her. Before she could talk herself out of it, she placed a telephone call.

"Sheriff's department."

"Sheriff Lambert, please."

"He's not here. Can anybody else help?"

"No, thank you. I need to speak with him personally."

"Excuse me, ma'am, but is this Ms. Gaither?"

"Yes, it is."

"Where are you?"

"In my motel room. Why?"

"That's where Reede's headed. He should be there by now." Then he paused and asked, "Say, are you all right?"

"Of course I'm all right. I think I hear the sheriff pulling up now. Thank you." Alex hung up and moved to the window in time to see Reede get out of his truck and rush toward her door.

She flung it open. He drew up abruptly, almost losing his balance. "Please don't kick it in again."

"Don't be cute with me," he said, glowering darkly. "What the hell is going on?"

"Nothing."

"Like hell." He gestured toward the bedside telephone. Its innocence seemed to provoke him further. He pointed toward it accusingly. "I've been calling for hours, and all I got is a busy signal."

"I took it off the hook. What was so important?"

"I heard what happened this afternoon between you and Sarah Jo."

Her shoulders dropped dejectedly and she released a long breath. She had almost forgotten about that in her perplexity over Greg's summons.

She had never checked the date on her parents' marriage license. It wouldn't necessarily be conclusive, anyway. As an attorney, she knew that dates, even on so-called legal documents, could be falsified. The way everyone had reacted to Sarah Jo's revelation, she knew it was true. She had been conceived illegitimately.

"You should have been there, Sheriff. I made a spectacle of myself. You would have been thoroughly entertained."

Her flippancy didn't improve his mood. "Why'd you take your phone off the hook?"

"To get some rest. What did you think, that I took an overdose of sleeping pills or gave my wrists a close shave?"

He gave the sarcastic question credence. "Maybe."

"Then, you don't know me very well," she told him angrily. "I don't give in that easily. And I'm not ashamed that my parents had to get married."

"I didn't say you were or that you should be."

"That was their mistake. It has nothing to do with me as a person, okay?"

"Okay."

"So stop thinking…Oh, hell, I don't care what you're thinking," she said, rubbing her temples. She was more annoyed with herself than with him. Lashing out was only an indication of how upset she really was. "I need your help, Reede."

"What kind of help?"

"Can you fly me to Austin?"

The request took him by surprise. He pulled himself upright from where he had complacently slouched against the framework of the recently repaired doorway.

"Fly you to Austin? Why?"

"Business with Greg Harper. I need to be there at ten o'clock in the morning for a meeting."

Chapter 27

They were in the air less than an hour later, on a south-easterly course toward the state capital. Alex had used a quarter of that hour to get herself looking human again. She had washed her face in cold water, applied fresh makeup, brushed her hair, and changed into a pair of wool slacks and a sweater. Whatever she wore to the meeting in the morning could come out of her closet at home.

On the way to Purcell's municipal airfield, Reede stopped at a hamburger joint and picked up the order he'd phoned ahead for. There was a single-engine Cessna waiting for them on the tarmac when they arrived at the landing strip. The sheriff knew how to pull strings.

Purcell was no more than a patch of glittering light on the black carpet beneath them before she thought to ask, "Does this plane belong to you?"

"Minton Enterprises. Angus gave me permission to use it. Pass me one of those cheeseburgers."

She devoured almost half of hers—Sarah Jo's cucumber

sandwich hadn't gone far—before she came up for air. "When did you learn to fly?"

Reede munched a french fry. "I was about eight."

"Eight!"

"I had salvaged an old beat-up bike from a junkyard and repaired it well enough to get around on. I pedaled out to the airfield every chance I got."

"It must be three miles from town," she exclaimed.

"I didn't care. I'd have gone twice that far. The planes intrigued me. The old guy who ran the place was as testy as a rattlesnake, a real loner, but he kept a strawberry soda pop waiting for me in his ancient icebox. I guess I pestered the snot out of him, but he didn't seem to mind all my questions. One day, he looked over at me and said, 'I gotta check out this plane. Wanna go along for the ride?' I nearly peed my pants."

Reede probably didn't realize that he was smiling over the happy memory. Alex remained silent so he wouldn't be reminded that she was there. She enjoyed his smile. It attractively emphasized the fine lines at the outer corners of his eyes and those around his mouth.

"God, it was great," he said, as though he could feel the surge of pleasure again. "I hadn't discovered sex yet, so flying was the best thing that had happened to me. From up there, everything looked so peaceful, so clean."

An escape from the awful realities of his childhood, Alex thought compassionately. She wanted to touch him, but didn't dare. She was about to venture down a rocky, hazardous path. One wrong word or turn of phrase would spell doom, so she felt her way carefully.

Quietly, she asked, "Reede, why didn't you tell me that my mother was pregnant when she came back from El Paso?"

"Because it doesn't make any difference."

"Not now, but it did twenty-five years ago. She didn't want to marry my father. She had to."

"Now that you know, what does it change? Not a god-damn thing."

"Perhaps," she replied uncertainly. After another brief silence, she said, "I was the quarrel, wasn't I?"

He looked at her sharply. "What?"

Letting her head fall back on the headrest, she sighed. "I wondered why the two of you didn't kiss and make up when she got back that summer. Knowing how much and how long you had cared for each other, I wondered what could possibly keep you apart after a silly lovers' spat. Now, I know. It wasn't silly. It was more than a spat. It was me. I kept you apart. I was the quarrel."

"It wasn't you."

"It was."

Grandma Graham had said it was her fault that Celina had been killed. Everything Alex uncovered was bearing that out. Had Celina, by having another man's child, driven her passionate, jealous, possessive lover to kill her?

"Reede, did you murder my mother because of me?"

"Damn," he swore viciously. "I could strangle Sarah Jo for telling you about that. My quarrel with Celina wasn't over you—not originally, anyway."

"Then, what?"

"Sex!" Swiveling his head around, he glared at her. "Okay?"

"Sex?"

"Yeah, sex."

"You were pressuring her to and she wouldn't?"

His jaw tensed. "It was the other way around, Counselor."

"*What?*" Alex exclaimed. "You expect me to believe—"

"I don't give a rat's ass what you believe. It's the truth. Celina wanted to get a head start on our future, and I wouldn't."

"Next, you're going to tell me that you had an unselfish, noble reason," Alex said, tongue-in-cheek. "Right?"

"My own parents," he said without inflection. "My old man got my mother pregnant when she was barely fifteen. They had to get married. Look how great that turned out. I wouldn't take a chance on the same thing happening to Celina and me."

Alex's heart was thudding with gladness, disbelief, and emotions that were too complex to examine. "You mean that you never—"

"No. We never."

She believed him. There was no mendacity in his expression, only bitterness, and perhaps a trace of regret. "Hadn't you heard of birth control?"

"I used rubbers with other girls, but—"

"So there were others?"

"I'm not a monk, for crissake. The Gail sisters," he said with a shrug, "lots of others. There were always willing girls available."

"Especially to you." He shot her a hard look. "Why weren't you concerned that you'd impregnate one of them?"

"They all slept around. I would be one of many."

"But Celina would have slept only with you."

"That's right."

"Until she went to El Paso and met Al Gaither," Alex mused out loud. "He was just a means to make you jealous, wasn't he?" On a humorless laugh, she added, "She overshot her mark and manufactured me."

They lapsed into silence. Alex didn't even notice. She was lost in her turbulent thoughts about her mother, Reede, and their unconsummated love affair.

"It's really beautiful up here at night, isn't it?" she said dreamily, unaware that almost half an hour had passed since they had last spoken.

"I thought you'd fallen asleep."

"No." She watched a bank of clouds drift between them and the moon. "Did you ever take my mother flying?"

"A few times."

"At night?"

He hesitated. "Once."

"Did she like it?"

"She was scared, as I recall."

"They gave her hell, didn't they?"

"Who?"

"Everybody. When word got out that Celina Graham was pregnant, I'll bet the gossip spread like wildfire."

"You know how it is in a small town."

"I kept her from graduating high school."

"Look, Alex, you didn't keep her from doing anything," he argued angrily. "All right, she made a mistake. She got too hot with a soldier boy, or he took advantage of her. However the hell it happened, it happened."

With the edge of his hand, he chopped the air between them in a gesture of finality. "You didn't have anything to do with the act or the consequences of it. You said so yourself, just a few hours ago. Remember?"

"I'm not condemning my mother or stigmatizing myself, Reede. I feel sorry for her. She couldn't attend school, even though she was legally married."

Alex wrapped her arms around her sides, giving herself a huge hug. "I think she was a very special lady. She could have given me up for adoption, but she didn't. Even after my father was killed, she kept me with her. She loved me and was willing to make tremendous sacrifices for me.

"She had the courage to carry me in a town where everybody was talking about her. Don't bother denying it. I know they did. She was popular; she fell from grace. Anyone harboring malice toward her was delighted. That's human nature."

"If they were, they didn't dare show it."

"Because you were still her knight, weren't you?"

"Junior and me."

"You closed ranks around her."

"I guess you could put it like that."

"Your friendship probably meant more to her then than at any other time." He gave a noncommittal lift of his shoulders.

She studied his profile for a moment. The rocky path had led her to the cliff, and she was about to take the plunge. "Reede, if Celina hadn't died, would you have gotten married?"

"No."

He answered without a second's hesitation. Alex was surprised. She didn't quite believe him. "Why not?"

"Lots of reasons, but essentially, because of Junior."

She hadn't expected that. "What about him?"

"While Celina was pregnant, they became very close. He just about had her talked into marrying him when she... died."

"Do you think she would have, eventually?"

"I don't know." He slid Alex a sardonic glance. "Junior's quite a ladies' man. He can be very persuasive."

"Look, Reede, I told Sarah Jo, now I'm telling you, that—"

"Shh! They're passing us off to Austin radar." He spoke into the headset. When the formalities had been dispensed with, he coaxed someone in the airport tower to arrange a rental car for him. By the time he had gone through that procedure, they were approaching the lighted runway. "Buckled up?"

"Yes."

He executed a flawless landing. Alex thought later that she must have been in a daze, because she barely remembered getting from the plane to the rented car. Without having to concentrate, she gave Reede directions to her condo.

It was located in a fashionable, yuppie neighborhood where Evian was the drink of preference, every kitchen had a wok, and membership in a health club was as mandatory as a driver's license.

A line of thunderstorms hadn't hampered their flight, but had moved in over the city by the time they reached her street. Raindrops began to splatter the windshield. Thunder rumbled.

"The one with all the newspapers scattered in the yard," Alex told him.

"You're a public prosecutor. Don't you know better than to

advertise to thieves that you're out of town? Or is that your way of drumming up business?"

"I forgot to stop delivery."

He pulled to the curb, but he didn't turn off the motor. Several days ago, Alex would have been jubilant at the thought of returning home, just for a temporary respite from the Westerner Motel, but as she looked at the front door now, she felt no enthusiasm for going inside. The tears that clouded her vision weren't tears of joy.

"I've been gone for almost three weeks."

"Then I'd better walk up with you." He turned off the ignition and got out, impervious to the rain. He walked with her up the sidewalk, picking up the outdated newspapers as he went. He tossed them into a corner of her covered porch as she unlocked the door. "Don't forget to throw those papers away tomorrow," he said.

"No, I won't." She reached inside and cut off her alarm system, which had begun to hum the moment she opened the door. "I guess that means it's safe inside."

"Do you want to meet at the airport tomorrow, or what?"

"Uh…" She couldn't think beyond him driving away, leaving her alone in her condo. "I hadn't thought about it."

"I'll drop by the D.A.'s office around noon and ask for you. How's that?"

"Fine. I should be finished by then."

"Okay, see ya." He turned to leave.

"Reede." Instinctively she reached for him, but when he turned, she pulled her hand back. "Would you like some coffee before you go?"

"No, thanks."

"Where are you going now?"

"I won't know till I get there."

"What did you have in mind?"

"Messing around."

"Oh, well..."

"You'd better get inside."

"I haven't paid you yet."

"For what?"

"The plane, your time."

"No charge."

"I insist."

He cursed. "The one thing I'm not going to argue with you about is money. Got that? Now, good night."

He turned and took two long strides before she called his name again. When he came back around, his eyes bore into hers. "I don't want to be alone tonight," she admitted in a rush. Even with all the crying she'd done that afternoon, her supply of tears hadn't been exhausted. They began to roll down her cheeks as steadily as the rainfall. "Please don't go, Reede. Stay with me."

He moved back beneath the overhang, but his hair and shoulders were already damp. Placing his hands on his hips, he demanded, "Why?"

"I just told you why."

"You've got to have a better reason than that, or you wouldn't have asked."

"All right," she shouted at him, "I feel like crap. Is that reason enough?"

"No."

"I'm hurting for what my mother must have suffered for my sake," she said, making a swipe at her leaking eyes.

"I'm no doctor."

"I need to be held."

"Sorry. I've got other plans."

"Don't you care that I'm appealing to you for help?"

"Not really."

She hated him for making her beg. Nevertheless, she threw down the last vestiges of her pride and said, "My Grandma Graham died resenting me for ruining Celina's life. She wanted her to marry Junior, and blamed my untimely birth when that didn't happen. Now, dammit," she said, "I need to know that you don't despise me, too.

"Can you imagine how terrible I feel, knowing that I'm the reason my mother married another man when she loved you? If it hadn't been for me, you could have married her, had children, loved each other for the rest of your lives. Reede, please stay with me tonight."

He closed the distance between them, backed her into the wall, and gave her a hard shake. "You want me to hold you and tell you that everything is okay, and that the sun will come out tomorrow and things will look better?"

"Yes!"

"Well, for your information, Counselor, I don't do bed-time stories. When I spend the night with a woman, it's not because I want to comfort her if she's hurting, or cheer her up if she's sad." He took a step closer. His eyes narrowed until they were mere slits. "And it's for damn sure not because I want to play *daddy*."

Chapter 28

———◦◦◦———

Gregory Harper, district attorney of Travis County, Texas, was clearly furious. He was on his third cigarette in five minutes. His anger was directed toward his assistant, who was seated on the other side of his desk, looking like she'd been socked hard in both eyes.

"Who've you been sleeping with, Dracula? You look like you've been sucked dry," Greg remarked with characteristic abrasiveness.

"Could we stick to one crushing blow at a time, please? Don't confuse the issue."

"Crushing blow? Oh, you mean the part where I told you that your investigation is over and done with and you're to return to Austin pronto, posthaste, lickety-split, do not pass go, do not collect two hundred dollars, haul ass?"

"Yes, that crushing blow." Alex flattened her hands on the edge of his desk. "Greg, you can't ask me to drop it now."

"I'm not asking—I'm telling." He left his swivel chair and moved to the window. "What the *fuck* have you been doing out there, Alex? The governor called me yesterday, and he was pissed. I mean p-i-s-s-e-d."

"He's always pissed at you."

"That's beside the point."

"Hardly. Greg, everything you do is politically motivated. Don't pretend it isn't. I don't blame you for it, but don't play Mr. Clean with me just because your hand got slapped."

"The governor thinks his racing commission can do no wrong. To admit that the commission made a mistake in selecting Minton Enterprises for a license is tantamount to the governor admitting that he made an error in judgment, too."

"Minton Enterprises is above reproach, as far as the horse-racing business goes."

"Oh, I see. The only hitch is that you suspect one of the Mintons is a murderer, or if not them, a peace officer. Gee, for a minute there, I thought we had a problem."

"You don't have to get sarcastic."

He rubbed the back of his neck. "To hear the governor yesterday, Angus Minton is a cross between the tooth fairy and Buffalo Bill Cody."

Alex smiled at the analogy, which was uncannily accurate. "That's a fair assessment, but that doesn't mean he's incapable of killing someone."

"What happened to his barn the other night?"

"How'd you know about that?"

"Just tell me what happened."

Reluctantly, she told him about Fergus Plummet and the vandalism done to the Minton ranch. When she was finished, Greg ran a hand down his face. "You've upset a real big applecart, full of shiny, bright apples." He selected another cigarette and spoke around it. It bobbed up and down with each word, making lighting it difficult. "I didn't like this case to start with."

"You loved it." Alex's nerves were already frayed, so it annoyed her even more that he was shifting all the blame to her. "You thought it might embarrass the governor, and you relished that thought."

He braced his arms on his desk and leaned over it. "You said you were going out there to reopen your mother's murder case. I didn't know you were going to get a loony preacher whipped into a frenzy, a man's barn nearly burned down, a valuable racehorse shot in the head, and offend a respected judge, who has a reputation as spotless as God's."

"Wallace?"

"Wallace. Apparently, he called our esteemed governor and complained about your unprofessional conduct, your handling of the case, and your unfounded accusations." He sucked smoke into his lungs and blew it out in a gust. "Shall I go on?"

"Please," she said wearily, knowing he would anyway.

"Okay. Chastain's scared shitless of Wallace."

"Chastain's scared shitless of his own shadow. He won't even return my calls."

"He's disclaimed you, washed his hands cleaner of you than Ivory soap could have done. He says you've been seen partying with your suspects."

"'Partying'? I've seen them on a few social occasions."

"Dangerous business, Alex. We've got three gentlemen suspects and one lady prosecutor whose association with each goes way back. It's all as murky as filé gumbo."

She tried not to squirm under his incisive stare. "New tack." Standing, she circled her chair. "This is an unsolved murder case. The investigation is viable, no matter who conducts it."

"Okay," he said complacently, folding his hands behind his head and leaning his chair back, "I'll play. What have you got? No body to dig up. No murder weapon. No—"

"It was lifted out of the vet's bag."

"What?"

"The murder weapon." She told him what Dr. Ely Collins had told her. "The scalpel was never returned to the elder Dr. Collins. I've been meaning to check the evidence room on the outside chance that it's still there, but I doubt that it is."

"So do I. The bottom line is that you've still got no weapon. Has an eyewitness come forward?"

She sighed. "During this telephone call, did the governor mention a ranch hand named Pasty Hickam?"

"So, it's true."

"It's true. And please don't insult me by trying to trap me like that again. I was going to tell you."

"When? When were you going to slip it into the conversation that a representative of this office got involved with a cowboy who turned up dead?"

"Care to hear my side of it?" She told him about Pasty. He was frowning more than ever when she finished. "If you're right, not only is it stupid and politically imprudent to continue this investigation, it's dangerous. I don't suppose anyone's confessed."

She made a face at him. "No. But one of them killed Celina, and probably Hickam."

Cursing, he mashed out his cigarette. "Let's stick to one murder at a time. If you had to arrest one of them tomorrow for killing your mother, who would it be?"

"I'm not sure."

"Why would the old man have iced her?"

"Angus is cantankerous and shrewd. He wields a lot of power, and definitely enjoys being the boss."

"You're smiling."

"He's extremely likeable, I'll admit." She kept Angus's comment about having a daughter like her to herself. "He's inordinately rough on Junior. But, a slasher?" she asked rhetorically, shaking her head. "I don't think so. It's not his style. Besides, Angus didn't have a motive."

"What about Junior?"

"There's a possibility there. He's glib and very charming. I'm sure that everything he tells me is the truth; he just doesn't tell me everything. I know he loved Celina. He wanted to marry her after my father was killed. Maybe she said no one too many times."

"Conjecture and more conjecture. So, that leaves Lambert. What about him?"

Alex lowered her head and stared at her bloodless fingers. "He's the most likely suspect, I believe."

Greg's chair sprang forward. "What makes you say that?"

"Motive and opportunity. He might have felt his best friend was displacing him and killed her to prevent it."

"Pretty viable motive. What about opportunity?"

"He was at the ranch that night, but he left."

"Are you sure? Has he got an alibi?"

"He says he was with a woman."

"Do you believe him?"

She gave a short, bitter laugh. "Oh, yes. I can believe that. Neither he nor Junior has a problem with women."

"Except your mother."

"Yes," she conceded quietly.

"What has Lambert's alibi got to say?"

"Nothing. He won't tell me her name. If she exists, she's probably still around. Otherwise, what difference would it make? I'll work on tracking her down when I get back."

"Who says you're going back?"

Up till now, Alex had been pacing. Returning to her chair, she appealed to him. "I've got to go back, Greg. I can't leave it up in the air like this. I don't care if the murderer is the governor himself, I've got to see it through to the finish."

He nodded toward the telephone on his desk. "He's going to call me this afternoon and ask me if you're off the case. He expects me to say yes."

"Even if that would mean leaving a murder unsolved?"

"Judge Wallace convinced him that you've got a bee up your ass and that this is a personal vendetta."

"Well, he's wrong."

"I don't think so."

Her heart stopped beating. "You think that, too?"

"Yep, I do." He spoke softly, more like a friend than a boss. "Call it quits, Alex, while we're all still speaking to each other, and before I get my tail in a real crack with the governor."

"You gave me thirty days."

"Which I can rescind."

"I've got just a little more than a week left."

"You can do a lot of damage in that amount of time."

"I could also get to the truth."

He looked skeptical. "That's a long shot. I've got cases here that need your expert touch."

"I'll pay my own expenses," she said. "Consider this my vacation."

"In that case, I couldn't sanction anything you did out there. You'd no longer have the protection of this office."

"Okay, fine."

He shook his head stubbornly. "I wouldn't let you do that, any more than I'd let my teenage daughter go on a date without a rubber in her purse."

"Greg, please."

"Jesus, you're a stubborn broad." He withdrew a cigarette from the pack, but didn't light it. "You know the one thing that intrigues me about this case? The judge. If he turned out to be as crooked as a dog's hind leg, it'd really get our governor's goat."

"You're mixing metaphors."

"What have you got on him?"

"Nothing more solid than dislike. He's a persnickety little man, nervous and shifty-eyed." She thought a moment. "There is something that struck me as odd, though."

"Well?" he asked, sitting forward.

"Stacey, his daughter, married Junior Minton weeks after Celina's death."

"Unless they're brother and sister, that wasn't illegal."

She shot him a sharp look. "Stacey's not...well, not Junior's type, you know? She still loves him." She recounted the incident in the powder room at the Horse and Gun Club. "Junior's very attractive. Stacey isn't the kind of woman he would marry."

"Maybe she's got a golden pussy."

"I'll admit, I never thought of that," Alex said dryly. "He didn't have to marry her to sleep with her. So why did he, unless there was a very good reason? In addition to that, Stacey lied to me. She said she was home unpacking after a trip to Galveston, but failed to mention she'd been in the stable that day."

Greg gnawed on his lower lip, then poked the cigarette in his mouth and flicked the lighter at it. "It's still too weak, Alex." He exhaled. "I've got to go with my gut instincts and call you off."

They stared at each other a moment, then she calmly opened her handbag and withdrew two plain white envelopes. She pushed them toward him. "What's this?"

"My letter of resignation, and a letter of intent to file a civil suit against the Mintons and Reede Lambert."

He almost swallowed his cigarette. "What? You can't."

"I can. I will. There's enough evidence to bring a civil suit against them for the murder of my mother. I'll sue them for so much money in damages that opening a racetrack will be out of the question. Reede Lambert's career will be shot to hell, too. They won't go to jail, but they'll be ruined."

"*If* you win."

"It won't matter if I do or not. In a civil suit, they can't plead the Fifth to avoid incrimination. No matter what they say, everyone will presume they're lying. The racing commission would have no choice but to reverse its decision and revoke the gambling license."

"So, what this all boils down to is money?" he cried. "Is that what you've been after all along?"

Her pale cheeks sprouted dots of color. "It's beneath even you to say something like that to me. I demand your apology."

Greg muttered a string of oaths. "Okay, I'm sorry. But, you mean this, don't you?"

"Yes, I do."

He deliberated for a full minute longer before grumbling, "I ought to have my head examined." Pointing a stern finger at her, he said, "Stay the hell out of trouble. Make sure you've loaded both barrels before you go after somebody, particularly Wallace. If you screw up and I get my ass chewed on, I'll claim you were a naughty girl and that I had nothing to do with your actions. And, your original deadline sticks. Got that?"

"Got it," she said, coming to her feet. "You'll be hearing from me as soon as I know something."

"Alex?" She was already at the door. When she looked back at him, he asked, "What's going on with you?"

"What do you mean?"

"Any reason in particular why you look like the ghost of Christmas, dead and buried?"

"I'm just tired."

He didn't believe her, but he let it go. After she'd left, he reached for the two envelopes she'd shoved across his desk. He ripped open the first, then more hastily, the second.

Greg Harper practically hurdled his desk and lunged for the door of his office. "Alex, you bitch!" he roared down the empty corridor.

"She just left," his startled secretary informed him. "With a man."

"Who?"

"A cowboy in a fur-trimmed leather jacket."

Greg returned to his desk, wadded the two empty envelopes into balls, and shot them at the wastebasket.

It was close to sundown when Reede wheeled his Blazer into the parking lot of the Westerner Motel.

"Just drop me at the lobby, please," Alex told him. "I need to check for messages."

Reede did as she asked without comment. They'd had very little to say to each other since their awkward reunion outside the D.A.'s office. The flight home had been uneventful. Alex had dozed most of the way.

Reede had passed the time watching Alex doze.

No less than a thousand times during the night, he'd almost gone back to her condo. Looking at the crescent-shaped circles beneath her eyes while she slept, he didn't know how he could have walked away from her. She had needed someone with her last night. He'd been the only one available.

But no one had ever presented him a prize for being a good Boy Scout. If he had stayed, he couldn't have kept his hands, or his mouth, or his cock, away from her. That's why he had left. Their needs hadn't been compatible.

Now, she was hesitating, half in, half out of the truck. "Well, thank you."

"You're welcome."

"Are you sure you won't let me pay you?"

He didn't honor that with an answer. Instead, he asked a question of his own. "What was the big powwow about?"

"A case I was working on before I left. The other prosecutor needed some facts cleared up."

"And they couldn't be cleared up over the phone?"

"It was complicated."

He knew she was lying, but saw no reason to pursue it. "So long."

She stepped to the ground and, pulling the strap of her heavy bag onto her shoulder, went into the motel lobby, where the clerk greeted her and handed her a stack of messages. Reede backed up and turned the truck around. He was about to pull out when he noticed that Alex had slowed down to read one of the messages. Her face had grown even paler than it already was. He shoved the transmission into Park and got out.

"What's that?"

She squinted up at him, then hastily refolded the letter and stuffed it back into the envelope. "My mail."

"Let me see it."

"You want to see *my* mail?"

He snapped his fingers rapidly three times and opened his palm. Her exasperation was plain when she slapped the envelope into his hand. It didn't take him long to read the letter. It was short and to the point. Tawny brows merged over the bridge of his nose as he frowned. "'An abomination unto God'?"

"That's what he's calling me."

"Plummet, no doubt. Mind if I keep this?"

"No," Alex said shakily. "I've memorized it."

"Be sure to keep your door locked."

"You're not taking his threat seriously, are you?"

He wanted to shake her, hard. She was either stupid or naïve, and either one could get her hurt. "Damn right, I am," he said. "And so should you. If he makes any attempt to contact you, call me. Understand?"

She looked ready to argue, but eventually nodded her head. Her exhaustion was evident. She seemed on the verge of collapsing in the parking lot. Reede knew he could take partial credit for that, but instead of making him feel smug, it made him feel terrible.

Closing his mind to it, he returned to his truck. He didn't drive away from the motel, however, until Alex was locked safely inside her room.

Chapter 29

Reede turned his head when the corrugated tin door of the hangar crashed open. The sinking sun was behind her, so Alex's face was in shadow, but he didn't need to see her expression to know that she was furious. She looked as tense as a pulled hamstring. The vivid light shining through her hair made it appear to crackle like flame.

He calmly finished washing his hands at the industrial metal sink, rinsed them, and reached for a paper towel from the wall dispenser.

"To what do I owe this unexpected pleasure?" he asked pleasantly.

"You're a liar, probably a cheat, possibly a murderer."

"That's been your opinion of me from the beginning. Tell me something I don't already know."

He dropped down onto a stool and hooked the heels of his boots on the lowest rung. Mindlessly, his hands slid up and down the tops of his thighs. He'd never wanted to touch a woman so badly in his life.

She advanced on him militantly, a package of quivering

energy. She looked soft, but so goddamn alive and vibrant that he could almost feel her skin against his palms. He wanted to clutch her hair while crushing her smart mouth with nonstop kisses.

She was wearing the fur coat that never failed to elicit an erotic curl deep in his groin. Her tight jeans gloved thighs that he could think of better uses for than supporting a woman obviously on the brink of exploding with rage.

When they were but inches apart, she shook a paper in his face. He recognized the letter she'd received from the concerned citizens soon after her arrival in Purcell. The shit was about to hit the fan, all right. He'd been waiting for it. This showdown had been due to happen the minute she figured it out.

"I knew something didn't jive with this," she said through clenched teeth, "but today as I was poring over the material I have, looking for clues, I finally realized what was out of sync."

Pretending that he didn't smell her tantalizing fragrance, which made him crazy, he folded his arms over his middle. "Well?"

"There is one more business cited in the letter than there are signatures at the bottom. Moe Blakely Airfield," she said, stabbing her finger repeatedly at the typed paragraph. "But Moe Blakely didn't sign it."

"That would have been tough to do, since he died about seven years ago."

"Moe Blakely was the old man you told me about, wasn't he? The one who taught you to fly and treated you to strawberry soda pops."

"You're batting a thousand, so far."

"You own this airfield, Mr. Lambert."

"Right down to the tumbleweeds and tarantulas. Moe willed it to me. Surprised?"

"Flabbergasted."

"Most folks around here were. Pissed off some of them, too—the ones who would have liked to get their hands on the property. That was when they were poking holes in the ground, drilling for oil under every rock."

"We discussed this letter at length," she grated. "You said you'd already seen it, but you failed to mention that your business was listed."

"The people who drafted the letter didn't consult me first. If they had, I would have told them to leave me out of it."

"Why? Your sentiments match theirs perfectly."

"That's right, they do, but I don't make veiled threats. I told you to your face to get your ass back to Austin. Besides, I'm not a joiner, never have been. Group projects aren't my thing."

"That still doesn't explain why you didn't tell me that the airfield was yours, when you've had so many opportunities to do so."

"I didn't because I knew you'd blow it all out of proportion."

She drew herself up. "I am not blowing it out of proportion. You own this airfield free and clear, and you've got big plans for expansion and improvement."

He came off the stool slowly and loomed above her, no longer amused. His eyes were icy. "How do you know about that?"

"I did my homework this afternoon. Representing myself as your secretary, I called three commuter airlines and asked about the status of *our* application for service. If they had never heard of you, I would have known my hunch was wrong."

She gave a dry laugh. "They'd heard of you, all right. They were very anxious to extend their congratulations to you for ME being guaranteed the racing license. All three are excited about your charter service ideas and are currently preparing proposals. They'll be in touch as soon as their market research is completed. By the way, you owe me ten dollars in long-distance charges."

He grabbed her arm. "You had no right to meddle into my business affairs. This hasn't got a goddamn thing to do with your murder case."

"I have every right to conduct this investigation as I see fit."

"Just because I own an airfield that will prosper if that racetrack is built, doesn't mean that I took a scalpel to Celina."

"It might mean that you're protecting whoever did," she shouted.

"Who? Angus? Junior? That's crap and you know it."

She wrested her arm out of his grip. "You've hampered this investigation every step of the way. You've got a badge, so that's supposed to make you an officer of the law. Ha! Now *that's* crap!

"You don't want me to discover the killer, whoever he is, because any indictment would mean bye-bye racetrack and the end of your moneymaking schemes. No wonder your loyalty to the Mintons is so steadfast," she said scornfully. "It has nothing to do with friendship or compensation for past favors. You're selfishly protecting your financial interests."

Her breasts quivered beneath her sweater when she pulled in an uneven breath and added, "I might just as well tell you, I think you're it."

"What, the murderer?" His voice was sharp and sinister. He backed her against the fuselage of the airplane he'd been tinkering with before she had arrived.

"Yes. I think you killed her. I think I know why."

"I'm all ears."

"You loved Celina to distraction, but she betrayed your love. I was a constant reminder of her betrayal, even before I was born. You couldn't forgive and forget, but Junior could. He welcomed the chance to take your place. He began to court her, and his efforts were effective.

"When you noticed that she was falling in love with him, you just couldn't stand losing her to your best friend and chief competitor, so you killed her. If you couldn't have her, then, by God, nobody, especially Junior, was going to."

He let one eyelid sink into a slow, congratulatory wink. "Very good, Counselor. But you got a big, fat problem with that pile of tripe." He took a step closer and lowered his face nearer hers. "You can't prove it, not a frigging bit of it. It's all conjecture. You've got nothing on me, nothing on anybody. So, why don't you just make life easier on all of us and give it up?"

"Because I can't."

He heard the desperation behind her words and knew that he was more than halfway to breaking her. "Why can't you?" he taunted.

"Because I want to punish whoever killed her."

"Uh-uh," he said, shaking his head. "You're not doing this for Celina. You're doing it for yourself."

"I am not!"

"Your granny built Celina up to be larger than life in your

eyes, and you can't forgive yourself for coming along at the wrong time in her life and messing it up."

"Now who's talking psychological bullshit?" she asked angrily. "I know enough about you to know that you're self-ish, Reede Lambert. The idea of another man touching what you considered your personal property would be intolerable to you."

Her expression was triumphant and challenging. "What did you find the hardest to forgive, Reede? That Celina went to bed with another man? Or couldn't you forgive yourself for not taking her when you had the chance?"

"Why are you so hung up on who I did or didn't *take*?" He nudged her body with his, then inclined forward until they were touching middle to middle. "I warned you once to keep your curiosity at bay," he whispered. "Isn't that what you've been doing with Junior, satisfying your curiosity about why your mama found him so appealing?" He took perverse pleasure in watching the color drain from her face.

"No," she denied hoarsely.

"I think it is."

"You're sick."

"Not me, baby." His breath trailed across her lips. "You're the one who's curious."

He bent his head and kissed her. She stubbornly resisted the pressure of his mouth, but he finally succeeded in maneu-vering her lips apart. His tongue raked her teeth and the inner linings of her lips.

She opened to him. He felt the breath leave her body on a ragged sigh. It was moist and warm and sweet inside his mouth. His erection stretched, pushing painfully against his fly, against hers. He reached inside her coat and covered her breast with his hand. Beneath his revolving thumb her nipple hardened, and when he swept it lightly, a low moan rose out of her throat.

He raised his head and looked down into her face. Her head was resting against the body of the airplane, her throat arched and exposed. She was breathing hard. Her chest rose and fell swiftly. He could feel her heart, like a small, wild, frightened creature that had become trapped in his palm. Her lips were slightly parted, wet and glistening. Her eyes were closed. Slowly, they came open. They looked at each other with wariness and confusion.

Oh Jesus, was Reede's last coherent thought. His mouth lowered to hers again, hungrier, but much more temperate. He pressed his tongue into her mouth, giving, not taking. He fondled her breast with more finesse.

Eventually losing patience with her clothing, he dropped his hand to her waist. Her sweater was pushed up, the cup of her bra was pushed down, and her warm, soft flesh filled his hand. Reflexively, she arched her back, plumping her breast against his callused fingers and palm. He kneaded it and continued to agitate its tight, feverish center with the pad of his thumb.

Kissing her as though this was his first kiss ever, or the last one he would ever be granted, he worked her legs apart with his knee and angled his hips toward her cleft. From the edge of his mind it registered that she made a helpless little sound and lifted her arms to encircle his neck, but he could focus on nothing except her mouth, his invasion of it, and how damn much he wanted to be buried snugly inside her.

His free hand slid over her butt, down the back of her

thigh, and caught her behind the knee. He lifted it, propped it on his hip, and made a grinding motion against her. He fit his rigid body into the notch of her thighs and stroked her there until the tempo escalated to a breathless pace. She spoke his name on a sudden, catchy little breath that fanned his passions hotter.

Several seconds later, he heard his name again, coming to him dimly and from afar. Vaguely, he wondered how she had managed to speak when her tongue was so actively engaged with his.

He heard his name called again and realized that it wasn't Alex's voice.

"Reede? Where are you, boy?"

His head snapped up. Alex blinked her eyes back into focus. He hastily withdrew his hand from inside her sweater. She yanked her coat closed.

"In here." His voice sounded like he'd recently gargled nails.

Angus stepped through the door Alex had left open.

Reede noticed that the sun had set.

Chapter 30

To her credit, Alex recovered remarkably well, Angus thought. Except for the dazed expression in her eyes and her slightly swollen lips, she seemed perfectly composed.

"Hello, Angus," she said.

"Hi, Alex. Get things straightened out in Austin?"

"Yes. Thank you for lending me your airplane."

"Don't mention it."

"I, uh, was just on my way out." To Reede she said, "I'll get back to you about this later." She left in a hurry. Reede picked up a wrench and stuck his head into the exposed engine of the small aircraft.

"What's she up to now?" Angus asked as he lowered himself onto the stool Reede had occupied earlier.

"She discovered that I own this place. I never kept it a secret, but I never advertised it, either. She figures I'd have a lot to lose if she takes this case to a grand jury, whether I'm the killer or not."

"She's right," the older man observed. Reede merely shrugged, tossed the wrench on a worktable, and closed the

motor casing. "Ely told me she came to his office asking questions about his daddy's scalpel and the day of the murder."

"The scalpel, huh?"

"Yeah. Know anything about that?"

"Hell, no, do you?"

"Hell, no."

Reede went to a cabinet where he kept a supply of liquor
and beer. He poured himself a hefty shot of Jack Dan-
iel's and tossed it down. He tilted the bottle toward Angus.
"Want one?"

"Sure, thanks." As he sipped the whiskey, he watched
Reede slam back another one.

Catching Angus's curious stare, he said, "It's been that
kind of day."

"Alex?"

Reede ran his hands through his hair like a man plagued
by demons. "Yeah. Damn, she's tenacious."

"There's no telling what kind of crap Merle Graham filled
her head with."

"No wonder she's vengeful." He blew out a breath of
extreme agitation. "If ME doesn't get that racetrack, all my
future plans will be affected."

"It's that important to you, huh?"

"What did you think, that I want to be a fucking sheriff for
the rest of my life?"

"You worry too much, boy!" Angus said heartily. "We'll
get it, and your future looks nothing but sunny. That's what I
came out here to talk about."

Reede regarded him curiously. "My future?"

Angus finished his whiskey in one hefty swallow and
crushed the paper cup in his fist. He pushed his cowboy hat

back further on his head and looked up at Reede, smiling devilishly.

"I want you to come back and be an active part of Minton Enterprises again."

For a moment, Reede was rendered speechless by shock. He fell back a step, laughed, and said, "Are you shittin' me?"

"Nope." Angus raised a callused hand. "Before you say anything, hear me out."

He had already outlined in his mind what he was going to say. After receiving disturbing calls from two worried members of the racing commission who had read about Alex's investigation in the Austin newspaper, he'd decided he'd better get more aggressive about putting a stop to it. This thing wasn't going to blow over, like he'd originally hoped.

The long-distance conversations had ended on an optimistic note. He'd pooh-poohed Alex's allegations, told them a few dirty jokes, and had them laughing by the time they hung up. He wasn't gravely concerned yet, but he definitely saw the need for ME to present a solid front. Having Reede as an integral part of the corporation again would be a positive step in that direction.

Now, his rehearsed words flowed smoothly. "You know almost as much as I do about racehorses, and more than Junior ever took the time or effort to learn. You'd come back into the company as an executive. I'd divide responsibilities equally between you and Junior, though you'd have different functions.

"I know how much this airfield means to you. You've got a sentimental attachment to it, but you also see its moneymaking potential. So do I. I'd incorporate it into ME. The corporation could afford to finance the rebuilding and expansion you want to do. We'd also have a lot more clout with the airlines."

His smile broadened. "Shit, I'd even throw in a few shares of ME stock as incentive. You can't pass up a deal like that, boy."

He was disappointed in Reede's reaction, which he had hoped would be astonishment tinged with pleasure. Instead, it appeared to be astonishment tinged with suspicion.

"What brought this on?"

A picture of equanimity, Angus said, "You belong with us—always have. I'm in a position to get things moving for you. You'd be foolish not to take advantage of my offer."

"I'm not a boy who still needs your charity, Angus."

"I never considered you a charity case."

"I know that," Reede said evenly, "but no matter how we dress it up with fancy words, that's what I was." He peered deeply into the older man's eyes. "Don't think I'm not grateful for everything you've done for me."

"I never asked you for gratitude. You always did an honest day's work for anything I sent your way."

"I wouldn't have had any advantages at all if it hadn't been for you." He paused before going on. "But I paid you back, several times over, I think. When I left your company, I did it because I needed independence. I still do, Angus."

Angus was perturbed, and made no secret of it. "You wanna be begged, is that it? Okay." He took a deep breath. "I'm getting close to retirement age. Some would consider me past it. The business needs your leadership qualities to survive." He spread his hands wide. "There. Does that satisfy your confounded ego?"

"I don't need to be stroked, Angus, and you damn well know it. I'm thinking about somebody else's ego."

"Junior's?"

"Junior's. Have you told him about this?"

"No. I didn't see any reason to, until..."

"Until there was nothing he could do about it."

Angus's silence was as good as an admission.

Reede began to pace. "Junior is your heir, Angus, not me. He's the one you should be grooming to take over. He needs to be ready when the time comes."

Angus paced, too, while he collected his thoughts. "You're afraid Junior won't get ready as long as you're around to do everything for him and cover his tracks when he messes up."

"Angus, I don't mean—"

"It's all right," he said, raising his hand to ward off Reede's objections. "I'm his daddy. You're his best friend. We should be able to discuss him freely without wading through bullshit. Junior isn't as strong as you."

Reede looked away. Hearing the truth warmed him inside. He knew how difficult it was for Angus to say it.

"I always wanted Junior to be more like you—aggressive, assertive, ambitious—but..." Angus gave an eloquent shrug. "He needs you, Reede. Hell, so do I. I didn't bust my balls all these years to see everything I've built up fall down around me. I've got my pride, but I'm a practical businessman. I face facts, bad as they sometimes are. One of those facts is that you're competent, and Junior isn't."

"That's my point, Angus. He *can* be. Force his hand. Delegate him more responsibility."

"And when he fucks up, you know what'll happen? I'll lose my temper, start yelling at him. He'll sulk and run to his mama, who'll mollycoddle him."

"Maybe at first, but not for long. Junior'll start yelling back one of these days. He'll figure out that the only way to deal with you is to give you tit for tat. I did."

"Is that what you're doing now, getting back at me for some slight I'm not even aware of?"

"Hell, no," Reede answered crossly. "Since when have I ever been afraid to tell you off, or anybody else, if something wasn't to my liking?"

"All right, I'll tell you since when," Angus snapped. "Since Celina was killed. That changed everything, didn't it?" He moved closer to Reede. "I don't think any of us has had an honest conversation with the other since that morning. The thing I always feared most was that she'd come between you and Junior." He laughed with rancor. "She did anyway. Even dead, she put a blight on the friendship."

"Celina has nothing to do with my decision to say no. I want to feel that what's mine is mine. Completely. Not a part of your conglomerate."

"So, it's strictly economics?"

"That's right."

The wheels of Angus's brain were whirring with fresh arguments. "What if I decided to build an airfield of my own?"

"Then we'd be competitors," Reede replied, unruffled. "But there's not enough business to support two, and both of us would lose."

"But I can afford to. You can't."

"You wouldn't get any satisfaction from bankrupting me, Angus."

Angus relented and snorted a laugh. "You're right. Hell, boy, you're like family."

"*Like* family, but not. Junior is your son, not me."

"You're turning down this opportunity on account of him, aren't you?" It was a shrewd guess and, he saw by Reede's reaction, a correct one.

Reede gave his wristwatch a needless glance. "Look, I've got to run."

"Reede," Angus said, grabbing his arm. "You reckon Junior'll ever realize just how good a friend you are to him?"

Reede tried to sound jocular. "Let's not tell him. He's conceited enough as it is."

Angus smelled defeat, and it was obnoxious to him. "I can't let you do it, boy."

"You've got no choice."

"I won't let you say no. I'll keep after you," he promised, his crafty blue eyes gleaming.

"You're not shook up because you'll miss me. You're shook up because you aren't getting your way."

"Not this time, Reede. I need you. Junior needs you. So does ME."

"Why now? After all these years, why does ME's future rely on me coming back?" Reede's features sharpened with realization. "You're scared."

"Scared?" Angus repeated with affected surprise. "Of what? of whom?"

"Of Alex. You're scared that she might pluck the candy apple right out of your hand. You're trying to pack all the power you can behind you."

"Wouldn't we all be stronger against her if we stood together?"

"We are standing together."

"Are we?" Angus fired.

"You've got my loyalty, Angus, just like I've got yours."

Angus stepped closer to Reede. "I damn sure hope so. But I recall the look on your face when I walked through that door a while ago," he whispered. "You looked like you'd been walloped in the nuts, boy. And she looked all rosy and wet around the mouth."

Reede said nothing. Angus hadn't expected him to. He would have considered a babbling denial or an apology a weakness. Reed's strength was one reason he'd always admired him.

Angus relaxed his tension. "I like the girl, myself. She's saucy, and cute as a button. But she's too smart for her own good." He pointed a stern finger at Reede. "See that you don't get your cock up so high you can't look around it at what she's trying to do. She wants to bring us to our knees, make us atone for Celina's murder.

"Can you afford to lose everything you've worked for? I can't. Furthermore, I won't." Ending the discussion on that grim promise, he stamped out of the hangar.

"Where's my boy?" he stormily demanded of the bartender, almost an hour after leaving Reede. During that time, he'd been making the rounds of Junior's haunts.

"In the back," the bartender answered, indicating the closed door at the back of the tavern.

It was a shabby watering hole, but it had the largest poker pot in town. At any time of day or night, a game was in progress in the back room. Angus shoved open the door, nearly knocking over a cocktail waitress carrying a tray of empty long-necks on her shoulder. He plowed through the cloud of tobacco smoke toward the overhead beam that spotlighted the round poker table.

"I need to talk to Junior," he bellowed.

Junior, a cigar anchored in one corner of his mouth, smiled

up at his father. "Can't it wait till we finish this hand? I've got five hundred riding on it, and I'm feeling lucky."

"Your ass is riding on what I've got to tell you, and your luck just ran out."

The other players, most of whom worked for Angus in one capacity or another, quickly swept up their stakes and scuttled out. As soon as the last one cleared the door, Angus banged it shut.

"What the hell's going on?" Junior asked.

"I'll tell you what's going on. Your friend Reede is about to get the best of you again, while you're here in the back room of this dump pissing your life away."

Junior meekly extinguished his cigar. "I don't know what you're talking about."

" 'Cause you've got your head up your ass, instead of on your business, where it belongs."

By an act of will, Angus calmed himself. If he hollered, Junior would only pout. Yelling never got him anywhere. But it was tough to keep his disappointment and anger from showing.

"Alex was at the airfield this afternoon with Reede."

"So?"

"So, if I'd gotten there ten seconds later, I'd've caught them screwing against the side of an airplane!" he roared, forgetting his resolution to restrain his temper.

Junior bolted from his chair. "The hell you say!"

"I know when animals are in heat, boy. I make part of my living breeding them, remember? I can smell when they want each other," he declared, touching the end of his nose. "He was doing what you should have been, instead of gambling away money you didn't even earn."

Junior flinched. Defensively, he said, "Last I heard, Alex was out of town."

"Well, she's back."

"All right, I'll call her tonight."

"Do better than that. Make a date, see her."

"Okay."

"I mean it!"

"I said, okay!" Junior shouted.

"And something else, just so you'll hear it from me first. I've asked Reede to rejoin ME."

"Huh?"

"You heard me."

"What . . . what'd he say?"

"He said no, but I'm not taking that as final." Angus walked toward his son until they were nose to nose. "I'll tell you something else. I haven't decided who'll be working for whom if he takes the job."

Junior's eyes reflected his pain and anger.

Angus poked him in the chest. "You'd better get busy and do what I told you to do, or one of two things could happen. Either Reede'll be sitting at your desk, assigning you jobs like cleaning out the stables, or all of us will be making license plates in the Huntsville prison. Either way, you won't have afternoons to while away playing poker."

Angus stepped back and gave the edge of the table a vicious kick with the pointed toe of his lizard boot. It toppled over, sending cards, poker chips, ashtrays, and bottles of beer crashing to the floor.

Then he marched out, leaving Junior to clean up the mess.

Chapter 31

The waitress set down two chicken salads served in fresh, hollowed-out pineapples and garnished with sprigs of mint. She asked Junior Minton if he and his guest needed refills on iced tea.

"We're fine for now, thanks," he said, flashing her his hundred-watt smile.

The country club's dining room offered a view of the golf course. It was one of the few rooms in Purcell County that didn't reek of Texana. The soothing pastel decor would have fit in anywhere. Junior and Alex were among a small number of luncheon diners.

She applied her fork to an almond sliver. "This is almost too pretty to eat. It beats the B & B Café's blue-plate special all to heck," she told him as she munched on the nut. "I'm sure if I ever saw the inside of the kitchen, I'd never eat there. It's probably crawling with roaches."

"Naw, they chicken-fry them and serve them as appetizers." Junior smiled. "Do you eat there often?"

"Often enough. I've had gravy, which comes on everything, and chili up to here."

"Then, since you refused to go out with me last night, I'm glad I insisted on lunch today. I've frequently had to rescue ladies who work downtown from the high-calorie clutches of the B & B. The menu is hazardous to their waistlines."

"Not that this is much more slenderizing," she said, tasting the rich, creamy salad dressing.

"You don't need to worry about that. You're as slender as your mother."

Alex rested her fork on the edge of her plate. "Even after having me?"

Junior's blond head was bent over his plate. He raised it, noticed her earnest curiosity, and blotted his mouth on the stiff linen napkin before answering. "From the back you'd be taken for twins, except that your hair is darker and has more red in it."

"That's what Reede said."

"Really? When?"

His smile faltered. The question had been posed a little too casually to be taken that way. A telltale crease formed between his brows.

"Soon after we met."

"Ah." The furrow between his brows smoothed out.

Alex didn't want to think about Reede. When she was with him, the practical, methodical, professional detachment she prided herself on disappeared. Pragmatism gave way to emotionalism.

One minute she was accusing him of first-degree murder, the next, kissing him madly and wishing for more. He was dangerous, not only from her viewpoint as a prosecutor, but as a woman. Both facets of her, one as vulnerable as the other, suffered under his assault.

"Junior," she said, after they'd finished eating, "why couldn't Reede forgive Celina for having me? Was his pride that badly damaged?"

He was staring out the window at the golf greens. When he felt her eyes on him, he looked at her sadly. "I'm disappointed."

"About what?"

"I thought—hoped—that you accepted my invitation to lunch because you wanted to see me." He let out a discouraged breath. "But you just want to talk about Reede."

"Not Reede, Celina. My mother."

He reached across the table and squeezed her hand. "It's okay. I'm used to it. Celina used to call me and talk about Reede all the time."

"What did she say when she called and talked about him?"

Junior propped his shoulder against the window and began to play with his necktie, idly pulling it through his fingers. "I usually heard how wonderful he was. You know, Reede this, Reede that. After your father got killed in the war, and she was available again, she was afraid that she'd never get Reede back."

"She didn't."

"No."

"Surely, she didn't expect him to be glad about Al Gaither and me."

"No, she knew better than that. Neither of us had wanted her to go away for the summer, but there wasn't much we could do about it once she'd made her mind up," Junior replied. "She went. She was there. We were here, three-hundred-plus miles away. One night, Reede decided to borrow a plane and fly us there to bring her back.

"That son of a bitch had convinced me that he could get us there and back safely before anybody realized the plane was missing. The only person who would notice would be Moe Blakely, and in his book, Reede could do no wrong."

"My God, you didn't do it?"

"No, not then. One of the stable hands—Pasty Hickam, in fact—overheard us plotting it and told Dad. He gave us hell and threatened us within an inch of our lives not to ever try something that crazy. He knew all about Celina trying to make Reede jealous and advised us to let her have her fun. He assured us that she would eventually tire of it and come home, and everything would be just like it had been before."

"But Angus was wrong. When mother came back to Purcell, she was pregnant with me. Nothing was ever the same."

She toyed with her iced tea spoon for a long, silent while. "How much do you know about my father, Junior?"

"Not much. How about you?"

She raised her shoulders in a small shrug. "Only that his name was Albert Gaither, that he was from a coal-mining town in West Virginia, that he was sent to Vietnam within weeks of his marriage to my mother, and that he stepped on a land mine and died months before I was born."

"I didn't even know where he came from," Junior told her regretfully.

"When I got old enough, I thought about going to West Virginia and looking up his family, but I decided against it. They never made any attempt to contact me, so I felt it best to leave it alone. His remains were shipped to them and interred there. I'm not even certain if my mother attended his funeral."

"She didn't. She wanted to, but Mrs. Graham refused to give her the money to make the trip. Dad offered to pay her way, but Mrs. Graham wouldn't hear of that, either."

"She let Angus pay for Mother's funeral."

"I guess she thought that was different, somehow."

"Al Gaither wasn't any more to blame for the hasty marriage than Mother."

"Maybe he was," Junior argued. "A soldier going off to war, that kind of thing. Celina was a pretty girl out to prove her allure."

"Because Reede wouldn't sleep with her."

"He told you about that, huh?"

Alex nodded.

"Yeah, well, some of the girls he did sleep with flaunted it in Celina's face. She was out to prove she was woman enough to snare a man. Gaither no doubt took advantage of that.

"To your grandma, his name was a dirty word. Because of him, your mother missed her senior year of high school. That didn't go down too well with your grandma, either. No, she had a real ax to grind with Mr. Gaither."

"I wish she had at least saved a picture of him. She had thousands of pictures of Celina, but not a single one of my father."

"To Mrs. Graham, he probably represented evil, you know, the thing that changed Celina's life forever. And for the worse."

"Yes," she said, thinking that Junior's words could apply to how her grandmother felt about her, too. "I don't even have a face to associate with the name. Nothing."

"Jesus, Alex, that must be rough."

"Sometimes, I think I just sprang up out of the ground." In an effort to lighten the mood, she said, "Maybe I was the first Cabbage Patch Kid."

"No," Junior said, reaching for her hand again, "you had a mother, and she was beautiful."

"Was she?"

"Ask anybody."

"Was she beautiful inside as well as out?"

His brows drew together slightly. "As much as anyone is. She was human. She had faults as well as virtues."

"Did she love me, Junior?"

"Love you? Hell, yes. She thought you were the most terrific baby ever conceived."

Basking in the glow of his words, Alex left the country club with him. As he held open the passenger door of his Jag, he stepped close to her and laid his hand along her cheek. "Do you have to go back to that stuffy old courthouse this afternoon?"

"I'm afraid so. I have work to do."

"It's a gorgeous day."

She pointed at the sky. "You liar. It looks like it's about to rain—or snow."

He bent his head and kissed her quickly. Leaving his lips in place, he whispered, "Then an even more pleasurable way of passing time indoors comes immediately to mind."

He kissed her more firmly, and expertly parted her lips. But when his tongue touched hers, she recoiled. "No, Junior." She was angered by the impropriety of his kiss and shocked by its failure to stir her sensually.

His kiss didn't cause her veins to expand and her blood to

pump through them with a new, feverish beat. It didn't cause her womb to contract with a craving so severe she didn't think it could ever be appeased. It didn't make her think that, God, if he didn't become a part of her, she was going to die.

About all Junior's kiss did was alert her to the fact that he had misinterpreted her friendship. Unless she stopped it now, some dangerous groundwork, disturbingly reminiscent of the past, would be laid.

She eased her head back. "I need to work, Junior. And I'm sure you've got work to do, too." He mumbled profanely, but conceded with good humor.

It was as he stepped back so she could get into the car that they saw the Blazer. It had crept up on them, and was now only a few yards beyond the hood ornament of the Jag.

The driver, whom they could see through the windshield, had his hands folded over the steering wheel and was watching them from behind opaque aviator glasses. He was sitting dangerously still and unsmiling.

Reede pushed open the door and stepped to the ground. "I've been looking for you, Alex. Somebody told me you'd left the courthouse with Junior, so I played a hunch and came here."

"What for?" Junior asked touchily, laying his arm across Alex's shoulders.

"We've located Fergus Plummet. One of the deputies is bringing him in now."

"And that gives you the right to interfere with our date?"

"I don't give a shit about your date," Reede said, his lips barely moving. "She said she wanted to be there when I questioned Plummet."

"Will both of you please stop talking about me as though

I'm not here?" The tension that had arisen between the two of them because of her was untenable. It resembled the triangle between them and her mother too well. She shrugged off Junior's arm. "He's right, Junior. I want to hear what Plummet has to say for himself."

"Now?" he whined.

"I'm sorry."

"I'll come with you," he said brightly.

"This is official. Duty calls, and I'm on the state payroll. Thank you for lunch."

"You're welcome." He gave her a soft peck on the cheek and said, loud enough for Reede to hear, "I'll call you later."

"'Bye." She rushed toward the Blazer and climbed in, though her high heels and slender skirt posed some problems. Reede pretended to be impervious to her difficulties. He sat behind the steering wheel glowering at Junior while Junior glowered right back. The second her bottom landed in the seat, Reede floored the accelerator.

When they reached the highway, he swung onto the macadam with enough impetus to plaster Alex against the passenger door. She gritted her teeth and hung on until he straightened out his turn and they were speeding along the center stripe.

"Have a nice lunch?"

"Very," she answered crisply.

"Good."

"Are you upset because you saw Junior kissing me?"

"Hell, no. Why should I be?"

"Exactly."

Secretly, she was glad he had arrived when he had. The interruption had relieved her of having to turn Junior down flat. Feeling a trifle guilty over that, and trying to set things back on a professional track with Reede, she asked, "Where did they find Plummet?"

"Right where I suspected. He was hiding inside one of his deacons' houses. He came up for air, and one of my deputies nabbed him."

"Did he come peaceably?"

"He's no idiot. He's only being questioned. We really can't make a formal arrest yet. They should beat us to the court-house by just a few minutes."

As moods went, Junior was in the black hole of Calcutta. There was no peace to be found anywhere, though his Jag streaked through the streets of town at an indiscriminate speed in pursuit of it.

Angus was on his back. His mother was on his back because Angus was. Last night she had sternly commissioned him to get off his ass—not in those terms, exactly—and do something that would make his father proud.

Sarah Jo found the idea of having Reede Lambert back at ME untenable and, using a harsher tone than she had ever used with him before, told her son that it simply must never happen.

"Angus wants *you*, not Reede."

"Then, why did he offer him a job?"

"To wake you up, darling. He's only using Reede as a sub-tle threat."

Junior promised her he'd do his best. But when he had called Alex and asked her to have dinner with him, she'd turned him down, saying she had a headache. She did agree to meet him for lunch today. And then, when everything had been going great, Reede had showed up and snatched her out of his grasp again.

"Business, my ass," he muttered as he pulled into the wide, circular driveway of the judge's home and brought the car to a jarring halt. He jumped the flower bed and landed a hard blow on the front door with his fist.

Stacey didn't get to the door quite fast enough to suit him. He was practically frothing at the mouth by the time she answered.

"Junior!" she exclaimed gladly when she saw him. "This is a sur—"

"Shut up. Just shut up." He slammed the door behind him, rattling every piece of china and glassware in the house. Taking Stacey by both arms, he backed her into the wall of the foyer and covered her stunned, gaping mouth with his.

He kissed her roughly while his hands attacked the buttons on her blouse. They scattered like BBs across the marble floor when he got too impatient to work them out of their holes and ripped them open.

"Junior," she gasped, "what—"

"I gotta have you, Stacey," he mumbled, plunging his face between her breasts. "Please, don't give me a hard time about it. Everybody gives me a hard time about everything. Just shut up and let me fuck you."

He flipped up her skirt and slip, worked down her panty hose, and then opened his trousers. He rammed into her dryly, and she cried out.

He was causing her pain. While he knew it and hated himself for hurting her when she didn't deserve it, he was glad, in a dark part of his soul, that somebody else besides himself was suffering. Why should he be the only person in the whole freaking world to be miserable?

Everybody picked on him. It was time he got to pick on somebody. Stacey was available ... and he knew he could get away with it.

Her dismay, her debasement made him feel powerful. His release came from subjugating her, not from the sex itself. When it was over, he collapsed against the wall, sandwiching her between himself and the floral wallpaper.

He regained his breath and his reason gradually. He eased away from her and stroked her cheek. "Stacey?" Slowly, she opened her eyes. He gave her a disarming smile and a soft kiss. Realizing that she was dressed up, he asked, "Did I keep you from going somewhere?"

"A meeting at church."

The dimple in his cheek grew deeper as his smile widened. Playfully, he tweaked an exposed breast. "You don't look much like going to a church meeting now."

As he knew she would, she responded to his caresses, which got bolder. "Junior," she whimpered breathlessly when he pushed her blouse off her shoulders, yanked down her brassiere, and fastened his mouth to her raised nipple. She chanted his name, interspersing it with avowals of love. He moved his head down her body, pushing aside clothing as he went.

"Junior?" she asked timorously when he dropped to his knees.

He smiled up at her beguilingly as he slipped his thumbs between the lips of her sex and spread them apart.

"Junior! Don't. No. I can't. You ... can't."

"Yes, I can, honey. What's more, you're just dying for me to." He licked her lightly, enjoying the taste of himself on her, the musky smell of aroused female, her uneasiness. "Still want to go to church?" he whispered, nuzzling her with his mouth. "Huh, Stacey?"

When her orgasmic sobs echoed off the walls of the empty house, he pulled her down to straddle him as he lay on his back on the cold marble floor. He emptied himself into her again. Afterward, when she was curled against him like a rag doll, he felt better than he had in weeks.

When he moved to sit up, Stacey clung to him. "Don't go."

"Hey, Stacey," he said teasingly, "look what a mess I've made of you. You'll have to spruce up, or the judge will know the mischief you've been into while he was at work today."

He stood, readjusted his clothing, smoothed back his hair. "Besides, I've got work to do myself. If I stay a minute longer, I'll cart you off to bed and waste the entire afternoon there. Not that it would be a waste, mind you."

"Are you coming back?" she asked plaintively as she trailed him to the door, covering her nakedness as best she could.

"Of course."

"When?"

He frowned, but concealed it from her by turning to open the front door. "I'm not sure. But after the other night and today, you don't think I could stay away, do you?"

"Oh, Junior, I love you so much."

He cupped her face and kissed her lips. "I love you, too."

Stacey closed the door behind him. Mechanically, she headed upstairs, where she bathed her aching body in warm water and scented bubble bath. Tomorrow, she'd likely be black and blue. She would cherish each bruise.

Junior loved her! He had said so. Maybe after all this time, he was finally growing up. Maybe he had come to his senses, and realized what was good for him. Maybe, at long last, he had expunged Celina from his heart.

But then Stacey remembered Alex, and the calf eyes Junior had had for her at the Horse and Gun Club. She recalled how closely he'd held her while they twirled around the dance floor, laughing together. Stacey's insides turned rancid with jealousy.

Just like her mother, Alex was what stood between her and total happiness with the man she loved.

Chapter 32

As soon as Reede and Alex arrived at the courthouse, they went into the interrogation room, followed by a court reporter. Fergus Plummet was seated at a square, wooden table. His head was bowed in prayer over an open Bible, his hands clasped tightly together.

Mrs. Plummet was there, too. Her head was also bowed, but when they came in, she jumped and looked up at them like a startled deer. As before, her face was void of makeup and her hair was drawn back into a severe knot on the back of her head. The clothes she wore were drab and shapeless.

"Hello, Mrs. Plummet," Reede said politely.

"Hello, Sheriff." If Alex hadn't seen her lips moving, she wouldn't have been certain the woman had spoken. She appeared to be scared out of her wits. Her fingers were knotted together in her lap. She was squeezing them so tightly, they had turned bluish-white.

"Are you okay?" Reede asked her in that same kind tone. She bobbed her head and glanced fearfully toward her husband, who was still fervently praying. "You're entitled to have a lawyer present when I and Miss Gaither question you."

Before Mrs. Plummet could offer a reply, Fergus concluded his prayer on a resounding, "Ah-men," and raised his head. He fixed a fanatical stare on Reede. "We've got the best lawyer on our side. I will get my counsel from the Lord God, now and through eternity."

"Fine," Reede said drolly, "but I'm putting it on the record that you waived the right to have an attorney present during questioning."

Plummet's eyes snapped to Alex. "What is the harlot doing here? I'll not have her in the presence of my sainted wife."

"Neither you nor your sainted wife have anything to say about it. Sit down, Alex."

At Reede's directive, she lowered herself into the nearest chair. She was grateful for the chance to sit down. Fergus Plummet was a prejudiced, ill-informed fanatic. He should have cut a comic figure, but he gave her the creeps.

Reede straddled a chair backward and stared at the preacher across the table. He opened a file one of his deputies had prepared.

"What were you doing last Wednesday night?"

Plummet closed his eyes and tilted his head to one side, as though he were listening to a secret voice. "I can answer that," he told them when he opened his eyes seconds later. "I was conducting Wednesday-night services at my church. We prayed for the deliverance of this town, for the souls of those who would be corrupted, and for those individuals who, heedless of the Lord's will, would corrupt the innocent."

Reede affected nonchalance. "Please keep your answers

simple. I don't want this to take all afternoon. What time is prayer meeting?"

Plummet went through the listening act again. "Not relevant."

"Sure it is," Reede drawled. "I might want to attend sometime."

That elicited a giggle from Mrs. Plummet. None of them was more surprised than she by her spontaneous outburst. Mortified, she looked at her husband, who glared at her in reproof.

"What time was prayer meeting over?" Reede repeated in a voice that said he'd tired of the game and wasn't going to be a good sport any longer.

Plummet continued to give his wife a condemning stare. She lowered her head in shame. Reede reached across the table and yanked Plummet's chin around.

"Stop looking at her like she's a turd floating in a punch bowl. Answer me. And don't give me any more bullshit, either."

Plummet closed his eyes, shuddering slightly, greatly put-upon. "God, close my ears to the foul language of your adversary, and deliver me from the presence of these wicked ones."

"He'd better send a whole flock of angels down to save you fast, brother. Unless you start answering my questions, I'm gonna slam your ass in jail."

That broke through Plummet's sanctimonious veneer. His eyes popped open. "On what charge?"

"The feds would like to start with arson."

Alex looked quickly at Reede. He was bluffing. Racehorses were considered interstate commerce, and therefore would come under the Treasury Department's jurisdiction. But government agents didn't usually get involved in an arson case unless damage amounted to more than fifty thousand dollars. Plummet didn't fall for the bluff, either.

"That's ridiculous. Arson? The only fire I've started is in the hearts of my believers."

"If that's so, then account for your time from last Wednesday night until today, when Deputy Cappell spotted you slinking out the back door of that house. Where'd you go after prayer meeting let out?"

Plummet laid a finger against his cheek, feigning hard concentration. "I believe that was the night I visited one of our sick brothers."

"He can vouch for you?"

"Unfortunately, no."

"Let me guess—he died."

Plummet frowned at the sheriff's sarcasm. "No, but while I was in attendance, the poor soul was delirious with fever. He won't remember a thing." He made a tsking sound. "He was very ill. His family, of course, could attest to my presence at his bedside. We prayed for him through the night."

Reede's incisive eyes sliced toward Wanda Plummet. She guiltily averted her head. Reede then swiveled around and looked at Alex. His expression said that he was getting about as far as he had expected to. When he turned back around, he asked abruptly, "Do you know where the Minton ranch is?"

"Of course."

"Did you go there last Wednesday night?"

"No."

"Did you send someone out there last Wednesday night?"

"No."

"Members of your congregation? The believers whose hearts you had stoked a fire in during prayer meeting?"

"Certainly not."

"Didn't you go out there and vandalize the place, paint on the walls, shovel shit into the drinking troughs, break windows?"

"My counselor says I don't have to answer any more questions." He folded his arms across his chest.

"Because you might incriminate yourself?"

"No!"

"You're lying, Plummet."

"God is on my side." He worked his eyes like the focusing lens of a camera, making them wide, pulling them narrow. "'If God is on our side,'" he quoted theatrically, "'then who can be against us?'"

"He won't be on your side for long," Reede whispered threateningly. Leaving his chair, he circled the table and bent over Plummet. "God doesn't favor liars."

"Our Father, who art in heaven—"

"Come clean, Plummet."

"—hallowed be thy name. Thy—"

"Who'd you send out there to trash the Minton ranch?"

"—kingdom come, thy—"

"You *did* send members of your congregation, though, didn't you? You're too much of a gutless coward to go yourself."

The praying ceased abruptly. The preacher's breathing became choppy and light. Reede had struck a chord. Knowing that, he pressed on. "Did you lead your ratty little army out there, or did you just furnish the spray paint?"

Reede had told Alex earlier that he'd made the rounds

of variety and hardware stores, checking out places where spray paint was sold. So far, none of the merchants recalled a significant demand for it on a single day.

Plummet was probably too clever to have bought it all in one store; perhaps he'd gone out of town. Reede couldn't hold him indefinitely because he had no evidence, but Plummet might be fooled into thinking he'd left behind an incriminating clue.

For the second time, however, he called Reede's bluff. Having composed himself, he stared straight ahead and said, "I can't imagine what you're talking about, Sheriff Lambert."

"Let's try this again," Reede said with a heavy sigh. "Look, Plummet, we—Miss Gaither and I—know you're guilty as hell. You all but told her to get tough with the sinners, or else. Wasn't the vandalism out at the Minton ranch the *or else*?"

Plummet said nothing.

Reede took another tack. "Isn't confession supposed to be good for the soul? Give your soul a break, Plummet. Confess. Your wife can go home to your kids, and I'll be able to take off early today."

The preacher remained silent.

Reede began at the top and methodically worked down his list of questions again, hoping to trap Plummet in a lie. Several times, Reede asked Alex if she wanted to question him, but she declined. She had no more to link him to the crime than Reede had.

He got nowhere. The preacher's story never changed. Reede didn't even trip him up. At the conclusion of another exhaustive round of questions, Plummet grinned up at him guilelessly and said, "It's getting close to supper time. May we be excused now?"

Reede, frustrated, ran his hand through his hair. "I know you did it, you pious son of a bitch. Even if you weren't actually there, you planned it. You killed my horse."

Plummet reacted visibly. "Killed your horse? That's untrue. You killed it yourself. I read about it in the newspaper."

Reede made a snarling sound and lunged across the room at him. "You're responsible." He leaned down close to Plummet again, forcing him backward in his chair. "Reading about that probably gave you a real thrill, didn't it, you little prick? You're gonna pay for that animal, if I have to wring a confession from your scrawny neck."

So it went for at least another hour.

Alex's bottom grew tired and sore from sitting in the uncomfortable chair. Once, she stood up and paced the length of the room, just to restore circulation. Plummet's fanatical eyes tracked her, making her feel so ill at ease that she returned to her seat.

"Mrs. Plummet?"

The preacher's wife flinched when the sheriff suddenly spoke her name. Her shoulders had been sagging forward with fatigue; her head had been kept slightly bowed. Both came erect and she looked up at Reede with awe and respect.

"Yes, sir?"

"Do you go along with everything he's told me?"

She shot Plummet a quick, sidelong glance, swallowed hard, and wet her lips nervously. Then, she lowered her eyes and bobbed her head up and down. "Yes."

Plummet's face remained impassive, though his lips were twitching with a smug smile longing to be full-blown. Next, Reede looked down at Alex. She gave him an almost imperceptible shrug.

He stared at the floor for ponderous seconds before barking out a deputy's name. The officer materialized in the doorway as though he'd been expecting his chief's restrained but furious summons.

"Let him go."

Plummet closed his Bible with a resounding clap and stood up. He marched toward the door like a crusader dressed in full battle armor. He ignored his wife, who meekly trailed in his righteous wake.

The deprecations Reede muttered were vile and scathing. "Have somebody keep an eye on the house," he told the deputy. "Let me know if anything he does looks suspicious or even slightly fishy. Damn, I hate to let that bastard walk out of here."

"Don't blame yourself," Alex said sympathetically. "You conducted a thorough interrogation, Reede. You knew going in you didn't have any real evidence."

He whirled on her, his eyes stormy. "Well, that sure as hell hasn't ever stopped you, has it?" He stamped out, leaving her speechless with indignation.

Alex returned to her cubicle, fumbled for the key in the bottom of her handbag, and bent to unlock the door. She felt a prickling sensation at the back of her neck that warned her a heartbeat before the sinister whisper reached her ears.

"You've been corrupted by the ungodly. You're consorting with Satan, showing no more shame than a whore who sells herself." She spun around. Plummet's eyes had regained their zealous glint. Spittle had collected to form white foam in the corners of his mouth. His breathing was labored. "You betrayed my trust."

"I didn't ask for your trust," Alex countered, her voice husky with alarm.

"Your heart and mind have been polluted by the ungodly. Your body has been tarnished by the stroke of the devil himself. You—"

He was caught from behind and slammed against the wall. "Plummet, I warned you." Reede's face was fierce. "Get out of my sight or you're going to be spending some time in jail."

"On what charge?" the preacher squealed. "You've got nothing to hold me on."

"Accosting Miss Gaither."

"I'm God's messenger."

"If God has anything to say to Miss Gaither, He'll tell her Himself. Understand? *Understand?*" He shook Plummet again, then released him. He rounded on Mrs. Plummet, who had flattened herself against the wall in horrified silence. "Wanda, I'm warning you, take him home. Now!" the sheriff bellowed.

Demonstrating more courage than Alex would have expected from her, she grabbed her husband's arm and virtually dragged him toward the staircase. Together, they stumbled up the steps and disappeared around the corner at the landing.

Alex didn't realize how shaken she was until Reede's eyes moved to the hand she had pressed against her pounding heart.

"Did he touch you, hurt you?"

"No." Then, shaking her head, she repeated, "No."

"Don't bullshit me this time. Did he make any threats? Say anything I could use to nail his skinny ass?"

"No, just garbage about me selling out to the unrighteous. He considers me the traitor in the camp."

"Get your things. You're going home."

"You don't have to ask me twice."

He took her coat off the rack near the door. He didn't hold it for her; in fact, he almost threw it at her, but Alex was touched by his evident concern for her safety. He pulled on his leather, fur-trimmed jacket and cowboy hat as they went upstairs and out the front door.

The Plummets must have taken his advice and left. They were nowhere around. Darkness had fallen. Most of the square was deserted. Even the B & B Café had closed for the night. It catered to the breakfast and lunch crowd.

Her car was cold when she slid beneath the steering wheel. "Start your motor to warm it up, but don't leave till I come around in my truck. I'll follow you to the motel."

"That's not necessary, Reede. As you said, he's probably a coward. People who make threats rarely carry them out."

"Yeah. Rarely," he said, stressing the word.

"I can take care of myself. You don't have to worry about me."

"I'm not. It's me I'm worried about. You asked for trouble when you came here, and you're getting it. But no female assistant D.A. is gonna get raped, maimed, or killed in my county. Got that?"

He slammed her car door. Alex watched him disappear down the dark sidewalk, wishing she'd never heard of him or his infernal county. She commissioned him to the fiery hell Plummet frequently expounded upon.

When she saw the headlights of the Blazer approaching, she backed her car into the street and aimed it in the direction of the motel that had been home for far too long. She resented being escorted home.

She let herself into her room and locked the door behind her, without even waving her thanks to Reede. Dinner was a tasteless meal ordered off the room service menu. She thumbed through the yearbooks again, but was so familiar with them by now that the pictures hardly registered. She was tired, but too keyed up to go to sleep.

Junior's kiss haunted her thoughts, not because it had sparked her sensual imagination, but because it hadn't. Reede's kisses haunted her because he had so effortlessly accomplished what Junior had wanted to.

Angus hadn't needed a script to know the kind of scene he'd walked into when he had entered the hangar and found her with Reede. His expression had been a mix of surprise, disapproval, and something she couldn't quite put a name to. Resignation?

She tossed and turned out of fatigue, frustration, and yes, fear. No matter how many times she denied it, Plummet disturbed her. He was a wacko, but his words held a ring of truth.

She had come to care what each of her suspects thought of her. Winning their approval had become almost as important as winning her grandmother's. It was a bizarre fact, one she had difficulty admitting to herself.

She didn't trust Reede, but she desired him and wanted him to reciprocate that desire. For all his laziness, she liked Junior and felt a twinge of pity for him. Angus fulfilled her childhood fantasies of a stern but loving parent. The closer she came to uncovering the truth about their connection to her mother's death, the less she wanted to know it.

Then, there was the cloud of the Pasty Hickam murder lurking on the horizon. Reede's suspect, Lyle Turner, was still at large. Until she was convinced that he had killed the Mintons' former ranch hand, she would go on believing that

Pasty had been eliminated as an eyewitness to Celina's murder. His killer considered her a threat, too.

So, in the middle of the night, when she heard a car slowly drive past her door, when she saw its headlights arc across her bed, her heart leaped in fright.

Throwing off the covers, she crept to the window and peeped through the crack between it and the heavy drape. Her whole body went limp with relief and she uttered a small, glad sound.

The sheriff's Blazer executed a wide turn in the parking lot and passed her room once more before driving away.

———◈———

Reede thought about turning around and going to where he knew he could find potent liquor, a welcoming smile, and a warm woman, but he kept the hood of his truck pointed toward home.

He was sick with an unknown disease. He couldn't shake it, no matter how hard he tried. He itched from the inside out, and his gut was in a state of constant turmoil.

His house, which he had always liked for the solitude it provided, seemed merely lonely when he opened the squeaky screen door. When was he ever going to remember to oil those hinges? The light he switched on did little to enhance the living room. It only illuminated the fact that there was nobody to welcome him home.

Not even a dog came forward to lick his hand, wagging its tail because it was glad to see him. He didn't have a goldfish, a parakeet, a cat—nothing that could die on him and leave another vacuum in his life.

Horses were different. They were business investments. But every once in a while, one would become special, like Double Time. That had hurt. He tried not to think about it.

Refugee camps in famine-ravaged countries were better stocked with provisions than his kitchen. He seldom ate at home. When he did, like now, he made do with a beer and a few saltines spread with peanut butter.

On his way down the hall, he adjusted the furnace thermostat so he wouldn't be frozen stiff by morning. His bed was unmade; he didn't remember what had gotten him out of it so suddenly the last time he'd been in it.

He shed his clothes, dropping them in the hamper in the bathroom, which Lupe's niece would empty the next time she came. He probably owned more underwear and socks than any man he knew. It wasn't an extravagance; it just kept him from having to do laundry frequently. His wardrobe consisted of jeans and shirts, mostly. Having several of each done up at the dry cleaner's every week kept him decently clothed.

While he brushed his teeth at the bathroom sink, he surveyed his image in the mirror. He needed a haircut. He usually did. There were a few more gray hairs in his sideburns than the last time he'd looked. When had those cropped up?

He suddenly realized how lined his face had become. Anchoring the toothbrush in the corner of his mouth, he leaned across the sink and peered at his reflection at close range. His face was full of cracks and crevices.

In plain English, he looked old.

Too old? For what? More to the point, too old for whom?

The name that sprang to mind greatly disturbed him.

He spat and rinsed out his mouth, but avoided looking at himself again before he turned out the cruelly revealing overhead light. There was no need to set an alarm. He was always up by sunrise. He never overslept.

The sheets were frigid. He pulled the covers to his chin and waited for heat to find his naked body. It was at moments like this, when the night was the darkest and coldest and most solitary, that he wished Celina hadn't ruined him for other relationships. At any other time, he was glad he wasn't a sucker for emotions.

At times like this, he secretly wished that he'd married. Even sleeping next to the warm body of a woman you didn't particularly love, or who'd gone to fat months after the wedding, or who had let you down, or who harped about the shortage of money and the long hours you worked, would be better than sleeping alone.

Then again, maybe not. Who the hell knew? He would never know because of Celina. He hadn't loved her when she died, not in the way he'd loved her most of his life up until then.

He had begun to wonder if their love could outlast their youth, if it was real and substantial, or merely the best substitute they had for other deficiencies in their lives. He would always have loved her as a friend, but he had doubted that their mutual dependence was a healthy foundation for a life together.

Perhaps Celina had sensed his reservations, and that had been one of the reasons she'd felt the need to leave for a while. They had never discussed it. He would never know, but he suspected it.

Months before she left for El Paso that summer, he had been questioning the durability of their childhood romance. If his feelings for her changed with maturity, how the hell was he going to handle the breakup? He had still been in a muddle about it when she had died, and it had left him wary of forming any future relationships.

He would never let himself get that entwined with another human being. It was deadly, having that kind of focus on another person, especially a woman.

Years ago, he'd sworn to take what women could expediently give him, chiefly sex, but never to cultivate tenderness toward one again. He would certainly never come close to loving one.

But the short-term affairs had become too complicated. Invariably, the woman developed an emotional attachment that he couldn't reciprocate. That's when he'd started relying on Nora Gail for physical gratification. Now, that had soured. Sex with her was routine and meaningless, and lately, he was having a hard time keeping his boredom from showing.

Dealing with a woman on any level demanded a much higher price than he was willing to pay.

Still, even as he lay there mentally reciting his creed of eternal detachment, he found himself thinking about *her*.

At this advanced stage of his life, he'd started daydreaming like a sap. She occupied more of his thoughts than he would have ever thought possible. At the edges of these thoughts was an emotion very akin to tenderness, nudging its way into his consciousness.

Nipping at the heels of it, however, was always pain: the pain of knowing who she was and how irrevocably her conception had altered his life, of knowing how decrepit he must appear to a woman her age, of seeing her kiss Junior.

"Dammit."

He groaned into the darkness and covered his eyes with his forearms as his mind tricked him into witnessing it again.

It had produced such an attack of jealousy, it had frightened him. His fury had been volcanic. It was a wonder he hadn't erupted from the roof of the Blazer.

How the hell had it happened? Why had he let her get to him when absolutely nothing could come of it, except to widen the gulf between him and Junior that had been created by her mother?

A relationship—the word alone made him shudder— between him and Alex was out of the question, so why did it bother him to know that to a smart, savvy career woman like Alex, he must look like a hick, and an *old* one, at that?

He and Celina had had everything in common, but she'd been unattainable, so how the hell did he imagine there was common ground on which he and Alex could meet?

One other small point, he thought wryly. *Celina's murder.* Alex would never understand about that.

None of that sound reasoning, however, kept him from wanting her. An influx of heat surged through his body now, and with it, desire. He wanted to smell her. He wanted to feel her hair against his cheek, his chest, his belly. Imagining her lips and tongue against his skin cost him precious breath, but the lack of sufficient air was worth the image. He wanted to taste her again and tug on her nipple with his mouth.

He whispered her name in the darkness and focused on that instant when he had slipped his hand into the cup of her bra and caressed forbidden flesh. He was consumed by the fire of his imagination. It burned brightly and fiercely.

Eventually, it dimmed. When it did, he was left feeling empty and alone in the cold, dark, lonely house.

Chapter 33

———◈———

Good morning, Wanda Gail."

Fergus Plummet's wife fell back a step. "What'd you call me?"

"Wanda Gail," Alex repeated with a gentle smile. "That's your name, isn't it? You're one of the Burton triplets, informally known as the Gail sisters."

Mrs. Plummet had answered her door with a dishrag in her hands. Shocked by Alex's knowledge of her past, she took a quick little breath. Her eyes darted about the yard, as though looking for artillery backing Alex up.

"May I come in?"

Alex didn't wait for permission, but used the other woman's astonishment to step inside and close the front door. She had discovered Mrs. Plummet's identity quite by accident while idly perusing the pages of the yearbooks over her morning coffee. After she'd glanced past it a hundred times, the classroom picture had suddenly leaped off the page. She'd thought her eyes were deceiving her until she verified the name in the margin. Wanda Gail Burton.

Hardly able to contain her excitement, she'd consulted the telephone directory for the address and driven straight to the parsonage. She had parked well down the block and hadn't approached the house until Fergus had driven away in his car.

The two women stood face-to-face in the dim hallway. Alex was curious. Wanda Gail Plummet was clearly afraid.

"I shouldn't be talking to you," she whispered nervously.

"Why? Because your husband warned you against it?" Alex asked softly. "I don't mean to cause you any trouble. Let's sit down."

Assuming the role of hostess, Alex led Wanda Gail into the drabbest, most unattractive room she had ever been in. There wasn't a single spot of color or gaiety. There were no plants, no pictures—other than one of a bleeding, crucified Christ—no books or magazines. There was nothing to relieve the cheerless atmosphere that pervaded the house. Alex had seen three thin, dejected-looking children leave with their father. She and Wanda Gail were alone.

They sat side by side on a tacky, threadbare sofa that reflected the overall penury of the house. Wanda Gail was wringing the damp towel between her hands. Her face was working with anxiety. She was obviously scared to death, either of Alex, or of her husband's reprisal should he find out she had been in their home.

Alex tried to reassure her by calmly stating, "I just want to talk to you. I accidentally discovered that your name was Wanda Gail Burton."

"Not anymore. Not since I found Jesus."

"Tell me about that. When was it?"

"The summer after I graduated. A bunch of us——"

"Your sisters?"

She nodded. "And some friends. We all piled into some-body's car and drove to Midland. We were looking for fun," she said, casting her eyes downward. "We saw this big tent set up in a cow pasture on the outskirts of town. There was a revival going on. We thought we'd go, see what it was about. We went on a lark, you know, to poke fun at the people and to laugh at the gospel."

She made a grimace of remorse. "It all seemed real funny, 'cause we'd been drinking and smoking pot somebody had brought back from Eagle Pass." She folded her hands together and offered up a brief prayer of repentance.

"What happened? Did you have a religious experience that night?"

She confirmed Alex's guess by briskly nodding her head. "There was this young preacher there. After the singing and praying, he took the microphone." Her eyes assumed a dreamy aspect as she was transported back. "I don't even remember what he preached on. His voice alone put me in a trance. I remember feeling his energy pouring through me. I couldn't take my eyes off him."

Her vision cleared. "The others had had enough and wanted to leave. I told them to go on and pick me up later. I wanted to stay. When he was finished preaching, I went down to the altar with dozens of others. He laid his hands on my head and prayed for my deliverance from sin." Misty-eyed, she announced, "I gave my heart to Jesus and to Fergus Plummet that same night."

"How soon after that were you married?"

"Two days."

Alex didn't know a delicate way to approach her next

question. Out of deference to the woman's Christian conversion, she addressed her by her married name. "Mrs. Plummet, you and your sisters…" She paused, wet her lips. "I've heard…"

"I know what you've heard. We were harlots."

Alex didn't approve of her harsh, condemning estimation of herself and tried to soften it. "I know that you dated a lot of men."

Wanda began to twist the towel again. "I confessed all my transgressions to Fergus. He forgave me, just like God did. He embraced me in love, in spite of my wickedness."

Alex had a more jaundiced opinion of the preacher's largesse. He had probably wanted a wife who felt privileged that he had so unselfishly forgiven her, one who would consider his grace equal to God's.

God forgot sins; Alex doubted that Fergus Plummet did. He probably kept scrupulous accounts of transgressions and used Wanda Gail's past as a tool to keep her under his thumb. He surely made her life miserable with constant reminders of how lucky she was to have his forgiveness.

It was apparent, however, that whatever had happened to Wanda Gail in that revival tent had been profound and irreversible. Her decision that night to create a different life for herself had withstood twenty-five years. For that, she had earned Alex's admiration.

"Two of the boys you dated in high school were Reede Lambert and Junior Minton."

"Yes," Wanda said with a reflective smile, "they were the two best-looking, most popular boys in school. All the girls wanted to date them."

"Including Stacey Wallace?"

"The only boy she could ever see was Junior Minton. It was kind of pitiful, you know, because Stacey was so crazy about him and he was stuck on Celina."

"And Celina belonged to Reede."

"Well, sure. Reede was, and still is, basically good. He didn't treat me and my sisters like trash, even though that's what we were. He was always nice about...well, you know, whenever he took us out. He always said thank you afterward."

Alex smiled sickly.

"Liked to have drove him plumb nuts when Celina got married. Then, when she died..." She sighed sympathetically. "He acts kinda mean sometimes now, but down deep, he's still good." She averted her head. "I know he doesn't like Fergus, but he still treated me nice yesterday."

This woman and Reede were former lovers. Alex looked at her closely. It was impossible to envision Wanda Gail in the throes of ecstasy with any man, but especially with Reede.

Her face retained enough of its former prettiness for Alex to have recognized her picture in the yearbook, but her skin was loose, her throat flabby. The full, teased hairdo she'd been sporting in the class photo had been replaced by the severe and unflattering bun. The eyes that had been dramatically enhanced with cosmetics for the picture wore no makeup at all now. Her waist had thickened to match the dimensions of her bust and hips, which, when she was a teenager, must have been voluptuous.

Wanda Gail looked at least ten years older than her classmates, Reede and Junior—even Stacey. Alex wondered if it had been her previous wild life, or her married life with Plummet that had accelerated her aging process. She would bet on the latter. He couldn't be much fun to live with. For all his piousness, he brought no joy or love to those around him. To Alex, that's what one's faith should be about. Her admiration for this woman was tinged with pity.

It became even more so when Wanda Gail looked up at her and shyly remarked, "You were nice to me, too. I didn't expect you to be nice, 'cause you're so fancy and have such pretty things." She gave Alex's fur coat and eel handbag a wistful glance.

"Thank you," she replied. Then, because Wanda Gail seemed stricken with self-consciousness, Alex resumed the questioning. "How did your sisters react to your marriage?"

"Oh, I'm sure they didn't like it."

"You don't know?"

"Fergus thought it would be best if I didn't mix with them anymore."

"He separated you from your family?"

"It was for the best," Wanda said, immediately rising to his defense. "I left my old life. They were part of it. I had to turn my back on them to prove to Jesus that I was forsaking sin."

Alex chalked up another reason to despise the preacher. He had brainwashed his wife against her family and used her immortal soul as leverage. "Where are your sisters now?"

"Peggy Gail died a few years ago. I read about it in the newspaper. She had cancer," she said, her face sorrowful.

"What about the other one? Nora Gail?"

Wanda's lips narrowed with stern disapproval. "She's still living her sinful ways."

"Here in town?"

"Oh my, yes." Again, she clasped her hands beneath her

chin and said a quick prayer. "I pray to God that she'll see the light before it's too late."

"She never married?"

"No, she likes men too much, all men. She never wanted one in particular. Maybe Reede Lambert, but he didn't want anything permanent."

"She liked him?"

"Very much. They enjoyed each other physically, but it never amounted to love. Maybe they were too much alike. Stubborn. They both have a mean streak, too."

Alex tried to make the next question sound casual. "Do you know if he still sees her?"

"I expect he does," she said, folding her arms across her middle and sniffing righteously. "He liked us all, but Nora Gail was always his first choice. I don't know if they still sleep together, but they've gotta stay friends 'cause they know too much about each other. Ever since the night Celina was killed, there's been—"

"What about it?" Alex interrupted.

"What about what?"

"The night Celina was killed."

"Reede was with Nora Gail."

Alex's heart fluttered. "He was with your sister that night? You're sure?"

Wanda gave her a puzzled look. "I thought everybody knew that."

Everybody but me, Alex thought bitterly.

She asked Wanda where Nora Gail lived. Reluctantly, Wanda gave her directions to the house. "I've never been there, but I know where it is. I don't think you can miss it."

Alex thanked her for the information and rose to leave. At

the door, Wanda became nervous again. "I don't think Fergus would like it that I talked to you."

"He won't hear about it from mc." Wanda Gail looked reassured until Alex added, "I'd advise him against any more vandalism, and I would appreciate not getting another condemning letter in the mail."

"Letter?"

She appeared not to have any knowledge of the letter that had been waiting for Alex when she had returned from Austin, but Alex felt sure that she must. "I won't place you in a position of having to lie for your husband, Mrs. Plummet, but I should warn you that Reede has the letter and considers it a police matter. I feel certain he'd make an arrest if I receive another one."

She hoped the subtle threat would work. By the time she reached her car, however, her mind had already moved forward to her interview with Reede's alibi.

———◆———

The two-story frame structure reminded Alex of the Prohibition-era roadhouses she'd seen in gangster movies. It had no signs out front and was invisible from the highway, but there were several commercial rigs in the parking lot, along with a few pickup trucks, and even a recent-model Cadillac.

The stone sidewalk was bordered with valiant, dusty pansies. A series of steps led up to a deep veranda. There was an old-fashioned pull bell next to the front door. Muted honky-tonk music wafted through the walls, but the windows appeared to have been blacked out; she couldn't see through them.

The door was answered by a bear of a man with a full, salt-and-pepper beard covering the lower two-thirds of a face as florid as a sirloin steak. He was wearing a white tuxedo shirt and black satin bow tie, over a full white apron. He was also wearing a fearsome, intimidating frown.

"I—" Alex began.

"Are you lost?"

"I'm looking for Nora Gail Burton."

"Whaddaya want with her?"

"I want to talk to her."

"What about?"

"It's personal."

He squinted suspiciously. "You selling something?"

"No."

"You got an appointment?"

"No."

"She's busy."

He started to close the door, but a man approached it on his way out. He squeezed between them, doffing his bill cap to Alex and muttering thanks to the doorman. Alex took advantage of the interruption and stepped over the threshold into a formally decorated vestibule. "I'd like to see Ms. Burton, please. I promise not to take too much of her time."

"If you're looking for work, miss, you'll need to fill out an application and provide pictures. She doesn't see a girl until she's looked over her pictures."

"I'm not looking for work."

He considered her for another long moment before coming to a favorable conclusion. "Name?"

"Alexandra Gaither."

"Wait right here, you hear?"

"Yes, sir."

"Don't move."

"I promise."

He retreated toward the back of the house, moving along the staircase with a grace and lightness of tread unusual for a man his size. His order for her to stay put had been so emphatic that it had nailed her shoes to the floor. She didn't think anything could prize her away.

Within seconds, however, the music beckoned her toward its source. Low conversation and soft laughter lured her toward the violet brocade drapes that separated the hallway from the room beyond. The edges overlapped so she couldn't see anything. Raising her hand tentatively, she pushed them apart and peeked through the slit.

"Ms. Gaither."

She jumped and spun around, dropping her hand guiltily. The bearded giant was looming over her, but his soft, pink lips were twitching with amusement.

"This way," the mammoth said. He led her behind the stairwell and stopped in front of a closed door. After giving it three sharp raps, he pushed it open and stepped aside for Alex to enter. He closed the door behind her.

Alex had expected the madam to be reclining on satin sheets. Instead, she was seated behind a large, functional desk banked by metal file cabinets. From the number of ledgers and folders and stacks of correspondence scattered across the desk, it looked as though she conducted as much business here as in the boudoir.

Nor was her clothing what Alex would have expected. Instead of a scanty article of lingerie, she was wearing a tailored wool business suit. She was, however, elaborately jeweled, and all the pieces were genuine and exquisite.

Her hair had been bleached snow-white and looked like a sculpted mound of cotton candy. Somehow, though, the outdated style suited her. Like her sister Wanda, her figure gravitated toward plump, but she carried that well, too. Her complexion was her best feature. It was flawless, smooth, and milky white. Alex doubted it had ever been exposed to the damaging West Texas sun.

The blue eyes with which she assessed Alex were as calculating as those of the cat that was occupying the corner of the desk nearest her right hand.

"You have better taste than your mother," she said without preamble, giving Alex a slow once-over. "Celina had pretty features, but no sense of style. You do. Sit down, Miss Gaither."

"Thank you." Alex sat down in the chair across the desk. After a moment, she laughed and shook her head with chagrin. "Forgive me for staring."

"I don't mind. No doubt I'm your first madam."

"Actually, no. I prosecuted a woman in Austin whose modeling agency proved to be a prostitution ring."

"She was careless."

"I did my homework. We had an airtight case against her."

"Should I take that as a warning?"

"Your operation doesn't fall into my jurisdiction."

"Neither does your mother's murder case." She lit a slender black cigarette as a man would, with an economy of motion, and offered one to Alex, who declined. "A drink? Forgive me for saying that you look like you could use one."

She gestured toward a lacquered liquor cabinet that was inlaid with mother-of-pearl.

"No, thank you. Nothing."

"Peter said you declined to fill out an application, so I guess you're not here looking for a job."

"No."

"Pity. You'd do very well. Nice body, good legs, unusual hair. Is that its natural color?"

"Yes."

The madam grinned wickedly. "I know several regulars who would enjoy you a lot."

"Thank you," Alex said stiffly, the compliment making her feel like she needed a bath.

"I guess you're here on business. Yours," she said with a lazy smile, "not mine."

"I'd like to ask you some questions."

"First, I'd like to ask one of my own."

"All right."

"Did Reede send you here?"

"No."

"Good. That would have disappointed me."

"I found you through your sister."

One eyebrow arched a fraction of an inch higher. "Wanda Gail? I thought she believed that speaking my name aloud would turn her into a pillar of salt, or some such nonsense. How is she? Never mind," she said when she sensed Alex's hesitation.

"I've seen Wanda Gail from a distance. She looks terrible. That little pecker who professes to be a man of God has nearly ruined her health, as well as her looks. Her kids go around like ragamuffins. If she wants to live like that, fine, but why impose poverty on them?"

She was genuinely indignant. "There's no righteousness in being poor. I'd like to help her financially, but I'm sure she would rather starve than take a cent from me, even if her husband would allow it. Did she just come right out and tell you that her sister was a whore?"

"No. She only gave me directions here. I guess she assumed that I already knew your...occupation."

"You didn't."

"No."

"My business has been lucrative, but I'm branching out. I used to screw men for fun, Ms. Gaither. I'm still screwing them, but now I do it mostly for money. And you know what? Money's even more fun." Her laugh was throaty and complacent.

She had none of Wanda Gail's timidity. Alex got the impression that Nora Gail wasn't afraid of Satan himself, that she would walk up to him and spit in his eye without an ounce of trepidation. After that, she would probably seduce him.

"In fact," she continued, "you were lucky to catch me in. I just returned from a meeting with my banker. No matter how busy he is, he makes room in his schedule to see me."

She gestured down at the portfolio lying open on top of the desk directly in front of her. Even reading it upside down, Alex recognized the logo on the letterhead.

"NGB, Incorporated," she mouthed silently. When her eyes met the madam's again, Nora Gail's were gloating. "*You* are NGB, Incorporated? Nora Gail Burton," she said faintly.

"That's right."

"You signed the letter the businesspeople sent to me."

"I helped draft it." Her long, beautifully manicured

nails sank into the cat's lush fur as she scratched it behind the ears. "I don't like what you're trying to do here, Miss Gaither. I don't like it at all. You're about to throw a goddamned wrench into all my carefully orchestrated plans for expansion."

"As I recall, NGB, Incorporated proposes to build a resort hotel near Purcell Downs."

"That's right. A resort complete with golf course, putting greens, tennis courts, racquetball, swimming. You name it, it'll have it."

"And does a whore come with every room?"

Nora Gail gave another of her bawdy laughs, taking no offense. "No. But who knows better how to show folks a good time than an old whore? I've got the best resort architects in the country working on the layout. It'll be spectacular, gaudy as hell, which I've decided the tourist trade likes. Everybody who comes to Texas from out of state, particularly from back east, expects us to be loud, raucous, and tasteless. I don't want my customers to be disappointed."

"Have you got the money to build a place like that?" Alex asked, her peevishness giving way to curiosity.

"I've got enough put aside to borrow against. Honey, more cowboys, truckers, roughnecks, white-collar types, statesmen, and would-be statesmen have trooped up those stairs than I could count," she said, pointing toward the staircase. "Actually, I could tell you exactly how many, how long each stayed, what he did, what he drank, what he smoked, whatever you wanted to know. My records are that meticulous.

"I'm a whore, but I'm a goddamned smart one. You don't go into this business just knowing how to make a john come. You go into it knowing how to make him come quickly so you can move on to the next one. You've also got to know how to get him to drop more dollars than he intends to while he's visiting."

She sat back and stroked the cat. "Yes, I've got the money. More important, I've got the brains to pyramid it into a fortune. With that resort, I can go legitimate. I'll never have to give a blow job to another stiff cock unless it's one of my own choosing, or listen to another hard-luck story from a man about how his wife doesn't understand him.

"I'm living for the day I can move out of this place and into town, hold my head up, and say, 'Kiss my ass,' to anybody who doesn't like me moving into his neighborhood." She pointed her cigarette toward Alex. "I don't need a cheerleader like you to come in here and fuck it up for me."

It was quite a speech. In spite of herself, Alex was fascinated, though not cowed. "All I'm trying to do is solve a murder case."

"Not for the sake of law and order you're not. The state doesn't give a damn about Celina Gaither's killing, or it would have been looked into years ago."

"You've just admitted that the case warrants being reopened."

Nora Gail gave an elegant shrug. "Maybe from a legal standpoint, but not from a personal one. Listen, sugar, take my advice. I'm talking to you now like I would to one of my girls when things aren't working out for her." She leaned forward. "Go home. Leave things here the way they were. Everybody'll be happier, especially you."

"Do you know who murdered my mother, Ms. Burton?"

"No."

"Do you believe that Gooney Bud killed her?"

"That harmless idiot? No."

"So, you suspect someone else. Who?"

"I'd never tell you."

"Even under oath on the witness stand?"

She shook her head of glorious white hair. "I wouldn't incriminate my friends."

"Like Reede Lambert?"

"Like Reede Lambert," Nora Gail repeated firmly. "We go way back."

"So I've heard."

Nora Gail's husky chuckle brought Alex's head up. "Does it bother you to know that Reede and I used to screw our brains out?"

"Why should it?"

Without taking her eyes off Alex, Nora Gail sent a plume of smoke ceilingward and ground out her cigarette in a crystal ashtray. "You tell me, sugar."

Alex drew herself up, attempting to reestablish herself as a tough prosecutor. "Was he with you the night my mother was killed?"

"Yes," she answered without a second's hesitation.

"Where?"

"I believe we were in my car."

"Screwing your brains out?"

"What's it to you?"

"My interest is strictly professional," Alex snapped. "I'm trying to establish Reede Lambert's alibi. I need to know where you were, what you were doing, and for how long."

"I fail to see the relevance."

"Let me decide the relevance. Besides, what difference

does it make if you tell me now? I'm sure you gave the answers to the officers who questioned you before."

"No one ever questioned me."

"What?" Alex exclaimed.

"No one ever questioned me. I guess Reede told them that he was with me and they believed him."

"Was he with you all night?"

"I'd swear to that in court."

Alex gave her a long, steady look. "But was he?"

"I'd swear under oath that he was," she said, her eyes openly challenging.

That was a dead-end street. Alex decided to stop butting her head against the bricks. It was giving her a headache. "How well did you know my mother?"

"Well enough not to cry over her death." Her candor matched Stacey Wallace's. Alex should have been inured to it by now, but she wasn't. "Look, sugar, I hate to put it to you so bluntly, but I didn't like your mother. She knew that Reede and Junior both loved her. The temptation was just too strong."

"What temptation?"

"To play them against each other, see how far she could go. After your daddy got killed, she started playing up to them again. Reede was slow to forgive her for getting pregnant, but not Junior. I guess he saw his chance and took it. Anyway, he started courting her in earnest.

"His folks didn't like it. Stacey Wallace was about to come apart at the seams over it. But it looked like Junior was going to get Celina, after all. He made it known to anybody who wanted to listen that as soon as he graduated, he was going to marry her. Tickled your grandma to death. She'd always been jealous of Reede and fancied Junior Minton as a son-in-law."

She paused to light another cigarette. Alex waited impatiently, a knot of tension drawing tighter in her chest. After Nora Gail's cigarette was lit she asked, "How did Reede feel about the pending marriage between Celina and Junior?"

"He was still pissed at Celina, but he cared—a hell of a lot. That's why he came to me that night. Celina had gone out to the ranch for supper. Reede expected Junior to pop the question. By morning, he expected them to be engaged."

"But by morning, Celina was dead."

"That's right, sugar," Nora Gail replied coolly. "And in my opinion, that was the best solution to their problem."

As though punctuating her startling statement, a shot rang out.

Chapter 34

"Good Lord, what was that?" Alex sprang to her feet.

"A gunshot, I believe." Nora Gail remained admirably calm, but she had already reached the door by the time the man who had greeted Alex flung it open. "Is anyone hurt, Peter?"

"Yes, ma'am. A customer's been shot."

"Phone Reede."

"Yes, ma'am."

Peter lurched toward the telephone on the desk. Nora Gail left the office. Alex followed her. The madam flung open the drapes with a theatrical flourish and took in the scene at a glance. With apprehension and curiosity, Alex peered over Nora Gail's shoulder.

Two men whom Alex assumed were bouncers had subdued a man and were restraining him against the ornate bar. Several scantily clad young women were cowering against the purple velvet furniture. Another man was lying on the floor. Blood was pooling beneath him, making a mess on the pastel Oriental rug.

"What happened?" When Nora Gail got no answer, she repeated her question with noticeably more emphasis.

"They got in a scuffle," one of the prostitutes answered finally. "Next thing we knew, the gun went off." She pointed down. A revolver was lying on the floor near the prone man's feet.

"What were they fighting over?" After a lengthy silence, one of the girls fearfully raised her hand.

"Go to my office and stay there." Nora Gail's tone was as brittle as cracking ice. It suggested that the girl should have known how to prevent an incident like this. "The rest of you get upstairs, and stay there until further notice."

No one argued. Nora Gail ran a tight ship. The young women flitted past Alex like a flock of butterflies. They were met on their way upstairs by several men stampeding down, pulling on their clothes as they ran. Without exception, they looked neither right nor left as they exited through the front door.

It was a farcical scene, but giggling over it was out of the question. Alex was mortified. She had been on the fringes of violence before, but reading about criminal action in a police report was different from experiencing it firsthand. There was something very startling and real about the sight and scent of fresh, human blood.

Nora Gail gestured Peter, who had rejoined them, toward the bleeding man. He knelt beside him and pressed his fingers against the man's carotid artery. "He's alive."

Alex saw some of the starch go out of Nora Gail's posture. She'd handled the situation with aplomb, but she wasn't made of stone. She had been more worried about the situation than she had let on.

Hearing the wail of a siren, Nora Gail turned toward the

door and was on the threshold to greet Reede when he came barging in. "What happened, Nora Gail?"

"There was a dispute over one of the girls," she informed him. "A man's been shot, but he's alive."

"Where is he? The paramedics are—" Reede stopped short when he spotted Alex. At first he just gaped at her with patent disbelief; then, his face turned dark with rage. "What the hell are you doing here?"

"Conducting my investigation."

"Investigation, my ass," he growled. "Get the hell out of here."

The wounded man moaned, drawing Reede's attention. "I suggest you tend to your own business, Sheriff Lambert," Alex said tartly.

He cursed as he knelt down beside the man. When he noticed the amount of blood, however, his concentration switched immediately from Alex to the victim. "How're you doing, cowboy?" The man moaned. "What's your name?"

His eyes fluttered open. He comprehended the question, but didn't seem able to answer. Reede gently moved aside his clothing until he found the source of the blood. The bullet had pierced his side at about waist level. "You'll live," he told him. "Just hang in there a few more minutes. An ambulance is on its way."

He came to his feet and walked toward the man still in the bouncers' custody. He was standing with his head bowed.

"What about you? Got a name?" Reede asked, jerking the man's chin up. "Well, howdy, Lewis," he drawled. "Thought we'd seen the last of your miserable hide. Didn't take my warning seriously, did you? Can't tell you what a pleasure it's gonna be to have you residing in my jail again."

"Go fuck yourself, Lambert," the man sneered insolently.

Reede hauled back his fist, then reached for the man's spine through about a foot and a half of abdominal tissue. Lewis doubled at the waist, but only until Reede's fist connected with his chin, bringing it up with a powerful blow. He was then lifted by the lapels of his jacket and shoved against the wall.

"You've got a big mouth, Lewis," Reede said calmly, barely winded by the exertion. "We'll see how smart you talk after a month or two in a place where the bad boys will make you eat their dicks for breakfast every morning."

The man whimpered helplessly. When Reede released him, he slid down the wall to form a pathetic heap on the floor. Two deputies stepped into the room, gawking at their plush surroundings.

"He resisted arrest," Reede calmly said, pointing at Lewis, then curtly ordered him handcuffed, Mirandized, and booked for attempted murder. He consulted with the paramedics who had come in behind the deputies and were dealing with the injured man.

"He's lost a lot of blood," one of them reported to Reede as he slid a needle into the victim's arm. "It's serious, but not critical."

Satisfied that everything was being handled properly, Reede's attention reverted to Alex. Taking her upper arm in a firm grip, he hauled her toward the door.

"Let me go."

"Unless Nora Gail hired you on, you've got no business here. Nora Gail, shut down for the night."

"This is Friday, Reede."

"Tough. Don't let anybody leave, either. Somebody'll be along soon to start the questioning."

He roughly shepherded Alex down the steps and into his Blazer, nearly cramming her into the seat before he slammed the door shut. He climbed in behind the wheel.

"My car is over there," she told him stubbornly. "I can drive myself back to town."

"I'll have one of the deputies pick it up later." He ground the key in the ignition. "What in God's name possessed you to come here?"

"I didn't know what it was until I arrived."

"Well, when you figured it out, why didn't you leave?"

"I wanted to talk to Nora Gail. She's a very old and dear friend of yours, I understand," she said with phony sweetness.

At the intersection with the highway, they met one of his patrol cars turning in. He signaled the deputy to stop and rolled down his window. "Give me your keys," he told Alex. She passed them to him because he wasn't going to give her a choice, and because, in spite of her brave front, she was trembling.

Reede tossed her keys to the deputy and instructed him to have his partner drive Ms. Gaither's car to the Westerner Motel when they were finished with the preliminary investigation of the shooting. With that taken care of, he zoomed onto the highway.

"Don't you feel the least bit guilty?" Alex asked him.

"For what?"

"For turning a blind eye to a whorehouse operating in your county?"

"No."

She looked at him, completely flabbergasted. "Why not? Because the madam is an old flame of yours?"

"Not entirely. Nora Gail's place keeps potential troublemakers concentrated in one spot. Her bouncers keep them in line."

"Today they didn't."

"Today was an exception. That scumbag is bad news no matter where he is."

"I should report you for police brutality."

"He had that coming, and then some. He got off on a technicality the last time he passed through our judicial system. This time he'll spend a nice, long time in prison.

"And, by the way, they caught Lyle Turner in New Mexico. He confessed to slitting Pasty's throat for screwing around with Ruby Faye. It had nothing whatsoever to do with you, so you can stop looking over your shoulder for bogeymen."

"Thanks for telling me." The news relieved her, but this latest development was still on her mind. "Don't try to get me off the subject. I'm not going to sweep this under the carpet. Pat Chastain would love to know that there's a bordello operating right under his nose."

Reede laughed. He took off his hat, ran his hand through his hair, and shook his head in dismay over her naïveté. "Have you ever met Mrs. Chastain?"

"What does that—"

"Have you?"

"No. I've talked to her on the telephone."

"She's a country club hag, tanned skin stretched over solid bone. She wears more gold jewelry than a pimp, even when she plays tennis. She thinks her shit don't stink. Got the picture? She likes being the D.A.'s wife, but doesn't like the D.A., particularly in bed."

"I'm not interested in—"

"Her idea of foreplay is, 'Hurry up, but don't mess up my hairdo,' and she would probably rather die than let him come in her mouth."

"You're disgusting."

"Pat's got a favorite out at Nora Gail's who'll swallow it and pretend to like it, so he's not going to lift a finger to shut the place down. If you were smart, which I'm beginning to seriously doubt, you won't embarrass him by letting on you even know that Nora Gail's place is out there. And don't even think about tattling to Judge Wallace. He never partakes, but all his friends do. He sure as hell isn't going to stop their party."

"My God, is everybody in this county corrupt?"

"Oh, for crissake, Alex, grow up. Everybody in the whole goddamn world is corrupt. You might be the only person who ever went through law school and came out believing that the law is still based on morality. Everybody's guilty of something. Everybody's got a secret. If you're lucky, the next guy's secret is juicier than yours. You use his secret to keep him quiet about yours."

"I'm glad you brought that up. It was Nora Gail you were with the night Celina was killed."

"Congratulations. You finally got one guess right."

"It wasn't a guess. Wanda Plummet told me."

He grinned. "When did you figure her out?"

"I didn't," she admitted with some reluctance. "I recognized her picture in the yearbook. You could have told me, Reede."

"I could have, but you'd have started pestering sooner."

"I didn't pester her. She was most cooperative."

"She was scared. You can't tell by looking at her now what a hell-raiser she used to be."

"I'd rather talk about her sister, Nora Gail. The night my mother was killed, were you with her all night?"

"Wouldn't you love to know?"

"What were you doing?"

"Three guesses, and the first two don't count."

"Making love?"

"Screwing."

"Where?"

"Her house."

"Nora Gail said you were in her car."

He whipped his Blazer around a farmer in a pickup truck. "Maybe we were. Car, house, what's the difference? I don't remember."

"You had been to the ranch earlier."

"Yeah, so?"

"You ate dinner there."

"We've been over this already."

"This was a special night—Celina was there for dinner."

"Don't you remember talking about this?"

"I remember. You told me that you'd left before dessert because apple pie wasn't one of your favorites."

"Wrong. Cherry pie. It's still not one of my favorites."

"That's not why you left, Reede."

"No?" He risked taking his eyes off the road to glance at her.

"No. You left because you were afraid Junior was going to propose to Celina that night. You were even more afraid that she was going to accept."

He brought the truck to a jarring stop outside her motel room. He got out and came around to her door, almost jerking it off its hinges when he opened it. Grabbing her arm again, he pulled her to the ground and pushed her toward her door. She resisted and turned to confront him.

"I'm right so far, aren't I?"

"Yeah, I went out with Nora Gail to blow off some steam."

"Did it work?"

"No, so I sneaked back to the ranch and found Celina in the mares' barn. How the hell I knew she was going to be there is something you've yet to figure out, Counselor," he sneered.

"I took the scalpel out of my pocket. Why I'd taken it from the vet's bag when I could have strangled her with my bare hands is something else you'll have to muddle through. While you're at it, think about where I'd hidden it when I took off all my clothes to screw Nora Gail, who would in all probability have noticed a scalpel.

"Anyway, I used the scalpel to stab Celina repeatedly. Then, I just left her body there on the outside chance that Gooney Bud would come wandering by, see her, try to help her, and, in the process, get her blood all over himself."

"I think that's exactly how it was done."

"You're full of shit, and a grand jury will think so, too."

He angrily gave her another shove toward her door. In a quavering voice, she said, "There's blood on your hands."

He looked down at them. "I've had blood on them before."

"The night you murdered Celina?"

His eyes moved back to Alex's. His voice was raspy with menace when he lowered his face close to hers and said, "No, the night she tried to abort you."

Chapter 35

Alex stared at him blankly for several seconds. Then, she attacked him. She went for his face with her nails, his shins with the toes of her shoes. He grunted in pain and surprise as she landed one solid kick against his kneecap.

"You liar! You're lying! *Lying*!" She took a swing at his head. He managed to dodge it.

"Stop it." He grabbed hold of her wrists to protect his face. She tried to wrest her hands free, while still kicking out with her feet and knees. "Alex, I'm not lying to you."

"You are! You bastard. I know you are. My mother wouldn't do that. She loved me. She *did*!"

She fought like a wildcat. Fury and adrenaline pumped through her system, endowing her with additional strength. She was still no match for him. Holding her wrists together in his left hand, he shook her key out of her handbag and used it to open the door. They stumbled inside together. Reede kicked the door shut.

She bucked against him, shouting deprecations, trying to

work her hands out of his grip, slinging her head from side to side like someone demented.

"Alex, stop this," he ordered fiercely.

"I hate you."

"I know, but I'm not lying."

"You are!" She twisted and turned and tried to stamp on his feet.

He forced her down on the bed, and secured her there with his own body. Keeping an iron grip on her wrists, he placed his other hand over her mouth. She tried to bite it, so he applied more pressure, making any motion of her jaw impossible unless she wanted to break the bones.

Her eyes were murderous as she glared at him over the back of his hand. Her breasts rose and fell dramatically with each breath. He hung his head above hers, his hair falling over his brow, gulping in draughts of air until he regained his breath.

Finally, lifting his head, he stared deeply into her eyes. "I didn't want you to know," he said in a low, throbbing voice, "but you just kept pushing me. I lost my temper. It's out, I can't take it back, and damn me if it's not the truth."

She tried to shake her head no, the denial in her eyes vehement. She arched her back in an effort to throw him off, but she remained pinioned beneath him.

"Listen to me, Alex," he said, angrily straining the words through his teeth. "Nobody even knew Celina was pregnant until that night. She'd been back from El Paso for several weeks, but I hadn't gone to see her yet, hadn't even called. My pride was still hurting. In a juvenile way, I was letting her sweat it out."

He closed his eyes and shook his head ruefully. "We were playing games with each other, childish, foolish, silly, boy-girl games. Finally, I decided to forgive her." He smiled with bitter self-derision.

"I went to see her on a Wednesday night because I knew your grandmother would be at prayer meeting at the Baptist church. After the service she always stayed for choir practice, so I knew that Celina and I would have a couple of hours alone to sort things out.

"When I got to her house, I knocked several times, but she didn't come to the door. I knew she was there. The lights were on in the back of the house where her bedroom was. I thought maybe she was in the shower or was playing the radio so loud she couldn't hear my knocking, so I went around to the back."

Alex lay still beneath him. Her eyes were no longer narrowed with animosity, but shiny with unshed tears.

"I looked through her bedroom window. The lights were on, but Celina wasn't in there. I tapped on the window. She didn't respond, but I noticed her shadow moving on the bathroom wall. I could see it through the door. It was opened partway. I called her name. I knew she could hear me, but she wouldn't come out. Then—"

He squeezed his eyes shut and bared his teeth in a grimace of pain before going on. "I was getting mad, see, because I thought she was just playing coy. She opened the bathroom door wider, and I saw her standing there.

"For a few seconds I just looked at her face because it had been so long since I'd seen her. She was staring back at me. She looked puzzled, like she was asking, "What now?" And that's when I noticed the blood. She was wearing a night-gown, and the lower front of it was streaked with red."

Alex's eyes closed. Large, cloudy tears slid from beneath her quivering eyelids and ran onto Reede's fingers.

"It scared the hell out of me," he said gruffly. "I got into the house. I don't even remember how. I think I raised the window and slipped through. Anyway, a few seconds later, I was in her bedroom, holding her. We both ended up on the floor and she just sort of crumpled in my arms.

"She didn't want to tell me what was wrong. I was scream-ing at her, shaking her. Finally, she turned her face toward my chest and whispered, 'Baby.' Then I realized what all the blood meant and where it had come from. I scooped her up, ran outside, and put her in my car."

He paused for a moment to reflect. When he picked up the story, the emotion that had racked his voice was gone. He spoke matter-of-factly.

"There was this doctor in town who did abortions on the sly. Everybody knew it, but nobody talked about it because abortions were still illegal in Texas then. I took her to him. I called Junior and told him to bring some money. He met us there. He and I sat in the waiting room while the doctor fixed her up."

He gazed down at Alex for a long time before removing his hand. It had left a stark white imprint on the lower half of her face, which in itself was ghostly pale. Her body was now pliant beneath his, and as still as death. With the pads of his thumbs, he wiped the tears off her cheeks.

"Damn you to hell if you're lying to me," she whispered.

"I'm not. You can ask Junior."

"Junior would back you up if you said the sky was green. I'll ask the doctor."

"He's dead."

"Figures," she remarked, laughing dryly. "What did she use to try to kill me?"

"Alex, don't."

"Tell me."

"No."

"What was it?"

"It doesn't matter."

"Tell me, damn you!"

"Your grandma's knitting needle!"

It had started out a soft exchange but ended on a shout. The sudden, resulting silence was deafening.

"Oh, God," Alex whimpered, clamping her teeth over her lower lip and turning her face into the pillow. "Oh, God."

"Shh, don't cry. Celina didn't hurt you, just herself."

"She wanted to hurt me, though. She didn't want me to be born." Her sobs shook her whole body. He absorbed them with his. "Why didn't the doctor just take me while he was fixing her up?"

Reede didn't answer.

Alex turned her head and stared up at him. She caught handfuls of his shirt in her fists. "Why, Reede?"

"He suggested it."

"Then, why didn't he?"

"Because I swore that if he did, I'd kill him."

An emotion zephyred between them. It was so strong it knocked the breath out of her and made her chest ache. She uttered an involuntary, wordless sound. Her fingers momentarily relaxed in the cloth of his shirt, only to grip it tighter and draw him nearer. Her back arched off the bed again, not in an attempt to throw him off, but to get closer.

He sank his fingers into her hair, tilted his dark blond head, and pressed his open mouth against hers. Her lips were parted and damp and receptive. He sent his tongue deep into her mouth.

Frantically, she worked her arms out of her coat sleeves and locked them around the back of his neck. He raised his head suddenly and looked down at her. There were dark shadows from weeping beneath her eyes, but the blue irises were crystal clear as they steadily gazed back at him. She knew exactly what she was doing. That's all he needed to know.

He ran his thumb over her lips, which were moist and swollen from his hard kiss. All he could think about was kissing her again, harder, and he did.

Her throat was arched and vulnerable to his lips when they left hers. He drew her skin lightly against his teeth, then soothed it with whisks of his tongue. He nuzzled her ear and the base of her neck, and when her clothing got in his way, he pulled her to a sitting position and peeled her sweater over her head.

As they lay back down, their breathing was loud and uneven, the only sound in the room. He unclasped her bra and pushed the cups aside.

His fingers skimmed over her flesh, which was warm and flushed with arousal. He cupped one breast, pushed it up, and took the center between his lips. He sucked it with enough pressure to elicit a tingle in her womb, but with enough finesse to tantalize. When the nipple drew taut, he flicked it roughly with the tip of his tongue.

Alex cried his name in panic and joy. He buried his face between her breasts and held her close while he rolled her above him and fought his way out of his jacket at the same time. She began tearing free the buttons of his shirt. He unzipped and unbuttoned her skirt, then shoved it down over her hips, taking her half-slip along with it. Alex ran her fingers through the thick pelt of hair on his chest, dropped random kisses on his supple muscles, and rubbed her cheek against his distended nipple.

They reversed positions again. She managed to get off her shoes and stockings before he stretched out on top of her. He placed his hand low on her belly and slid it down into her underpants.

His hand covered her mound completely and possessively. With his thumb, he parted the lips of her sex and exposed the tight, responsive kernel of flesh. His fingertips dipped into her creaminess and anointed that tiny nub with the dew of her own desire.

When she moaned her pleasure, he bent his head and kissed her stomach. Removing her panties, he nuzzled the fiery dark curls between her thighs and touched her with his open mouth.

Clumsily, he undid his fly and, taking her hand, pressed it against his erection. He hissed a curse when her fist closed tightly around him. Nudging her thighs apart, he settled himself between them.

The smooth tip of his penis slipped between the folds of her body. He covered her breasts with his hands and lightly ground the raised centers with his palms. He gave a steady, smooth thrust of his hips that should have planted him firmly inside her.

It didn't.

He readjusted his hips slightly and tried again, encountering the same resistance. Levering himself up, he stared at her with disbelief. "You mean…?"

Her breath was choppy, and her eyes fluttered in an effort to stay focused on him. She was making small yearning noises in her throat. Her hands moved restlessly, searchingly, over his chest and neck and cheeks. Her fingertips glanced his lips.

The utter sexiness of all that and the satiny heat that was gloving him so tightly were his undoing. He applied more pressure and sank into her completely. Her ragged sigh of surprise and discovery was the most erotic sound he'd ever heard. It inflamed him.

"Christ," he groaned. "Oh, Christ."

Mating instincts took over and he moved his hips against hers with the ancient compulsion to possess and fill. Sandwiching her head between his hands, he kissed her mouth with rampant carnality. His climax was an avalanche of sensation. It was soul-shuddering. It seemed to go on forever… and it still wasn't long enough.

Several minutes elapsed before he roused himself enough to disengage. He didn't want to, but when he gazed down at her, any thoughts of prolonging their coupling fled.

She was lying with her head turned away, one cheek on the pillow. She looked fragile and haunted. Looking down at the faint pulse in her throat, seeing the bruise his kiss had branded there, Reede felt like a rapist. Filled with regret and self-loathing, he worked his fingers free of the snare of her hair.

They both reacted violently to the knock on the door. Alex quickly reached for the rumpled bedspread and pulled it over herself. Reede's feet landed hard on the floor. He hiked his jeans up over his hips.

"Reede, you in there?"

"Yeah," he called through the door.

"I, uh, I got Ms. Gaither's keys here. Remember, you told me to—"

The deputy broke off when Reede opened the door. "I remember." He extended his hand through the crack and the deputy dropped the keys into them. "Thanks," he said tersely, and closed the door.

He tossed the keys on the round table in front of the window. The clatter they made when they landed on the wood veneer was as loud as a cymbal's crash. Reede bent down to retrieve his shirt and jacket, which he'd slung over the side of the bed at some point that escaped his memory now. As he pulled them on, he spoke to Alex over his shoulder.

"I know you're hating yourself right now, but it might make you feel better to know that I wish it hadn't happened either."

She turned her head and gave him a long, searching look. She looked for compassion, tenderness, love. His features remained impassive, his eyes those of a stranger. There was no softness or feeling in his remote gaze. He seemed untouched and untouchable.

Alex swallowed hard, burying her hurt. In retaliation for his aloofness, she said, "Well, we're even now, Sheriff. You saved my life before I was born." She paused, then added, huskily, "And I just gave you what you always wanted, but never got, from my mother."

Reede curled his hands into fists, as though he wanted to strike her. Then, with jerky, disjointed motions, he finished dressing. At the open door, he turned back. "Whatever your reason for doing it, thanks. For a virgin, you were a fairly good fuck."

Chapter 36

Junior slid into the orange vinyl booth of the Westerner Motel's coffee shop. His engaging smile collapsed the instant he saw Alex's face. "Darling, are you sick?"

She smiled wanly. "No. Coffee?" she asked, signaling the waitress.

"Please," he told her distractedly. When the waitress tried to hand him a large, plastic menu, he waved it off. "Just coffee."

After she had poured him a cup, he leaned across the table and lowered his voice to a whisper. "I was real tickled to hear from you this morning, but something is obviously very wrong. You're as pale as a sheet."

"You ought to see me without the sunglasses." She bobbed them up and down in an attempt at humor that fell flat.

"What's the matter?"

She leaned back against the bright vinyl and turned her head to gaze through the tinted window. It was bright outside; her sunglasses wouldn't appear out of place. That about exhausted the merits of this day. "Reede told me about Celina's attempted abortion."

At first, Junior said nothing. Then, he cursed expansively beneath his breath. He sipped his coffee, started to say something he thought better of, and finally, shook his head in apparent disgust. "What the hell's wrong with him? Why'd he tell you about that?"

"So, it's true?"

He lowered his head and stared into his coffee. "She was only seventeen, Alex, and pregnant by a guy she didn't even love, a guy on his way to Saigon. She was scared. She—"

"I know the pertinent facts, Junior," she interrupted impatiently. "Why do you always defend her?"

"Habit, I guess."

Alex, ashamed of her outburst, took a moment to compose herself. "I know *why* she did it. It's just incomprehensible to me that she *could*."

"To us, too," he admitted reluctantly.

"Us?"

"To Reede and me. He gave her only two days to recover before he and I flew her back to El Paso to take care of it." He sipped his coffee. "We met out at the airstrip, right after sunset."

Alex had asked Reede if he'd ever taken Celina flying at night. "Once," he had told her. Celina had been scared, he'd said. "He stole a plane?"

"*Borrowed* is what he called it. I think Moe knew what Reede was up to, but he looked the other way. We landed in El Paso, rented a car, and drove to the army base. Reede bribed the guards into telling Al Gaither that he had relatives waiting to see him. He was off duty, I guess. Anyway, he came to the gate and we, uh, talked him into getting in the car with us."

"What happened?"

He looked at her, shamefaced. "We took him to a deserted spot and beat the shit out of him. I was afraid Reede was going to kill him. He probably would have, if Celina hadn't been there. She was practically hysterical."

"You coerced him into marrying her?"

"That same night. We drove across the border into Mexico." He shook his head wryly at the memory of it. "Gaither was barely conscious enough to recite his vows. Reede and I supported him between us through the ceremony, then dumped him back at the gate of Fort Bliss."

"One thing puzzles me. Why did Reede insist on Celina getting married?"

"He kept saying he wouldn't let her baby be born a bastard."

Alex looked at him intently from behind her shaded glasses.

"Then, why didn't he marry her himself?"

"He asked her."

"So, what was the problem?"

"Me. I asked her, too." Seeing her confusion, he blew out his breath. "This all happened the morning following the, uh—"

"I understand. Go on."

"Celina was still real shaken up and said she couldn't think clearly. She begged us to stop badgering her. But Reede said she had to get married in a hurry, or everybody would find out what had happened."

"Everybody found out anyway," she said.

"He wanted to protect her from the gossip as long as possible."

"I must be dense, but I still can't figure it. Celina has two men who love her begging her to get married. Why didn't she?"

"She refused to choose between us." A furrow of concentration formed between his brows. "You know, Alex, that's the first smart, adult decision Celina ever made. We were seniors in high school. God knows Reede didn't have any money. I did, but my folks would have gone ape shit if I'd've gotten married before I even graduated, especially with Celina carrying another man's baby.

"She had another reason, though, more important than finances or parental approval. She knew that if she chose one of us over the other, it would alter the friendship forever. There would be an odd man out. When it came right down to it, she wouldn't break up the triangle. Funny, isn't it? That happened anyway."

"What do you mean?"

"It was never quite the same between the three of us after we got back from El Paso. We were on guard all the time, where before, we were always nakedly honest with each other."

His voice turned sad. "Reede didn't see as much of her as I did while she was pregnant, and that wasn't very often. We were busy with school and she stayed close to home. Oh, we went through the motions of still being best buddies, but when we were together, we tried too hard to pretend that everything was normal.

"That night she tried to abort you stood between us like a solid wall. None of us could ever go up, over, around, or through it. It was there. Conversations became an effort. Laughter was forced."

"But, you didn't desert her."

"No. The day you were born, Reede and I rushed to the hospital. Besides your grandmother, we were the first people you were introduced to."

"I'm glad of that," she said thickly.

"So am I."

"If I'd been Celina, I would have snagged one of you when I had the chance."

His grin slowly faded. "Reede stopped asking."

"Why?"

Junior signaled for the waitress to refill his coffee cup. Then, cradling it between his hands, he stared into its dark depths. "He never forgave her."

"For Al Gaither?"

"For you."

Stricken, Alex raised her hand to cover her mouth. The guilt she had borne all her life pressed in on her like a vise.

Junior, sensing her anxiety, rushed to say, "It wasn't because she'd conceived you. He couldn't forgive that abortion business."

"I don't understand."

"See, Alex, Reede's a survivor. Hell, if anybody was ever destined to turn out rotten, it was Reede. He didn't have a snowball's chance in hell of making anything out of himself. Social workers, if Purcell had had any, would have pointed at him and said, 'There goes a wasted life in the making. He'll go bad. Watch and see.' But no, not Reede. He thrives on adversity. He's a scrapper. He's strong. He gets knocked down and comes up fighting.

"Now me," he said with a scoffing laugh, "I can overlook other people's weaknesses because I've got so many of my own. I could understand the panic and fear Celina must have felt. She took desperate measures because she was afraid to stick it out.

"Reede can't understand taking the path of least resistance. He couldn't tolerate that weakness in her. He expects so goddamn much out of himself, he imposes the same standards on everybody else. Those standards are virtually impossible to live up to. That's why he's constantly disappointed in people. He sets himself up to be."

"He's a cynic."

"I can see where you'd think that, but don't let that tough pose fool you. When people let him down, as they invariably do because they're human, it hurts him. When he's hurt, he turns mean."

"Was he mean to my mother?"

"No, never. Their relationship being what it was, she had the power to hurt and disappoint him more than anybody could. But he couldn't turn mean toward Celina because he loved her so much." He looked at Alex levelly. "He just couldn't forgive her."

"That's why he stepped aside and gave you the advantage."

"Which I unabashedly took," he said with a short laugh. "I'm not as hard to please as Reede. I don't demand perfection in myself or anybody else. Yes, Alex, in spite of her mistakes, I loved your mother and wanted her to be my wife on any terms."

"Why didn't she marry you, Junior?" Alex asked, genuinely perplexed. "She loved you. I know she did."

"I know she did, too. And I'm damned good-looking." He

winked and Alex smiled. "Few would believe this because of the way I live now, but I would have been faithful to Celina and made you an excellent daddy, Alex. I wanted to try, anyway." He clasped his hands together on the table. "But Celina said no, no matter how many times I asked her."

"And you went on asking her, right up until the night she died."

His eyes snapped up to hers. "Yes. I invited her out to the ranch that night to propose."

"Did you?"

"Yes."

"And?"

"Same as always. She turned me down."

"Do you know why?"

"Yes." He shifted uncomfortably in the booth. "She still loved Reede. Always and forever, it was Reede she wanted."

Alex looked away because she knew it was a painful admission for him to make. "Junior, where were you that night?"

"At the ranch."

"I mean after that, after you took Celina home."

"I didn't take her home. I presumed Dad would."

"Angus?"

"I was upset because she had refused me again. See, I'd told my parents to get used to the idea of having a daughter-in-law and a grandchild in the house soon." He spread his hands in a helpless gesture. "I got mad and stormed out—just flew the coop and left Celina there."

"Where did you go?"

"I hit all the places that would sell liquor to minors. I got drunk."

"Alone?"

"Alone."

"No alibi?"

"Junior doesn't need an alibi. He didn't kill your mother."

They had been so immersed in the conversation that neither had noticed Stacey Wallace's approach. When they looked up, she was standing at the edge of the table. Her stare was even more hostile than it had been at their first meeting.

"Good morning, Stacey," Junior said uncomfortably. He seemed less than pleased by her sudden appearance. "Sit down and have a cup of coffee with us." He moved over to make room for her on his side of the booth.

"No, thank you." Glaring down at Alex, she said, "Stop bothering Junior with your endless questions."

"Hey, Stacey, I'm not bothered," he said, trying to smooth over the situation.

"Why don't you just give it up?"

"I can't."

"Well, you should. It would be best for everybody."

"Especially the murderer," Alex said quietly.

Stacey's thin, straight body quivered like a bowstring just plucked. "Get out of our lives. You're a self-serving, vindictive bitch, who—"

"Not here, Stacey." Junior, intervening quickly, scooted out of the booth and took her arm. "I'll walk you to your car. What are you doing out this morning? Oh, your bridge group is having breakfast," he said, noting the table of women watching curiously. "How nice." He gave them a jaunty little wave.

Alex, as aware as Junior of all the prying eyes, slipped a five-dollar bill beneath her saucer and left the coffee shop only a few moments behind Junior and Stacey.

She gave Stacey's car a wide berth, but watched from the

corner of her eye as Junior pulled Stacey into an embrace and rubbed her back consolingly. He gave her a soft kiss on the lips. She clung to him, appealing to him about something that had caused her consternation. His answer seemed to soothe her. She went limp against his chest.

Junior worked himself out of her clutches, but in such a charming way that Stacey was smiling when he tucked her into the driver's seat of her car and waved her off.

Alex was already inside her room when he tapped on the door and said, "It's me."

She opened the door. "What was that all about?"

"She thought I'd spent the night with you, since we were having breakfast together in the coffee shop."

"Lord," Alex whispered. "People in this town certainly have fertile minds. You'd better leave before anybody else gets that impression."

"What do you care? I don't."

"Well, I do."

Uneasily, Alex glanced toward the unmade bed. On any other morning the housekeeper was knocking while she was still in the shower. This morning, of all mornings, she was running late. Alex was afraid that the bed would give away her secret. The room was redolent of Reede. His essence lingered on each surface like a fine coating of dust. She was afraid Junior would sense that.

Gently, he removed her sunglasses and traced the lavender half-moons beneath her eyes. "Bad night?"

That's an understatement, she thought. "You might as well hear it from me. I'm sure it will get around. Late yesterday afternoon I went to Nora Gail's place."

His lips parted with surprise. "Son of a bitch."

"I needed to talk to her. It seems she's Reede's alibi for the night Celina was killed. Anyway, while I was there, a man got shot. There was blood, an arrest."

Junior laughed with incredulity. "You're kiddin' me."

"I wish I were," she said grimly. "Here I am, representing the D.A.'s office, and I get involved in a shootout between two cowboys in a whorehouse."

Suddenly it all collapsed on her. Instead of crying, she began to laugh. Once she started, she couldn't stop. She laughed until her sides ached and tears were rolling down her cheeks. "Oh, God, can you believe it? If Greg Harper ever hears about this, he—"

"Pat Chastain won't tell him. He has a girl out at—"

"I know," she said, "Reede told me. He responded to the call and hustled me out. He didn't seem to think there would be any repercussions." She shrugged in an offhanded manner that she hoped didn't look as phony as it felt.

"It's good to hear you laughing for a change," Junior commented, smiling down at her. "I'd like to stick around and cheer you up even more." He placed his hands on her derriere and began to move them up and down. Alex pushed him away.

"If you wanted to cheer someone up, you should have gone with Stacey. She looked like she could use it."

He glanced away guiltily. "It doesn't take much to make her happy."

"Because she still loves you."

"I don't deserve her."

"That doesn't matter to her. She'll forgive you anything. She already has."

"Of murder, you mean?"

"No. Of loving someone else—Celina."

"Not this time, Alex," he whispered and dipped his head to kiss her.

She dodged his well-aimed lips. "No, Junior."

"Why not?"

"You know why."

"Am I still only a pal?"

"A friend."

"Why just a friend?"

"I keep getting the present mixed up with the past. Hearing you talk about wishing you could have been my father stifled my romantic inclinations."

"When I look at you now, I can't relate you to that tiny baby in the crib. You're an exciting woman. I want to hold you, love you, and not like a daddy."

"No." She shook her head adamantly. "It just doesn't sit right, Junior. It's out of whack."

This was the speech she should have made to Reede. Why hadn't she? Because she was a phony, that's why. And because the same rules didn't always apply to similar situations, even when one wanted them to. And because she didn't have any control over whom she fell in love with. She and Celina had that in common.

"We can never be lovers."

He smiled and said without rancor, "I'm stubborn. Once this is over, I'll make certain that you see me in a whole new light. We'll pretend that we're meeting for the first time and you'll fall hard for me."

If it soothes his ego, let him think so, Alex thought.

She knew it would never be, just as it could never have been with him and Celina.

And in both cases, Reede Lambert was the reason.

Chapter 37

Angus's secretary escorted Alex into his office at ME headquarters. It was an unpretentious complex, situated in a professional building between a dentist's office and a two-partner law firm. He stepped around his desk to greet her.

"Thank you for stopping by, Alex."

"I'm glad you called. I needed to talk to you anyway."

"Would you like a drink?"

"No, thanks."

"Seen Junior lately?"

"Yes. We had coffee together this morning."

Angus was pleased. His lecture had obviously worked. As usual, Junior had just needed a pep talk to get into gear.

"Before we get to my business," Angus said, "what's on your mind?"

"Specifically, the night my mother died, Angus."

His hearty smile faded. "Sit down." He guided her to a small upholstered couch. "What do you want to know?"

"When I spoke with Junior this morning, he confirmed

what I'd already been told—that he proposed to Celina that night. I know that you and Mrs. Minton opposed the idea."

"That's right, Alex, we did. I hate to tell you that. I don't mean to speak badly of your mother because I adored her as Junior's friend."

"But you didn't want her for his wife."

"No." He leaned forward and wagged his finger at her. "Don't think it was snobbishness on my part. It wasn't. Sarah Jo's opinion might have been swayed by class and economic distinctions, but not mine. I would have objected to Junior marrying anybody at that time in his life."

"Then why did you consent to his marriage to Stacey Wallace only a few weeks later?"

No dummy, this girl, Angus thought. He assumed an innocent pose. "The situation had changed by then. He'd been emotionally devastated by Celina's death. Stacey worshiped the ground he walked on. I thought she would be good for him. For a while, she was. I don't regret blessing that marriage."

"A prestigious judge's daughter was also a far more suitable match for the son of Angus Minton."

His blue eyes darkened. "You're disappointing me, Alex. What you're suggesting is downright tacky. Do you think I'd force my son into a loveless marriage?"

"I don't know. Would you?"

"No!"

"Even if the stakes were awfully high?"

"Listen," he said, lowering his voice for emphasis, "anything I've ever done for my boy has been for his own good."

"Does that include killing Celina?"

Angus jerked upright. "You've got your nerve, young lady."

"I'm sorry. I can't afford to be subtle. Angus, Junior says he left the ranch that night, angry and hurt, because Celina turned down his proposal."

"That's right."

"It was left to you to drive her home."

"Yes. Instead, I offered her one of the cars and gave her the keys. She told me good-bye and left the house. I assumed she drove herself home."

"Did anyone overhear this conversation?"

"Not that I know of."

"Not even your wife?"

"She went up to bed right after supper."

"Don't you see, Angus? You've got no alibi. There's no witness to what happened after Junior left."

It pleased him enormously that she seemed worried about it. Her features were anxious and drawn. Lately, he'd found it hard to think of this girl as his enemy. Evidently, she was nursing that same ambiguity.

"I slept with Sarah Jo that night," he said. "She'll vouch for that. So will Reede. We were in bed the next morning when he came running in to tell us that he'd found Celina's body in the stable."

"Wasn't my grandmother worried about her? When Celina didn't come home, didn't she telephone the ranch?"

"In fact, she did. Celina had already left the house. She had bragged that you were already sleeping through the night, so I guess Mrs. Graham went back to bed, assuming that she was on her way. She didn't realize until the following morning that Celina hadn't made it home."

"What time did Grandma Graham call?"

"I don't remember. It wasn't very late because I was still

up. I usually go to bed early. I was especially tired after the day we'd spent in the stable with that mare."

Alex was frowning in concentration. He grinned. "Sound plausible?"

Grudgingly, she returned his smile. "Yes, but it's riddled with holes."

"It's damn sure not enough to ask a grand jury for a murder indictment. It's nothing like a blood-soaked Gooney Bud holding a scalpel."

Alex said nothing.

Angus reached out and covered her hand. "I hope I didn't hurt your feelings, talking frankly about your mother like that."

"No, you didn't," she replied with a weak smile. "In the last few days I've learned that she was far from an angel."

"I would never have approved of her for Junior. My disapproval didn't have anything to do with whether she was a saint or a sinner."

He watched her wet her lips anxiously before asking, "What was your main objection, Angus? Was it because she had me?"

So that's it, he thought. *Alex blames herself for her mother's fate.* Guilt had driven her to get to the bottom of this case. She craved absolution for the sin Merle Graham had laid on her. What a spiteful thing for the old bitch to do to a kid. Still, it served his purpose well.

"My disapproval had nothing to do with you, Alex. It was Reede and Junior." Humbly, he folded his hands and studied them as he spoke. "Junior needs somebody to goad him every now and then. A strong daddy, a strong friend, a strong woman." He looked up at her from beneath lowered brows. "You'd be a perfect mate for him."

"Mate?"

He laughed and spread his arms wide at his sides. "Hell, I might as well come right out with it. I'd like to see a match between you and Junior."

"*What!?*"

Angus wasn't sure whether she was actually stunned, or a damn good actress. Either way, he was glad he'd chosen to prod this thing along himself. Left alone, Junior wasn't getting the job done.

"We could use a smart lady lawyer in this family. Think what a contribution you'd make to the business, not to mention the empty bedrooms at the ranch. In no time you'd fill 'em up with grandbabies." He lowered his eyes to her pelvic region. "You've got the build for it, and you'd bring new blood to the stock."

"You can't be serious, Angus."

"I've never been more serious in my life." He patted her on the back. "For now, though, let's just leave it at this: I'd be pleased as punch if something romantic was to spark between you and Junior."

She moved away from his touch. "Angus, I don't want to offend you or Junior, but what you're suggesting is…" She searched for the right word, then laughed and said, "preposterous."

"Why?"

"You're asking me to play the role my mother was cast for. You rejected her."

"You're suited to the role. She wasn't."

"I'm not in love with Junior, and I don't want the part." She stood up and moved to the door. "I'm sorry if there's been any misunderstanding or if I've misled anybody into thinking…" He gave her his darkest, most fearsome frown, the one that usually struck terror into the hearts of those who opposed him. She withstood it well. "Good-bye, Angus. I'll be in touch."

After she left, Angus poured a drink to calm himself down. His fingers closed around the glass so tightly, it was a wonder it didn't shatter under the pressure.

Angus Minton rarely had his ideas questioned, and even less frequently, snickered at. They were sure as hell never called preposterous.

Alex left feeling greatly disturbed. In spite of her best intentions, she had offended him. She regretted that. But what disturbed her most was that she'd seen into the man behind the good ole boy demeanor.

Angus Minton liked to have things go his way. When they didn't move along fast enough, he boosted them. He didn't take kindly to being crossed.

More than ever, Alex pitied Junior, whose pace was so different from his father's. No doubt that had always been a source of friction between them. She could also understand why a man as self-sufficient as Reede had left Minton Enterprises. He wouldn't have functioned well under Angus's heavy thumb.

She returned to her car and began to drive aimlessly, leaving the city limits and taking to the back roads. The scenery wasn't much to brag about. Tumbleweeds were snagged on barbed-wire fences that seemed to stretch forever. Oil wells, black outlines against the colorless earth, pumped desultorily.

The drive helped; it gave her privacy in which to think.

Like her mother, she had become entangled with three men, all of whom she liked. She didn't want to believe one of them was a killer.

Lord, what a muddle. She was gradually peeling away layers of deception. If she kept at it long enough, surely she would eventually get to the truth.

But her time was running out. She had only a few days left before Greg would demand to see some results. If she couldn't produce something concrete, he would demand that she desist.

As she approached the city limits on her return, she became aware that the vehicle behind her was following too closely.

"Jerk," she muttered, glancing into her rearview mirror. For another mile the pickup rode her rear end like a shadow. The sun was at an angle to prevent her from seeing the driver. "Come on around if you're in such a hurry."

She tapped her brake pedal, enough for the taillights to blink on. He didn't take the hint. On this rural highway, the gravel shoulder was so narrow it hardly qualified as such. She edged toward it anyway, hoping that the driver of the truck would pass her.

"Thank you very much," she said when the truck straddled the center yellow stripe and sped up to pass her.

It pulled even with her. She was aware of it from the corner of her eye. She didn't realize that the driver had a more nefarious purpose than vehicular horseplay in mind until he stayed even with her, a hazard at the speed they were driving.

"You fool!" She whipped her head around to glance out the window. The pickup accelerated suddenly and deliberately swerved, catching her front left bumper with his right rear one. She lost control of the car.

She clutched the steering wheel and stamped on the brakes, but to no avail. Her car skidded off the loose shoulder and plowed into the deep, dry ditch. Alex was held in by her seat belt, but flung forward hard enough to bang her head on the steering wheel. The windshield shattered upon impact, showering the back of her head and hands with glass. It seemed to rain down forever.

She didn't think she had lost consciousness, but the next thing she knew, there were voices speaking to her. They were soft and melodious, but she couldn't understand what they were saying.

Groggily, she raised her head. The motion gave her a searing headache. She fought down rising nausea and struggled to focus her eyes.

The men surrounding the car and looking at her with concern were speaking Spanish. One opened her door and said something that was gently inquiring.

"Yes, I'm all right," she answered automatically. She couldn't imagine why they were looking at her so strangely until she felt the wet trickle against her cheek. She raised her hand and investigated. Her trembling fingers came away red.

<hr />

"I'd rather you spent the night here at the hospital. I can arrange for a room," the doctor said.

"No, I'll be fine in the motel. After a couple of these, I should sleep till morning." She shook the brown plastic bottle of pills.

"You don't have a concussion, but take it easy for a couple of days. No sports, or anything like that."

She winced at the very mention of physical exertion. "I promise."

"In a week, we'll take out the stitches. Good thing that gash was on the top of your head and not on your face."

"Yes," Alex replied uncertainly. He'd had to shave a small patch of her scalp, but with artful combing, her hair would cover it.

"Are you up to having a visitor? There's somebody waiting to see you. Since this is a weeknight, things are kind of slow, so use the room for as long as you like."

"Thank you, Doctor."

He left the treatment room. Alex tried to sit up, but discovered that she was still too dizzy. The sight of Pat Chastain walking through the door didn't help her equilibrium. "Well, Mr. Chastain, long time, no see," she said with sarcasm.

He moved toward the examination table and sheepishly asked, "How are you?"

"I've been better, but I'll be fine."

"Is there anything I can do?"

"No. There was no need for you to come here. How'd you know about it, anyway?"

He pulled forward the only chair in the room and sat down. "Those Mexicans flagged down a passing car. The driver went to the nearest phone and called for an ambulance. The deputy who went out to investigate the accident speaks Spanish, so he heard from them what happened."

"They saw the truck force me off the road?"

"Yeah. Could you identify it?"

"It was white." She met the D.A.'s eyes. "And it had the Minton Enterprises logo stenciled on the side."

He looked troubled and nervous. "That's what the Mexicans said, too. The deputy couldn't locate Reede, so he called me." He nodded toward the bandage on her head. "Is that gonna be okay?"

"In two or three days. I can take the bandage off tomorrow. It required several stitches. And I've got these as reminders." She held up her hands, which were covered with tiny scratches where glass fragments had been tweezed out.

"Alex, did you recognize the driver?"

"No." The district attorney gave her a hard look, testing her truthfulness. "No," she repeated. "Believe me, if I had, I'd be after him myself. I didn't even catch a glimpse. All I could make out was a silhouette against the sun. I think he was wearing some kind of hat."

"Do you think it was a random incident?"

She came down on both elbows. "Do you?"

He patted the air, urging her to lie back down. "No, I guess it wasn't."

"Then don't tax my strength with stupid questions."

He ran a hand through his hair and swore. "When I told my old buddy Greg Harper that you'd have carte blanche, I didn't know that you were going to wreak havoc in my county."

Her patience with him snapped. "It's my head that mountains are being slammed against, Mr. Chastain. Why are you whining?"

"Well, dammit, Alex. Judge Wallace, who didn't like me much in the first place, is hotter than a pistol. I can't win a single point in his courtroom these days. You've all but called three of the county's leading citizens murderers. Pasty Hickam, a fixture in this town, turns up dead while you're with him. You were at Nora Gail Burton's whorehouse when a shooting took place. Goddamn it, why'd you have to open up that hornets' nest?"

She pressed her hand to her throbbing forehead. "It wasn't by choice. I was following a lead." She lowered her hand and gave him a pointed look. "And don't worry, your secret interest in Nora Gail's is safe with me."

He squirmed guiltily in his chair. "I tell you, Alex, you've got a bull by the horns here, and it almost got you killed tonight."

"Which should prove that I'm getting closer to the truth. Someone's trying to bump me off to protect himself."

"I guess," he said morosely. "What have you got that you didn't have before you got here?"

"Firmly established motives, for one thing."

"Anything else?"

"A shortage of concrete alibis. Reede Lambert says he was with Nora Gail. She admitted that she would perjure herself if necessary to corroborate that, which leads me to believe that he wasn't with her all night. Junior hasn't produced any kind of alibi."

"What about Angus?"

"He claims he was at the ranch, but so was Celina. If Angus was there all night, he would have had ample opportunity."

"So would Gooney Bud, if he'd followed her out there," Pat said, "and that's what a good defense attorney will tell the jury. No one gets life on probable cause. You've still got nothing that places one of them in that stable with a scalpel in his hand."

"I was on my way to your office this afternoon to talk to you about that when I was run off the road."

"Talk to me about what?"

"The vet's scalpel. What happened to it?"

An expression of surprise came over his face. "You're the second person this week to ask me that."

Alex struggled to prop herself up on one elbow. "Who else asked you about it?"

"I did," Reede Lambert said from the doorway.

Chapter 38

Alex's insides lifted weightlessly. She had dreaded the moment she would see him again. It was inevitable, of course, but she had hoped to appear unscathed by what had happened between them.

Lying on a hospital examination table, her hair clotted with blood, her hands painted with pumpkin-colored antiseptic, too weak and muzzy to sit up, she didn't exactly convey the impression of invincibility she had desired.

"Hello, Sheriff Lambert. You'll be pleased to know that I took your advice and stopped looking over my shoulder for bogeymen."

Ignoring her, he said, "Hi, Pat. I just got off the radio with the deputy."

"Then you heard what happened?"

"My first thought was that Plummet was involved, but the deputy said her car was struck by an ME truck."

"That's right."

"ME encompasses a lot of companies. Just about anybody in the county could get access to one of those trucks."

"Including you," Alex suggested snidely.

Reede finally acknowledged her existence with a hard stare. The D.A. looked at them uneasily. "Uh, where were you, Reede? Nobody could find you."

"I was out on horseback. Anybody at the ranch could tell you that."

"I had to ask," Pat said apologetically.

"I understand, but you ought to know that running somebody off the road isn't quite my style. Besides me, who do you think could have done it?" he asked Alex pointedly.

It was difficult for her to even conceive of the idea, much less speak it aloud. "Junior," she said quietly.

"Junior?" Reede laughed. "Why in hell?"

"I met with him this morning. He doesn't have an alibi for the night Celina was killed. He admits he was terribly angry." She glanced down. "I also have reason to believe he might be angry at me."

"Why?"

She glared up at him with as much defiance as she could muster. "He came to my room this morning." That's all she was going to supply him. He could draw his own conclusions.

His eyes narrowed fractionally, but he didn't ask what Junior had been doing in her room. Either he didn't want to know, or he didn't care. "Anybody else?" he asked. "Or have you narrowed it down to the two of us?"

"Possibly Angus. I saw him this afternoon, and we didn't part on the best of terms."

"The three of us again, huh? Do you believe we're to blame for everything that happens around here?"

"I don't *believe* anything. I base my suspicions on facts." She was assailed by a wave of dizziness and nausea and had to close her eyes for a moment before going on. "I have another suspect in mind."

"Who?"

"Stacey Wallace."

Pat Chastain reacted like he'd been goosed. "Are you shittin' me?" He glanced toward the door to make certain it was closed. "God, please tell me I'm dreaming. You aren't going to publicly accuse her of anything, are you? Because if you're even thinking about it, I have to tell you right now, Alex, that you'll be on your own. I'm not sticking my neck out again."

"You haven't stuck your neck out for anything, yet!" Alex shouted, causing a blast of pain through her skull.

"Where would Stacey get access to an ME truck?" Reede asked.

"I don't have any solid facts," Alex said wearily. "It's just a hunch."

"Which is all you ever seem to have," Reede said. Alex gave him a menacing look, which she hoped packed more punch than she felt it did.

Pat intervened. "About Stacey, what do you base your allegations on?"

"She lied to me about where she was on the night of the murder." She related what Stacey had told her in the ladies' room at the Horse and Gun Club. "I know she still loves Junior. I don't think I'd get an argument from anyone on that."

The two men exchanged a glance that signified agreement. "She's like a mother hen to her father, and she doesn't want his reputation ruined. And," she added with a sigh, "she hates me for the same reason she hated Celina—Junior.

She thinks I'm stealing his affection from her, just as my mother did."

Pat jingled the change in his pockets as he rocked back and forth on the balls of his feet. "Sounds logical when you put it that way, but I just can't imagine Stacey using physical force."

"And here lately, your guesses have been way off base, Counselor."

Alex struggled to a sitting position. "Let's go back to the scalpel." She was so dizzy she had to grip the edge of the table to remain upright. "When did Reede ask you about it, Pat?"

"If you have something to ask, ask me." Reede moved to stand directly in front of her. "I mentioned the scalpel to him a few days ago."

"Why?"

"Just like you, I wanted to know what happened to it."

"If you had located it before me, would you have destroyed it, or turned it over as evidence?"

A muscle in his cheek twitched. "The point is moot. It's no longer in the evidence room."

"You checked?"

"Damn right. I couldn't find a trace of it. It probably hasn't been there for years. Most likely, it was thrown out because the case was."

"Out of consideration to the Collins family, wouldn't someone have offered to give it back?"

"I have no answer for that."

"Was it ever dusted for fingerprints?"

"I took the liberty of asking Judge Wallace that."

"I'm sure you did, Sheriff. What did he say?"

"He said no."

"Why not?"

"The handle was bloody. Gooney Bud's prints were all over it. It was hardly necessary to dust it."

They regarded each other with so much animosity that Pat Chastain broke out in a sweat. "Well, we'd better give these people back their treatment room. Your car is trashed, Alex, so I'll drive you to the motel. Are you up to walking to the car, or should I call for a wheelchair?"

"I'll take her to the motel," Reede said, before Alex could respond to Pat's offer.

"Are you sure?" Pat felt obligated to inquire, though he was obviously relieved that Reede was taking her off his hands. "Since the sheriff has offered," she told Pat, "I'll let him drive me."

The D.A. scuttled out before either could change his mind. Alex watched his rapid departure with derision. "It's no wonder crime is so prevalent in this county. The D.A. is as chicken-livered as they come."

"And the sheriff is corrupt."

"You took the words right out of my mouth." She slid off the edge of the examination table and braced herself against it long enough to get her balance. She tried to take a step, but swayed unsteadily. "The doctor gave me a painkiller. I'm so woozy, maybe you'd better ask them for a wheelchair."

"Maybe you'd better check in for the night."

"I don't want to."

"Suit yourself."

He scooped her into his arms before she could protest and carried her out of the examination room. "My purse." She gestured weakly toward the check-in desk. Reede retrieved it. Then, with the emergency room staff enthralled by the sight, Reede carried her out and deposited her in the front seat of his Blazer.

She rested her head on the back of the seat and closed her eyes. "Where were you this afternoon?" she asked, once they were underway.

"I told you already."

"You were riding even after sundown?"

"I ran some errands."

"You couldn't be reached on your radio. Where were you, Reede?"

"Lots of places."

"Specifically."

"I was at Nora Gail's."

Alex was surprised at how much that hurt her. "Oh."

"I had to question the witnesses about that shooting."

"Then, you were working?"

"Among other things."

"You still sleep with her, don't you?"

"Sometimes."

She prayed that he would die a slow, painful death.

"Maybe Nora Gail dispatched one of her heavies to do me in," she said, "as a favor to you."

"Maybe. It wouldn't surprise me. If she doesn't like something, she doesn't hesitate to take care of it."

"She didn't like Celina," Alex said softly.

"No, she didn't. But I was with Nora Gail the night Celina died, remember?"

"That's what I'm told."

So, was Nora Gail another suspect for Celina's murder?

The thought made her head ache. She closed her eyes. When they arrived at the motel, she reached for the door handle. Reede ordered her to wait and came around to assist her out. With his left arm around her waist, lending support, they made a shuffling trip to the door.

Reede unlocked it and helped her to the bed. She lay down gratefully. "It's freezing in here," he said, rubbing his hands together as he looked for the thermostat.

"It always is when I first come in."

"I didn't notice it last night."

They glanced quickly at each other, then away. Again unable to cope, Alex closed her eyes. When she opened them, Reede was rummaging in the top drawer of the bureau opposite the bed.

"What are you looking for this time?"

"Something for you to sleep in."

"Any T-shirt. It doesn't matter which one."

He returned to the bed, gingerly sat down on the edge, and removed her boots. "Leave my socks," she told him. "My feet are cold."

"Can you sit up?"

She could by leaning heavily against his shoulder while he fumbled with the buttons on the front of her dress. The tiny round things were no bigger than pills, and were covered in the same fabric as her dress. There was a row of them that ran from neck to knee. He was viciously cursing them by the time he got to her waist.

He eased her back down on the pillow, pulled her arms from the tight long sleeves, and worked the dress over her hips and down her legs. Her slip didn't give him pause, but her bra did. Once he seemed to make up his mind about it, he unclasped it with businesslike efficiency and helped her slide the straps off her shoulders.

"I thought you only had a gash on the head and some scratches on your hands?" Evidently, he'd consulted the doctor.

"That's right."

"Then, what's all th—"

He stopped suddenly, realizing that the abrasions on her upper torso were whisker burns. The corner of his mouth twitched with a spasm of regret. She felt compelled to lay her hand against his cheek and reassure him that it was all right, that she hadn't minded having his hot, eager mouth at her breasts, his deft tongue stroking her nipples into stiff rosiness.

Of course she didn't. His dark frown stifled anything she might have said. "You're gonna have to sit up again," he told her curtly.

With a hand behind each shoulder, he pulled her into a sitting position again and propped her against the head-board. He gathered the T-shirt up and tried to pull it over her head. Alex winced the instant he set it against her hair.

"This isn't working," he muttered. Then, with a single, violent motion, he ripped the neck of the shirt wide enough to slip over her head without causing any pain.

When she lay back down, she touched the long tear in the fabric. "Thanks. This was one of my favorites."

"Sorry." He pulled the covers up to her chin and stood up. "Are you going to be all right?"

"Yes."

He looked doubtful. "Are you sure?"

She nodded weakly. "Do you need anything before I go? Water?"

"Okay. Put a glass of water on the nightstand, please."

When he returned to the side of the bed, carrying the glass of water, she had already fallen asleep. Reede stood above her. Her hair, fanned out over the pillow, had bloodstains in it. There was an unnatural wanness to her complexion. It made him sick at his stomach to think how close she'd come to serious injury or death.

He set the glass of water on the nightstand and gingerly lowered himself to the edge of the bed. Alex stirred, murmured unintelligibly, and extended her hand, as though reaching for something. Responding to that silent, subconscious appeal, Reede carefully covered her cut hands with his strong, callused ones.

He wouldn't have been surprised if her eyes had popped open and she had started rebuking him for taking her virginity. How the hell could he have known?

And if I had known, he thought to himself, *I would have done it anyway.*

She didn't wake up. She only snuffled softly and trustingly curved her fingers over his knuckles. Good sense and impulse warred within him, but the fight didn't last long, and the outcome had been decided before his conscience raised its head.

He eased himself onto the bed, until he was stretched out full beside her, facing her, feeling her gentle, drug-induced breaths against his face.

He marveled over the delicate bone structure of her face, the shape of her mouth, the way her eyelashes lay upon her cheeks.

"Alex." He whispered her name, not to awaken her, but merely for the pleasure of speaking it out loud.

She sighed deeply, drawing his attention down to the torn

T-shirt. Through the tear he could see the smooth slope of her breasts. Her cleavage was dusky in the faint lamplight, shadowy and velvety, and he wanted to press his open mouth there.

He didn't. Nor did he kiss her vulnerable mouth, even though his mind was wildly occupied with how softly and deeply and wetly she kissed.

He thought of fondling the tempting mounds of her breasts. He could see the dark impressions of their centers behind the soft cloth of the T-shirt, and knew that with the merest touch of his tongue or fingertips, they would become taut. And that damned T-shirt was far sexier than any fancy negligee and garter belt that Nora Gail had ever worn.

It was hell to lie this close to her and not touch, but it was heaven to have this much access, to stare his fill. When the pleasure and pain of it got to be too much, he reluctantly withdrew his hand from hers and left the bed.

After making certain that she had enough blankets, that the medication had her completely sedated, he slipped quietly out of the room.

Chapter 39

"Come in." Junior was sitting up in bed watching TV and smoking a joint when Reede entered his room. "Hi. What brings you around?" He offered Reede the marijuana.

"No, thanks." Reede dropped into the easy chair and propped his boots on the matching ottoman.

The room had undergone very few changes since the first time Reede had been invited into it, although Junior had updated the furniture when he elected to move home after his last divorce. It was a spacious room, designed with comfort in mind.

"Lord, I'm tired," Reede said, running his fingers through his hair.

Junior pinched out the smoldering cigarette and put it away. "You look it."

"Thanks." He grinned ruefully. "How come I always look like forty miles of bad road and you're always perfectly groomed?"

"Genes. Look at Mother. I've never seen her mussed."

"I guess so. God knows my father didn't cotton to good grooming."

"Don't expect any pity from me. You know your rugged good looks are irresistible to the ladies. We're different types, that's all."

"Together, we'd be great."

"We were."

"Huh?"

"Remember the night we shared one of the Gail sisters behind the National Guard armory. Which one was it?"

Reede chuckled. "Damned if I remember. I'm too tired to think, much less remember."

"You've been putting in a lot of overtime, haven't you?"

"It's taken that," he paused strategically, "just to keep an eye on Alex and keep her from getting hurt."

Reede saw the interest spark in Junior's eyes. "She's a handful, all right."

"I'm not joking. She almost got killed this afternoon."

"What?" Junior swung his feet over the side of the bed to the floor. "What happened? Is she hurt?" Reede told Junior about the incident on the highway. "I'd better call her," he said as soon as Reede finished.

"Don't. When I left her, she was asleep. They gave her a painkiller at the hospital and it was already working."

He could feel the weight of Junior's inquisitive stare, but he didn't acknowledge it. He wasn't going to explain why he'd felt it necessary to tuck Alex in. It had taken all his willpower to walk out of that room and deny himself the luxury of lying beside her all night.

"Some Mexicans witnessed the whole thing. They said

it was an ME truck, and it deliberately ran her off the road."

Junior looked confused. "My first guess would be that preacher."

"Where would he get one of your company trucks?"

"A devoted member of his flock could be an employee."

"I've got a man checking out that possibility, although I doubt anything'll turn up."

The two friends were silent for a moment. Finally, Reede said casually, "I understand you had breakfast with Alex this morning."

"She called and asked me to meet her."

"Why?"

"She said you told her about Celina's attempted abortion." Reede averted his head. "Yeah."

"I don't like to second-guess you, friend, but—"

"Then, don't." Reede rolled out of the chair and came to his feet.

"Okay, okay. I just fail to see why it was necessary."

Reede didn't intend to talk about last night at all. "What else did you discuss over breakfast?"

"The night Celina died. Alex wanted to know if I'd proposed." Junior recounted that morning's conversation with Alex.

"Did she believe you when you said you went out and got drunk alone?"

"I guess so. She seemed to. Everybody else believes me."

The look they exchanged lasted a few seconds too long to be comfortable for either. "Yeah, right." Reede gazed out the window. "Alex said Stacey showed up and was none too friendly."

Junior fidgeted. "I've, uh, I've been seeing Stacey lately."

Reede swiveled around, surprised. "Seeing or screwing? Or are they automatically synonymous to you?"

"Guilty to both charges."

Reede cursed. "Why are you fanning that fire?"

"Convenience."

"Nora Gail's is convenient."

"But not free—at least, to no one but you."

Reede's lip curled. "You sorry son of a bitch."

"Look, it's not hurting anybody. Stacey needs the attention. She wants it."

"Because she loves you, you jerk."

"Awww." Junior dismissed that notion with a wave of his hand. "One thing I do know. She's all bent out of shape about Alex. Stacey's afraid she'll ruin all of us, but especially, her old man."

"She might do it. She's determined to find a culprit and send him to prison."

Junior slouched against the headboard again. "Does that really worry you?"

"Yes," Reede said. "I've got a lot to lose if ME doesn't get that racing license. So do you."

"What are you getting at, that *I* ran Alex off the road? Is this an interrogation, Sheriff?" he asked in a tone that didn't flatter the office Reede held.

"Well?"

Junior's handsome face flushed with anger. "Good God, are you crazy?" He left the bed and came to stand eye to eye with Reede. "I wouldn't harm a hair on her head."

"Were you in her room this morning?"

"Yes. So?"

"What for?" Reede shouted.

"What do you think?" Junior shouted back.

Reede's head gave a little snap backward. It was a reflex-ive action, one he couldn't prevent from happening or hide once it had.

Several moments of silence elapsed before Junior said, "She said no."

"I didn't ask."

"But you wanted to," Junior said intuitively. "Does Alex and her reason for being here have anything to do with you turning down Dad's offer to come back to ME?" He returned to the bed and sat down on the edge of it, giving Reede a wounded and inquisitive look. "Weren't you even going to mention it, Reede?"

"No."

"Why?"

"There was no point. When I left the company, it was for good. I don't want to become a part of it again."

"Of *us*, you mean."

Reede shrugged. Junior thoughtfully gazed at his friend. "Because of Celina?"

"Celina?" Reede whispered with a soft, sad laugh. "Celi-na's dead and buried."

"Is she?"

The friends stared at each other frankly, with all pretense stripped away. After a moment, Reede answered, "Yes."

"It hasn't been the same between us since she died, has it?"

"It couldn't be."

"I guess not," Junior said morosely. "I regret that."

"So do I."

"What about Alex?"

"What about her?"

"Is she the reason you won't come back in with us?"

"Hell, no. You know the reason, Junior—or at least, you should. You've heard me talk about it often enough."

"That crap about independence? That's no reason. You work your way around Angus a lot better than I do."

Junior sucked in a quick breath, suddenly realizing that he'd hit pay dirt. "That's it, isn't it? You're steering clear of ME for my sake."

"You're wrong." Reede's denial came a little too fast.

"The hell I am," Junior growled. "You see yourself as a threat to me, the heir apparent. Well, thanks a lot, but don't do me any favors!"

As suddenly as Junior's anger had erupted, it evaporated. "Who the fuck am I kidding?" He gave a scoffing laugh. "Sure as hell not myself." He raised his head and looked at Reede imploringly. "I'd love to have you back. We need you, especially after that racetrack is built."

"Now who's talking crap?"

"You know I'm right. Dad makes things happen, but he operates like a robber baron. Business doesn't work like that nowadays. I've got charm, but charm is as wasted on a breeding ranch as snow skis in Jamaica. Unless you're a gigolo—a career I've often thought of pursuing—you can't bank charm."

"It comes in handy."

"Dad's smart enough to see that you could hold us together, Reede. You could be the buffer between us." He looked down at his hands. "He'd rather have you than me around."

"Junior—"

"No, let's be honest about this for once, Reede. We're getting too old to lie to ourselves or to each other. Dad would swear on a stack of Bibles that he's proud that I'm his son, but I know better. Oh, I know he loves me, but I'm one screwup after another. He'd rather me be like you."

"That's not true."

"I'm afraid it is."

"Uh-uh," Reede said, sternly shaking his head. "Angus knows that in a pinch, when all the cards are down, you come through. There have been times—"

"What times?"

"Many times," Reede stressed, "when you did what you knew you had to do. Sometimes it has to get to that last-gasp stage before you accept your responsibility," Reede said, "but when you know it's up to you or else, you do it." He laid his hand on Junior's shoulder. "It's just that sometimes some-body has to put a boot to your butt to get you going."

It was time to end the discussion, before it got sloppily maudlin. Reede socked Junior's shoulder, then headed for the door. "Don't go selling that dope to schoolkids or I'll have to haul you in, okay?" He had opened the door and was on his way out before Junior halted him.

"I was mad as hell the other day when you showed up at the country club to pick up Alex."

"I know. It couldn't be helped. It was business."

"Was it? What about the airfield? Was that business, too? That wasn't Dad's impression."

Reede remained stonily silent, neither admitting or deny-ing anything.

"Jesus," Junior breathed, drawing his hand down his face. "Is it happening again? Are we falling in love with the same woman?"

Reede walked out, quietly closing the door behind him.

Chapter 40

Stacey Wallace slid her father's half-eaten tuna salad out of the way and replaced it with a bowl of fruit cocktail. "I don't think we'll have her to worry about much longer," she said with assurance. The topic of conversation was Alexandra Gaither. "Did you hear about her accident?"

"From what I understand, it wasn't an accident."

"All the more reason for her to want to leave town."

"Angus doesn't think she's going to leave," the judge said as he toyed with the cherry floating in the syrup. "He says she's convinced somebody wanted to scare her into leaving before she exposed the killer."

"Do you take everything Angus says as carved in granite?" Stacey asked with exasperation. "How does he know what she's going to do?"

"He's going by what she told Junior."

Stacey laid her fork aside. "Junior?"

"Hmm." Judge Wallace sipped his iced tea. "He sat with her yesterday."

"I thought she left the hospital and was back at her motel."

"Wherever she is, Junior's been her only contact with the outside world." The judge was so caught up in his own worries, he didn't notice Stacey's suddenly preoccupied gaze.

He pushed away from the table. "I'd better go or I'll be late. We've got a jury selection this morning and a pretrial hearing for that character who shot a man out at Nora Gail Burton's the other night. I'm expecting a plea bargain, but Lambert's got Pat Chastain pushing for attempted murder."

Stacey was only half listening. Her mind had lodged on a mental picture of the beautiful Alex Gaither languishing on her motel room bed while Junior waited on her hand and foot.

"By the way," the judge said as he pulled on his overcoat, "did you get that message I left you yesterday?"

"To call Fergus Plummet?"

"Yes. Isn't he that evangelical preacher who raised Cain because they had bingo at the Halloween carnival last year? What'd he want with you?"

"He's canvassing support to keep pari-mutuel gambling out of Purcell County."

The judge snickered. "Does he know he'd just as well try and hold back our next dust storm?"

"That's what I told him when I returned his call," Stacey said. "He knows I belong to several women's organizations and wanted me to plead his case with them. I declined, of course."

Joe Wallace picked up his briefcase and opened the front door. "Reede is convinced that Plummet was responsible for that vandalism out at the Minton ranch, but he's got no evidence to hold him." The judge didn't think twice about discussing cases with Stacey. She had earned his confidence years ago. "I don't think Plummet has the sense to pull off something like that, not without somebody directing him. Reede has been harping on it, but right now, Plummet is the least of my worries."

Concerned, Stacey caught her father's arm. "What worries, Dad? Alex Gaither? Don't worry about her. What harm could she possibly do you?"

He faked a smile. "Absolutely none. You just know how I like things neat and tidy. I've got to run. Good-bye."

———◆———

Wanda Gail Burton Plummet happened to be sweeping off her front porch when the postman arrived. He handed her the stack of mail and she thanked him. She sorted through it as she made her way back into the house. As usual, all the mail was addressed to her husband. It was mostly bills and church-related correspondence.

One envelope, however, was different from the others. It was made of high-quality beige paper. There was an embossed return address on it, but it had been exed out on a typewriter, making it illegible. Their address had been typed on it, too.

Curiosity won out over her husband's strict instructions that he was to open their mail. Wanda tore open the envelope. It contained only a blank piece of paper, folded around five one-hundred-dollar bills.

Wanda stared at the money as though it was a message from an alien planet. Five hundred dollars was more than the offering plate contained after a well-attended revival service. Fergus only took out a pittance to support his family. Almost everything collected went to the church and its "causes."

No doubt this money had been sent by a donor who wanted to remain anonymous. For the last several days, Fergus had been calling up folks on the telephone, asking for volunteers to picket at the gates of the Minton ranch. He solicited money. He wanted to place full-page antigambling ads in the newspaper. Well-publicized crusades were expensive.

Most people hung up on him. Some had called him ugly names before slamming down their receivers. A few had listened and given halfhearted pledges to send a supportive offering.

But, *five hundred dollars.*

He'd also spent time on the phone in secretive, whispered conversations. Wanda didn't know what these covert calls were about, but she suspected they had something to do with that business at the Minton ranch. One of the hardest things she'd ever had to do was lie to her old friend, Reede. He had known she was lying, but he'd been gentlemanly enough not to accuse her of it.

Afterward, when she had expressed concern to Fergus about her sin of lying, he had told her that it had been justified. God didn't expect his servants to go to jail, where they would be ineffectual.

She timidly pointed out that Paul had spent a lot of time in prison, and had done some of the most inspired writing in the New Testament while behind bars. Fergus hadn't appreciated the comparison and had told her that she should keep her mouth shut about matters that were too complicated for her to comprehend.

"Wanda?"

She jumped at the sound of his voice and reflexively clutched the money to her sagging breasts. "What, Fergus?"

"Was that the postman at the door?"

"Uh, yes." She glanced down at the envelope. The money was surely related to those furtive telephone calls. Fergus wouldn't want to talk about them. "I was just bringing you the mail."

She went into the kitchen. He was seated at the Formica dining table that served as his desk between meals. She laid the stack of mail on the table. When she returned to the sink to finish washing dishes, the fancy envelope and its contents were in her apron pocket.

She would give it to Fergus later, Wanda promised herself, as a surprise. In the meantime, she would fantasize about all it could buy for her three kids.

Alex had had thirty-six hours to think about it. While nursing her debilitating headache, she'd lain in bed, reviewing everything she knew and filling in what she didn't know with educated guesses.

She couldn't continue to run around in circles indefinitely. She was probably as close to the truth as she was ever going to get, short of taking desperate measures. The deadline Greg had set was imminent. It was time to force someone's hand, to get aggressive, even if she had to bluff.

Days ago, she had reached the heartbreaking conclusion that she had been the catalyst for Celina's murder, but she didn't plan to bear the burden of that guilt alone for the rest of her life. Whoever had done the actual deed must suffer for it also.

That morning when she woke up, she still had a headache,

but it was one she could live with. She spent the morning reviewing her notes and doing some research, and was waiting in Judge Wallace's anteroom when he returned from lunch. He didn't look pleased to see her.

"I told Ms. Gaither that you had a full schedule today," Mrs. Lipscomb said defensively when he turned a baleful glance on her. "She insisted on waiting for you."

"She's right, Judge Wallace, I did," Alex said. "Can you spare me a few minutes?"

He consulted his wristwatch. "A very few."

She followed him into his office. He took off his overcoat and hung it on a brass coat tree. Not until he was situated behind his desk, trying to look intimidating, did he say, "What is it this time?"

"What did Angus Minton use to entice you?"

His face became instantly mottled. "I don't know what you're talking about."

"Yes, you do. You confined an innocent man to a state mental hospital, Judge Wallace. You knew he was innocent, or at least strongly suspected that he was. You did that at Angus Minton's request, didn't you? And in exchange, you demanded that Junior marry your daughter, Stacey."

"This is incredible!" He banged his fists on his desktop.

"It's extremely credible. On the morning after Celina Graham Gaither was found murdered in a stable on the Minton ranch, you received a phone call or a visit from Angus. Bud Hicks had been arrested nearby, covered in blood and in possession of a scalpel presumed to be the murder weapon. That was never ascertained because the scalpel wasn't thoroughly analyzed. The autopsy report specified that she died of repeated stab wounds, but a forensic expert didn't have access to the body before it was cremated, so she could have been stabbed by anything."

"Gooney Bud stabbed her with Dr. Collins's scalpel," he stated stubbornly. "He found it in the stable and killed her with it."

"Where is it now?"

"Now? It's been twenty-five years. You don't expect it to be lying around in the evidence room, do you?"

"No, but I would expect to have a record of its dispensation. No one ever called the late Dr. Collins or his son, asking if they might want it back, even though it was known to have been a gift from his wife. Doesn't that strike you as unusual?"

"God knows what happened to it, or to the records concerning it."

"I think that you disposed of it, Judge. You, not the sheriff's office, were the last one recorded to have possession of it. I checked this morning before coming here."

"Why would I dispose of it?"

"Because if someone came along later—an investigator like me—it would be easy and believable to pass off its disappearance as a clerical error. Better to be accused of sloppy bookkeeping than miscarriage of justice."

"You are obnoxious, Miss Gaither," he said stiffly. "Like most avengers, you're reacting emotionally, and have no basis whatsoever for your horrid allegations."

"Nevertheless, this is what I intend to present to the grand jury. Actually, I'm doing you a favor by telling you what I have. You'll be able to consult with your attorney ahead of time about the answers you will give. Or will you take the Fifth?"

"I won't need to do either."

"Do you want to call your lawyer now? I'll gladly wait."

"I don't need a lawyer."

"Then I'll proceed. Angus asked you for a favor. You asked for one in return."

"Junior Minton married my daughter because he loved her."

"I find that impossible to believe, Judge Wallace, since he's told me himself that he asked my mother to marry him the night she was killed."

"I can't explain his fickleness."

"I can. Junior was the trade-off for your ruling on Gooney Bud."

"The district attorney's office—"

"He was on vacation in Canada at the time. I confirmed that with his widow this morning. His assistant had enough evidence to arraign Bud Hicks for murder."

"A trial jury would have convicted him, too."

"I disagree, but we'll never know. You prevented that." She drew a deep breath. "Who was Angus protecting—himself, Junior, or Reede?"

"No one."

"He must have told you when he called that morning."

"He didn't call."

"He had to have called as soon as Hicks was arrested. What did Angus tell you?"

"He didn't tell me anything. I never heard from him."

She came out of her chair and leaned over his desk. "He must have said, 'Look, Joe, I've gotten myself in a jam here.' Or, 'Junior's taken this boys-will-be-boys thing a little too far this time,' or 'Can you help Reede out? He's like a son to me.' Isn't that what happened?"

"No, never."

"You might have argued that you couldn't do it. You probably asked for time to think about it. Being the nice guy that he is, Angus granted you a few hours to mull it over. That's when you came back saying that you would do this little favor for him in exchange for a marriage between Stacey and Junior."

"I won't have you—"

"Maybe you even discussed your dilemma with her and Mrs. Wallace."

"This is defamation of—"

"Or maybe Stacey was the one to suggest the terms of the deal."

"Stacey never knew anything about it!"

He shot out of his chair and stood nose to nose with Alex, shouting the words in her face. When he realized what he'd admitted, he blinked, wet his lips, then eased away from her and turned his back. Nervously, he ran his fingers over the row of brass studs on the back of his leather chair. It had been a gift from his daughter, his only child.

"You knew how much Stacey loved Junior Minton."

"Yes," he said softly. "I knew that she loved him more than he deserved."

"And that her affection wasn't returned."

"Yes."

"And that Junior slept with her whenever he felt like it. You thought you had better protect her reputation and the possibility of an unwanted pregnancy by getting her married as soon as possible."

The judge's shoulders slumped forward and he answered in a low, heartbroken voice. "Yes."

Alex closed her eyes and let go a long, silent breath. Tension ebbed from her like a wave receding from the shore. "Judge Wallace, who killed my mother? Who was Angus protecting when he asked you to hustle Buddy Hicks through the legal system?"

He faced her. "I don't know. As God is my witness, I don't. I swear it on my years as a judge."

She believed him and said so. As unobtrusively as possible, she collected her things. When she reached the door of his office, he spoke her name in a thin voice.

"Yes?"

"If this ever comes to trial, will it be essential to your case for all this to come out in court?"

"I'm afraid so. I'm sorry."

"Stacey…" He paused to clear his throat. "I wasn't lying when I said she didn't know about my agreement with Angus."

Alex repeated, "I'm sorry."

He nodded gravely. She stepped into the anteroom and closed the door behind her. The secretary shot her a resentful look, which wasn't entirely undeserved. She had badgered him into telling the truth. It had been necessary, but she hadn't enjoyed doing it.

She was waiting for the elevator when she heard the gunshot. "Oh, God, no." She whispered the words, but wasn't even aware of saying them as she dropped her briefcase and raced back toward the end of the corridor. Mrs. Lipscomb was at the door to his office. Alex shoved her aside and ran in ahead of her.

What she saw brought her to an abrupt halt. Her scream froze in her throat, but the secretary's echoed through the chamber and into the hallways.

Chapter 41

A stream of secretaries, bailiffs, and other courthouse employees had gathered at the door of Judge Wallace's chambers within sixty seconds of the gunshot.

Reede, the first person to make it upstairs from the basement, shouldered his way through them, barking orders to the deputies who had followed him. "Clear everybody out!"

He instructed one to call an ambulance and another to cordon off the hallway. He placed a comforting arm around Mrs. Lipscomb, who was weeping hysterically, and commissioned Imogene, Pat Chastain's secretary, to take her away. He then bore down on Alex.

"Go to my office, lock yourself in, and stay there, understand?" She stared back at him blankly. "Understand?" he repeated loudly, giving her a shake. Still incapable of speech, she nodded.

To another deputy, he said, "See that she gets to my office. Don't let anybody in."

The officer led her away. Before she left the judge's

chambers, she saw Reede look toward the grisly sight at the desk. He ran his hand through his hair and muttered, "Shit."

In his office on the lower level, Alex passed the time by pacing, weeping, gnashing her teeth, staring into space. She agonized in her own private hell over Judge Joseph Wallace's suicide.

Her head was pounding so fiercely, the stitches in her scalp felt like they would pop. She had failed to bring along her medication. A frantic search through the sheriff's desk didn't even produce an aspirin tablet. Was the man totally immune to pain?

She was light-headed and nauseated and her hands refused to get warm, though they perspired profusely. The ancient plaster ceiling conducted every sound from above, but she couldn't identify them. There was an endless parade of footsteps. The office provided her refuge from the confusion, but she was desperate to know what was happening in the rooms and hallways overhead.

She was chin deep in despair. The facts pointed toward an inexorable truth that she didn't want to acknowledge. Judge Wallace's confession to a cover-up further implicated her chief suspects.

Caught in a bind, Angus would have looked out for himself without feeling any remorse. By the same token, he would have bribed the judge in order to protect Junior, and probably done no less for Reede. But of the three, which had actually gone into the stable that night and murdered Celina?

When Reede flung open the door, Alex whirled around, startled. She'd been staring out the window. She didn't know how long she had waited in the room, but she realized suddenly that it was getting dark outside when he flipped on the light switch. She was still ignorant of what was transpiring upstairs and at the front of the courthouse.

Reede gave her a hard look, but said nothing. He poured himself a cup of coffee and sipped from it several times. "Why is it lately that every time something happens in this town, you're involved?"

Tears instantly formed in her eyes. One moment they weren't there, the next they were heavily pushing against her eyelids. She aimed a shaking index finger at his chest. "Don't, Reede. I didn't know that—"

"That when you backed Joe Wallace into a corner he'd blow his brains out. Well, that's what happened, baby. They're dripping over the edge of his desk."

"Shut up."

"We found clumps of hair and tissue on the opposite wall."

She covered her mouth, swallowing a scream behind her hands. Turning her back on him, she shuddered uncontrollably. When he touched her, she flinched, but his hands were firm on her shoulders as he turned her around and pulled her against his chest.

"Hush now, it's done." His chest expanded against her cheek as he drew in a deep breath. "Forget it."

She shoved herself away. "Forget it? A man is dead. It's my fault."

"Did you pull the trigger?"

"No."

"Then, it's not your fault."

There was a knock at the door. "Who is it?" Reede asked crossly. When the deputy identified himself, Reede told him to come in. He signaled Alex into a chair while the deputy rolled a sheet of paper into the typewriter. She looked at Reede in bewilderment.

"We have to take your statement," he said.

"Now?"

"Best to get it over with. Ready?" he asked the deputy and got a nod. "Okay, Alex, what happened?"

She dabbed her face with a tissue before she began. As briefly as possible, she told what had transpired in the judge's chambers, being careful not to mention any names or issues that had been discussed.

"I left his office and got as far as the elevator." She stared down at the soggy Kleenex that she'd been mutilating between her hands. "Then, I heard the shot."

"You ran back in?"

"Yes. He was slumped over. His head was lying on his desk. I saw blood and... and knew what he'd done."

"Did you see the pistol?" She shook her head. Reede said to the deputy, "Make a note that she answered no and that she couldn't have seen it because it had fallen from the victim's right hand to the floor. That's all for now." The deputy discreetly withdrew. Reede waited several moments. His foot swung to and fro from the corner of the desk where he was seated. "What did you and the judge talk about?"

"Celina's murder. I accused him of tampering with evidence and accepting a bribe."

"Serious allegations. How did he respond?"

"He admitted it."

He took something out of his shirt pocket and tossed it onto his desk. The sterling-silver scalpel landed with a dull, metallic sound. It had oxidized, but was otherwise clean.

Alex recoiled from the sight of it. "Where'd you get that?"

"From the judge's left hand."

They exchanged a long stare. Finally, Reede said, "It was his instrument of self-abuse, kept in his desk drawer, a constant reminder that he was corruptible. Knowing how proud he was of his years on the bench, it's no wonder he cashed in. He'd rather blow off the side of his head than watch his career be ruined."

"Is that all you can say?"

"What do you expect me to say?"

"I expect you to ask me who bribed him? With what? Why?" Her tearful eyes dried instantly. "You already know, don't you?"

He eased himself off the desk and stood up. "I wasn't born yesterday, Alex."

"So, you know that Angus got Judge Wallace to lock Gooney Bud away, presumably as Celina's murderer, in exchange for Junior marrying Stacey."

"Where does that leave you?" Planting his hands on his hips, he loomed above her. "It's speculation. You can't prove it. Neither of them would have been stupid enough to record a conversation to that effect, if one did take place. Nobody wrote anything down. There's enough reasonable doubt there for downtown Dallas to fit into. A man's dead, his reputation as a fine judge has been shot to hell, and you've still got nothing to base a murder rap on."

He tapped his chest, his fingertips making angry stabs at his shirt. "I had to drive to the judge's house and notify Stacey that her old man had emptied his head onto his desk because of your loosely based charges that would probably have been no-billed by the grand jury."

He stopped and regained control of his temper. "Before I get really pissed off at you, I suggest we get out of here and go someplace where it's safe."

"Safe? For whom?"

"For you, dammit. Haven't the repercussions of this sunk in yet? Pat Chastain's near cardiac arrest. Greg Harper has already called three times today, wanting to know if you could possibly have had anything to do with this prominent and respected judge's suicide. Stacey is incoherent with grief, but in her lucid moments, she's cursing you to perdition.

"We've got Plummet and his army of crazies out there on the courthouse steps, carrying pickets that say this is just the beginning of the end. All this chaos is because of you and your half-baked murder case, Counselor."

Alex felt as though her chest was going to cave in, but she fought back. "Was I supposed to let Wallace go free just because he was a really nice guy?"

"There are more subtle ways to handle delicate situations like that, Alex."

"But, no one handled it at all!" she cried. "Is that your philosophy of the law, Sheriff Lambert? Some rules don't apply to people? When a friend of yours crosses over, do you conveniently look the other way? Apparently so. Case in point—Nora Gail Burton and her whorehouse. Does that same exclusion from justice apply to you, as well?"

He didn't answer. Instead, he went to the door and opened it, saying curtly, "Let's go."

She stepped into the hallway with him; he steered her toward the rear elevator. "Pat loaned me his wife's car," she told him. "It's parked out front."

"I know. There's a swarm of reporters camped right beside it, all of them eager to know the gory details of the judge's suicide. I'm sneaking you out the back door."

They left the building unseen. It was completely dark outside, and Alex wondered what time it was.

They were halfway between the building and the parking lot when a form disengaged itself from the shadows and blocked their path.

"Stacey," Reede exclaimed softly. Subconsciously, his hand closed around the butt of his pistol, although he didn't remove it from the holster.

"I thought I'd catch you trying to hide."

Stacey's eyes were fixed on Alex. The hatred in them made Alex want to cower against Reede for protection, but she maintained her proud stance. "Before you say anything, Stacey, I want you to know that I'm terribly sorry about your father."

"Are you?"

"Very sorry."

Stacey shivered, whether with cold or revulsion, Alex couldn't tell. "You came here to ruin him. Instead of being sorry, you should feel very proud of yourself."

"I had nothing to do with your father's past mistakes."

"You're the reason for the whole mess! Why couldn't you just leave him alone?" Stacey cried, her voice cracking. "What happened twenty-five years ago wasn't important to anybody but you. He was old. He planned to retire in a few months anyway. What harm was he doing you?"

Alex remembered the judge's last words to her. Stacey hadn't known about the shady deal he had struck on her behalf. Alex could spare her that pain, at least until she'd had time to absorb the shock of her father's death. "I can't discuss the case with you. I'm sorry."

"Case? *Case?* This was never about a case. This was about your trashy mother, who used and manipulated people— *men*—until someone got tired of it and killed her." Her eyes narrowed threateningly and she took a malevolent step closer. "You're just like her, stirring up trouble, a user of people and a whore!"

She launched herself at Alex, but Reede stepped between them, catching Stacey against his chest and holding her there until her rage was spent and she was clinging to him weakly, sobbing.

He stroked her back and murmured words of comfort. Behind her back, he passed Alex the keys to his Blazer. She took them and let herself in, locking the door behind her. Watching through the windshield, she saw him lead Stacey around the corner of the building and out of sight. Several minutes later, he came jogging back. She unlocked the door for him and he climbed in.

"Will she be all right?" Alex asked.

"Yeah. I turned her over to some friends. They'll see that she gets home. Someone will stay with her tonight." His lips narrowed into a bitter line. "Of course, the man she wants isn't there for her."

"Her father?"

He shook his head. "Junior."

Because it was all so pitifully sad, Alex began to cry again.

Chapter 42

She didn't raise her head until the Blazer jounced over a chuckhole. She tried to get her bearings by looking through the windshield, but it was a dark night, and the road had no markings. "Where are we going?"

"My place." No sooner had he said it than his headlights picked up the house.

"Why?"

He cut the truck's engine. "Because I'm afraid to let you out of my sight. People turn up dead or wounded when I do."

He left her sitting in the truck while he went to unlock the front door. She thought about driving off, but he'd taken the keys. In some ways, Alex was relieved she'd been robbed of taking the initiative. She wanted to defy him, but didn't have the physical or mental energy. Tiredly, she pushed open the Blazer's door and got out.

The house looked different at night. Like a woman's face, it fared better under soft lighting that helped camouflage its flaws. Reede had gone in ahead of her and turned on a lamp.

He was crouched in front of the fireplace, putting a long match to the kindling beneath the stacked logs.

When the dry wood started crackling, he stood up and asked her, "Are you hungry?"

"Hungry?" She repeated the word like someone unfamiliar with the language.

"When did you eat last? Lunch?"

"Junior brought a hamburger to my room last night."

He made a grumpy, grunting sound and headed for the kitchen. "I don't promise anything as fancy as a hamburger."

Thanks to Lupe's niece, the pantry had been recently stocked with more than peanut butter and crackers. After taking a quick inventory, he recited their choices. "Canned soup, canned spaghetti, frozen tamales, bacon and eggs."

"Bacon and eggs."

They worked in companionable silence. Reede did most of the actual cooking. He had little regard for tidiness and none for culinary finesse. Alex enjoyed watching him. When he slid a plate in front of her and dropped into the chair across the small table, she smiled at him pensively. He noticed her expression and did a double take as he lifted the first forkful to his mouth.

"What's the matter?"

She shook her head and shyly lowered her eyes. "Nothing."

He didn't seem ready to accept her answer. Before he could pursue it, however, the telephone rang. He reached for the wall extension.

"Lambert. Oh, hi, Junior." He looked toward Alex. "Yeah, it was a real mess." He listened. "She, uh, she had a meeting with him right before it happened . . . I'm afraid she saw everything."

He paraphrased Alex's official statement. "That's all I know...Well, Christ, tell them to calm down. They can read about it in tomorrow's paper, like everybody else...Okay, look, I'm sorry," he said, "it's been a bitch of a day and I'm tired.

"Give Sarah Jo one of her pills and tell Angus he's got nothing to worry about." He caught Alex's frown, but kept his expression bland. "Alex? She's fine...Well, if she doesn't answer her phone, she's probably in the shower. If you want to play Good Samaritan, there's somebody who needs you more than Alex tonight...Stacey, you idiot. Why don't you go over there and sit with her for a while...Okay, see you tomorrow."

After he broke the connection, he left the phone off the hook and went back to his food. Alex asked, "Why didn't you tell him I was here?"

"Did you want me to?"

"Not particularly. I just wondered why you didn't."

"He didn't need to know."

"Will he go see Stacey?"

"I hope so, but you never can tell about Junior. Actually," he said, swallowing a bite, "you seem to be all he's thinking about."

"Me, personally, or what I heard from Judge Wallace?"

"A combination of both, I guess."

"Angus is upset?"

"Naturally. Joe Wallace was an old friend."

"Friend and coconspirator." Reede didn't rise to the bait; he didn't even divert his attention from his supper. "I must talk to Angus, Reede. I want you to drive me over there as soon as we finish eating." He calmly reached for his coffee cup, sipped, returned it to the saucer. "Reede, did you hear me?"

"Yes."

"Then, you'll drive me over?"

"No."

"I've got to talk to him."

"Not tonight."

"Yes, tonight. Wallace implicated him in a cover-up. I've got to question him about it."

"He's not going anywhere. Tomorrow's soon enough."

"Your loyalty is commendable, but it can't protect Angus forever."

He set his silverware on his empty plate and carried it to the sink. "Tonight, I'm more concerned about you than Angus."

"Me?"

He glanced at her plate and, satisfied that she was finished, cleared it away. "Seen yourself in a mirror lately? You look like hell. Several times I've braced myself to catch you, afraid you were about to keel over."

"I'm fine. If you'll just take me back to the motel, I'll—"

"Uh-uh," he said, shaking his head. "You're staying here tonight, where you can get some sleep without being pestered by reporters."

"Do you really think I would be?"

"A judge's death is hot news. A judge's suicide is even hotter. You were the last person to talk to him. You're conducting an investigation that has the racing commission worried. Yeah, I think the press will be tramping down the bushes around the Westerner to get to you."

"I'd be okay if I locked myself in my room."

"I'm not taking any chances. As I've told you before, I don't want one of Harper's pets to get herself killed in my county. You've generated enough negative publicity for us these last few weeks; we sure as hell can't stand any more. Does your head hurt?"

She had rested her head in her hand and was subconsciously massaging her temples. "Yes, a little."

"Take some medicine."

"I don't have it with me."

"I'll see if I can round up something for your pain."

He circled the back of her chair and scooted it away from the table. As she stood up, she said, "You keep a stash of drugs, too? That's against the law, you know."

"Is that all you ever think about—the law? Whether something is right or wrong? Is the line between them so clearly defined for you?"

"Isn't it for you?"

"If it had been, I'd have gone hungry lots of times. I stole food to feed myself and my old man. Was that wrong?"

"I don't know, Reede," she said wearily.

Her head hurt from trying to keep up with their argument. She trailed him down the hallway, not really realizing where he was headed until he switched on the light in his bedroom.

Her face must have registered alarm because he grinned sardonically and said, "Don't worry. I'm not trying to seduce you. I'll sleep on the sofa in the living room."

"I really shouldn't stay here, Reede."

"We could both be grown-up about this...if you were a grown-up to start with."

Not in the least amused, she lashed out at him. "There are a million reasons why I shouldn't spend the night here.

Number one on the list is that I should be questioning Angus right now."

"Give him one more night of grace. What could it hurt?"

"Pat Chastain will probably expect to hear from me."

"I told him you were near collapse and that you would contact him in the morning."

"You planned ahead, I see."

"I wasn't taking any chances. When allowed to roam free, you're dangerous."

She leaned against the wall and closed her eyes for a moment. Too proud to capitulate, but too exhausted not to, she compromised. "Just answer one question."

"Shoot."

"May I use your shower?"

***

Fifteen minutes later, she turned off the taps and reached for a towel hanging on the bar. He had loaned her a pair of pajamas to put on. They looked brand new.

When she had commented on it, he said, "Junior brought them to me in the hospital when I had my appendix taken out several years ago. I only wore them so I could get out of that ass-baring gown. Can't stand the things."

Smiling at the distasteful face he'd made when he'd said that, she slid her arms into the blue silk top and buttoned up the front. Just then he tapped on the bathroom door. "I found some pain pills."

Well covered to midthigh, she opened the door. He handed her the prescription bottle. "This is strong stuff," she remarked, reading the label. "You must have been in severe pain. The appendectomy?"

He shook his head. "Root canal. Feeling better?"

"The shower helped. My head's not hurting so bad anymore."

"You washed your hair."

"Against doctor's orders. I wasn't supposed to for a week, but I couldn't stand it any longer."

"Better let me take a look at your stitches."

She tipped her head forward and he gently parted her hair. His fingers were light and deft. The most pressure she felt was his breath against her scalp.

"Everything looks all right."

"I washed around it."

Reede stepped away, but continued to look at her. She looked back. They stayed that way for a very long, silent time. Eventually, in a low, rough voice, Reede said, "Better take your pill."

She turned toward the sink and filled his toothbrush glass with tap water. She shook a tablet from the plastic bottle, tossed it back, and took a long drink. As she was bringing her head forward, she caught his eyes in the mirror. She replaced the snap-on lid of the pill bottle and turned, drying her mouth on the back of her hand.

Inexplicably, and totally unexpectedly, tears formed in her eyes. "I know you don't regard me too highly, Reede, but you must know how terrible I feel about what Judge Wallace did." Her lower lip began to tremble; her voice became husky with emotion. "It was awful, horrible."

She stepped toward him, put her arms around his waist,

and laid her cheek against his chest. "Be kind for once and just hold me. Please."

He groaned her name and curled his arm around her waist. His other hand cradled the back of her head to hold her face against his chest. He massaged her scalp soothingly and pressed soft kisses on her brow. At the first touch of his lips, she tilted her head up. She kept her eyes closed, but she could feel the heat of his gaze on her face.

His lips brushed hers, and when hers separated, he murmured another low groan and kissed her deeply. His hands sifted through her wet hair, then caressed her neck.

"Touch me again, Reede," she pleaded.

He unbuttoned the pajama top, then slid his hands inside it, encircling her body and drawing it up high against him. His shirt lightly rubbed against her nipples. She felt the cold bite of his belt buckle on her bare belly and the bulge of his fly nudging her mound as it nestled in the soft hair between her thighs.

Each sensation was more electrifying than the last. She wanted to savor each one individually, but the combination of them was too immense and overwhelming for her to concentrate. Every blood vessel in her body expanded with passion. She was inundated with him.

Suddenly, he moved away from her. She looked up at him, bewildered, wide-eyed, and already feeling the loss. "Reede?"

"I have to know."

"What?"

"Have you been to bed with Junior?"

"I don't have to answer that."

"Yes, you do," he said resolutely. "If you want this to go one step further, you do. Have you been to bed with Junior?"

Desire won out over pride. She shook her head and gave him a soft, whispery answer. "No."

After several ponderous seconds, he said, "Okay, then, this time we're going to do it right."

Taking her hand, he led her into the living room, which surprised her because the bed had been turned down while she was in the shower. In the living room, the only light was from the fire burning in the fireplace. He had already made up the couch for himself, but he whipped the bedding off now and spread it out on the floor in front of the hearth. She knelt on the pallet while he calmly began to undress.

His boots, socks, shirt, and belt were cast aside with dispatch. Alex, acting on impulse, moved aside his hands when they went to undo his fly. Slowly, her fingers pushed the stubborn metal buttons through the holes. When all were undone, she opened the wedge wider, leaned forward, and kissed him.

Groaning, Reede gently cupped her head between his hands. Her mouth opened warmly and wetly over his belly, just below his navel. "That's my favorite thing," he rasped.

Sliding her hands into the back of his jeans, she eased them over his buttocks, while her lips continued to whisk airy, breathy kisses over his lower body. Finally, her tongue glanced the tip of his penis.

"Stop, Alex. Stop," he moaned. "That's killing me, baby."

Quickly, he stepped out of the jeans and kicked them aside. Naked, he was tall and rangy and rugged, the appendectomy scar only one of many.

His body hair caught the glow of the fire. It showed up as

a golden fuzz over his tanned skin, except around his sex, where it was dark and dense. Lean muscles rippled with each movement.

"Get out of that goddamn pajama top before I tear it off."

Sitting back on her heels, Alex eased the pajama jacket off her shoulders and let it go. The sensuous fabric pooled around her. Reede dropped to his knees in front of her. His eyes drank in every inch of her.

Alex thought he seemed hesitant to touch her, but finally, he lifted his hand to her hair and rubbed the damp auburn strands between his fingertips. He watched his hand's slow progress down her neck and chest to her breast. His thumb made light, deft passes across the nipple until it hardened.

Catching her breath, she sighed, "I thought you weren't trying to seduce me."

"I lied."

They lay down together. He pulled the covers up over them, took her in his arms, drew her close, and kissed her with more tenderness than passion.

"You're very small," he whispered against her lips. "Did I hurt you the other night?"

"No." He angled his head back and looked at her suspiciously. She ducked her head timidly. "Only a little."

His hand curved around her throat; he stroked it with his thumb. "How was I supposed to know you were a virgin?"

"You weren't."

"How come you were, Alex?"

She tilted her head to one side and gazed up at him. "Are the reasons why so important, Reede?"

"Only because you let me."

"*Letting* you never entered my mind. It just happened."

"Any regrets?"

She laid her hand along his cheek and drew his head down. They kissed long and avariciously. His hand had found its way to her breast again by the time he ended the kiss. Pushing back the covers, he watched his fingers caress her nipple.

"Reede," she said, her voice tentative, "I'm embarrassed."

"I want to look. Just tell me if you get cold."

"I'm not cold."

She was making small, yearning sounds even before he lowered his head and closed his lips around her nipple. He sucked on it with masterful skill. His hand moved down to appreciate the curve of her waist, then smoothed over the shape of her hip and thigh. He touched her navel playfully, and lightly scrubbed the area beneath it with his knuckles. He touched the delta of springy hair, and his eyes turned dark.

"I want you to come this time," he murmured.

"I want to."

He slid his hand between her thighs. She raised her hips slightly to accommodate him. She was already wet. He slipped his fingers inside her.

"Reede," she gasped with pleasure.

"Shh. Just enjoy."

His thumb idly fanned back and forth across that vulnerable gem of flesh while he planted kiss after fervent kiss on her fertile mouth.

"I think it's about to happen," she panted between kisses.

"Not yet. Talk to me. I never get to talk in bed."

"Talk?" She couldn't even think. "About what?"

"Anything. I just want to hear your voice."

"I . . . I don't . . ."

"Talk, Alex."

"I like watching you cook," she blurted.

"What?" He chuckled against her lips.

"It was very manly, the way you banged and rattled the pans. You're messy. You didn't crack the eggs, you smashed them. Your ineptitude was endearing."

"You're crazy."

"You're making me crazy."

"Am I?"

He inched his head down and stroked her belly with his tongue. His thumb continued to finesse her slowly, provocatively, maddeningly, while his fingers slid in and out. Sensations began to bubble warmly within her lower body. The pressure centered on the idle movement of his thumb, so that when he replaced it with the tip of his tongue, she cried out.

She clutched handfuls of his hair and tilted her hips upward toward the heat of his avid mouth, toward the swirling magic of his tongue.

Not until the aftershocks had subsided did she open her eyes. His face was bent low over hers. Damp strands of hair clung to her cheeks and neck. He lifted them away and laid them on the pillow.

"What does a woman say at a time like this, Reede?"

"Nothing," he replied gruffly. "Your face said it all. I've never watched a woman's face before."

Alex was deeply touched by his admission, but tried to make light of it. "Good. Then you won't know if I did it right or not."

He glanced down at her flushed breasts, at the moisture that had caused her pubic hair to glisten. "You did it right."

Lovingly, she combed her fingers through his hair. "It

could have happened before it did, you know—like, that evening at the airfield. And the time in Austin when you took me home. I begged you to stay with me that night. Why didn't you?"

"Because you wanted me there for the wrong reasons. I wanted a woman, not a little lost girl looking for her daddy." He studied her doubtful expression. "You don't seem convinced."

Unable to meet his incisive eyes, she looked at a point beyond his shoulder. "Are you positive that's the reason? Or were you looking for somebody else?"

"You don't mean somebody, you mean Celina." Alex turned her head aside. Reede gripped her jaw and forced her to look at him. "Listen to me, Alex. You made me mad as hell by saying what you did the other night, that crap about taking from you what I'd always wanted from Celina. I want you to understand something. We're the only two people here now. There's nobody between us. No ghosts, either. You got that?"

"I think—"

"No." He shook his head so emphatically that strands of dark blond hair fell over his green eyes. "Don't just think—*know*. You're the only woman in my head right now. You're the only woman that's been in my head since I met you. You're the only woman I'm dying to fuck every minute I'm awake and that I dream about fucking when I'm asleep.

"I'm too old for you. It's stupid and probably wrong for me to want you. It's complicated as hell. But, right or wrong, no matter whose daughter you are, I want you." He imbedded himself firmly inside her. "Understand?" He pushed higher, harder, hotter, and groaned, "Understand?"

He made himself understood.

Junior woke up before sunrise, a rarity for him. He'd had a bad night. Following Reede's suggestion, he'd spent several hours with Stacey. Her physician had given her a sedative, but it hadn't worked well enough. Each time Junior thought she was asleep and left his chair at her bedside, she would wake up, clutch his hand, and beg him not to leave her. He hadn't gotten home until well after midnight. Then he'd slept fitfully, worrying about Alex.

The instant his eyes opened, he reached for the telephone on his nightstand and dialed the Westerner Motel. He instructed the clerk, who was tired and cranky during those waning minutes of his long shift, to connect him with her room. The phone rang ten times.

Breaking the connection, he called the sheriff's office. He was told that Reede hadn't come in yet. He asked to be patched into his mobile unit, but the switchboard operator told him it wasn't in use. He called Reede's house and got a busy signal.

Frustrated, he got out of bed and began to pull on clothes. He couldn't stand not knowing where Alex was. He would find out for himself, starting with Reede.

He crept past his parents' bedroom, although he heard stirrings behind the door. He was sure Angus would want to talk to him about the deal with Judge Wallace concerning his marriage to Stacey. Junior didn't feel up to discussing that yet.

He left the house and climbed into his Jag. It was a clear but cold morning. The drive to Reede's house took him no more than a few minutes. He was glad to see that the Blazer was still parked out front and that smoke was curling out of the chimney. Reede was an early riser. Hopefully, he had a pot of coffee already perking.

Junior jogged across the porch and knocked on the front door. He stood there, hopping from one foot to another and blowing on his hands in an effort to get warm. After a long wait, Reede pulled open the door. He was wearing only a pair of jeans and a rumpled, sleepy, disagreeable expression.

"What the hell time is it?"

"Don't tell me I got you out of bed," Junior said incredulously, opening the screen door and stepping into the living room. "It's late for you, isn't it?"

"What are you doing here? What's going on?"

"That's what I was hoping you could tell me. Alex hasn't answered her phone all night. Do you have any idea where she is?"

From the corner of his eye, he noticed the pallet in front of the hearth, then a movement. Turning slightly, he saw her standing in the hallway leading to Reede's bedroom. Her hair was tousled, her lips full and red, her legs bare. She was wearing the top to the pajama set he'd given Reede when he'd had his appendectomy. She looked wanton and well-screwed.

Junior fell back a step as the breath left his body. Slumping against the wall, he looked toward the ceiling and uttered a short laugh.

Reede laid a hand on his arm. "Junior, I—"

Junior angrily shook off his friend's hand. "It wasn't enough you had her mother, was it? You had to have her, too."

"It's not like that," Reede said in a steely voice.

"No? Then, you tell me, what's it like? You gave me the green light the other night. You said you didn't want her."

"I said nothing of the kind."

"Well, you damn sure didn't say hands off. You moved faster than a sidewinder when you found out I was interested, didn't you? What was your rush? Were you afraid that if she slept with me first, she'd never want to give up quality for low life?"

"Junior, stop it!" Alex cried.

Junior didn't even hear her. He was focused on Reede. "Why is it, Reede, that whatever I want, you take? Football trophies, my own father's respect. You didn't even want Celina anymore, but you made damn sure I didn't get her, didn't you?"

"Shut up," Reede snarled, taking a threatening step forward.

Junior aimed his finger at the center of Reede's chest. "Stay away from me, you hear? Just stay the hell away from me."

He slammed out the front door. The racket echoed through the small house. After the Jag's roar had faded, Reede headed toward the kitchen. "Want some coffee?"

Alex was stunned by what Junior had said, and even more shocked by Reede's cavalier reaction. She ran into the kitchen. Coffee grounds showered from the metal scoop when she grabbed his arm and spun him around.

"Before I fall completely in love with you, Reede, there's something I've got to ask one final time." She took a sharp breath. "Did you kill my mother?"

Several heartbeats later he replied, "Yes."

Chapter 43

Fergus Plummet stood at the side of the bed, looking down at his sleeping wife, his body quivering with indignation. "Wanda, wake up." His imperious tone of voice could have awakened the dead.

Wanda opened her eyes and sat up, groggy and disoriented. "Fergus, what time—" Everything sprang into clarity when she saw what he was holding in his hand—five incriminating one-hundred-dollar bills.

"Get up," he ordered before marching from the room.

Trembling in fear, Wanda got out of the bed. She dressed as quickly as she could and ruthlessly raked her hair back, not wanting him to find more fault with her.

He was waiting for her in the kitchen, sitting straight and tall at the table. Like a penitent, she timorously approached him.

"Fergus, I . . . I was saving it as a surprise."

"Silence," he bellowed. "Until I tell you to speak, you will remain silent and soul-searching." His accusing eyes pierced straight through her. She bowed her head in shame.

"Where did you get it?"

"It came in the mail yesterday."

"In the mail?"

Her head wobbled up and down in a frantic nod of affirmation. "Yes. In that envelope." It was lying on the table beside his cup of coffee.

"Why did you hide it from your husband, to whom you are supposed to be submissive, according to holy scripture?"

"I," she began, then stopped to wet her lips, "I was saving it to give you as a surprise."

His eyes smoldered with suspicion. "Who sent it?"

Wanda raised her head and looked at him stupidly. "I don't know."

He closed his eyes and swayed as though entranced. "Satan, I command you to release her from your evil power. You have control of her lying tongue. Give it back, in the name—"

"No!" Wanda shouted. "I'm not lying. I thought it probably came from one of those folks you've been talking to on the phone about what you did out at the Minton ranch."

He was out of his chair like a shot. Rounding the table, he bore down on her. "How dare you mention that? Didn't I tell you never, *never* to utter a word about that?"

"I forgot," she said, cowering. "I thought maybe the money came from somebody who appreciated what you did."

"I know who it came from," he hissed.

"Who?"

"Come with me." He grabbed her hand and dragged her toward the door that connected the kitchen to the garage.

"Where are we going, Fergus?"

"Wait and see. I want the sinners to meet face-to-face."

"The kids are—"

"God will watch over them until we get back."

With Wanda sitting shivering in the front seat beside him, Plummet drove through the sleeping streets of town. At the highway, he headed west. He seemed unaware of the cold, warmed by his coat of righteousness. When he took the turn-off, Wanda stared at him in total disbelief, but he shot her a look of such condemnation that she wisely refrained from uttering a peep.

He pulled up in front of the large house and ordered his wife to get out of the car. His footsteps landed hard on the hollow steps and his knock rang out loudly in the stillness of early morning. No one answered his first knock, so he pounded harder on the door. When still no one came, he emphatically banged on the window nearest him.

Nora Gail herself pulled open the door and aimed the barrel of a small handgun directly at his forehead. "Mister, you'd better have damned good reason for beating down my door and getting me out of bed at this ungodly hour."

Fergus raised his hands above his bowed head and called upon God and a host of angels to cleanse the sinner of her wrongdoing.

Nora Gail pushed him aside and moved toward her sister. They faced each other. Nora Gail, her platinum hair radiant, looked marvelous for someone who had just gotten out of bed. The constant use of expensive night creams guaranteed her a glowing complexion. She was resplendent in a rose satin robe trimmed with seed pearls. By contrast, Wanda looked like an overweight brown wren.

"It's cold out here," Nora Gail remarked, as though they'd seen each other only yesterday. "Let's go inside." She led her gawking sister across the threshold of the whorehouse. Nudging Fergus in his skinny ribs as she went past, she said, "Preacher, if you don't shut up that noisy praying, I'm going to shoot your balls off, you hear?"

"Ah-men!" he cried, suddenly ending his prayer.

"Thank you," Nora Gail said with amusement. "I'm sure I can use the prayers. Come on in. I've been wanting to talk to you."

Several minutes later, they were collected around the table in her kitchen, which looked very ordinary and not the least bit sinful. Coffee had been brewed and poured into fine china cups. Fergus commanded Wanda to avoid it, as though it was a poisonous concoction.

"You can't defeat us," Fergus said heatedly. "God is on our side, and He's sorely provoked at you, a whore who leads weaker brothers astray."

"Save it," Nora Gail said with a casual wave of her hand. "I fear God, all right, but what's between Him and me is personal, and no business of yours. The only thing that scares me about you, preacher, is your stupidity."

He took umbrage. His face puffed up like an adder. "Did you send my wife some of your ill-gotten money?"

"Yes. From the looks of her and your kids, I thought she could put it to good use."

"We don't need your money."

Nora Gail sat forward and, with a lazy smile, spoke softly to Fergus. "You haven't thrown it back in my face, either, have you?"

His mouth puckered like a drawstring purse. "I never reject a gift that God so generously bestows."

"No, I'm sure you don't." Nora Gail complacently

dropped two cubes of sugar into her coffee. "That's why I want to make a deal with you, *Reverend* Plummet."

"I don't deal with the ungodly. I came here as a messenger of God, to warn you of His wrath, to hear your confession of—"

"How would you like a new church?"

The flow of evangelism ceased abruptly. "Huh?"

Idly, Nora Gail stirred her coffee. "How would you like a new church? A big, grand church that would put all the others in town to shame, even the new First Baptist." She paused to sip her coffee. "I can see I've left you speechless, which in itself is a blessing."

Again, she smiled like a cat that had just licked clean a saucer of cream. "As soon as Purcell Downs is completed, I'm going to be very rich and very respectable. It would be to your benefit, preacher, to accept my generous donations, which would be sizable and given on a regular basis. Then, when *Texas Monthly* or *60 Minutes* comes out here to interview me as one of the state's richest businesswomen, they can also report what a generous and benevolent person I am.

"And in return for this fancy church I'll build you," she said, leaning forward again, "I would expect you to keep your loud mouth shut about racetrack gambling. There are plenty other sins to keep you occupied. If you run out of sermon material, I'll be more than glad to provide you a list of sins, because I've committed them all, sugar."

He was gaping like a fish washed ashore. The madam definitely had his attention.

"And, you wouldn't be pulling any more stunts like you did at the Minton ranch a week or so back. Yes," she said, holding up her heavily jeweled hand to stem his denials, "I know you did it. You caused a valuable horse to get put down, and that really chaps my ass."

Her eyes narrowed on him. "If you do anything that stupid again, I'll pull the pulpit right out from under you, preacher man. I make plans, see, and I knock down anybody who stands in the way of them. If you have a problem you want solved, come to me. Leave the revenge-getting to somebody who knows how to get it and not get caught." She leaned back in her chair. "Well?"

"You've . . . you've given me a lot to think about."

"Not good enough. I want your answer today. Right now. Do you want to become a religious big shot with a shiny new church, or do you want to go to jail? Because, you see, if you don't say yes to my offer, I'll call my good buddy Reede Lambert and tell him I've got an eyewitness to that vigilante raid out at the ranch. What's it gonna be, sugar—a pulpit or prison?"

Fergus swallowed visibly. He struggled with himself, with his conscience, but not for long. His head gave one swift nod of agreement.

"Good. Oh, one other thing," Nora Gail continued in the same lilting voice. "Stop treating my sister like a doormat. You were overheard dressing her down in public at the sheriff's office the other night. If I ever get wind of it happening again, I'll personally cut off your pitiful pecker and feed it to the next dog I see. Okay?"

He swallowed hard.

"I'm sending Wanda Gail to a spa up in Dallas, where she'll stay and be pampered for two weeks, which is little enough vacation from you. How do you expect to attract folks to your new church if your own wife looks like a downtrodden toad? This summer your kids'll go to camp. They're gonna have new bicycles and baseball gloves, because I'm overturning your rule about no games of any kind and signing them up for Little League next spring." She winked. "Their Aunt Nora Gail is gonna be the best goddamn thing that ever happened to those kids. Are you getting all this, preacher?"

Again, Plummet gave a brusque nod.

"Good." She sat back in her chair, calmly swinging a shapely leg back and forth through the slit of her robe. "Now that we've cleared the air, let's talk terms. You'll receive the first donation the day after the licensing is finalized, and one on the first of each month after that. The checks will be drawn on the NGB, Incorporated account. I'm going to need the tax deduction," she said with a throaty laugh.

Then, dismissing Fergus, she looked at her sister. "Wanda Gail, don't wait till I send you to Dallas. Use the money I sent you the other day to buy you and your kids new clothes. And for crissake, do something with your hair. It looks like shit."

Wanda's eyes misted. "Thank you, thank you."

Nora Gail reached out to touch her sister's hand, but thought better of it and lit one of her black cigarettes instead. Through a dense cloud of acrid smoke, she replied, "You're welcome, sugar."

Chapter 44

Junior?"

He turned away from the bar, where he'd been mixing his second drink in ten minutes. "Good morning, Mother. Would you like a Bloody Mary?"

Sarah Jo crossed the room and yanked the bottle of vodka from his hand. "What's the matter with you?" she asked, speaking in a much harsher tone than she usually used with him. "Why are you drinking this early?"

"It's not that early, considering what time I got up."

"You went out. I heard you leave. Where'd you go?"

"I'd like to know that myself," Angus said, coming into the room. "I need to talk to you."

"Let me guess," Junior said with feigned cheerfulness, "it's about Judge Wallace."

"That's right."

"And my marriage to Stacey."

"Yes," Angus said reluctantly.

"I'll bet you're going to tell me why it was so all-fired important that I marry her when I did."

"It was for your own good."

"That much you told me twenty-five years ago. It was a trade-off, wasn't it? You got him to close Celina's murder case in exchange for my marriage to Stacey. Am I getting warm? Apparently, so was Alex. When she confronted the judge with her hypothesis, he killed himself."

Looking faint, Sarah Jo covered her mouth. Angus responded with anger. His hands flexed into fists at his sides. "It was the best thing to do at the time. I couldn't allow an in-depth investigation. To protect my family and my business, I had no choice but to ask the judge that favor."

"Did Stacey know about it?"

"Not from me. I doubt that Joe ever told her."

"Thank God for that." Junior dropped into a chair. His head hung dejectedly. "Dad, you know as well as I do that Gooney Bud was innocent."

"I know no such thing."

"Come on. He was harmless. You knew he didn't kill Celina, but you let him be punished for it. Why didn't you just let things take their natural course? In the long run, we'd all have been better off."

"You know that's not so, Junior."

"Do I?" He raised his head and looked at his parents with hot, intense eyes. "You know who Reede has in his bed this morning, looking all soft and sexy and satisfied? Alex." He flopped back against the easy chair's cushions and rested his head. With a bitter, humorless laugh, he said, "Celina's *daughter.* Jesus, can you beat that?"

"Alex spent the night with Reede?" Angus thundered.

Sarah Jo made a sniffing sound of disgust. "That doesn't surprise me."

"Why didn't you keep it from happening, Junior?" Angus demanded.

Junior, sensing his father's rising temper, shouted, "I tried!"

"Evidently, not hard enough. It's your bed she's supposed to be in by now, not Reede's."

"She's a grown woman. She didn't need my permission to go to bed with him. With anybody." Junior pushed himself out of the chair and headed for the bar.

Sarah Jo blocked his path. "I don't like the girl. She's as trashy as her mother, but if you wanted her for yourself, why did you let Reede Lambert have her?"

"It's more critical than that, Sarah Jo," Angus said tightly. "Our future rested on Alex's opinion of us. I was hoping she would become part of the family. As usual, Junior fell down on the job."

"Don't criticize him, Angus."

"Why the hell not? He's my son. I'll criticize him if I damn well feel like it." Then, curbing his impatience with her, he exhaled a heavy sigh. "Too late now to be bawling over spilled milk. We've got a bigger problem than Junior's love life. I'm afraid we're extremely vulnerable to prosecution." He left the room and slammed out the front door.

At the bar, Junior poured himself a straight vodka. Sarah Jo grabbed his arm as he raised the glass to his lips. "When are you going to learn that you're as good as Reede? *Better*. You've disappointed your father again. When are you going to do something to make him proud of you? Junior, my darling, it's time you grew up and seized the initiative for a change."

Alex stared at Reede with wordless disbelief. He calmly swept the spilled coffee grounds off the counter with the back of his hand and continued to fill the filtered basket of the coffee maker. Once it was dripping boiling coffee into the glass carafe, he turned to face her.

"You look like you've swallowed a marble. Isn't that what you expected to hear?"

"Is it true?" she asked hoarsely. "Did you kill her?"

He looked away, staring at nothing for several moments, then back into her eyes, penetrating them. "*No*, Alex. I did not kill Celina. If I had wanted to, I would have done it before that night, and with my bare hands. I would have felt that it was justifiable homicide. I wouldn't have gone to the trouble of stealing a scalpel. I sure as hell wouldn't have let that unfortunate retarded man take the rap for me."

She stepped into the circle of his arms and hugged him tight. "I believe you, Reede."

"Well, that's something, I guess." Holding her close, he moved his hands over her back. She nuzzled his chest.

He made a low sound of arousal, but set her away from him. "The coffee's ready."

"Don't push me away, please. I'm not ready to stop hugging."

"Neither am I," he said, stroking her cheek, "but hugging isn't all I want to do, and I have a strong feeling that our conversation isn't going to be conducive to romance." He poured two mugs of coffee and carried them to the table.

"Why do you say that?" She sat down across from him.

"Because you want to know if I know who went into the barn that night."

"Do you?"

"No, I don't," he said with an emphatic shake of his head. "I swear to God I don't."

"But you know it was either Junior or Angus."

He shrugged noncommittally.

"You've never wanted to know which, have you?"

"What difference does it make?"

She was aghast. "It makes a difference to me. It should to you."

"Why? Knowing won't change a damn thing. It won't bring Celina back. It won't alter your unhappy childhood or mine. Will it make your grandmother love you? No."

Reading her horrified expression, he said, "Yes, Alex, I know that's why you've appointed yourself Celina's avenger. Merle Graham always had to have a scapegoat. Whenever Celina did something she considered wrong, I usually caught the blame for it. 'That Lambert kid,' she used to call me, always with a sour expression on her face.

"So it doesn't surprise me that she laid a lifelong guilt trip on you. She wouldn't take the blame for Celina's mistakes upon herself. And she wouldn't admit that Celina, like every other human being ever to grace this earth, did what she damn well pleased when she damned well felt like it, with or without motivation. That left you, the only real innocent in this whole goddamn affair, to place the blame on."

He drew in a deep breath. "So, with all that in mind, what good can it possibly do anybody to know who killed her?"

"I've got to know, Reede," she said, close to tears. "The

murderer was also a thief. He robbed me. My mother would have loved me if she had lived. I know she would have."

"For crissake, she didn't even want you, Alex," he shouted. "No more than my mother wanted me. I didn't go on any quests after her."

"Because you're afraid to," she yelled back.

"Afraid?"

"Afraid of being hurt by what you find out."

"Not afraid," he said. "Indifferent."

"Well, I'm not, thank God. I'm not as cold and unfeeling as you."

"You thought I was hot enough last night," he sneered. "Or did you stay a technical virgin this long by going down on all your dates?"

She flinched as if he'd struck her. Hurt beyond belief, she stared at him across the table. His expression was closed and hostile, but her vulnerability defeated him. He muttered a string of swear words and dug into his eye sockets with his thumb and middle finger.

"I'm sorry. That was uncalled for. It's just that you're so goddamn aggravating when it comes to this." He lowered his hand. His green eyes appealed to her. "Give it up, Alex. Relent."

"I can't."

"Won't."

She reached for his hand. "Reede, we're never going to agree on this, and I don't want to argue with you." Her face turned soft. "Not after last night."

"Some people would think that what went on in there," he said, indicating the living room, "would erase the past."

"Is that why you made it happen, hoping that I'd forgive and forget?"

He yanked his hand away. "You're dead set on pissing me off, aren't you?"

"No, I'm not trying to provoke you. Just please understand why I can't give up when I'm this close."

"I *don't* understand."

"Then just accept it. Help me."

"How? By pointing a finger at either my mentor or my best friend?"

"Junior didn't sound like a best friend a while ago."

"That was injured pride and jealousy talking."

"He was jealous the night Celina was killed, too. She had injured his pride. She turned down his marriage proposal because she was still in love with you. Could that have driven him to murder her?"

"Think about it, Alex," he said with annoyance. "If Junior did blow his top at her, would he have had that scalpel handy to start slashing? And do you honestly think, no matter how enraged he was, that Junior could kill anybody?"

"Then, it was Angus," she said softly.

"I don't know." Angrily, Reede slung himself out of his chair and began to pace. This was a familiar, haunting hypothesis. "Angus was against Junior marrying Celina."

"Angus is more volatile than Junior," she said, almost to herself. "I've seen him angry. I imagine that when he's crossed, he could be capable of killing, and he certainly took desperate measures to have the case closed before the evidence could come around to him."

"Where are you going?" Reede jerked to attention when she left her chair and headed toward the bedroom.

"I've got to talk to him."

"Alex!" He went after her. He rattled the knob of the bathroom door, but she'd locked it behind herself. "I don't want you to go over there."

"I've got to." She opened the door, already dressed, and stuck out her hand. "Can I borrow your Blazer?"

He stared at her hard. "You'll wreck his life. Have you thought of that?"

"Yes. And every time I feel a pang of regret, I remind myself of the lonely, loveless childhood I spent while he was prospering." She closed her eyes and pulled herself together. "I don't want to destroy Angus. I'm only doing my job, doing what's right. I actually like him. If circumstances were different, I could grow very fond of him. But the circumstances are what they are, and I can't change them. When a person does something wrong, he's got to be punished."

"All right." He grabbed her arm and drew her up close. "What's the punishment for a prosecutor sleeping with a suspect?"

"You're no longer a suspect."

"You didn't know that last night."

Furious, she wrestled her arm free and ran through the house, grabbing his keys off the end table where she'd seen him drop them the night before.

Reede let her go and placed a call to his downtown office. Without preamble, he barked, "Get me a car out here on the double."

"They're all out, Sheriff. All except the Jeep."

"That'll do. Just get it here."

Chapter 45

Stacey Wallace Minton shocked her friends by walking into the living room fully dressed, dry-eyed, and seemingly composed. They had been speaking in hushed tones in deference to her suffering. They had believed that she was getting some much-needed rest in preparation for the ordeal facing her.

Tupperware and Pyrex dishes, filled with salads and casseroles and desserts, had been delivered to the house by a steady stream of concerned acquaintances. Without exception, all had asked, "How's she taking it?"

By all appearances, Stacey was taking her father's death very well. As always, she was impeccably dressed and groomed. Except for the grayish circles beneath her eyes, she could have been on her way to a club meeting.

"Stacey, did we wake you? We put a note on the door, asking people to knock instead of ringing the bell."

"I've been awake for a while," she told her friends. "What time did Junior leave?"

"Sometime during the night. Would you like something to eat? Lordy, there's enough food in there to feed an army."

"No, thank you, nothing right now."

"Mr. Davis called. He needs to discuss the funeral arrangements with you, but said that could be at your convenience."

"I'll contact him later this morning."

As her friends watched in stupefaction, she went to the hall closet and took out her coat. They exchanged concerned and bewildered glances.

"Stacey, dear, where are you going?"

"Out."

"We'll be glad to run errands for you. That's what we're here for."

"I appreciate the offer, but this is something I've got to do myself."

"What are we supposed to tell people when they drop by to see you?" one asked, anxiously following her to the front door.

Stacey turned and calmly replied, "Tell them whatever you like."

———◦———

Angus didn't seem surprised to see Alex when she walked into his den unannounced. He was seated on the leather sofa, massaging the toe that continued to give him pain. "I didn't hear you come in," he said. "I just got in from the stables myself. We've got a two-year-old gelding with shin bucks, which can't be a damn bit more painful than gout."

"Lupe told me you were back here."

"Do you want some breakfast? Coffee?"

"No, thank you, Angus." Hospitable to the bitter end, Alex thought. "Is this a convenient time for us to talk?"

He laughed. "As convenient a time as any, I reckon, considering what we're going to talk about." She sat down beside him on the sofa. He studied her with shrewd blue eyes. "Did Joe spill his guts before he killed himself?"

"He didn't invite me to his office to take a confession, if that's what you mean," she answered, "but I know about your deal with him. How did you talk Junior into going along with it, Angus?"

"At that point in time," he said, making no effort to deny her allegations, "the boy didn't care about what happened to him. Celina's death hit him so hard, he was married to Joe's girl almost before he realized it. Know what? I'm not sure he could have made it those first few months if Stacey hadn't taken such good care of him. I never regretted making that deal with Joe."

"Who were you protecting?"

Changing the subject abruptly, he said, "You look a little worse for wear this morning. Did Reede ride you that hard last night?"

Embarrassed, Alex ducked her head. "Junior told you?"

"Yes." He pulled on his boot, wincing as he worked the sore toe into it. "Can't say that I'm surprised—disappointed, but not surprised."

She lifted her head. "Why?"

"Like mother, like daughter. Reede always had an edge over every other man with Celina. Who knows why? That's just the way it was. Chemistry, I think they call it nowadays."

He set his foot on the floor and leaned back against the tufted sofa. "What's between you two?"

"It's more than chemistry."

"So, you love him?"

"Yes."

He drew a worried expression. "I'll caution you like a daddy would, Alex. Reede's not an easy man to love. He has a tough time showing affection, and an even tougher time of accepting it. As old as he is, he's still bitter about his mama up and leaving him when he was a baby."

"Is that why he found it impossible to forgive Celina for getting involved with Al Gaither and having me?"

"I think so. He tried not to let on like it hurt him. Walked around here with a chip on his shoulder as big as Texas. He hid his feelings behind that I-don't-give-a-damn veneer, but he was crushed just the same. I could tell. He didn't hold it against you, you understand, but he could never quite forgive your mother for cheating on him."

"What about Junior?"

"Junior couldn't forgive her for loving Reede more than she loved him."

"But neither one of them killed her." She met him eye to eye. "It was you, wasn't it?"

He stood up and moved to the window. He gazed out on all that he had built from nothing and was liable to lose. The ponderous silence in the room lasted for several minutes. Finally, he said, "No, I didn't." Then, turning slowly, he added, "But I wanted to."

"Why?"

"Your mother played games, Alex. She liked to. When I

first met her, she was still a little tomboyish. Things might have gone fine if she'd stayed like that. But she grew older and realized that she had a power over both of those boys— sexual power. She began to use that in her games."

Alex's heart began to ache. She scarcely breathed. It was like watching a horror movie and waiting for the monster to finally rear its head. She wanted to see the whole picture, but yet, she didn't. It would probably be ugly.

"I could see it happening," Angus was saying, "but there wasn't much I could do about it. She played them against each other."

His words echoed what Nora Gail had told her. *The temptation was just too strong.*

"The older they got, the worse it got," Angus continued. "The solid friendship between the boys was like a shiny apple. Celina ate away at the core of it like a worm. I didn't like her very much." He returned to the sofa and sat down. "But I desired her."

When Alex was sure her ears hadn't deceived her, she couldn't hold back her gasp. *"What?"*

Angus smiled crookedly. "Remember, this was twenty-five years and thirty pounds ago. I didn't have this," he said, rubbing his protruding belly, "and I had more hair. If I do say so, I was still considered a lady-killer."

"It's not that I doubt your appeal, Angus, it's just that I had no idea—"

"Neither did anyone else. It was my little secret. Even she didn't know...until the night she died."

Alex groaned his name. The monster of truth wasn't only ugly, it was hideous.

"Junior stormed out on his way to drown his sorrows

in booze. Celina came into this room. She sat right there, where you're sitting now, and cried. She told me she didn't know what to do. She loved Reede in a way she'd never love another man. She loved Junior, but not enough to marry him. She didn't know how she was going to raise you alone. Every time she looked at you, she was reminded of the mistake that had changed her future forever.

"On and on she went, expecting me to sympathize, when all I could see was what a selfish little bitch she was. She'd brought all her hardships on herself. She didn't give a damn how she hurt other people or played with their lives. She only cared about how things affected her."

He shook his head with self-derision. "That didn't stop me from wanting her. I wanted her more than ever. I think I justified it to myself because I figured she deserved no better than lust from a horny old man like me." He took a deep breath. "Anyway, I made my pitch."

"You told her you...desired her?"

"I didn't come right out with it, no. I offered to set her up in a house out of town, someplace close. I told her I'd pay for everything. She wouldn't have to lift a finger, just be accommodating when I could come see her. I expected her to bring you along, of course, and Mrs. Graham, too, though I doubt your grandma would ever have agreed to it. In short," he concluded, "I asked her to be my mistress."

"What did she say?"

"Not a goddamn thing. She just looked at me for several seconds, and then she burst out laughing." His eyes chilled Alex to the bone when he added raspily, "And you know how I hate having my ideas laughed at."

"You filthy son of a bitch."

Simultaneously, they turned toward the intrusive voice. Junior, his face contorted with outrage, was standing in the open doorway. He pointed a shaking, accusatory finger at his father. "You didn't want me to marry her because you wanted her for yourself! You killed her because she turned down your despicable proposal! You goddamn bastard, you killed her for that!"

The road seemed bumpier than usual. Or maybe she was just hitting all the ruts because her eyes were blurred with tears. Alex fought to keep the Blazer on the road to Reede's house.

When Junior had launched himself at Angus and begun to beat him with his fists, she had run from the room. She couldn't stand to watch. Her investigation had turned son against father, friend against friend, and she simply couldn't stand any more. She had fled.

They'd all been right. They'd tried to warn her, but she had refused to listen. Compelled by guilt, headstrong and fearless, armed to the teeth with an unshakable sense of right and wrong, cheered on by the recklessness of immaturity, she had excavated in forbidden territory and disturbed its sanctity. She had aroused the ire of bad spirits long laid to rest. Against sound counsel, she had kept digging. Now those spirits were protesting, making themselves manifest.

She had been brainwashed to believe that Celina was a fragile heroine, tragically struck down in the full bloom of womanhood, a heartbroken young widow with a newborn infant in her arms, looking out on the cruel world with dismay. Instead, she had been manipulative, selfish, and even cruel to the people who had loved her.

Merle had made her believe that she had been responsible for her mother's death. With every gesture, word, and deed, whether overt or implied, she had made Alex feel inadequate and at fault.

Well, Merle was wrong. Celina was responsible for her slaying. By an act of will, Alex unburdened herself of all guilt and remorse. She was free! It no longer really mattered to her whose hand had wielded that scalpel. It hadn't been because of her.

Her first thought was that she must share this sense of freedom with Reede. She parked the Blazer in front of his house, got out, and ran across the porch. At the door, she hesitated and knocked softly. After several seconds, she pulled it open and stepped inside. "Reede?" The house was gloomy and empty.

Moving toward the bedroom, she called his name again, but it was obvious that he wasn't there. As she turned, she noticed her handbag, lying forgotten on the nightstand. She checked the adjoining bathroom for items she might have left behind, gathered them up, and dropped them into her handbag.

As she snapped it closed, she thought she heard the unfamiliar squeak of the screened front door. She paused and listened. "Reede?" The sound didn't come again.

Lost in the sweet reverie of the night before, she touched Reede's things on the nightstand—a pair of sunglasses, a comb that was rarely used, an extra brass belt buckle with the state seal of Texas on it. Her heart swelling with love, she turned to go, but was brought up short.

The woman standing in the doorway of the bedroom had a knife in her hand.

Chapter 46

‮‮"W‬hat the hell is going on here?"

Reede grabbed Junior's collar and hauled him off Angus, who was sprawled on the floor. Blood was dribbling down his chin from a cut on his lip. Oddly enough, the old man was laughing.

"Where'd you learn to fight like that, boy, and why haven't you done it more often?" He sat up and extended his hand to Reede. "Help me up." Reede, after giving Junior a warning glance, let go of his collar and assisted Angus to his feet.

"One of you want to tell me what the devil that was all about?" Reede demanded.

When the Jeep arrived, he had driven straight to the ranch house, where an anxious Lupe had greeted him at the door with the news that Mr. Minton and Junior were fighting.

Reede had run into the den and found the two men locked in combat, rolling on the floor. Junior had been throwing earnest, but largely ineffective, punches at his father's head.

"He wanted Celina for himself," Junior declared, his chest heaving with exertion and fury. "I overheard him telling

Alex. He wanted to set Celina up as his mistress. When she said no, he killed her."

Angus was calmly dabbing at the blood on his chin with a handkerchief. "Do you really believe that, son? Do you think I would sacrifice everything—your mother, you, this place—for that little chippy?"

"I heard you tell Alex that you wanted her."

"I did, from the belt down, but I didn't love her. I didn't like the way she came between you and Reede. I sure as hell wouldn't gamble away everything else in my life by killing her. I might have felt like it when she laughed at my offer, but I didn't." His eyes roved over both the younger men. "My pride was spared when one of you did it for me."

The three men exchanged uneasy glances. The past twenty-five years had dwindled down to this crucial moment. Until now, none of them had had the courage to pose the question. The truth would have been too painful to bear, so they had let the identity of the murderer remain a mystery.

Their silence had been tacitly agreed upon. It had protected them from knowing who had ended Celina's life. None had wanted to know.

"I did not kill that girl," Angus said. "As I told Alex, I gave her the keys to one of the cars and told her to drive herself home. The last time I saw her, she was leaving by the front door."

"I was upset because she turned me down," Junior said. "I made the rounds of the beer joints and got shit-faced. I don't remember where I was or who I was with. But I think I would remember slashing Celina to ribbons."

"When dessert was passed around I left," Reede told

them. "I spent the night humping Nora Gail. I got to the stable about six that morning. That's when I found her."

Angus shook his head in bafflement. "Then everything we've told Alex is true."

"Alex?" Reede exclaimed. "Didn't you say she was just here?"

"Dad was talking to her when I came in."

"Where is she now?"

"She was sitting right there," Angus said, pointing at the empty spot on the sofa. "I didn't see anything after Junior came sailing toward me and knocked me down. Felt like a goddamn bull falling on me," he said, jovially socking his son beneath the chin. Junior grinned with boyish pleasure.

"Would you two cut it out and tell me where Alex went?"

"Calm down, Reede. She's gotta be around here somewhere."

"I didn't see her when I came in," he argued stubbornly as he rushed into the hall.

"It couldn't have been but a couple of minutes in between," Junior said. "Why are you so anxious about—"

"Don't you get it?" Reede asked over his shoulder. "If none of us killed Celina, whoever did is still out there, and he's just as pissed off at Alex as we've been."

"Jesus, I didn't think—"

"You're right, Reede."

"Come on."

The three men rushed through the front door. As they were clambering down the steps, Stacey Wallace wheeled into the drive and stepped out of her car.

"Junior, Angus, Reede, I'm glad I caught you. It's about Alex."

Reede drove the Jeep like a bat out of hell. At the crossroads of the highway and the Mintons' private road, he caught up with the deputies who had delivered him the Jeep and flagged down the patrol car.

"Have you seen my Blazer?" he shouted to them. "Alex Gaither was driving it."

"Yeah, Reede, we did. She was headed back toward your place."

"Much obliged." To his passengers he shouted, "Hang on," and executed a hairpin turn.

"What's going on?" Stacey asked. The Jeep's top was off, so she was clinging to the roll bar for dear life. In her staid world, nothing this death-defying had ever happened.

Trying to detain the Mintons and Reede had been impossible. They had almost mowed her down in their haste to scramble into the Jeep. She'd been summarily told that if she must speak with them right then, she had to go along. She had climbed into the backseat with Junior, while Angus sat in the front seat, next to Reede.

"Alex could be in danger," Junior shouted into Stacey's ear to make himself heard. The cold north wind sucked the words out of his mouth.

"Danger?"

"It's a long story."

"I went to her motel," Stacey shouted. "The desk clerk told me she might be at the ranch."

"What's so important?" Reede asked over his shoulder.

"I didn't get everything off my chest last night. She didn't hold the pistol or pull the trigger, but she caused Daddy's suicide."

Junior placed his arm around her, drew her close, and kissed her temple. "Stacey, let it drop. Alex isn't the reason Joe killed himself."

"It's not just that," Stacey said, distraught. "Her investigation has raised questions about...well, we got married so soon after Celina was killed. People thought...you know how suspicious and narrow-minded they can be. They're talking about it again." She gazed up at him imploringly. "Junior, why did you marry me?"

He placed a finger beneath her chin. "Because you're a beautiful, dynamic woman, the best damn thing that ever happened to me, Stacey," he said, meaning it. He couldn't love her, but he appreciated her kindness and goodness, and her unflagging love for him.

"Then, you do love me a little?"

He smiled down at her and, for her sake, said, "Hell, girl, I love you a lot."

Her eyes glistened with tears. The radiance with which her face shone made her almost pretty. "Thank you, Junior."

Angus suddenly leaned forward and pointed toward the horizon. "My God, that looks like—"

"Smoke," Reede grimly supplied, and floored the accelerator.

Chapter 47

———◆———

Sarah Jo!" Alex cried. "What on earth are you doing?"

Sarah Jo smiled placidly. "I followed you here from my house."

"Why?"

Alex's eyes were on the knife. It was an ordinary kitchen knife, but it didn't look all that ordinary in Sarah Jo's hand. Always before, her hand had looked feminine and frail. Now it looked skeletal and ominous around the handle of the knife.

"I came to rid my life of another nuisance." Her eyes opened wide, then narrowed. "Just like I did back in Kentucky. My brother got the colt I wanted. It wasn't fair. I had to get rid of him and that colt, or I could never be happy again."

"What . . . what did you do?"

"I lured him into the stable by telling him the colt had colic. Then, I locked the door and started the fire."

Alex swayed in terror. "How horrible."

"Yes, it was, actually. You could smell burning horseflesh for miles. The stench hung on for days."

Alex raised a trembling hand to her lips. The woman was obviously psychotic, and therefore, all the more terrifying.

"I didn't have to start a fire the night I murdered Celina."

"Why not?"

"That idiot man, Gooney Bud, had followed her to the ranch. I met him on my way out of the stable. He scared the living daylights out of me, standing there in the shadows so quiet. He went in and saw her. He fell down on top of her and started carrying on something awful. I saw him pick up Dr. Collins's knife." She smiled gleefully. "That's when I knew I wouldn't have to start a fire and destroy all those lovely horses."

"You killed my mother," Alex stated tearfully. "You killed my mother."

"She was a trashy girl." Sarah Jo's expression changed drastically, becoming spiteful. "I prayed every night that she would marry Reede Lambert. That way, I'd get both of them out of my life. Angus didn't need but one son, the one I gave him," she cried, thumping her chest with her free fist. "Why did he have to keep that mongrel around?"

"What did that have to do with Celina?"

"That stupid girl let herself get pregnant. Reede wouldn't have her after that." She clenched her teeth, distorting her delicate features. "And I had to watch when Junior stepped in to take Reede's place. He actually wanted to marry her. Imagine a Presley marrying a lowlife with an illegitimate baby. I wasn't going to let my son ruin his life."

"So, you looked for an opportunity to kill her."

"She dropped it into my lap. Junior left the house that night, disconsolate. Then, Angus made a complete fool of himself over her."

"You overheard their conversation?"

"I eavesdropped."

"And you were jealous."

"Jealous?" she said with a musical little laugh. "Good heavens, no. Angus has had other women for almost as long as we've been married. I might not even have minded him having Celina, so long as he set her up out of town and away from Junior. But that silly bitch laughed at him—laughed in my husband's face after he had poured out his heart to her!"

Her eyes were blinking rapidly now, and her meager breasts were rising and falling with each strenuous breath. Her voice had grown shrill. Alex knew that if she was going to talk Sarah Jo out of this, she had to tread softly. She was still trying to choose her next words when she caught the first whiff of smoke.

Her eyes moved beyond Sarah Jo to the hall. It was filling with smoke. Flames were licking up the walls of the living room beyond.

"Sarah Jo," Alex said in a quavering voice, "I want to talk to you about this, but—"

"Stay where you are!" Sarah Jo commanded sharply, brandishing the knife when Alex took a hesitant step. "You came here and started causing trouble, just like her. You favor Reede over my Junior. You're breaking his heart. Angus is upset and worried over Joe Wallace's death, which is all your fault. You see, Angus thought one of the boys killed her."

She smiled impishly. "I knew he would. I knew that the boys wouldn't ask any questions, either. I depended on their loyalty to each other. It was the perfect crime. Angus, thinking he was protecting the boys, made his deal with the judge. I hated that Junior had to get married so young, but I was glad it was to Stacey rather than Celina."

The smoke was growing thicker. It was swirling around Sarah Jo, though she seemed unaware of it. "You started asking too many questions," she told Alex, drawing a sad face. "I tried to scare you off with that letter. I made it look like it had come from that crazy Reverend Plummet, but I sent it." She seemed quite pleased with herself. Alex used her complacency to creep forward, moving slowly, one step at a time.

"You still didn't take the hint, so I ran you off the road with one of the company pickups. Judge Wallace would probably still be alive, and the deal Angus made with him would still be a secret, if only you had died when your car crashed." She seemed genuinely perturbed. "But, after today, I won't have to—"

Alex lunged forward and struck Sarah Jo's wrist. She was stronger than she appeared. She managed to maintain her grip on the knife. Alex grabbed her wrist and hung on, trying to dodge the stabbing motions aimed toward her body.

"I won't let you destroy my family," Sarah Jo grunted as she plunged the knife toward Alex's midsection.

The two women struggled over control of the knife. They fell to their knees. Alex tried to dodge the downward arcs of the blade, but the smoke was getting too thick for her to see it well. Her eyes filled with tears. She began to choke. Sarah Jo knocked her into the wall. Upon impact, she felt the stitches in her scalp pop open.

Somehow, she managed to get to her feet, and began dragging Sarah Jo down the hallway, where smoke was billowing around them. All the rules of fire escape fled Alex's mind. She tried to hold her breath, but her lungs demanded oxygen for the difficult task of pulling Sarah Jo along with her.

They had almost reached the living room before Sarah Jo

realized that Alex had gained the upper hand. She renewed her efforts and came back stronger than ever. The knife slashed Alex's ankle and she screamed. Its serrated edge caught her again in the calf, and she staggered back toward the living room.

Suddenly, she lost her grip on Sarah Jo. While seconds ago, she'd been fighting for her freedom, she now panicked at the thought of losing her attacker in the suffocating black smoke. It was so thick that she couldn't even distinguish an outline of the other woman.

"Sarah Jo! Where are you?" Alex gagged on a mouthful of smoke. Stretching her arms far out in front of her, she groped for the woman, but touched nothing except the searing air.

Then, survival instincts took over. She turned, ducked, and plunged through the hallway. In the living room, she dodged burning furniture and ran blindly in the direction of the door. The door was intact, but smoldering. She grabbed the knob; it branded the palm of her hand.

Screaming in fear and pain, she barreled through the door and out onto the porch.

"Alex!"

She stumbled in the direction of Reede's voice and saw through smoke-damaged eyes the wavering image of a Jeep coming to a screeching halt only yards in front of her.

"Reede," she croaked, reaching for him. She fell. He leaped from behind the steering wheel and bent over her. "Sarah Jo," she wheezed. With an effort, she raised her hand and pointed toward the house.

"My God, Mother!" Junior went over the side of the Jeep and hit the ground at a run.

"Junior, come back!" Stacey screamed. "No, God, no!"

"Son, don't!" Angus reached for Junior's arm as he sped past. "It's too late!"

Reede was already on the porch when Junior knocked him aside. Reede fell backward down the steps and onto the ground. He made an unsuccessful grab for Junior's ankle. "Junior, you can't!" he roared.

Junior turned and looked down at him. "This time, Reede, I'll get the glory."

He flashed Reede his most beautiful smile, then ran into the burning house.

Epilogue

—◈—

I thought you might be here."

Reede gave no impression of having heard Alex approach until she spoke to him. He glanced at her over his shoulder, then back at the two fresh graves. For a moment, there was an awkward silence, then he said, "I promised Angus I would come out every day to check on things. He's not feeling quite up to it yet."

Alex moved nearer. "I stopped by to see him this afternoon. He made a feeble attempt to be the hail-fellow-well-met," she remarked sadly. "He's entitled to grieve. I told him so. I hope he took it to heart."

"I'm sure he appreciated your visit."

"I'm not so sure." Reede came around to face her. She nervously swept back her hair, which the strong wind was blowing across her face. "If I'd never come here, never reopened the case—"

"Don't do that to yourself again, Alex," he said fiercely. "None of it was your fault. Nobody guessed the extent of Sarah Jo's insanity, not even Angus, and he was married to her. Junior ... Well ..." He stopped speaking, his throat working convulsively.

"You'll miss him."

"Miss him?" he repeated with phony nonchalance. "The dumb bastard. Running into a burning house about to collapse. Only a goddamn fool would do something that stupid."

"You know why he did it, Reede. He felt he had to." The tears shimmering in his eyes made Alex's throat ache with the need to cry. She stepped forward and laid a hand on his arm. "You loved him, Reede. Is that so hard to admit?"

He stared down at the flower-banked grave. "People always talked about how jealous he was of me. Nobody ever guessed how jealous I was of him."

"You were jealous of Junior?"

He nodded. "Of the advantages he had." He gave a dry, derisive laugh. "I stayed mad at him most of the time for squandering those advantages."

"We love people in spite of what they are, not because of what they are. At least, that's the way it should be."

She dropped her hand from his arm and, trying to keep her voice light and conversational, said, "Angus told me that he plans to go ahead with the racetrack."

"Yeah. He's a stubborn old cuss."

"Your airfield will prosper."

"It better. I'll be out of a job by the end of the year," he told her. In response to her puzzled expression, he said, "I resigned. I can't sheriff and make anything out of that airport at the same time. It was time I either tackled it or let it go. I decided to tackle it."

"Good. I'm glad for you. Angus says you're considering incorporating with him."

"We'll see. I'm going to buy another racehorse with Double Time's insurance money. I'm thinking about training it myself. Angus wants to help."

She wasn't fooled by his casual treatment of the subject, but she didn't pressure him about it. If she were a gambler, she'd put her money on a future alliance. This time it would be for Angus's benefit more than Reede's.

"What about you?" he asked. "When will you be going back to work?"

She dug her hands into her coat pockets and drew her shoulders up. "I'm not sure. In light of my injuries—"

"How are they, by the way?"

"Everything's healing fine."

"No pain?"

"Not any longer. Basically, I'm as good as new, but Greg told me not to rush back to work. He knows the strain I've been under." She plowed into the soft earth with the toe of her boot. "I'm not sure I want to go back at all." Sensing his start of surprise, she smiled up at him. "You'll find this amusing, Sheriff. I've recently realized how much empathy I have for the accused. I might try defense law for a change."

"Public defender?"

"Possibly."

"Where?"

She looked deeply into his eyes. "I haven't decided."

Reede began to rearrange the freshly turned earth beneath his boots, too. "I, uh, I read your statement in the newspaper. It was decent of you to close the case for lack of evidence," he said in a low voice.

"It really wouldn't serve much purpose to quarrel with the original ruling, would it?"

"No, it wouldn't, especially not now."

"Probably from the beginning, Reede." He raised his head and gave her an appraising look. "You were right, all of you. This investigation was self-serving. I used it and the people involved to prove my grandmother wrong." She drew a shaky breath. "It's too late for Celina to rectify her mistakes, but I can certainly do something about mine."

She inclined her head toward the nearby grave, the older, overgrown one, which now had a single red rose lying at the base of the headstone. "Did you put that there?"

Reede looked across the two fresh graves toward Celina's. "I thought Junior would like sharing a flower with her. You know how he felt about the ladies." It was healthy that he could smile when he said it.

"You know, I didn't realize that this was the Minton family plot until the funeral the other day. Mother would like that, being here with him."

"And he's where he always wanted to be. Near Celina, with nobody between them."

Emotion welled up in Alex's throat and eyes. "Poor Stacey. She never had a chance with Junior, did she?"

"No woman did. For all his philandering, Junior was a one-woman man."

By tacit agreement, they turned and started down the hill toward their cars.

"Was it your idea for Stacey to move into the ranch house for a while?" Alex asked, as she picked her way across the grass.

He seemed reluctant to admit it. An affirmative rolling motion of his shoulders was all he gave her for an answer.

"That was a thoughtful suggestion, Reede. She and Angus

will be good for each other." The late judge's daughter would never feel kindly toward her, but Alex understood and could forgive her animosity.

"Stacey needs somebody to fuss over," Reede said, "and Angus needs that kind of attention right now."

Having reached her car, Alex turned to him and asked huskily, "What about you? Who'll fuss over you?"

"I've never needed it."

"Oh, yes, you have," she said, "you just never let anybody." She took a step closer to him. "Are you going to let me leave town, walk out of your life, without making any effort to stop me?"

"Yes."

She regarded him with love and frustration. "Okay, I'll tell you what, Reede. I'll just go on loving you for as long as I live, and you just go on resisting it." It was spoken as a dare. "See how long you can hold out."

He angled back his head and gauged the determination in her posture, her voice, her eyes. "You're too big for your britches, you know that?"

Her responding smile was tremulous. "You love me, Reede Lambert. I know you love me."

The wind lifted the tawny hair on his head as he nodded slowly. "Yeah, I do. You're a pain in the ass, but I love you." He cursed beneath his breath. "That still doesn't change anything."

"Like what?"

"Like our ages. I'll get old and die long before you, you know."

"Does that matter today—this very minute?"

"It sure as hell should."

"It doesn't."

Infuriated by her calm logic, he crammed his fist into his opposite palm. "God, you're persistent."

"Yes, I am. When I want something badly enough, when I feel that it's right, I never give up."

For several long moments he stared at her, at war with himself. He was being offered love, but he was afraid to accept it. Then, swearing liberally, he grabbed a handful of dark auburn hair and pulled her toward him.

He reached inside her coat, where she was warm and soft and giving. "You make a damn strong argument, Counselor," he growled.

Backing her into the side of her car, he touched her heart, her belly, then placed a hand on her hip and bowed her body against his. He kissed her with passion and love and something he'd always had very little of—hope.

Breathlessly tearing his lips from hers, he buried his face in the warmth of her neck. "In my whole life, I've never had anything that belonged to me first, that wasn't a hand-me-down or a handout—nothing, until you. Alex, Alex..."

"Say it, Reede."

"Be my woman."

Prologue

That night in 2000

Talking about it is the surefire way to get caught."

He let the statement settle, then looked each of his three companions straight in the eye one at a time, using the deliberation rather than additional words to serve as a warning.

The huddled quartet was coming down from an adrenaline high. It hadn't been a crash landing but a gradual descent. Now that they were no longer in immediate danger of being caught red-handed, their heartbeats remained stronger than normal, but had slowed to a manageable rhythm. Breaths gusting into the humid air were just as hot, though not as rapid as they'd been.

However, what hadn't let up, not by a single degree, was the tension among them.

They couldn't risk being seen together tonight, but before going their separate ways, they must forge an understanding. If, during the process of creating that bond, a threat was implied, so much the better. It would discourage any one of them from breaking the pact to keep their mouths shut. One stuck to the vow of silence, or else.

"Do not talk about it." The speaker's hair was a paprika-colored thatch that grew straight up out of a sidewall. A freckled scalp showed through the bristle. "Don't tell any-damn-body." He made five stabbing motions toward the ground to emphasize each word.

Somewhat impatiently, the oldest of the group said, "Of course not."

The one vigorously gnawing his fingernails spat out a paring while bobbing his head in assent.

The fourth, the youngest of them, had maintained an air of cool detachment and remarkable calm throughout the evening's endeavor. A laconic shrug conveyed his unspoken *Goes without saying.*

"One of us boasts about it, or drops a hint, even joking, it'll have a domino effect that could—"

"You can stop going on about it," the oldest interrupted. "We got it the first time, and didn't need a lesson from you to start with."

The ditch in which they were hunkered was choked with weeds, some thriving, some lying dead in the mud, having drowned during the last hard rain. The ravine was four feet deep and made for an ugly scar that cut between the narrow road and a listing barbed-wire fence demarcating a cow pasture that reeked of manure. Without a breeze to disperse the odor, the sultry atmosphere kept it ripe.

At the center of the circle formed by the four was the cause of the resented lecture: a canvas bag stuffed with stolen cash.

It was a hell of a lot bigger haul than they had anticipated, and that unexpected bonus had been both exhilarating and sobering. It made the stakes seem higher, which wound the tension tighter.

Following the rebuke about unnecessary lessons, no one moved or said anything until the young, aloof one reached up and ground a mosquito against the side of his neck, leaving a smear of blood. "Nobody'll hear about it from me. I don't cotton to the idea of jail. Already been there."

"Juvie," the redhead said.

"Still counts."

The older one said, "Only a fool would blab about it. I'm no fool."

The redhead thought it over, then nodded as though reassured. "All right, then. Another thing. We see each other on the street, we act the same as always. We don't go out of our way to avoid each other, but we don't get chummier, either. We recognize each other on sight, maybe we're well enough acquainted to speak, but that's it. That's why this will work. The only thing we have in common is this." He nudged the canvas bag with the steel-tipped toe of his boot.

The other pair of cowboy boots in the circle weren't silver-toed. They weren't worn for show but lived in. This wasn't the first time they'd been caked with mud.

The pair of brown wingtips had sported a shine before sliding down into the ditch.

The navy blue trainers had some mileage on them.

"Six months is a long time to wait to divide it up," the eldest said, eyeing the carrot-top. "In the meanwhile, why do you get to keep the money? We didn't vote on that."

"Don't you trust me with it?"

"What do you think?"

If the one with the gingery thatch took offense, he didn't show it. "Well, look at it this way. I'm the one taking all the risks. Despite our pledge not to talk it up, if one of you lets something slip, and somebody who wears a *badge* gets wind of it and starts snooping, I'm the one holding the bag."

The other three hadn't missed the emphasis he placed on that certain word. They exchanged glances of patent mistrust toward the self-appointed banker, but no one argued with him. The youngest gave another one-shouldered shrug, which the redhead took as consensus.

"Once you get your share," he said, "you can't go spending cash like crazy. No new cars, nothing flashy, nothing—"

The older one cut him off again, testier than before. "You know, I could well do without these instructions of yours."

"No call to get touchy. Anything I tell you is a reminder to myself, too." The redhead fashioned a placating smile, but it wasn't in keeping with his eyes, which reflected the meager moonlight like twin straight razors. He then turned to the nail-biter, who was running out of fingers on which to chew. "What's the matter with you?"

"Nothing."

"Then stop with the nervous fidgeting. It'll single you out like a red neon arrow."

The older seconded that. "He's right. If you come across as nervous, you had just as well confess."

The nail-biter lowered his hand from his mouth. "I'll be okay." His Adam's apple forced down a hard swallow. "It's just...you know." He looked down at the bag. "I still can't believe we actually did it."

"Well, we did," the redhead said. "And when you report for work on Monday morning and are informed that the safe was cleared out over the weekend, you've got to pretend to be as shocked as everybody else. But don't overreact," he said, raising his index finger to underscore the point.

"Just a soft 'holy shit' will do. Something like that to show disbelief, then keep your trap shut. Don't do anything to call attention to yourself, especially if detectives start interviewing all the store employees, which it's certain they will. When your turn comes, you stay ignorant and innocent. Got that?"

"Yeah."

"*Got that?*" demanded the older.

"Sure. I know what to do." But even as he acknowledged his responsibility, he dried his palms by running them up and down his pants legs, a gesture that didn't inspire confidence among the other three.

The older sighed, "Jesus."

The nervous one was quick to reassure the other three. "Look, don't worry about me. I've done my part, and I'll continue to. I'm just jumpy, is all. Out here in the open like this." He made a sweeping motion with his arm that encompassed the pasture and deserted stretch of country road. "Why'd we stop out here, anyway?"

"I thought we should come to an understanding," the redhead said.

"And now we have." The oldest one started up the embankment and gave the nervous one a warning glare. "You had better not screw this up."

"I won't. By Monday I'll be okay." He wet his lips and formed a shaky grin. "And six months from now, we'll all be rolling in clover."

As a group, they climbed out of the ditch, but the adjourning optimistic prediction didn't pan out.

By morning, their plan had been shot to hell.

One of them was in the hospital.

One was in jail.

One was in the morgue.

And one had gotten away with the haul.